# PENDRAGON

### JOURNAL OF AN ADVENTURE THROUGH TIME AND SPACE

## Book Five:

## Black Water

## D. J. MacHale

Aladdin Paperbacks

New York   London   Toronto   Sydney

First Aladdin Paperbacks edition August 2004
Copyright © 2004 by D. J. MacHale

ALADDIN PAPERBACKS
An imprint of Simon & Schuster
Children's Publishing Division
1230 Avenue of the Americas
New York, NY 10020

Designed by Debra Sfetsios
The text of this book was set in Apollo and Helvetica.

Printed in the United States of America
6  8  10  9  7  5

Library of Congress Control Number 2003096186
ISBN 0-689-86911-8

*Kitties for Keaton*

## ACKNOWLEDGMENTS

Greetings to all.

It's time once again to join Bobby Pendragon and the Travelers in their quest to protect Halla from the evils of the demonic Saint Dane. It's been quite an adventure for Bobby since that night when Uncle Press whisked him away to learn of his true destiny. It's also been quite a journey for me, who had no idea it was going to be so much fun writing about it. But here we are five books later, halfway home, and sharing Bobby's adventures with you all is getting more exciting all the time.

I've had the pleasure of receiving countless letters and e-mails from readers who want to discuss their theories, predictions, and concerns for the future of Halla. There are a lot of creative thinkers out there! I feel as if I'm being treated to the collective creativity of a whole new generation of fantasy-adventure writers. How awesome is that? A big thank-you to everyone who has written.

Of course, I'm not the only one responsible for bringing Bobby's adventures to you. There is a lot of credit to go around and I'd like to spread some of it here. Many thanks go to Rick Richter, Julia Richardson, Ellen Krieger, Samantha Schutz, Jennifer Zatorski and all the good folks at Simon & Schuster Children's Publishing for continuing to support the Pendragon books. As always, Debra Sfetsios and Victor Lee did an incredible job designing and creating an awesome cover. Heidi Hellmich, ace copy editor, has once again done a miraculous job in making me look as if I actually know proper grammar. My own small team of acolytes consisting of Peter Nelson, Richard Curtis, and Danny Baror remain my guardian angels. And of course, my wife, Evangeline, continues to assure me that what I write each day is actually worth reading. Believe me, that is an invaluable service.

Thanks to you all, and to all those who helped bring this latest chapter in the Pendragon saga to print.

I've discovered that writing a continuing story spread out over several books is tricky. Even though each book contains a unique complete story, it's also a piece in a much larger puzzle. Trouble is, not everybody will get the chance to read the books in order, and starting in the middle of a series can be confusing. That means every book has to be written as if it were the first and only book in the series. Yikes! For everyone who has been with me since the beginning, you know that's no small task, because a lot of ground has been covered since *The Merchant of Death*. So with each book, I try to sneak in enough back story to get new readers up to speed, but not so much that veteran readers will get bored. If you're new to Pendragon, don't panic. As you go along, many of your questions as to what the heck is going on will be answered. If you're a veteran, try not to doze off when I remind you of what's happened in the past. I've spread it out all over the place, and if you're not paying attention, you might miss something new. That's a warning to keep you on your toes.

Okay, that's all from me. For those of you who freaked after reading the cliffhanger in last chapter of *The Reality Bug*, your wait is over. For those of you who are new to the series, welcome. You're about to enter a world of demons, heroes, and destiny. All you've got to do is take a breath, turn the page, and step into the flume.

Hobey ho,


D. J. MacHale
March 2004

# PENDRAGON

JOURNAL OF AN ADVENTURE THROUGH
TIME AND SPACE

## Book Five:

## Black Water

# ☙ PROLOGUE ☙

**Acolytes.**

That's what this was all about.

It was also about saving humanity from being crushed by a villainous demon named Saint Dane, but that was a little much for Mark Dimond and Courtney Chetwynde to tackle right off the bat. They figured becoming acolytes was the best way to ease into the whole universe-saving thing. The two friends sat together on a musty old couch in a small New York City apartment. They were there to learn the mysterious ways of the acolytes. Not exactly dramatic surroundings, considering they were hearing words that would change their lives forever.

"You are the acolytes from Second Earth now," said Tom Dorney, whose apartment it was. "With Press gone, I'm no longer needed. It may be an easy job compared to what the Travelers do, but I think you'll agree it's an important one."

"We do. Absolutely. Yessir," Mark and Courtney assured him.

Dorney turned to look out his window and frowned. He was an old guy with short-cropped gray hair and excellent posture. He was once a soldier. Old habits die hard.

"Is there something you're not telling us?" Courtney asked.

Dorney sighed and said, "It's just a feeling."

"What?" she demanded.

"I don't know," Dorney said, troubled. "I didn't like what I heard about Veelox."

"Yeah, no kidding," Courtney said.

"What I mean to say is, be careful. Saint Dane has finally had a victory, and there's no telling what's next. From this point on, I can't guarantee that the old rules still apply."

This was chilling news for Mark and Courtney on their first official day as acolytes. Dorney's ominous warning was very much on their minds as they left his apartment and took the train back to Stony Brook, Connecticut. Just before the train pulled into Stony Brook Station, Mark announced, "I want to go to the flume."

"Why?" Courtney asked.

"We'll bring some of our clothes to leave there."

"But nobody told us they needed clothes," Courtney countered.

"I know. Just thinking ahead."

"That's just an excuse to go there, isn't it?" Courtney asked.

Mark didn't argue. "I guess I just want to see it again. To prove it's real."

"I hear you," Courtney said. "I do too."

When they got off the train, they both went home and gathered up a bunch of clothes they thought a Traveler from some distant territory might need on a visit to Second Earth. That's what acolytes did. They supported the Travelers on their mission to protect Halla. Courtney picked out a bunch of simple, functional things like jeans, T-shirts, a sweater, socks, hiking boots, and underwear. She debated about bringing one of her bras, but figured that was overkill. Mark gathered up a bunch of clothes that were totally out of style. It wasn't like he had a choice. That's all he had. He found sweatshirts with logos that meant nothing, no-name jeans, and generic sneakers. Style was not something Mark concerned himself with. He hoped the Travelers felt the same way.

Mark brought one extra item, but hoped he wouldn't need it. It was the sharp poker from his parents' fireplace. It was a woefully inadequate weapon to deal with an attacking quig-dog, but it was all he could find.

Shortly after, Mark and Courtney met at the iron gates in front of the empty Sherwood house. They silently walked around to the side and climbed the tree to get over the high stone wall that surrounded the spooky, abandoned estate. Once over, Mark held the fireplace poker out in front of him, ready to ward off a rampaging quig. Mark's hand was shaking like warm Jell-O, so Courtney gently took the weapon from him. If either of them had a chance of fighting off a charging quig, it would be Courtney.

Luckily they didn't run into any of the yellow-eyed beasts. They made it through the big empty mansion, down into the basement, and into the root cellar that held the newly created flume. No problem. They emptied their backpacks and neatly folded the clothes in a pile. Courtney looked at some of the geek clothes Mark brought, and chuckled.

"Oh yeah, Bobby's gonna blend right in wearing a bright yellow sweatshirt with a red logo that says, *'Cool Dude!'*"

"Give me a break," Mark said defensively. "It's my favorite sweatshirt."

Courtney shook her head in disbelief. When they were finished, they both gazed into the dark tunnel to the territories. The flume. They stood together, each with his/her own thoughts as to what the future might hold.

"I'm scared and excited at the same time," Mark said.

"Really," Courtney added. "I want to be part of this, but it's scary not knowing what to expect."

"Can you imagine being a Traveler?" Mark asked while stepping into the mouth of the tunnel.

"Well, no," Courtney answered, "to be honest."

"Well, I've thought about it a lot!" Mark declared. "It would be awesome, stepping into a flume and announcing the next amazing place you'd like to go."

"It's pretty unbelievable," Courtney agreed.

"Look at this thing!" Mark said, scanning the flume. "It's kinda like having a jet fighter."

"It is?" Courtney asked with a chuckle.

"Yeah. You know what it's capable of, but have no idea what to do to make it go."

"It's not all that hard," Courtney said. "If you're a Traveler."

Mark smiled, turned to face the dark tunnel, and shouted out, *"Eelong!"*

He looked back to Courtney and said, "Could you imagine if—"

"Mark!" Courtney shouted.

Mark saw the terrified look on Courtney's face. She was looking past him, deeper into the flume. Mark spun quickly and saw something he thought was impossible.

The flume was coming to life.

Mark jumped out of the tunnel and ran to Courtney. The two backed away toward the far wall of the root cellar, hugging each other in fear.

"D-Did I do that?" Mark asked.

"Or is somebody coming?" Courtney added.

The light appeared from the depths of the tunnel. The musical notes were faint at first but quickly grew louder. The rocky walls began to crackle and groan. They had seen all this before, but only when the flume was activated by a Traveler. Never, ever had a flume been activated by a non-Traveler—until now.

"I-I don't really want to go to Eelong," Mark cried. Courtney held him tighter, ready to hold him back if he got pulled in by the power of the flume.

The gray walls of the tunnel melted into glorious crystal as the bright light and sound arrived at the mouth. Mark and Courtney didn't dare put their hands in front of their eyes because they were too busy hanging on to each other. But neither felt the tug of the flume, because someone was headed their way. Through the bright light they saw a tall, dark silhouette appear and step out of the tunnel. Oddly, the sparkling light didn't go away. The jangle of music stayed too. This had never happened before, at least not that Mark or Courtney knew. But none of that mattered as much as the man who now stood facing them.

It was Saint Dane. He had arrived on Second Earth. The two had never seen him before, but there was no mistaking the tall demon with the long gray hair, piercing blue eyes, and dark clothes.

"And so it begins," Saint Dane cackled. "The walls are beginning to crack. The power that once was, will no longer be. It is a whole new game, with new rules."

Saint Dane roared out a laugh. With a sudden burst of light from deep inside the flume, his hair caught fire! His long gray mane exploded in flames, burning right down to his skull. Mark and Courtney watched in horror as the flames reflected in his demonic eyes. Saint Dane laughed the whole while, as if enjoying it.

Mark and Courtney didn't move, except to tremble.

The fire burned away all of Saint Dane's hair, leaving him completely bald, with angry red streaks that looked like inflamed veins running from the back of his head to his forehead. His eyes had changed too. The steely blue color had gone nearly white.

He fixed those intense eyes on the two new acolytes and smiled. He tossed a dirty, cloth bag at their feet.

"A present for Pendragon," Saint Dane hissed. "Be sure he gets it, won't you?" Saint Dane took a step back into the light of the flume. "What was meant to be, is no longer," he announced. With that, he began to transform. His body turned liquid as he leaned over to put his hands on the ground. At the same time his body mutated into that of a huge, jungle cat. It was the size of a lion. His coat was brown, but speckled with black spots. The big cat snarled at Mark and Courtney, and leaped into the flume. An instant later the light swept him up and disappeared into the depths. The music faded, the crystal walls returned to stone, and the light shrank to a pin spot.

But it didn't disappear entirely.

Before Mark and Courtney could get their heads back together, the light began to grow again. The music became louder and the gray rock walls transformed back into crystal.

"My brain is exploding," Mark uttered.

A second later the bright light flashed at the mouth of the tunnel to deposit another passenger before returning to its normal, dormant state.

"Bobby!" Mark and Courtney shouted. They ran to him and threw their arms around him in fear and relief.

"What happened?" Bobby demanded, all business.

Mark and Courtney were both supercharged with adrenaline. "It was Saint Dane!" Courtney shouted. "His hair burned! It was horrible!"

"He said the rules have ch-changed, Bobby," Mark stuttered. "What did he m-mean?"

Bobby took a step back from them. Mark and Courtney sensed his tension.

"What did you do?" Bobby demanded. It sounded like he was scolding them.

"Do?" Courtney said. "We didn't do anything!"

Mark and Courtney focused on Bobby. He was wearing rags. His feet were bare, his hair was a mess, and he had a coating of dirt all over his body. He didn't smell so hot either.

"What happened to you?" Mark asked.

"It doesn't matter," Bobby shot back. He was just as charged up as they were. "Did you activate the flume?"

Mark and Courtney looked to each other. Mark said, "Uh, I g-guess so. I said 'Eelong'—"

"No!" Bobby said in anguish.

"What's the matter?" Courtney asked. "We're not Travelers. We can't control the flume."

"Things have changed," Bobby shouted. "Saint Dane's power is growing. He's got his first territory. It's all about changing the nature of things."

"So . . . that means we can use the flumes?" Courtney asked.

"Don't!" Bobby demanded. "It'll just make things worse."

Mark remembered something. He ran back to the door of the root cellar and picked up the bag Saint Dane had thrown at them. "He said this was for you," Mark said, handing the bag to Bobby.

Bobby took it like it was the last thing in the world he wanted. He turned the rotten bag upside down, and something fell onto the floor. Courtney screamed. Mark took a step back in shock. Bobby stood firm, staring at the floor, his jaw muscles clenching. Lying at his feet was a human hand. It was large and dark skinned. As gruesome as this was, there was something else about it that made it nearly unbearable to look at. On one finger, was a Traveler ring.

"Gunny," Bobby whispered. It was the severed hand of the

Traveler from First Earth, Vincent "Gunny" VanDyke. Bobby took a brave breath, picked up the hand, and jammed it into the bag.

"Bobby, what's happening?" Courtney asked.

"You'll know when I send my journal," he said. He turned back and ran into the mouth of the flume, clutching the bag with Gunny's hand in it. "*Eelong!*" he called out. The flume sprang back to life.

"Is Gunny all right?" Mark asked, nearly in tears.

"He's alive," Bobby said. "But I don't know for how long."

"Tell us what to do!" Courtney pleaded.

"Nothing," Bobby answered. "Wait for my journal. And whatever you do, do *not* activate the flume. That's exactly what Saint Dane wants. It's not the way things were meant to be."

With a final flash of light and jumble of notes, Bobby was swept into the flume, leaving his two friends alone to begin their careers as acolytes.

It wasn't a very good beginning.

## ◦ SECOND EARTH ◦

**Four months had passed** since that incredible, frightening episode in the basement of the Sherwood house.

Mark Dimond and Courtney Chetwynde had done exactly what Bobby told them to do. Nothing. They stayed away from the flume and waited for the arrival of another journal. They waited. And waited. And waited some more. Mark found himself staring at his ring, willing it to activate. He so desperately wanted a sign that being an acolyte meant more than sitting around like a load, pretending all was normal. A few times he called Tom Dorney to see if he had gotten any messages from other acolytes. Dorney's answer was always the same: "Nope." No detail. No chitchat. Just "Nope." Dorney was a man of few words. To Mark, he was a man of *one* word. "Nope."

Mark went to the safe-deposit box at the National Bank of Stony Brook, where Bobby's journals were securely kept. He sat by himself for an entire day, reading them all, reliving the incredible journey that his best friend had been on for the last year and a half. So much had changed since that winter night when Bobby left Stony Brook with his uncle Press to discover that he was a Traveler, and that his destiny was to protect the territories of Halla.

The same night Bobby left, his family disappeared. Any record that they had ever existed disappeared right along with them. More importantly, the curtain was pulled back on the incredible truth that the universe didn't function the way everyone thought. Bobby's journals explained how every time, every place, every person and every thing that had ever existed, still did exist. It was called Halla. Halla was made up of ten territories that were connected by tunnels called flumes that only the Travelers could use. But the most frightening truth contained in the journals was that an evil Traveler named Saint Dane was doing his best to destroy Halla. Saint Dane would travel to a territory that was about to reach a critical point in its history, and do all that he could to push events the wrong way and send the territory into chaos. It was up to Bobby and the other Travelers to stop him. They had been pretty successful, too. Denduron, Cloral, First Earth—all victories over Saint Dane and his evil plots.

But then came Veelox.

Veelox was a territory doomed to crumble because people chose to live in Lifelight, the wonderful, virtual-reality world created by a supercomputer, instead of in real life. It marked Saint Dane's first victory over Bobby and the Travelers. Mark worried that the toppling of Veelox meant Saint Dane had even more power than before. He worried that the rules had changed and that the demon would now be more difficult to defeat. He worried that the battle would soon come to Second Earth. He worried that this was the beginning of the end for Halla. Mark worried a lot. He was good at it.

And on top of it all, Mark and Courtney were now acolytes. Up to this point their job had been to read Bobby's journals and keep them safe. Basically they had been librarians. Now they were in it. Being acolytes meant they would support any

Travelers who came to Second Earth and help them blend in with the local culture. They were psyched and ready for the challenge. Finally, they had the chance to take an active role in helping Bobby.

But in spite of all these exciting and scary developments, it turned out that there was nothing for them to do. Mark felt like an anxious racehorse stuck in a gate that wouldn't open. He'd walk through the halls of Davis Gregory High, where he was a sophomore, look at the other kids, and think, *Do they know the danger we're all in? Do they have any clue that I'm one of the few people in Halla who is trying to protect them?* The answer was, of course, no. To the other kids at school, Mark Dimond was nothing more than a nervous brainiac who ate too many carrots and didn't wash his unkempt, greasy black hair often enough. Guys like Mark were like wallpaper . . . always hanging around but totally invisible.

Things weren't going much better for Courtney. Life had changed drastically for her since entering high school. Courtney had always been the girl who had it all going on. She was pretty, with waist-length brown hair and deep gray eyes. She had lots of friends and, most notably, kicked butt in every sport she played. Courtney was a legend. It didn't matter what sport either: soccer, volleyball, softball, track . . . She even wanted to play football, but the rules wouldn't allow it. But since coming to Davis Gregory High, things had changed. Courtney wasn't the best anymore. Maybe it was because the other girls caught up. Maybe it was because she never had to try very hard, and it was paying off for those who did. Or maybe it was because she had lost something intangible. The spark. The magic. Whatever. The result was that Courtney looked bad. In soccer she was demoted from varsity to JV and then quit the team. That was big. Courtney never quit anything. Ever. But she quit soccer. She sought refuge in volleyball, her favorite sport. But things weren't any better. Courtney didn't even make the team. She got cut. *Cut!* Courtney had never been cut. It was humiliating. At first the other kids were happy to see the queen dethroned, but after a while they started feeling bad for her. Courtney didn't want pity. That was the worst.

If there was one word you could use to describe Courtney Chetwynde, it was "confident." But that confidence was taking a severe beating, and she was starting to question herself. It affected the rest of her life too. Her grades took a nosedive; she stopped hanging with her best friends; and she fought with her parents. She hated their constant, worried looks that silently asked, "What's wrong with you?" The frustrating truth was, she didn't know. It was eating her up.

But Courtney wasn't totally self-absorbed. She knew her troubles were puny compared to the bigger dangers lurking about. Bobby Pendragon, the guy she'd had a crush on since she was four years old, was flying around the universe battling an evil demon who wanted nothing less than the destruction of everything. Courtney realized that on a scale of one to ten where ten was the worst, getting cut from volleyball was around negative forty. Knowing this, Courtney felt guilty when she worried about her own little problems. But she couldn't help it, which made her feel worse. She couldn't control events in Halla; she could only deal with her own life . . . and she wasn't dealing so well.

Mark and Courtney were an odd couple. Under normal circumstances they would never have been on each others' radar. Shy nerds didn't hang with awesome jock girls. It was one of the realities of high school. But these two were joined by their friendship with Bobby. They knew Saint Dane had to be stopped and were prepared to do whatever it took to help their friend. But after months of being acolytes, they hadn't done a single thing that had anything to do with life outside of boring old Stony Brook, Connecticut.

It was making them absolutely, totally crazy.

The only thing that kept Mark from going off the deep end was the Sci-Clops science club at school. The summer before, Mark had designed and built a battling robot for the state science fair. He won first prize and got an invitation to join the prestigious club. Mark wasn't used to being rewarded for doing something that was usually considered geek territory, so he welcomed the chance. Mark found that Sci-Clops was full of brilliant students who shared his curiosity about the world around them. A Sci-Clops meeting was a minivacation from the relentless social pressure of high school. It also helped get his mind off the imminent destruction of the universe.

Four months to the day after they saw Bobby and Saint Dane at the flume, Mark anxiously watched the clock tick toward the end of the school day. Mr. Pike, the teacher who led Sci-Clops, promised that a special guest would be speaking that day, and Mark was dying to know who it might be. When the bell rang, he gathered his books and walked quickly toward the science wing. He hurried across the student center, entered the science wing, and was halfway up the back stairwell when his day began to unravel.

Standing on the landing, smoking a cigarette, was Andy Mitchell.

"Hey, Dimond," Mitchell wheezed. "Smoke?"

"Hate" is a strong word. The word "hate" shouldn't be used lightly. Mark hated Andy Mitchell. From the time they were little, Mitchell bullied Mark. It was the classic scenario: smart nerd vs. pathetic loser. Mark would stress over taking alternate routes around school to avoid crossing paths with him. Encounters invariably ended up with a punch in the arm, or an Indian burn or, as they got older, the threat of serious violence. Their relationship came to a head when Mitchell stole Bobby's Traveler journals. Mark and Courtney cleverly got them back and nearly got Mitchell arrested in the process. Having finally beaten Mitchell gave Mark a bit more confidence in dealing with the imbecile, but he still preferred not to.

Mark ignored Mitchell and walked past him up the stairs. He fully expected Mitchell to grab him for some obligatory noogie-type humiliation. Instead Mitchell stubbed out his cigarette and followed. Mark stopped and whipped him a look.

"What do you want?" Mark demanded.

"Nothin'," Mitchell answered while pushing his greasy blond hair out of his eyes. Mark could smell the cigarettes on his breath. Gross. He turned and started up the stairs again. Mitchell followed. Mark stopped and spun back.

*"What?"* he demanded.

"What 'what'?" Mitchell asked innocently. "I ain't doing nothing!"

"You're following me. Why? You gonna shove me in a locker or ask for money or . . . or . . ."

"I'm going to the Sci-Clops meeting," Mitchell answered.

On the list of answers Mark expected, this was below last. It was so far from last, it was in another state. Mark stared in shock, waiting for a punch line that didn't come.

"You're going to the Sci-Clops meeting?" Mark asked. "Why? We going to experiment on you?"

"That's real funny," Mitchell snarled. "Pike asked me to join."

If Mark didn't grab on to the railing, he would have fallen down the stairs. Had he heard right? Was the dreaded Andy Mitchell, professional ignoramus, truly asked to join the elite science club? Andy Mitchell was a moron, and that was paying him a compliment. Mr. Pike must have gotten Andy Mitchell mixed up with somebody else. Sci-Clops was made up of science brains who had dreams of attending MIT. Andy Mitchell was a lamebrain who dreamed about being old enough to buy beer and getting a tattoo. Mark concluded that it had to be a mistake.

"Oh, okay," Mark said, trying not to laugh. "Let's go. Don't want to be late for your first meeting."

"They'll wait," Andy snapped back snottily.

The two continued up the stairs to the physics floor. Mark couldn't wait to see Mitchell's reaction when the mistake was discovered. Wishing total humiliation for someone wasn't exactly noble, but after the years of havoc Andy Mitchell rained down on the dweebs of Stony Brook, he deserved it. When they entered Mr. Pike's classroom, most of the Sci-Clops members were already sitting and waiting to begin. They were a precise bunch. Mark took a seat in the back of the room because he was still one of the newer members. Unlike the bus where the cool kids sat in back, in Sci-Clops the senior members sat right up front. It was one of the many things Mark liked about the club. Andy Mitchell, on the other hand, chose a seat in the first row like he owned the place. Mark loved it. He couldn't wait until Mr. Pike called him out. It was every dweeb's dream come true. Twenty against one. An excellent nerd vs. terd ratio.

Mr. Pike walked to the front of the class. He was a pleasant-looking guy who Mark figured was in his thirties, with longish hair that was starting to go gray. "Exciting day today, guys," he began.

Mark hoped he would have opened up by kicking Andy Mitchell's butt out of the room. But he was willing to wait. He knew it would only be a matter of time.

"We're going to be talking about the creation of a new polymer material that is unique because of its extreme flexibility and tensile strength."

Tensile strength? Mark wasn't exactly sure what that was. The only tensile he knew about was the kind you put on Christmas trees. Whenever Mark wasn't sure about something at a meeting, he'd nod and pretend to understand. That was okay; he liked learning new things. The trick was not to look like an idiot and try to figure it out as they went along.

"Our guest today has been conducting some groundbreaking experiments in this field, and I, for one, am very excited that he's here to share his findings. So let's get right to it. Ladies and gentlemen, I give you . . . Andy Mitchell."

Mark sat bolt upright and let out an involuntary "Huh!" Nobody heard him. They were too busy applauding. He watched in shock as Andy Mitchell stood in front of the group and started digging into his backpack. Mark's brain wouldn't accept this. He looked around, expecting to see some guy in a suit and tie jump out with a microphone and shout, "Surprise! Candid Camera!"

Andy Mitchell coughed into his hand, then brushed his long greasy hair out of his face with the same hand.

Mark nearly puked.

Andy said, "I ain't great at giving speeches. I only know what I know."

Mark wanted to jump to his feet and shout, "Nothing! He knows nothing! He's an idiot!"

But instead, the other members shouted encouragement. "Don't worry about it. We're cool here. Just be yourself."

Mark was on the hairy edge of a scream. Most of the Sci-Clops members were juniors and seniors, so he figured they didn't know Andy Mitchell. But they were going to get to know him real fast. Mark was sure this charade would end as quickly as it began.

Mr. Pike announced, "Andy is a sophomore here, but he attends science classes in a special program at the University of Connecticut."

"You guys wouldn't know me," Andy explained. "Except for science, I'm not all that smart. You won't see me in any of your AP courses."

The members chuckled knowingly.

Mark squeezed the desk in anger. They liked him! They thought he was clever! This can't be happening! Andy Mitchell smart? Attending college science courses and researching subjects Mark never even heard of? Bantering with the Sci-Clops crowd? Mark had heard people say: "I thought I was dreaming," but always thought it was just a saying. He never thought anyone could really think they were dreaming. But right then, Mark seriously wondered if he was in dreamland.

Andy Mitchell reached into his backpack and pulled out a small, soft silver bag that looked like the kind of bag his mother used to put things in the freezer. "This is what I've been working on," he explained. "Looks like a regular old bag, right? It ain't." He grabbed the bag with two hands and pulled. The silver bag stretched out as wide as his arms would reach.

The kids gasped.

"The thing is," Andy said with a slight strain in his voice from the exertion, "even though it goes way out, it's still real strong. I could probably put a piano in here and it wouldn't break."

The only thing that was close to breaking was Mark. His mind locked. His mouth hung open. If anybody looked at him, they'd call for an ambulance. The kids of Sci-Clops applauded. Andy beamed. Mark didn't think he could take any more. . . .

And that's when his ring started to twitch.

He didn't react at first. He was too busy being stunned. But a second later, when the ring began to grow, he was yanked back to reality. It was the bright light that started to flash from the gray stone that did it. It was a good thing he was sitting in the back of the room because nobody else saw it. He quickly clamped his hand over the ring.

"You okay, Dimond?" Andy called from the front of the class.

Every one of the Sci-Clops members turned to look at Mark. Mark felt like he was in one of those dreams where you suddenly discovered you were only wearing underpants.

"Uhh, y-yeah. I'm fine," Mark stammered. He stood up, caught his foot on the leg of the desk, and nearly tumbled over. "I-I just remembered I g-got something—"

"Is everything all right?" Mr. Pike asked.

Mark could feel the ring growing on his finger. In a second everything *wouldn't* be all right.

"S-Sure," Mark stammered. "D-Don't mind me. B-Bye."

Mark half ran, half fell out of the room. He didn't care what he looked like. He had to get out of there. He sprinted down the hallway, gasping for breath, and blasted through the doors back to the stairway. It was too late to find anywhere more private. He pulled off his ring, put it on the floor and stepped back. It was already the size of a bracelet and still growing. The gray stone shot out lights that lit up the stairway like a storm of sparklers. The ring grew to the size of a Frisbee. Mark saw the dark opening in the center that he knew was a portal to the territories. The light show was followed by the familiar jumble of musical notes that grew louder, as if they were coming closer. Because they were. A brilliant light flashed out of the hole that forced Mark to cover his eyes. He had been through this before. He didn't have to see.

A second later it was over. The music was gone, the lights stopped flashing, and the ring returned to normal. Mark looked at the floor. He was close to hyperventilating. In that moment, all the waiting, all the frustration, all the anxiety of the last few months washed away. He didn't even care that Andy Mitchell was now addressing his beloved Sci-Clops. That's because sitting on the floor next to his ring was a rolled-up piece of parchment paper tied with a piece of green, plantlike twine. Mark looked at it for a moment, just to make sure it was real. After what he had been through over the last few minutes, he wasn't sure anything was real. He reached into his backpack and pulled out the cell phone his parents had given him for the holidays. It was only supposed to be used in emergencies. This qualified. He hit #1 on his speed dial and listened. After a few seconds . . .

"Courtney?" he said. "Hobey-ho, let's go."

He snapped the phone shut, bent over, and reverently picked up the next journal in the saga of his best friend.

Bobby Pendragon.

Traveler.

# EELONG

I'm in trouble, guys.

I know, I've said that a million times before. But here on Eelong I'm faced with something that is way different than anything I've ever had to deal with. As I'm writing this, I can honestly say I don't know what to do. This isn't about being afraid, or being confused about Traveler stuff or even about finding Saint Dane. Finding him is the least of my worries. My problem is that, unlike Cloral or Denduron or Veelox or the Earth territories, the intelligent beings that inhabit the territory of Eelong aren't normal. I know what you're thinking: has anyone I've run into since leaving home even come close to being considered normal? Not really. But here on Eelong, the inhabitants may be a lot of things, but there is one thing they definitely are not.

Human.

Yeah, you read right. They're not human. I've got to figure out what the turning point is here and stop Saint Dane just like on the other territories, but how can I do that when I can't communicate with the very people I'm supposed to help? This is impossible! I've been on the run from the first moment I landed here. I'm in constant danger, and the scariest part is that my biggest threat isn't Saint Dane—it's the inhabitants of Eelong. How wrong is that?

It gets worse.

Saint Dane told you that the rules have changed, right? Well, I can't say for sure what that means, but I think he's right. From the moment I left Veelox, I felt as if things were different. In some ways, I'm starting over. It's not a good feeling. But I've got to calm down, take a breath, and write this journal. This may be the only chance I'll get. I don't mean to sound dramatic, but I am really, really scared.

Where to begin? It already seems like a lifetime ago that I was on Veelox with Aja Killian. I've lost all track of real time. Jumping between territories will do that. A day in one territory isn't always twenty-four hours in another. What year is this? What month? What century? I'm totally lost. I gotta get a grip. Let me go back to where I finished my last journal and pick up my story from there. So much has happened, I hope I can remember all the details.

Aja Killian and I stood together in the dark, subterranean room that held the flume on Veelox, not sure of what to say to each other. Her normally well-kept blond hair was kind of a mess. I know that doesn't sound all that weird, but for somebody like Aja, who is all about being perfect, it was a huge statement. It was a tough moment because no matter how you cut it, we had lost. The Reality Bug had failed. No, worse than that. It had nearly killed every last person on Veelox. Calling it a failure is kind of an understatement. The virtual-reality computer called Lifelight was back online and most everybody on Veelox had jumped back inside to live in their own personal fantasy worlds. There was nobody left in reality to grow food, to maintain buildings, to uphold the law, or to do the million and one other basic things that a civilization needs to function. It would only be a matter of time before the territory itself began to fall apart. Bottom line was, Saint Dane had won his first territory. I couldn't let him win another, so staying on Veelox wasn't an option.

"Please finish my journal for me," I asked Aja. "Tell Mark and Courtney that I went to Eelong to find Gunny."

"You don't want to finish the journal yourself?" Aja asked.

Good question. Maybe I was too tired. Maybe I was drained after having snatched defeat from the jaws of victory. I could even say that I was in too much of a hurry to find Gunny. All that was true. But as I think back, I believe the real reason was because I was too embarrassed to admit defeat. Especially to you guys. I still don't know why I was chosen to be a Traveler, but I've been around the block enough times now to realize that whether I liked it or not, the job was mine. On Veelox, I had done a lousy job. I was angry, frustrated, and a little bit scared, because I didn't know what losing a territory was going to mean in the battle against Saint Dane. My head was not in a good place.

"No," I finally answered. "Please finish it for me."

She nodded and said, "I'm sorry, Pendragon; this was my fault." Aja was near tears. She took off her small, yellow glasses and cleaned them on her sleeve. Aja hated to admit defeat even more than I did. She was a brilliant computer scientist who never failed at anything she tried, until now. Too bad it had been the most important challenge of her life.

"Don't think that way," I said, trying to sound positive. "This isn't about any one of us. When we fail, we fail together." That was a totally cheesy, football coach–type statement, but I couldn't think of anything better to say.

Besides, it was the truth. I was as much to blame as Aja.

"What do I do now?" she asked. "Maybe I should go with you."

I have to admit, I thought about bringing her along. Every time I had gone to a territory for the first time, I had another Traveler with me. But it wouldn't have been right to take Aja away from Veelox. No, this time I had to fly solo. I was suddenly missing Uncle Press a whole bunch.

"No," I said. "You've got to keep Lifelight running for as long as possible. Remember, this is about all of Halla, not just Veelox. Saint Dane hasn't won yet. Anything can happen."

"So you think there's still hope for Veelox?" she asked.

"Absolutely," I answered. To be honest, I wasn't sure about that at all. But I had to give Aja hope. She grabbed me and hugged me close. It took me totally by surprise because Aja wasn't normally an affectionate person. But she held me so tight—it made me realize that telling her there was still hope was like throwing a lifeline to a drowning person. She needed to hear that, whether it was the truth or not. I hugged back. I liked Aja. I felt bad that she was hurting. But I was hurting too. Hugging her felt good. I guess misery loves company.

"Find Gunny," she said while still holding me. "And do me one favor."

"What's that?" I asked.

She pulled back from me. I looked into her deep, blue eyes. They once again flashed with the confidence I remembered from when we first met. "I want another crack at Saint Dane," she said with authority. "Get it for me."

I had to smile. Aja wasn't the type to feel sorry for herself for long. She had too much brass for that.

"I'll see what I can do," I answered.

Aja leaned forward and kissed me on the cheek. She held

her cheek against mine for a second longer and said, "I believe you." We stayed that way for a long moment. I have to admit, it felt kind of good.

My time on Veelox was over. I was on the wrong territory. I backed away from Aja and took two steps into the mouth of the flume. As I stood there staring into the infinite black void, my thoughts went to what I might find next. Truth was, I had no idea. Eelong was a total mystery. Gunny had left for Eelong only a few days before, in pursuit of Saint Dane. The plan was for him to get a quick look around and then meet me back on Veelox. He never returned. That could only mean trouble. So I had to flume to a new territory, alone, and be prepared to face whatever nastiness prevented Gunny from coming back. I suddenly wanted to step back out of the flume and hug Aja again. But that would have blown whatever small bit of cool I had managed to build.

"Eelong!" I shouted into the flume. The tunnel instantly came to life. The stone walls cracked and groaned; a distant pin spot of light appeared and the sweet magical jumble of notes could faintly be heard. They were coming to take me away.

"I won't let you down again, Pendragon," Aja called.

"You didn't let me down this time," I answered.

The stone walls of the tunnel began to dissolve to crystal as the light grew brighter and the music grew louder.

"Remember," she said with gritted teeth. "I want another chance."

"You'll get it," I replied, trying to sound as if I knew what I was talking about. But other than making Aja feel better, what I thought didn't matter. Veelox was then. The battle was moving to Eelong.

"Good luck, Pendragon," Aja shouted.

"And so we go," I said.

I squinted against the brilliant light as I felt the familiar tug that meant my trip was beginning. A second later I was lifted off my feet and launched through the flume. Next stop, Eelong.

I still had no clue as to what a flume actually was, or why they were able to send Travelers through time and space, but the experience was awesome. It was like floating through space on a bed of light. It was the closest you could get to playing Superman.

But this time something was different.

It wasn't a physical difference. The ride felt the same as always. The difference was with what I saw. I was surrounded by the usual star field, but there was something else. Something more. Beyond the crystal walls of the flume, I saw floating images. As I flew along, I'd see something far in the distance, then whip past it and watch it disappear behind me. The images were nearly transparent, which meant I could see the stars behind them like they were ghosts on the edge of becoming solid. Some looked to be my size, others were so huge it took me a few seconds to move past them. Some I even recognized. I saw a Bedoowan knight from Denduron on horseback, galloping through space. I saw what looked to be a school of swimmers in green swimskins from the underwater city of Faar, moving in formation. I saw a tall building that could have been the Manhattan Tower Hotel and an aquaneer on a skimmer from Cloral, riding the sky.

Other images I didn't recognize. There were two giant men who looked like twins, running across the sky. They looked powerful, though somewhat stiff, as if they were mechanical. I saw a vast field of people wearing nothing but rags. They were all raising their open hands into the air in some common gesture that looked like they were cheering. I also saw a huge, spotted jungle cat charging across the field of stars.

None of this was scary. In fact, it was kind of cool. It was like kicking back and watching a bunch of weird movies projected in space. But the more I saw, the more it bothered me. Why was it happening? What had changed? What did the strange images mean? I couldn't help but think back to what Saint Dane had warned. He said that once the first territory fell, the rest would fall like dominos. I didn't want to be paranoid or anything, but since Saint Dane had finally toppled a territory, I worried that there might have been some grand, cosmic change in Halla.

I didn't get the chance to stress about it for long because the musical notes began to play quickly. I was at the end of my trip. My thoughts turned to Eelong. Was I about to be dumped into a pool of water, like on Cloral? Would there be quigs waiting for me, licking their chops because the dinner bell had just rung?

A few seconds later the flume gently deposited me on my feet. Nothing dramatic at all. That was the good news. Bad news was that I was instantly engulfed in a tangle of thick, sticky ropes. At least I thought they were ropes. For all I knew it was a massive web and the quigs on Eelong were hungry spiders. But I didn't want to believe the worst, so I pushed my way through the dense tangle of ropes. I came out on the far side to find myself standing in a cave. A quick three-sixty showed me it was a grand, underground cavern with a high ceiling. Light leaked through random cracks high above. The ropes I had pushed through turned out to be a curtain of thick vines that cascaded down from the ceiling and covered the mouth of the flume.

"Roots," I said to myself.

Roots were good. Way better than spiderweb. The cavern

was full of these long, green sticky roots that covered the rock walls. I took a few steps toward the center, still on high alert. But there were no gangsters, no quigs, no pools of water, and no Saint Dane. So far, so good. I looked back to the flume to see it was hidden by the dense curtain of roots. I dug an arrow into the dirt floor with my heel, pointing to it. I wasn't taking any chances if I had to bolt out of there fast.

In the dead center of the cavern was a large flat rock. Lying on it was something I wasn't happy to see. It was a pile of clothing. As you know, acolytes put clothing at the flumes for visiting Travelers. According to the Traveler rules, I had to dress in these clothes. No problem, right? Wrong. The clothing on this rock was nothing more than a pile of dirty rags. I'm not exaggerating. At first I thought that's what they were. Rags. But when I lifted one up, I saw that it was a crudely made pair of cloth pants. It wasn't exactly soft, either. It felt like rough burlap. I picked up what looked like a shirt. I wasn't really sure at first, because I saw one sleeve and a hole that I thought would go around your neck, but the rest was in tatters. Not exactly something you'd find on the rack at the Gap. And they smelled, too. Like bad BO. (Is there such a thing as *good* BO?)

I also found some crude shoes made of cloth. I knew they were shoes because they were sort of foot-shaped with extra layers on the bottom. This was not good. I looked around, hoping there might be some other clothes that were a little less nasty, and saw something that made my heart jump. Lying on the ground next to the rock, neatly folded, was a black suit with a white shirt and a large pair of leather shoes.

"Gunny," I said out loud.

These were the clothes he'd worn when he left me on Veelox. There was no mistake; I was in the right place in the wrong clothes. I had to change. Those were the rules. I reluctantly took off my comfy green jumpsuit from Veelox and folded it next to Gunny's clothes. I then did something I absolutely hated, but didn't have a choice about. I had to lose my boxer shorts. In the past, no matter what territory I visited, I kept on the boxers. I figured that if the future of Halla rested on my choice of underwear, it was beyond saving. But these Eelong clothes were so raggy and threadbare, my boxers would have shown! There was no way I could wear them without arousing suspicion. Or at least looking like a total dork. I wanted to scream. It was the final injustice. I had to wear these rough, itchy, torn-up rags, without boxer protection. They were smelly, too. Did I mention that? I already felt like I was on Eelong for too long.

I put on the rags as best as I could, but they hung on me like, well, like rags. On the rock I spotted several strips of thin, braided vine about two feet long. I used them to tie up the cloth in places where it hung too loose. I used these vines on the cloth shoes, too, wrapping up both my feet to keep the ratty material on. After a while I felt like a Thanksgiving turkey, all trussed and ready for the oven. It was awful. Compared to these putrid rags, the leather skins on Denduron were like soft pajamas.

And they smelled, too. I must have mentioned that.

Now that I was all dressed up (or down) the next step was to find the gate and get out of this cavern. I figured the way out must be hidden by the hanging roots. I walked to the side and stuck my arm out to brush aside the dangling vegetables. I walked along, pushing aside the vines, peering beyond to look for something that might be an exit. I saw that the walls weren't entirely made of rock. There were thick sections of roots that had grown into and around the rock. I figured there must be some serious vegetation on the surface.

I had gotten more than halfway around the cavern when I started to worry that I might have missed it. That's when I saw something. Beyond the thick curtain of hanging vines, there was a vertical crack in the rock wall. This had to be the way out. I took a step through the vines and immediately tripped on something. I stumbled forward, hit the wall, and face-planted into the dirt. Ouch. When I opened my eyes, I was face-to-face with . . . a human skull!

"Ahh!"

I rolled away fast. When I got the guts to look back, I nearly retched. Lying on the dirt floor in front of the crack in the wall was a pile of bones. Human bones. I had seen enough horror movies to recognize people bones when I saw them. I couldn't tell how many victims these bones belonged to, and I wasn't about to do inventory, but I'm guessing they were the remains of about six poor souls. They must have been there for a while, because there was nothing left of them but bones, and raggy clothes like I was wearing. Their clothes actually looked a little better than mine, but I wasn't about to make a swap. Ick.

I began to question whether the opening in the rock was the way out, or the path to a gruesome death that would land me back on this pile. I saw crudely fashioned stairs, leading up. They looked to have been carved out of the root material that snaked through the rock. Better, I saw a faint hint of light coming from above. Light was good. I decided to take my chances. I gingerly stepped over the bones because the idea of stepping on something and hearing a *crack* would have pushed me over the edge into gak-dom. With a quick hop I was over, and slid through the opening in the rocks.

The steps were narrow and steep and wound around like

a spiral staircase. I could smell fresh air coming from above, so my confidence grew. I really, really wanted to be out of here. This place was starting to feel more like a crypt than a gate to the flumes. After climbing for a few minutes, I got to the top of the crude stairs and found myself in a dark space. I couldn't see the walls, and the ceiling was so low I couldn't stand. What now?

A few feet away I saw a thin sliver of light shining through what looked like more hanging vines. This had to be the way out. I stayed on my knees for fear of bonking my head and crawled toward the light. It was growing cooler, as if fresh air were only a few feet away. I found myself squeezing through a narrow passageway that at first gave me claustrophobia, but the urge to get the heck out was stronger. I picked up the pace, and a few seconds later the final veil of vegetation was pushed aside and I was hit with bright sunlight. I was out! I squeezed myself through, ready to be free of the dark tunnel and get my first look at the territory of Eelong.

I don't know what I expected, but it wasn't this.

Eelong was totally, absolutely, beautiful. I found myself about twenty yards from the edge of a cliff, looking out over a green, tropical forest. I don't think I've ever seen anything so awesome. I walked closer to the edge, on ground that was thick with grass so soft I probably didn't need the lame-o shoes. The view spread out before me was absolutely stunning. As far as I could see there was nothing but forest. The canopy of trees below was so dense, you couldn't see the ground. There were no structures, no roads, no towers, no sign at all of civilization. Just forest. A flock of birds that looked like pelicans soared by beneath me. They were bright yellow with brilliant red heads.

As dramatic as this was, there was another sight that made the view even more spectacular. Eelong didn't have a sun. At least not in the way we think of a sun. The sky was blue, just like at home. There were even clouds. But rather than a ball in the sky, there was a wide band of light, stretching from one horizon all the way across to the opposite, like a rainbow. It was directly overhead, and I wondered if it would move across the sky as the day wore on. It was hot, too. Jungle hot. This band of brilliant light gave off heat like a tropical sun.

Looking to either side, I found myself on a wide outcropping that must have been at least a couple of hundred yards above the forest below. But it was hard to judge, since I couldn't see the ground through the dense trees. Far to my right I saw a waterfall shoot from near the top of the rock and cascade down through the tree canopy below. I couldn't see where it landed, though. The trees were too thick.

And the smell. It was sweet, but not icky sweet like when you walk into a flower shop. Whatever flowers grew on Eelong, they had a faint smell that reminded me of lemons. To my left I saw some low, scrubby trees that were covered with deep blue flowers. I walked over to this bushy tree and took a deep whiff. Oh yeah, this is where the smell came from.

One word came to mind as I surveyed Eelong: "paradise."

The view was so breathtaking, I had completely forgotten to see where I had come from. That was important because the little tunnel I had crawled through was the gate to the flume. A quick look at my Traveler ring confirmed it. The gray stone in the center was glowing slightly. When in doubt, this ring would always lead me to the flume, so long as I was in the neighborhood. So I turned around to take a mental picture of where the gate was hidden.

What I saw made me catch my breath. I instantly knew that I wouldn't have any trouble finding the gate again. That's because looming up in front of me was the *hugest* tree I had ever seen. I'm not talking big. I mean immense. Colossal. Impossible. The trunk at the base must have been thirty yards across. Did you ever see a picture of those trees in California that have a tunnel cut through the base you could drive a car through? Well, if there were a tunnel cut into the base of this tree, you could drive a dozen eighteen-wheelers through, side by side, and still have room for a couple of Hummers. It was like a skyscraper covered with bark. Looking up, the branches didn't even begin for about fifty yards up. Then the tree spread out into a canopy that could shade Yankee Stadium. I don't know why, but being next to giant things like that makes my palms sweat, and they were definitely sweating. That's how awesome it was.

I looked to the base of the tree and saw the small opening that I had crawled out of. It was so small compared to this monster tree that if I hadn't known it was there, I'd have missed it. Sure enough, carved in the bark just above the opening was the star symbol that marked it as a gate to the flume. Unbelievable. Now the hanging vines in the cavern below made sense. They were the root system of this immense tree. I walked along the base, running my hand across the rough bark. You could live in this tree . . . with all of your friends and their families, and still have room for a Keebler cookie factory. I took a step back, looked up, and laughed. The impossible kept proving itself to be possible. What was I going to see next?

The answer came quickly, and it wasn't a good one.

I felt something hit the back of my leg. I looked down and instantly wished I hadn't, because lying on the ground next to my leg was an arm. A bloody, human arm. I quickly looked up to the direction it came from and felt like the wind was knocked out of me. If the big tree hadn't been there to catch me, I would have fallen back on my butt.

Standing ten yards away from me was a beast. It was like nothing I had ever seen before. The first thing I thought of was . . . dinosaur. It stood upright on two legs, with a long, thick tail that whipped back and forth angrily. It looked to be around seven feet tall, with powerful arms and hands that were three-finger talons. Same with its feet. Its entire body was bright green, like a lizard, with scales covering it. But what I couldn't take my eyes off of was its head. It was reptilian with a snoutlike nose. It had bright green hair that swept back from its forehead and fell halfway down its back. But most hideous was its mouth. It looked like a shark mouth, with multiple rows of sharp teeth that were all about tearing flesh.

And that's exactly what it was doing, because clasped in its jaws was another human arm. Blood ran into the beast's mouth and down its chin. If I hadn't been so scared, I would have gotten sick. We held eye contact. I could feel this monster sizing me up. Its eyes were red, and angry. Without looking away, it closed its jaws, crunching the arm like a dry twig. The sound made my stomach turn. The monster flipped out a green tongue and sucked the shattered arm into its mouth. One gulp later, the arm was gone. Swallowed. Bone and all. Gross. It turned back to me as its mouth twisted into a bloody grin.

I was next on the menu.

Welcome to Eelong.

# EELONG

It was a quig.

It had to be. Every territory had its own quigs that prowled the flumes. They were somehow put there by Saint Dane, but I hadn't figured out how that worked yet. On Denduron they were prehistoric-looking bears. On Cloral they were killer sharks. Zadaa had snakes, and Second Earth had vicious dogs. Veelox was strangely quig free, but I think that's because Saint Dane was already done with that territory by the time I showed up. Now it was looking like the quigs on Eelong were mutant, dinosaur-looking reptiles. I knew that's how it was looking, because I was looking at one. One thing was certain—it was a meat eater. Human meat. The bloody arm at my feet was proof of that. I didn't want to know where the rest of the body might be.

The beast locked its red eyes on me and drew back its lips, revealing yet another row of pointed teeth. Swell. Its long green hair spiked out, like an angry cat. It hissed, and I got a whiff of something nasty. It was sending out a disgusting scent that smelled like rotten fish. This thing was going to pounce, and it was going to hurt. I was totally defenseless. Worse, the giant tree was behind me. It was like being trapped in a dead end. I took a tentative step to my right. The beast mirrored my move. I took a step back to my left. So did the beast. I felt like I was playing basketball and this monster was playing defense. Only it didn't want to steal the ball. It wanted to steal my head.

That's when I saw a flicker of movement to my left. I looked quickly, afraid that another quig might be circling in. But what I saw was my salvation. Poking its head out from the hole at the base of the tree was a person! At least I thought it was a person. The guy had straggly hair and a long beard. I only saw him for an instant, because he popped his head back into the hole like a scared turtle. He must have poked his nose out, saw the quig, and changed his mind about coming out. Good thinking. I wished I had done the same. But seeing him reminded me that I had an escape route. The trick would be to get to the hole before the quig got to me.

The two of us stood facing each other like gunslingers. I hoped he didn't realize that I didn't have a gun and wasn't prepared to sling anything. I knew that if I bolted for the hole, the thing would leap at me and it would be all over except for the chewing. All I needed was a couple of seconds for a head start. But how?

An idea came to me. A hideous idea. If I hadn't been so desperate, there was no way I would have been able to pull it off. But if there is one thing I've learned since becoming a Traveler, self-preservation is a pretty strong motivator. Without taking another second to talk myself out of it, I slowly bent my knees and reached for the ground. I saw the hair on the back of the beast grow higher. It was waiting to see what I was going to do. I cautiously picked up the bloody arm that lay at my feet. I know, how gross can you get? I grabbed it by the elbow trying not to think about what it was. When I touched it, I almost gagged, because it was still warm. Whoever it belonged to had been using it not long before. I had to push that thought away or I'd have lost my lunch . . . and probably my life along with it. As soon as I picked up the arm, the rotten smell from the beast grew stronger. I think the sight of the bloody arm was getting it psyched, like blood in the water to a shark. That was okay. It meant I had a chance. I slowly stood back up and held the dismembered arm out to my side. The beast's red eyes followed it like it was some tasty morsel. Gross.

The next few seconds were critical. It was going to mean the difference between buying me the time I'd need to get to safety, and total failure, which meant it would eat me and then get the arm anyway. It all depended on how stupid this quig was. I waved the arm, tantalizing it. The beast stayed focused on it. The horrible smell grew stronger. Oh yeah, it wanted the arm, all right. I reared back and flung it off to my right.

The beast went for it. The instant it moved, I bolted for the hole like a base runner stealing second when the pitcher went into his windup. I could only hope the quig would keep going for the arm and not decide I was more interesting. I didn't stop to look back because every second counted. I ran for the hole and dove inside headfirst. I hit the ground and scrambled to crawl inside. I thought I had made it, when I heard a bellowing howl from outside and felt a burning sensation on my leg. The beast was back and it had me by the ankle! It was too big to follow me inside, but that wouldn't matter if it pulled me back out. I kicked for all I was worth and felt its sharp talons rake across my skin. But there was no way I was giving up. He was going to have to work for his supper. With one hard kick, I yanked my leg free of its grip. I was loose! I tried to bend my leg and get it inside, but couldn't. A quick look back showed me that one of the quig's talons had caught in the braided twine that held my cloth boot on. It still had me!

I frantically wriggled my foot, trying to pull it out of the boot. I actually cursed myself for doing such a good job tying the twine with half hitches and square knots I learned in Boy Scouts. Why did I have to do such a good job? I expected to feel the pain of the monster's jaws clamp down on my leg at any second, biting me like some giant Buffalo wing. But that didn't stop me from squirming to get away. Then suddenly I felt something snap. It wasn't my leg, I'm glad to say. The beast's claw must have severed the twine because my foot slipped out of the cloth shoe. I quickly tucked my knees up to my chest to keep my feet out of reach. Looking back, I saw the long, green scaly arm of the monster reaching inside the hole, groping to get at me. His sharp talons whipped back and forth blindly, finding nothing but air and a few dangling vines. He was pretty charged up. The rotten-fish smell got so bad it made me gag. But he had lost. With a final bellow of frustration, the beast pulled his arm out and gave up. I suppose he went back and got the bloody arm as a consolation prize.

I lay inside the dark space, breathing hard, trying to get my head back together. Now that I was safe, the reality of what had happened finally hit me. I had picked up a human arm and used it as bait to save me from getting eaten. How disgusting was that? I looked down at my leg and saw three long scrapes that ran from my knee to my ankle. I gingerly touched them and found that, luckily, they weren't very deep. They would just sting for a while. Eelong was shaping up to be a nasty place.

I had to figure another way out of this tree. I wasn't about to stick my head out of that hole. For all I knew, Little Godzilla was waiting outside, munching his arm snack and waiting me out. As much as I wanted to flume out of there, that wasn't an option either. I had to get away from this tree, away from the quigs, and find Gunny. So I got on my hands and knees and started to crawl around, pushing my way through the dangling vines, looking for another escape route. I figured there had to be one. If not, where did the guy come from who poked his head out of the hole? He hadn't been down in the flume cavern when I was there. And for that matter, who *was* that guy?

I passed by the hole that led down to the flume and continued crawling with one hand out in front in case I hit a dead end. But that dead end never came. I kept crawling deeper and deeper into the tree. What I first thought was a small space was actually a tunnel that brought me into the very core of this behemoth tree. As I crawled along, I saw that it was actually getting lighter. Of course, that didn't make sense, but when did something silly like "making sense" matter? I soon felt confident enough that I no longer held my hand out in front of me. Up ahead I saw light at the end of the tunnel. Literally. I hadn't been crawling for that long, so there was no way I had gone all the way through to the other side of the tree. It was way too big for that. But I didn't stop to wonder what to expect; I'd see for myself soon enough.

When I reached the mouth of the tunnel, I crawled out and stood up to view an incredible sight. The tree was hollow. Or at least, this part of it was. I found myself in a huge space that had been carved out of the core of the immense tree. I was kidding before about being able to live in this tree along with cookie-making elves, but this room proved it was possible. The walls were made of, well, of wood. Duh. Light came in through cracks that ran up and down and all around, like veins. I'm not sure if the hollowing out was natural, or done by hand. If it was by hand, then it had to have been done a long time ago, because everything looked aged, with bits of green moss growing everywhere. Looking straight up was like looking into the mouth of the flume. There was no ceiling. For all I knew, this tree was hollow all the way to the top. I saw multiple levels and ledges that led to other tunnels, like the one I just crawled out of. I wasn't sure how you got from one level to the next. I suppose you could climb the vines that clung to the walls . . . if you were Spider-Man.

Now that I was safe from the quig outside, I began to wonder who the people of Eelong were. Going by the look of that hairy guy who poked his head out of the hole, they didn't exactly seem to be a race of advanced mathematicians. I figured they were a primitive, tribal society who lived in these incredible trees. If they were more advanced than that, they certainly didn't prove it with the clothes they made. Besides, I had yet to see any sign of tools or buildings or anything else you'd expect to see from a society that had advanced beyond the Stone Age. I was beginning to think I would have to deal with cavemen. Or treemen.

"Hello?" I called out, my voice echoing. "Anybody here?" All I got back was the gentle groaning of the tree. I glanced around, trying to figure which tunnel I'd take to find another way out . . . when I was shoved from behind with such force, it nearly knocked me off my feet.

I spun quickly and came face-to-face with the guy who'd peeked out of the hole before. He was short, probably no more than five feet tall. His hair was long and tangled. So was his beard. In fact, I think his head hair was tangled up in his beard hair. Not a good look. His skin was white and filthy, and he wore the same kind of rags that I had on. The guy was crouched down low and breathing heavily. A line of drool ran from his mouth and through his gnarly beard. He may have looked human, but he was acting more like a wild animal.

"H-Hello," I said, trying to calm him. I held my hand out the way you hold your hand out to a dog that you want to show you're not a threat. "My name is—"

Before I could say another word, my arm was grabbed and yanked to the side. I looked in surprise to see that a vine had been thrown around my arm like a lasso. Holding the other end was another person, looking just as hairy and gnarly as the first. I opened my mouth to say something, when another lasso of vine was thrown around my shoulders from behind. It pulled snug around me, locking my arms onto my sides. I looked back to see a third guy yanking it tight. Another vine whipped around my ankles. This one was pulled so hard it yanked my feet out from under me. I hit the ground square on my back. Ooof.

"Wait . . . wait . . ." I gasped, trying to get air. I wanted to use my powers of Traveler mind persuasion, but things were happening so fast, I couldn't think straight. "I'm a friend!" was all I could get out. I know, not exactly convincing, but what else could I say? A second later it didn't matter, because one of the guys leaped at me and jammed a fistful of cloth into my mouth, making me gag. Not good. I didn't think any of these dudes knew the Heimlich maneuver. I figured they must have seen me as a threat. An invader. I needed to show them I meant no harm, because they seemed ready to put some serious hurt on me.

The guy who jammed the cloth in my mouth sat on my chest, staring down at me. I was pinned, unable to move. I looked up into his eyes and saw something that made any hope I had of reasoning with these people fly out the window. I don't know why I didn't realize it before, but I didn't. Now it was too late. The lizard beast that attacked me outside may have been deadly. It may have been trying to eat me. But there was one thing that it wasn't. Its eyes should have told me. Its eyes were red. Quigs didn't have red eyes. Quigs had yellow eyes. And as I looked up at the guy who was sitting on my chest, I saw that his eyes were yellow. And vicious. He opened his mouth into a grotesque smile to reveal rows of sharp, blood-stained teeth. A thin line of drool ran from his lips and fell onto my cheek.

In that one instant, the horrible truth hit me: The quigs on Eelong were human.

# EELONG

I was pinned to the floor with this foul-smelling quig-human sitting on my chest. He leaned down, inches from my nose, and I got a good look into the dark, soulless depths of his yellow eyes.

"I . . . won't hurt you," I stammered out weakly.

Yeah right. I thought maybe I could use some reverse psychology and not let him know that I was totally at his mercy. His answer was a steady stream of drool that fell onto my cheek. My bluff didn't work, no big surprise. I ignored the vile spittle and asked, "Do you understand me?"

The quig shrieked something that sounded like a monkey screaming in pain. I guessed that meant "no." These quigs may have been human, but there was no sign of intelligent life lurking between those hairy ears. These were Saint Dane's animals, and they only knew one thing: killing. My mind groped to come up with a way out. I thought maybe I would be okay, because I was a human too. But then a quick, unpleasant memory of the quigs on Denduron shot to mind. When one went down, the others ate it alive. Quigs were cannibals. That meant here on Eelong, being human didn't even come close to getting me off the hook. It probably made things worse.

The other two quigs held down my arms. They sniffed at me like, well, like animals. I actually hoped they'd be grossed out by the smelly rags I had on. It was a totally idiotic thought, but hey, I was desperate. I kicked my legs and tried to pull away, but the quigs held me tight and laughed. At least I thought it was a laugh. It sounded somewhere between a hyena howl and a pig grunt. It made my skin crawl. The quig on my chest raised his head and let out a horrifying howl. When he looked back down at me, his eyes were sparked with an insane fury. He was firing up for the kill. I feared my strange life was going to end right then and there. In that horrifying moment, I did the only thing left to do: I closed my eyes.

I heard another shriek. It didn't sound as if it came from the quigs, though. It sounded more like an animal roar. I opened my eyes in time to see the quig on my chest turn quickly to look behind himself. The other two quigs fled in fear. I was still flat on my back and didn't dare look up because I was sure another horrifying beastie had decided to drop in on our party. The quig on my chest tried to stand up, but suddenly whipped back around to face me, as if he had been spun by a powerful force. The look on his face had gone from one of bloodlust to terror. I quickly saw why. Across his chest were four deep slashes. Something had just attacked him. The wounds didn't kill him, though. The quig dove over my head and ran away. Whatever new monster had come into this hollow tree was capable of doing some serious damage, and these quigs knew it. But what was it? Was there an uber-quig dwelling in this giant tree? Or had one of those lizard thingies found a way to crawl inside?

Still on my back, I glanced up to see one of the quigs

scramble up a vine as easily as if he were running across the floor. He made it up to an overhead ledge and disappeared into a tunnel. The quig was terrified, and no wonder. I saw what was chasing him.

Climbing the vine behind him, was a big jungle cat. It was a powerful thing, maybe six feet long from head to butt. Its fur was mottled red and black, kind of like a tiger. Because it was moving so fast, I couldn't tell for sure, but it looked like most of its body was covered with some kind of cloth. If I didn't know better, I'd say it was wearing clothes. But that made no sense. The only kitty outfit I'd ever seen before was that cute pink sweater your mother, Mark, put on your cat, Dusty. But this beast wasn't a cute kitty; it was a predator, hot after its prey. It climbed the curtain of vines and darted into the tunnel after the quig. I had no doubt that the quig wouldn't be long for this territory.

Wow. I put my head back down on the floor and took my first breath in about a minute. I hadn't been on Eelong for an hour and I'd already come across a man-eating lizard, a quig-human, and a jungle cat that had a taste for quig-humans. Bottom line was, everything on Eelong was capable of eating me. But who was in charge? Where were the people? I was about to sit up when I heard a low, guttural growl. Uh-oh. I wasn't alone. Another *growl* made me realize the worst:

There was another cat in the room.

I slowly lifted my head and looked between my legs. Across the cavern I saw it, hunched low, stalking me. This one was a light brown color, like a mountain lion. It was big, too. Bigger than the one I saw chase the quig up the vines. Its large, brown cat eyes were fixed on me as it lurked closer. What did the Boy Scout Field Guide say to do in times like this? Should I stare at the beast? Should I play dead? Should I jump up and pretend to be really big and scare it? I sure remembered how to tie knots, but when it came to something useful like saving my butt from a monster, my Boy Scout training fell woefully short. While my mind clicked through these choices, the cat crept closer. Soon, it wouldn't matter what my plan was. It would be all about the cat's plan, and I didn't think I was going to like it.

The cat grumbled and bared its teeth. Oh yeah, there were a couple of long fangs in there. It crept closer until its nose was nearly at my feet. I saw its big brown nose working, sniffing me. I thought maybe I should give it a quick kick in the head and take off, but figured that would only get it mad. Mad and hungry weren't a good combination. At least now I had a faint hope that it would think I smelled foul, and leave me alone. I didn't move. I stopped breathing again. The cat took a few more steps, stood still for a second, and opened its mouth. This was it. It was going to attack. I was actually beginning to hope one of these Eelong beasts would finally get me and put me out of my misery. If this kept up, chances are I'd die of a heart attack anyway.

The big cat kept its eyes on me, opened its mouth wider, and said, "Are you Pendragon?"

Huh? Let me write that again. *Huh?* I went into brain lock. As hairy as everything had been so far, at least it made sense. The hanging roots, the jungle, the band of sun, the big tree, the scary lizard and the quig-humans. All fantastic, but all within my brain's ability to compute. This new development . . . wasn't. I searched for an explanation. I figured maybe when the lizard scratched my leg it released some kind of hallucinatory venom into my system that made me think I was seeing a jungle cat who not only talked, but knew my name. Or maybe this was like the Cheshire Cat in *Alice in*

*Wonderland*, which meant he'd smile and disappear and this would all turn out to be a dream. That would be cool, too.

"Can you talk?" the cat asked. "Or are you just a dumb gar?"

As you know, one of the bizarro perks of being a Traveler is that for some reason we're able to understand the various languages spoken on different territories. But as far as I knew, it didn't work with animals. If it did, there'd be a whole annoying Doctor Dolittle thing going on and we'd be able to understand conversations had by every crawling, swimming and flying creature we ran in to. But we couldn't do that. No way. That meant this cat could really talk.

"I-I'm Pendragon," I said softly.

"Then it's true!" the cat exclaimed. "Unbelievable!"

I took one more step into *The Twilight Zone* when the big cat stood up on its back legs and walked like a human! It must have been around my size, just under six feet. I saw that it too wore some kind of crude clothing. It was a simple, brown tunic that fit snugly to his body, but his outfit was in much better shape than my rags. The garment had no buckles or snaps or buttons. It looked to have been form fitted to his body.

"Sorry for sneaking up on you like that," the cat said. "But you can't be too careful with gars. Especially the ones that hang around here. The quigs, I mean."

I figured I had totally snapped. This talking cat knew about quigs! It held out its paw as if to help me up. Or maybe I should call it a hand. It looked to be a cross between a human hand and a big cat paw. It had a thumb like a human's, but was covered with fur and had some vicious-looking claws.

"My name's Boon," he said. "Welcome to Eelong."

His voice sounded as normal as mine. There was no hint that it was coming out of a nonhuman mouth. I looked up at his cat face and realized that maybe he wasn't a typical cat after all. Sure, his face and head and ears were definitely cat-like, but his snout wasn't as pronounced as a regular cat's. His mouth was a bit smaller too. But he was covered with fur, and his arms were too long for a human, and he had knees that bent at an odd angle. You know that dumb Broadway musical where everybody dressed in tights and cat makeup and ran around singing about how swell it was to be a cat? Well, forget that. This wasn't anything like that. This was no costume. This guy was definitely a cat, but with some human traits . . . not the least of which was talking.

"It's okay," he assured me. "I won't bite."

I tentatively reached up and took his hand. Or his paw. Or whatever. It felt like I was grabbing on to somebody wearing a furry glove, with rough pads in the palm. He was strong, too. And the claws that grazed the back of my hand were sharp. Note to self: Don't mess with the cat.

"I don't mean to stare," Boon said. "But I'm not used to talking with a gar. This is very strange."

Strange? Tell me about it.

"What's a gar?" I asked tentatively.

"You know. A gar. Like you. Two legs, no fur, no teeth, fairly useless. Seegen said you'd be a gar, but I didn't believe it until, well, until I saw you. We have to do something about the smell, though."

"Sorry," I said. "These clothes reek."

"Not the clothes, you!" Boon said sniffing. "Gars all have the same smell, like rotten fruit. No offense."

"I'm losing my mind," I muttered. Then I asked, "How

can you talk? Did humans teach you? I mean, did the gars teach you?"

Boon laughed. He actually laughed. I'd never heard a cat laugh. It was raspy, and trailed off with a croaking growl.

"A gar teach a klee to talk? That's funny. You're a funny one. I heard that about you."

My head was spinning. "Okay, I'm a gar, and you're a klee. Who's in charge here? I mean, are there other klees like you who can talk?"

Boon laughed again and patted me on the back like an old pal. It nearly knocked me over. He had a lot of energy and seemed like he was actually having fun. I had no idea how old he was, but it was beginning to feel like he was a young guy, around my age. At least I think he was a guy. I wasn't about to ask him for a peek between his legs.

"I hate to tell you this, Pendragon." He chuckled. "But things are a little different on Eelong. C'mon, I'll show you."

He walked to the far side of the tree room. I didn't move. I couldn't get my head around the fact that I was watching a six-foot-tall cat wearing clothes walk around on two legs. It was then that I noticed the one thing that kept Boon from truly looking like a regular old Second Earth mountain lion: He didn't have a tail. I supposed it could have been curled up inside his tunic, but I didn't think so. He glanced back to see I wasn't following.

"You're kind of stunned. I am too." He looked around at the cavern, then continued, "We don't normally come here to the gate. It's the quigs. Nasty bunch of little gars. We can usually handle them with no problem, but if they gang up on you . . . ouch. That's why I brought my buddy with me. He doesn't know about them being quigs, though. He just likes hunting wild gars."

I was getting nervous about this talking cat knowing so much about the Traveler biz, so I asked, "Are you a Traveler?"

"Me? Nah. Seegen is the Traveler from Eelong. I'm an acolyte. Actually, I'm not an acolyte yet, officially, but I will be someday. Seegen's told me everything, though. You like the clothes I picked out?"

"They stink."

"Right, you said that. Like I was saying, we don't normally come here. It's a long way from the city, but that's a good thing. Don't want anybody finding the flume, do we?"

The guy spoke fast, like he was excited. Or nervous. Whatever. "Seegen asked me to watch the flume in case the lead Traveler arrived. I couldn't believe it when he told me you were a gar, too. Just like the other Traveler who showed up and—"

"Gunny!" I jumped in. "Are you talking about Gunny?"

"Yes, Seegen said his name was Gunny."

"Yeah!" I exclaimed. "Where is he? Is he all right?"

"I don't know," Boon answered. "Seegen wouldn't tell me. One thing is for sure, though; I've never seen him in Leeandra."

"Leeandra? What's a Leeandra?" I asked.

"It's my home," he answered. "Seegen lives there too. We should go see him now."

"Absolutely," I agreed.

"Good!" Boon exclaimed happily. "This is going to be a great adventure!"

One of us was having a good time. It wasn't me.

"We've a long way to go," he explained. "You'll need another shoe."

Right. I had lost my "shoe" to the lizard thingy. Boon walked to the side of the tree room to a pile of dead vines. He lifted them up to reveal another pile of rag clothing.

"I keep my gar clothes here," he explained. "Going down there to the flume is kind of creepy."

I knew what he meant. Piles of bones will do that. Boon dug through the clothes and found another raggy shoe. It was amazing how he had the physical dexterity of a human. He tossed the shoe to me, saying, "Is this what you wear on your home territory?"

It was my turn to laugh. "Not even close," I chuckled. "So far there isn't a whole lot here that is like Second Earth."

Boon looked totally stunned. "Really?"

"Oh yeah," I answered while tying on the shoe. "What you call klees, we call cats. Some are big and wild, but most are small and gars keep them as pets."

I saw a frown cross Boon's face. Uh-oh. Maybe I shouldn't have told him that.

"You keep klees as pets?" he asked, incredulous.

"Not me, no," I was quick to answer, trying to do damage control. "But some people. A couple people. Not many, really. It's very rare." Yikes.

Boon walked toward me, and I once again realized that he was a dangerous predator. I was about to say something like, "Whoa, remember, I'm the lead Traveler!" But I didn't want to be lame. Instead I stood up and tried to act like the lead Traveler.

"Your ring," he said.

I looked down at my Traveler ring. It was the one item that was allowed to be brought between territories.

"What about it?" I asked.

"Hide it," Boon said. "If somebody sees you wearing a ring, they'll know something is wrong. The *best* thing they'll do is take it from you."

"Really?" I asked. "What's the *worst* thing they'll do?"

"Eat you" was his sober answer.

Gulp. I quickly took off my ring.

"Can I see it?" Boon asked.

I reluctantly handed it over to him. Boon took the ring and admired it like it was a priceless jewel.

"Incredible," he said with awe. "Someday I'll have one too."

I took the ring back and tied it around my neck with one of the braided vines that I used to lash on my stinky clothing.

"You should take me to Seegen now," I said with authority.

Boon looked at me with cold eyes. Had I pushed too far? Obviously, he wasn't used to being told what to do by a gar. We held eye contact for a moment longer, then Boon broke out in a big smile.

"This is going to be fun!" he exclaimed, and hurried off.

Fun? I can think of a lot of words to describe my first few minutes on Eelong. "Fun" wasn't one of them. But that didn't matter. I was here to find Gunny . . . and stop Saint Dane. Fun wasn't part of the equation. So I hitched up my shoes, hid my ring around my neck, and jogged after the walking, talking cat that was going to bring me to a place called Leeandra and the Traveler from Eelong.

# EELONG

Eelong is a strange and wonderful place. Strange because of the way evolution took such a different turn from on Second Earth . . . or any of the other territories I'd been to, for that matter. Wonderful because it's totally beautiful. Not since I first swam through the underwater world of Cloral had I been to a place where you could use the word "paradise" to describe it. I think this territory is about as close as it gets. But Eelong is one other thing. Dangerous. Strange, wonderful, and dangerous. That pretty much summed up my opinion.

Boon led me to the far side of the massive room inside the hollow tree and pointed up to a ledge that led to a hole in the wall. It must have been a hundred feet up.

"That's the tunnel we've got to take out of here," he said.

"You're kidding?" I answered. "It'll take me an hour to climb those vines."

Boon shook his head in pity. "How can gars on your territory be superior to klees if they can't even climb?"

"We have an agreement with cats," I answered. "They don't ask us to climb things and we don't ask them to do algebra."

Boon had no idea what I meant. But he shrugged and said, "No problem. We'll take the gar way up." He walked along the wall of the cavern until he came upon another tunnel into the tree, at ground level. "Follow me," he said, and disappeared into the opening. I stepped into the opening to find myself in the dark.

"Boon?" I called out.

Boon's head suddenly appeared from above, upside down, right in front of my face. I jumped back in surprise and saw he was hanging from his back feet, or paws.

"Climb the roots," he instructed. "It should be easy."

I looked up to see he was hanging from a dense tangle of thick roots that created a tunnel going straight up. "Why do we have to climb?" I protested. "Can't we just go outside and walk to Leeandra?"

"We could," Boon answered. "If you don't mind running into a tang."

Tang? The only "Tang" I knew was a fake orange drink that astronauts liked. "What's a tang?" I asked.

"Nasty creatures," Boon answered. "Predators. They eat gars, mostly, but that's because we klees are smart enough to keep to the trees. Tangs climb even worse than gars do."

"Are they green?" I asked. "With lots of teeth, and smell bad when they're hungry?"

"You know about 'em?" he asked.

"You might say that," I answered. "I nearly got eaten by one."

"Then you know what I'm talking about," Boon exclaimed. "That's why we climb."

Boon hoisted himself up and climbed the root system. I figured that if the price of avoiding those lizard creatures outside was to climb a tree, that was okay by me. Boon was right; it was easy. It was like climbing the jungle gym in the playground at Glenville School.

"What happens when we get up?" I called up to Boon. "Won't we be stuck?" I thought about making a joke about dumb cats getting stuck up in trees and having to be rescued by the fire department, but I didn't think Boon would get it.

"Trust me," he said. "I'll get you where you need to go."

This was his show, so I stopped asking questions. Since he hadn't eaten me yet, I had no reason to believe he meant me any harm. As strange as the whole situation was, I was beginning to feel that finding Boon was a good thing. And if he took me to Gunny, it would be an even better thing. We climbed quickly for about five minutes. When we reached the top, I hoisted myself out of the vertical tunnel and into another large, empty room. We were still inside the tree, but now high above the ground. The room was about a third of the size of the room at ground level. I could feel a slight swaying as the huge tree moved in the wind. The floor was made of wood planks that looked old and weathered, like they had been there a long time. Leading outside were three big archways cut into the walls. I felt a warm breeze blowing through and saw blue sky beyond.

"It's a tree house," I said. "Do people, uh, klees live here?"

"I told you, nobody comes here much anymore," Boon answered. "It's too far from civilization. But somebody must have lived here at one time, and built this dwelling."

"So now what?" I asked.

Boon walked for one of the archways. I followed him, but slowed before reaching the opening. I'm not good with heights. I expected to peer out of the archway and see a long drop to the ground. When I took a tentative peek outside, I was surprised to see that beyond the opening was a balcony about twenty feet wide. I took a cautious step outside and saw that it wrapped around the tree. The floor was made of the same wooden planks as inside. There was a handrail around the outside for safety. Better still was the view. I walked slowly toward the handrail and got another look at the incredible forest.

Boon joined me and said, "Pretty, isn't it?"

"It's awesome," I replied. I meant it.

"This is nothing," Boon scoffed. "Wait until you see Leeandra." He walked away from me as if he were actually going somewhere.

"Where are you going?" I asked. "We're in a tree!"

"To Leeandra," he shouted back without turning. "It's a long way, let's not waste any more time."

I followed him, but fully expected to circle this treetop balcony and end up right back where we started.

We didn't. After walking a few feet, I saw that there was a bridge leading off the balcony. It was about ten feet wide and held up by thick vines, like a suspension bridge. Boon stepped onto it like it was the most natural thing in the world, and kept walking. I, on the other hand, wasn't so sure. I stood at the beginning of the bridge and peered over the handrail. It was a long way down. A *long* way. The bridge seemed safe. It barely moved when Boon walked across it. Still, this was scary. I'd seen too many movies where people walked across these suspension bridges and the wooden slats started to break through and . . . look out below! I reached up and grabbed one of the suspension vines, giving it a good tug to see if it would hold.

"It's safe, Pendragon," Boon assured me. "I told you, klees live in the trees. We know how to build bridges."

"So everybody lives in tree houses?" I asked. "Klees and gars?"

"It's better than worrying about tangs all the time," he answered.

I gritted my teeth and took a step onto the wooden bridge. Obviously it didn't break, and I didn't plummet to a horrifying death. I took a few more tentative steps, and we were on our way to Leeandra. It turned out that the big tree that held the flume was only one of thousands. Every tree on Eelong was as big, if not bigger. The bridges were like roads in the sky, snaking beneath the canopy of leaves. Each new tree we reached had a similar platform that ringed it. Some had multiple platforms with stairs between them. I thought back to the first moment I stepped out of the tree and looked over the cliff. I now realized that the reason I didn't see any buildings was because they were hovering just below the treetops, out of sight from above. Incredible! An entire civilization existed high above the ground. It was a world of tree houses.

This world was full of life, too. I saw a swarm of tiny, orange hummingbird creatures float by like a small cloud. They each gave off a sweet, whistling sound that must have been their tiny wings beating. Together, the effect was like music. I glanced up to see a large hawk soaring overhead. It was pure white and floated on thermals like a lazy cloud. Directly across from us, on our level, was a tree full of green monkeys. They were cute little things that chattered and chased one another from branch to branch.

Looking over the side to the forest below, I saw that it was dense jungle, like a rain forest. Every so often I'd catch a glimpse of a green tail disappearing into the underbrush. These could only be more of the lizardlike tangs. I decided that if there were more of those bad boys hiding below, I was very happy to be walking above them, out of reach.

Boon walked quickly. I had to work to keep pace. After five minutes we had passed through a dozen trees, each with a couple of different choices as to which bridge to take next. I was going to need a roadmap to find my way back to the flume. That wasn't good.

"Tell me about Saint Dane," Boon said as we walked. "He's a gar, right?"

"I guess," was my answer. "But he can change himself to look like whatever he wants. I'll bet he could change himself into a tang if he wanted to."

"Really? That's hard to believe," was his response.

Hard to believe? I was walking along a wooden sky bridge talking to a cat. Don't tell me about hard to believe.

"You think he's here, on Eelong?" Boon asked.

"Yes, I do," was my answer.

"Finally!" Boon exclaimed. He hopped ahead of me with excitement and walked backward while talking quickly. "I've been waiting forever to meet this guy. Seegen said he'd be here someday, but I never thought the day would actually come! He's really bad, right? I mean, do you think he's going to try and do something horrible on Eelong? Let him try. I'll slash him like that quig in the flume tree!"

I realized that this man-eating cat was no more than an excited kid who thought the war with Saint Dane was some kind of exciting game.

"Uhh, this isn't like pro wrestling," I said. "This is real."

"I know that," Boon said defensively. "What's pro wrestling?"

I didn't like having to be the voice of reason. I was suddenly feeling like I had to act like an adult or something. I stopped walking and spoke in my most serious voice.

"Look, Boon, I don't know what Seegen told you, but this isn't going to be fun. Saint Dane is a killer. I've seen him start wars and destroy cities. He'll do anything he can to turn Eelong inside out."

"Let him try!" Boon shouted with defiance. "I'm not afraid and neither is Seegen."

"Yeah, well, I hate to burst your bubble, but maybe you should be."

"Why? He's a gar! There hasn't been a gar born that I can't handle."

"He isn't an ordinary gar, Boon, he's . . . Wait, what am I doing? I'm talking to a cat! You're a freaking cat! This is insane!"

Maybe it was because the shock of my first few moments on Eelong had finally worn off. Maybe it was because I was feeling alone. Or maybe it was because my mind had finally rejected the possibility that cats could talk, but I had had enough.

"I'm going back," I said, and turned back for the flume. I had no idea how to find it, but I was ready to try. Boon ran around in front to head me off, but I kept walking.

"You can't go back, you're supposed to be here!" he complained.

"No, I'm not," I shot back. "This territory is crazy. Quigs are humans. Cats talk and live in trees because they might get eaten by big lizards. And I'm supposed to follow somebody who thinks battling Saint Dane is going to be fun? I don't think so."

I kept walking. Boon kept pace. "But, but, Seegen will be really angry with me," he complained. "I was supposed to bring you to Leeandra."

"Tell you what," I said. "I'm going back home, to Second

Earth, where humans are humans and cats pee in a litter box. If this Seegen character wants my help, he can find me there. Let's see how *he* likes dealing with a world where he belongs in a zoo."

"But what about the other Traveler, Gunny?" Boon asked.

That made me stop. Gunny. I'd almost forgotten. Whatever problems I was having with Eelong, Gunny had them too. I couldn't leave without finding him.

*"Ahhhhh!"* A horrifying scream came from down in the jungle. Boon and I ran to the railing of the sky bridge and looked down. On the ground we saw a small band of klees run from the jungle into a clearing that was directly below us. They were running on all fours like, well, like cats.

"I thought the klees lived in the trees?" I asked.

"We do," Boon answered. "But we still need to spend time on the ground. Food doesn't grow on trees, you know."

There was a joke in there somewhere, but I didn't go after it. Running behind the band of cats we saw a group of humans. They were dressed in the same rags as I wore, but didn't look as wild as the quigs. They just looked like smallish, dirty people. There were about a dozen in all. Mostly men, but a few women as well. They all looked as if they were running in fear from something, and a second later I saw what it was.

A green shape sprang from the bushes and grabbed the last of the fleeing humans. It was a tang. The lizard wrapped its talons around the leg of the human, who had fallen on his stomach. The beast dragged the guy along the ground toward the bushes. The victim may have looked human, but his terrified screams sounded more like an animal. A *doomed* animal.

"We gotta do something!" I shouted.

"Like what?" Boon answered casually. "It's okay, Pendragon. This happens all the time."

It was horrible. Maybe Boon was used to seeing humans dragged off to a gruesome death at the hands of a hungry lizard, but this was alien to me. I'd never seen anything like this on the Discovery Channel.

"But he's going to die!" I shouted.

"That's how it works," Boon said patiently. "Survival of the fittest."

Even though we were high overhead, I could smell the deadly-sick odor come from the hungry tang. It was getting ready to feed. The human grabbed at the ground, digging its fingers in, desperately trying to pull away. It was futile. The other humans kept running. The cats, too. This guy was left to die. My stomach turned.

Then I saw a black shadow flash back into the clearing. One of the cats had returned. It ran toward the tang on all fours and stood up on its back two feet.

"Kasha!" Boon exclaimed.

"Who?"

"She's a friend of mine," he answered. "And she hates tangs."

The cat Boon called Kasha was jet black. Her fur was so black, it looked blue. It was shiny, too. She wore the same dark clothing as the other cats. In one hand she held a long stick. In the other she held what looked to be a coiled rope.

The tang stopped dragging the human. It eyed Kasha warily. The human let out a guttural plea, begging for Kasha's help.

"Kasha, let it go!" came another voice from below. The other cats had returned. They stood together in a group, on their back legs, keeping a safe distance from the action. Boon pointed to the big, gray cat who had yelled at Kasha.

"That's Durgen," he said. "He's in charge of the group."

"It's over, Kasha," Durgen yelled, sounding bored. "I want to go home."

Another cat called out, "He's past his prime anyway. The tang's doing you a favor."

The other cats laughed at the remark. Kasha ignored them. She crept closer to the tang and stopped about ten feet away. With her left hand she held the stick out as a threat. She swiped the air a few times, getting its attention. The tang kept its eye on the stick, but didn't let go of the human. What the tang didn't see, was that in Kasha's right hand, she held the lasso. I saw that one end of the rope split off into three threads. Hanging from each end was a ball about the size of a big lemon. Kasha turned her body sideways so the tang couldn't see that she was getting ready to throw it. She swept the air with the stick again. The tang snarled. It held tight to the leg of the human with one of its talon hands, and held the other up, ready to fend off the stick.

"Hurry up," Durgen yelled. "I'm already late for supper."

Kasha flashed the stick once more, the tang swiped at it, and Kasha hurled the rope. The three balls spun toward their target. The tang had no idea what hit him. The three balls wrapped around its neck, winding the vines along with it. Kasha quickly dropped the stick, grabbed the vine with both hands, and yanked hard. The tang screamed in pain and reached for the vine. Of course, by doing that he let go of the human, and the frightened guy scrambled to his feet and fled. When he ran past the group of cats, one of them shouted at him, "What? Not even a thank-you? Where are your manners?" The others laughed.

But it wasn't over. Kasha was still grappling with the tang. The lizard made a move for her, but Kasha danced away and yanked the rope again, making the tang scream in agony. As long as she held the rope, she could control the tang. But if she let go, the tang could attack. It was a standoff.

Kasha called to the others, "Uh, little help, please?" Her voice was definitely feminine, which is weird to say because she was a cat. She didn't sound scared, either. But it was clear she didn't want to be dealing with this tang on her own.

"Come on," Durgen said to the others, sounding like he was bored with the whole event. "Let's help her out . . . again."

The cats all picked up long sticks of their own and moved toward Kasha and the tang. Durgen said to Kasha, "What if we weren't here to help?"

Kasha replied, "But you are, so start."

The cats poked at the tang with their long sticks. Kasha let go of the rope and backed away. The tang made an angry move for her, but the other cats poked it back.

"Easy there, big fella," Durgen said to the tang. "Party's over. Go find dinner somewhere else."

The tang hissed at them and backed away. With a final shriek, it turned and rumbled into the bushes.

"Can we go now?" one of the cats asked Kasha.

"Yes, thank you," she answered.

They retreated as a group, in case the tang decided to make a counterattack.

"Why do you do that?" Durgen asked Kasha. "Risk your life for a gar?"

"To make you angry," Kasha replied playfully, and gave the cat a friendly shove.

"I'm serious," Durgen added. "One day you're going to get yourself killed."

"Then you won't have to worry about me anymore," Kasha said with a chuckle.

The cats dropped their sticks, got down on all fours, and

ran into the forest, once again looking like a pack of jungle cats.

"She's a friend of yours?" I asked Boon.

"Since we were little," Boon answered. "Her father is Seegen."

"Seegen? The Traveler?" I asked in surprise. "He has a daughter?"

"Yes. She doesn't know it yet, but Seegen told me she'll be the next Traveler from Eelong. And when that happens, I'll become her acolyte."

"Are you serious?" I asked, sounding more surprised than I meant to.

"Yes. What's wrong with that?"

"Oh, nothing."

"Let's keep going. We're almost there," Boon said, and continued walking.

I followed, but with a new, troubling thought. There was only one Traveler from each territory. My uncle Press was killed, making me the Traveler from Second Earth. Loor's mother and Spader's father died as well, making them the Travelers from their territories. Aja was an orphan. If Kasha was destined to be the next Traveler from Eelong, then I was very worried about the safety of Seegen, the current Traveler. It was suddenly more important than ever to meet him.

# EELONG

Leeandra.

I'm not sure if you'd call it a city, or a zoo, or a fantasy village in the trees. It was all of the above. When Boon told me we were going to his home, I expected to find a tree house that smelled like cat pee and had clumps of fur piled in the corners. After all, these jungle cats may walk and talk, but they were still animals. I thought Leeandra would be more like a zoo than someplace I would call a city.

Man, was I wrong. I suppose my first clue should have been the sky bridges and balconies. Near the flume tree they were old and unkempt, but the closer we got to Leeandra, the slicker these bridges became. There wasn't a rotten board in sight. The supports were taut and true. Whoever built these bridges was a heck of an engineer. Also, the farther we walked, the more complex the structures became. The trees held multiple platforms connected by sky bridges at all levels and angles. As I think back on the journey, I can describe it as being like a trip from the country into the city.

We also started seeing more cats. I should probably start calling them klees, but that's going to be tough because, well, they were cats. I saw klees of all different sizes and colors traveling the sky bridges. Some walked on their hind legs. Others ran on all fours, seemingly in a hurry to get somewhere important. I suppose I should have been scared, because any one of them could have turned me into Tender Vittles, but I wasn't. It all seemed so . . . civilized. I figured that unlike on Second Earth, predator cats and humans were able to live side by side. Weird, no?

It was about to get a whole lot weirder.

We were starting to cross another sky bridge when Boon stopped. He looked around to make sure nobody was watching or listening, then reached into his tunic and pulled out a thick, braided vine that was looped into two small circles on one end.

"We're almost at Leeandra," he explained. "I hate to do this, Pendragon, but there are city rules that don't apply in the jungle."

"What is it?" I asked.

"Restraints," he said with his head down, embarrassed.

"It's okay, I understand," I said and took the braided vine to place it around Boon's furry hands. "I won't make it too tight."

"No!" Boon said and pulled his hands back. "These are for you!"

I didn't react at first. It took a couple of seconds to understand what he was saying. He wanted to put the restraints on *me*!

"You gotta be kidding me!" I shouted and backed away.

"Sshhhh!" he said while looking around nervously. "You're a gar. We don't let gars walk around on their own inside the city."

"Why not? What's wrong with gars? Besides the smell, which you already pointed out."

Boon frowned. He grew nervous. "I . . . I'm sorry, Pendragon. Maybe you don't understand. I'm not really sure how to say this but, the gars here aren't like you."

"Yeah, I saw those quigs," I said.

"Not just the quigs," Boon said. "Pendragon, on Eelong, gars are like . . . animals."

I stared at Boon a long time, letting his words roll around in my head, hoping they would settle down in some way that would make sense. They didn't.

"I thought you knew," he said sheepishly. "Most gars can't even speak, that's why I was so surprised to hear you talk. I guess I didn't explain things so well."

"No, you didn't," I said nervously. "You're telling me humans on Eelong can't speak? Or think intelligently? Or work or read or laugh or write or . . . or play sports?"

"No, they play sports!" Boon assured me. "Gars play wippen all the time." He then dropped his voice low and said, "But lots of them are killed during the game."

"Oh, that's just swell!" I shouted. "Humans aren't capable of doing anything except getting killed playing games or being eaten by tangs. I feel so much better now."

"But everything will be fine if you stay with me . . . and put this on," Boon said, holding up the restraint.

"No . . . freakin' . . . way," I said. "You're not going to put a leash on me like some kind of . . . of . . . animal!"

"But that's what you are!" Boon pleaded. "Nobody here knows about other territories or Travelers or places where gars are intelligent. Believe me, I know about it, and I'm still having trouble accepting it."

"Well, that's just too bad," I shot back. "The hell with your leash laws. I'm here to help these cats. If they're going to treat me like a pet, then they can get somebody else to protect them from Saint Dane."

I was really mad. But more than that, I was freaked out. Can you imagine dropping down a few notches on the food chain and being treated like a lower life-form?

"Take me to Seegen," I demanded. "If he's the Traveler from Eelong, then I'm going to need his help. And I've got to find Gunny. The more time we waste playing zoo boy, the more time Saint Dane has to cause trouble."

Boon looked to the ground. "I understand how you feel, Pendragon," he said quietly. "I don't blame you. If I went to Second Earth, I'm sure I'd feel the same way."

"I guarantee it," I grumbled.

"But we've got a problem," he continued. "If you want to walk around Leeandra like you're a klee, you'll be picked up by the Stray Division and impounded."

"You mean like a loose dog?" I asked, horrified.

"I don't know what a dog is," Boon answered.

"What if you explained to them I'm a really smart gar, and I should be treated with respect?"

Boon looked at me like I had just said I was going to sprout wings from my ears and fly.

"Okay," Boon said calmly. "You win. I'll do whatever you want, you're the lead Traveler. But please, before you decide, let me show you something."

"What?" I asked.

"You need to understand how things work here," he explained. "There's a meeting going on right now. Maybe we can catch the end of it. It's being run by the viceroy of Leeandra."

"You want me to speak at a meeting?"

*"No!"* Boon said quickly, as if the idea actually scared him. "I want you to listen to what they're discussing. After you hear what they have to say, I'll go along with whatever you want."

I put my anger aside and decided that Boon was being pretty fair. He may have been naive about Saint Dane, and a little overeager, but he seemed to be a smart guy. He was trying.

"Okay, fine," I agreed.

Boon looked visibly relieved. "But please," he added. "Until that meeting is over, will you go along with me and slip these restraints on your wrists? The klees will think you're with me and we won't have any problems."

The idea of getting tied up and led around like a dog made my mouth go dry. It's hard to describe the feeling. It was very primal, like I was handing over control of my life and my intellect.

"Trust me," he added. "It will be much easier this way."

I answered by holding out my wrists. Boon nodded in thanks and gently slipped the two loops over my hands. He gently tugged the loops tight until they were snug around my wrists. My stomach twisted.

"Now," he said. "Let me show you Leeandra."

Boon stepped onto the bridge, and I was happy that he didn't pull the leash tight. He waited for me to walk beside him. That was good. If he had made me walk behind him I think I would have lost it again. It was then that I noticed the band of light in the sky had moved lower on the horizon. My guess was right; this thing was like the sun. This small revelation made me feel more comfortable. At least I was getting to understand Eelong, even if I wasn't so thrilled about most of what I was learning. I looked ahead over the sky bridge to a huge tree on the far side. The bridge led to a large portal in the tree, like we were walking over the drawbridge to the entrance of a giant castle. There was dense foliage to either side of it, blocking my view of what was beyond.

"You okay?" Boon asked.

"Yeah, whatever" was my answer. Truth was, I wasn't, but what could I do?

We walked through the portal to find that this hollowed-out tree held a guard station. Two large cats stood in front of a cage that blocked the way. They each held long sticks as weapons and had coils of ropes attached to their belts. They were the same weapons I saw the cat named Kasha use against the tang.

"Boon!" one of the cats shouted jovially. "Where have you been? You missed the wippen tournament!"

"Busy," Boon answered, trying to sound casual. "How'd it go?"

"Lousy," the other cat answered. "Those big klees from the north end were too good."

"They're no better than us," the first cat corrected. "They just train more."

The second cat added, "We needed you, Boon."

"Next time," Boon promised. He nodded to the cage door. The first cat swung it open for us.

"New gar?" the cat asked.

I had been looking to the ground the whole time. I was afraid if these big cats looked into my eyes, they might see some hint of intelligence they weren't used to. But now, I glanced to Boon to see his reaction. Boon gave me a quick, embarrassed look.

"Uh, yeah," he answered.

"Do yourself a favor," the first cat said. "Wash him down. He stinks."

It took every bit of willpower I had not to say something. The truth was, these cats didn't exactly smell like roses either.

"Yeah," Boon said. I heard a slight nervous quiver in his voice. "I'll do that. Thanks."

Boon led me through the door. I was a good little gar and followed with my head down. As we walked away from the cage, Boon whispered, "Sorry."

I decided not to give him a hard time. Instead I asked, "What's wippen?"

"It's the game I told you about," Boon said, relieved to be talking about something else. "We've all played since we were kids."

"Kittens," I said.

"Excuse me?"

"Forget it."

Before I had the chance to ask him any more about what to expect, we stepped out of the portal on the far side of the tree and I got my first view of Leeandra. Oh man. What a sight! Like I wrote before, it was a city built in the air. There were wooden huts of all sizes dotting the sides of the trees. Busy sky bridges were everywhere. The structures were built high overhead, and down low, with the lowest buildings only about twenty yards off the ground. I guessed they were still high enough to be safe from marauding tangs. The city was big. I saw no end to the buildings, either way. It all looked to be manufactured out of natural material. Wood, bamboo, and woven vines. I didn't see anything that looked like metal or plastic. Everything I saw was very much like I had seen on my way to Leeandra, but multiplied a few hundred times.

But there was more. Running alongside many of the sky bridges were vehicles that traveled on a single track, like a monorail. They were open-car trains that each carried about twenty klees. They moved silently and stopped at intersections where klees got off and on. I also saw elevators. There were round platforms that carried passengers up and down the outsides of the trees, to all levels. I saw fountains on many levels that emptied into square troughs where klees bellied up and lapped water like, well, like cats. That meant Leeandra had pumps, and plumbing. But maybe the most incredible sight was the streetlights. The entire city was covered by a thick canopy of foliage that didn't let in much light from the sunbelt in the sky. So even though it was daytime, it was pretty dark. But the streetlights took care of that. Every few yards along the sky bridges and walkways was an overhead light fixture that was made up of a handful of small, vertical tubes that looked like wind chimes. The lights gave off a warm glow that made the city look as if it were lit by giant fireflies. It was something out of a fairy-tale fantasy.

"You have electricity?" I asked Boon.

"What's that?"

"You know, power, juice."

Boon shrugged and shook his head. He had no idea what I was talking about.

I tried another tack. "What makes those trains run? I mean, I doubt if you have little birds inside running on a treadmill like the Flintstones."

"Oh! You mean energy!"

"Yeah, energy. What makes everything go?"

"Collectors, above the canopy," Boon explained. "We use crystals to collect and store energy from the light in the sky. It's very simple, really. But I don't know what a 'flintstone' is."

Amazing. This walking, talking jungle cat was telling me that this society of animals had figured out a way to collect enough solar energy to power their city, while our so-called advanced society on Second Earth had no clue as to how to make solar energy practical. If it was so simple, how come we couldn't do it?

"Don't you get your energy that way on Second Earth?" Boon asked innocently.

"Uh . . . yeah, sometimes," I said quickly, not wanting to admit the truth. "Where is this meeting?" I added, changing the subject.

"At the Circle of Klee," Boon answered. "This way."

The two of us walked through the city, crossing over several more sky bridges and taking two different elevators. Klees were everywhere—on the sky bridges, on the elevators, riding the monorails and hanging around on every level of the city. I didn't see many gars, though. The ones I did see were either walking along on leashes with klees, like I was with Boon, or doing some menial work, like lugging heavy materials or cleaning the monorail tracks. The gars may have been considered animals, but they were smart enough to do work. I was beginning to think there was a lot more to the social system on Eelong than Boon had explained to me. The gars were small people. The biggest guy I saw was maybe a little over five feet. They all wore rags like I did, and had wild hair that looked like it hadn't been brushed or cut since the day they were born. Only a few had beards, though. I wasn't sure if that's because they shaved, or they simply didn't have much facial hair.

What really freaked me out, though, was the look in their eyes. It was like nobody was home. They walked all hunched over, always glancing back toward the klees they walked with. I was beginning to realize what Boon meant when he said I'd stand out. Without thinking, I found myself hunching over a little bit.

One last note about the gars. Just before we reached the

Circle of Klee I saw something that was kind of odd. I'm not sure what it meant, but it was strange enough to write about here. We passed two gars who were tied up outside a tree house like dogs waiting for their master. They sat huddled together, staring at something that one gar held in the palm of his hand. It was a cube about the size of a box that a ring would come in. It was amber colored and could have been made of some kind of crystal. The odd thing was that the gars were both petting it like it was alive. They made this strange cooing sound, as if they were consoling a baby. It was totally creepy. They were so focused on this little cube that they didn't hear us coming, but as soon as we drew even with them, the one gar closed his hand around the cube and hid it so fast, it made me feel like it was either very valuable or very illegal. I made brief eye contact with the gar and could tell that the guy was scared I had seen his treasure. Or maybe he was scared that Boon saw it. Either way, he looked pretty nervous. I decided not to say anything to Boon, but filed it away to ask about later.

We took one last elevator and arrived at a platform that led to an archway into a hollow tree. As soon as we stepped off the elevator, I sensed that the tree was busy with activity. The general buzz gave it away. When Boon led me inside that archway, I saw that it was a meeting place. The room was big, with benches circling a round stage at the center. And it was packed. There must have been a hundred klees. What do you call a group of cats? A pack? A herd? A litter? They were all sitting on benches, looking toward the stage at center. Yes, they were sitting. They were cats, and they were sitting. Unbelievable.

Standing onstage was a tall cat dressed in a royal blue tunic. He actually looked somewhat like a lion, but his hair, or mane, wasn't as full as a lion's. It was long, though, and fell halfway down his back. He looked older, too. He stood center stage holding a long, wooden staff that had the carving of a snarling cat's head on top. I wasn't sure if he needed this for balance, or if it was a symbol of power. Behind him sat six more cats, each wearing tunics that were bright red.

"The Council of Klee," Boon whispered, as if reading my mind. "The governing body here in Leeandra."

He gently nudged me to an area away from the stage, where we could watch the proceedings while keeping our backs to the wall. That was a good idea. We didn't want any klees sneaking up from behind to hear us talking.

We had stepped into the middle of an argument. It wasn't chaotic, but it was close. Cats were yelling at each other, throwing up their hands for emphasis. Everybody was talking at once so I couldn't make out what anybody was saying. Whatever it was, emotions were definitely running high.

"Who's the guy on the stage?" I whispered to Boon.

"Ranjin, the viceroy of Leeandra," he answered.

Viceroy. I guessed that meant he was the boss. But the boss wasn't getting much respect. He held his paws up, calling for order, but nobody paid attention. Ranjin kept his cool, though. He glanced back to one of the cats in red, who was sitting politely, not joining in the argument. The cat nodded and lifted what looked like a carved, wooden horn to his mouth. He blew into it, sending out a long, low note. At the same time Ranjin raised his wooden staff over his head. Immediately the crowd grew quiet and looked to Ranjin. When he spoke, it was with a soft, calm voice that showed he was used to being in charge.

"What exactly is it that we are proposing here?" he said. "The repeal of Edict Forty-six?"

The cats all looked at one another nervously, as if none wanted to answer. I leaned close to Boon and whispered, "What's Edict Forty-six?"

Boon looked straight ahead, deliberately not answering.

"Boon?" I pressed. "What is Edict Forty-six?"

Boon sighed and said, "It's the law that forbids klees to hunt and eat gars."

Gulp.

"And they're thinking of getting rid of it?" I asked nervously.

"Yes," he answered. "You still want to risk getting picked up by the Stray Division?"

I was really starting to hate Eelong.

# EELONG

"We are not barbarians," Ranjin said with passion. "Edict Forty-six is what separates klees from the beasts of the jungle. As long as I am viceroy I will not allow this to happen."

Good man, Ranjin. Or good cat. Whatever.

"Then what do you suggest?" a cat shouted from the crowd. "The situation is getting worse. We can no longer grow enough food to feed our own young, let alone the gars."

Another cat jumped up and shouted, "Their numbers are growing daily. They have no concern for our society; they are savages."

I was beginning to realize why Boon wanted me to hear this. He wanted me to hear, firsthand, that humans weren't treated well here. Heck, they weren't even treated as well as cats on Second Earth. At least we didn't need laws to stop us from eating them. The more I heard, the less I minded being tied to Boon. That leash was starting to feel like a lifeline.

One of the cats in red who shared the stage with Ranjin stepped up to the viceroy. He bowed to the older cat respectfully. Ranjin nodded as if giving him permission to address the crowd.

"Who's that?" I whispered.

"His name is Timber," Boon answered. "He's one of the Council of Klee."

Timber, Ranjin, Boon, Seegen . . . I was in another one-name territory. How does that work? How many names have to be handed out before last names kick in?

"The Council of Klee gives advice to the viceroy," Boon continued. "But all decisions are the viceroy's to make."

That was good. From what I'd heard so far, the viceroy didn't want to declare open season on humans.

"Fellow Leeandrans," Timber began. "It is clear that we are in difficult times."

The big cat spoke with confidence. He had dark brown fur, with thousands of black spots, like a leopard. His mane was long, and it looked as if he actually combed it. How's that for an image? A big jungle cat with a slick hairdo? Amazing.

"Not one of us here today welcomes the idea of turning back the clock and returning to the ways of our primitive ancestors. Hunting gars has been outlawed for generations. The gars have become valuable to our very existence. Not just here in Leeandra, but throughout Eelong. Besides providing manual labor, they aid in our protection when traveling on the jungle floor. Some have even become beloved pets, family members, if you will."

The spotted cat was making it sound as if gars were pampered lapdogs. From what I had seen so far, it wasn't like that at all. But if this cat's speech was going to keep the cats from hunting humans, as far as I was concerned, Timber could spin the situation any way he wanted.

"However," Timber continued. "There are times when higher intentions must give way to harsh realities. The production of our farms can no longer keep up with the growing population of both klees and gars. At this rate, we will soon reach a point where there are dangerous shortages. We are always trying to find new ways to increase our yield, but even with the great strides we've made, we cannot keep up with the exploding gar population. I hate to say this in such dire terms, but soon there will not be enough food to go around."

Uh-oh. His speech was taking a bad turn.

"One of the beauties of our society is that we welcome free and open debate. We are encouraged to challenge our leaders in constructive ways. It is what has made Leeandra the most powerful city in Eelong, and I'm sure we all want it to remain that way. That is why I challenge the opinion of our esteemed viceroy."

His passion was growing, and so was the enthusiasm of his audience. Suddenly I wasn't liking Timber so much.

"As important as it is to keep sight of our loftier ideals," he continued, "noble intentions cannot take importance over our very survival!"

The crowd of cats cheered him on. Timber was feeding off their energy. This was looking very bad. I started to sweat.

"I for one cannot sit idly by and see our children go hungry in order for some lowly animals to fill their own bellies."

A big cheer. Public opinion was on his side. Being the only gar in the room, I was feeling pretty uncomfortable. I glanced to Boon. He wouldn't look at me. I looked to Ranjin, the viceroy. He stood firm, with his feet planted. He didn't seem angry, though I wasn't entirely sure what an angry cat looked like. Would he hiss? Would his ears go back?

"This is why I pledge to you today that I will use whatever humble influence I have on the Council of Klee to repeal Edict Forty-six until we have devised a way to increase our food supply. I believe the choice here is simple, my fellow

Leeandrans. If it comes down to the survival of our race, I say: Let them eat gar!"

Yikes. The crowd jumped to their feet with wild applause. It was like one of those political conventions you see on TV. I half expected balloons to start falling from the ceiling. My stomach turned. In a few short minutes I had gone from being insulted by having to wear a leash, to understanding that gars were treated worse than gerbils, to fearing it might soon be hunting season on gars . . . and like it or not, I was a gar. I looked back to the stage to see what Ranjin's reaction was to Timber's speech. What I saw made my blood freeze.

The klees in the audience were on their feet, stomping and clapping. On the stage, the red-robed Council of Klee all stood, calmly discussing something with Ranjin. They didn't seem upset or caught up in the emotion of the moment. But that's not what I focused on. My eyes went right to the big cat named Timber. I expected him to be on the edge of the stage, waving his arms to whip the crowd into a frenzy. But he wasn't. This cat stood by himself, away from the others. He didn't face the Council of Klee. He didn't face the crowd.

He was looking directly at me.

His gaze was solid and cold, like a predator who had located its prey. In some ways, that's what it was. I had been here before . . . and so had he.

"We gotta get outta here," I said to Boon.

"Let's wait till things calm down," he said.

"No!" I shouted. "Now!" I yanked my leash and pulled Boon toward the doorway. Boon quickly jumped in front of me. I'm sure he didn't want to be seen being led by a gar. It didn't matter to me. We had to get out of there. We got halfway through the large room when a crowd of klees spilled in front of us, laughing and cheering.

"Boon!" one cat yelled. It was the same cat who had chased the quig back in the tree with the flume. "You made it back in time!"

"Can't talk now!" Boon said as he tried to pull me through the crowd.

"But this is history!" The cat grabbed Boon and tried to pull him into the crowd. Boon struggled to get away, but these guys weren't letting him go.

Boon complained, "I need to bring my gar—"

"Forget the gar!" the cat said. He yanked the leash out of Boon's paw and tied me to a railing along the wall. "He'll be here when you get back . . . if he's lucky!" The cat laughed. He and the others grabbed Boon and pulled him into the crowd. Boon glanced at me, helpless. He was swept away in a jumble of fur and whiskers. Now I was alone . . . and trapped in a room full of predator cats who were getting all sorts of psyched about eating humans. As bad as that was, there was something that worried me more.

I heard the voice before I saw him. "Welcome to Eelong, Pendragon," he said calmly. "I trust you enjoyed my performance."

# EELONG

I didn't have to look. I knew who it was. He may have taken the form of a jungle cat named Timber, but I knew the truth.

"Hello, Saint Dane," I said. Trying to sound as if I wasn't surprised, or scared—because I was both. "You really must be getting desperate." I turned around to see him standing a few feet from me. He stood on two feet, staring down at me like some lowly bug. It was Saint Dane, all right.

"And why would you say that?" he asked.

"I can't change myself into a klee like you," I said. "It gives you an unfair advantage here. But maybe that's the only way you can beat me."

Saint Dane chuckled. "Oh, so brash for a young Traveler who failed so miserably on Veelox."

It took all my willpower not to scream at this creep. I didn't want to let him know that he was getting to me, which he was. "What have you done here?" I asked.

"Isn't it obvious?" he replied. "The word has such a nice ring to it, no?"

"What word?" I asked, not really sure I wanted to hear the answer.

"Genocide," Saint Dane said with finality.

"Genocide?" I repeated. "You want to wipe out the gars? Why? Aren't the gars like animals here? Wiping them out would be horrible, but not exactly a turning point for the territory."

"Ahh, but you're wrong," Saint Dane said. "The gars are much more integral to life on Eelong than the klees realize. Without the gars, the tangs will have no prey. It will only be a matter of time before those vicious lizards become desperate enough to rise up against the klees. The klees may be the superior race on Eelong, but they are no match for the tangs. So when I speak of genocide, the gars are simply the first step in the cycle of destruction."

It was a chilling thought. Saint Dane was monkeying with the food chain on Eelong. If he succeeded, the hunters would become the hunted, and Eelong would be left to a race of mindless, carnivorous dinosaurs . . . and he would have his second territory.

"You never told me your plan before. Why now?" I asked.

Saint Dane, or Timber as he called himself here, looked me in the eye. It took everything I had not to look away.

"Things have changed, Pendragon," he said with confidence. "As I said, once the first territory falls, the rest will topple like dominos. Veelox is on a path to destruction, thanks to your failure. My power is growing. Nothing is as it was. The order that ruled the territories is crumbling, and so is Halla." He backed away and added, "Which reminds me, it's time to pay a visit to your friends on Second Earth. What are their names? Oh yes, Mark and Courtney."

Hearing that, there was no way I could keep my cool anymore.

"Leave them alone!" I shouted. "They aren't Travelers. They have nothing to do with this."

"Everyone has a role in our little drama, Pendragon," Saint Dane shot back. "It's their turn. But don't blame me. It was you who chose them. I wonder how they'll use their new power."

"Power? What power?" I asked. "What's happened?"

Saint Dane backed toward the door. "Like I said, the walls are crumbling. I'll give them your regards." He held up a rotten, cloth bag and said, "Along with a small token from our friend Gunny." With that he turned and walked quickly for the door.

"Saint Dane!" I shouted, but it was useless. The big cat dropped down on all fours and sprang forward, leaping out of the doorway.

He was headed for the flume. For Second Earth. For you guys.

I knew I couldn't stop him, but you two had to be warned. I yanked at the leash, desperate to get loose and chase after the demon. All I did was pull the knot tighter. Idiot. Thankfully Boon came back.

"What are you doing?" he asked nervously. "Everybody's watching you!"

"It's Saint Dane," I said frantically. "Timber is Saint Dane."

"What?" Boon said, confused. "Timber has been on the Council of Klee since, well, since forever."

"Then Saint Dane has been here forever," I answered quickly. "Or he got rid of the real Timber and took his place. I told you, he can turn into whatever he wants, and he wants to be on the Council of Klee. That's what he does. He slimes himself into a territory and manipulates people and . . . now he's going after my friends on Second Earth. We've got to get back to the flume!"

"Maybe we should find Seegen first and—"

"No! We don't have time!"

Boon must have seen the desperation in my eyes. With one quick move he flashed one of his sharp claws and sliced through the leash. "Let's go," he said, all business. He grabbed the cut end of the leash for show, and the two of us ran out of the Circle of Klee. Good cat.

"I gotta beat him to the flume," I announced.

"If he's on the run, you'll never catch him," Boon warned.

"You gotta get me there, Boon," I said, not caring that other cats were watching us curiously. The thought flashed that I could jump on Boon's back and ride him to the flume, but Boon had another idea. He led me to an elevator platform and to my surprise, we went down . . . to the jungle floor.

"Whoa, isn't this dangerous?"

"You want to get there fast?" he asked. "This is the way."

We hit the ground, and Boon ran across the jungle beneath the trees. He stayed on two feet so I'd be able to keep up. But he was still faster than I was. It didn't help my speed any that I kept looking around, expecting a tang to leap out of a bush and start chewing on my butt.

"Don't worry. It's pretty safe inside Leeandra," Boon said without slowing down. "There are guards everywhere. We won't be in any real danger until we leave the city."

Good. No worries . . . for now. Boon led me to a tall fence made of bamboo that was around ten feet high. There was an opening with two klees standing guard. Boon ran up to one and said breathlessly, "I need a zenzen."

The guard answered, "What's your rush? The wippen tournament is over."

"And those guys from the north made us look bad," Boon said, thinking fast. "I want the extra practice."

The guard stepped aside and said, "Good! They aren't better than us, they just train more."

"Exactly!" Boon replied. "Watch my gar, would you?"

That was me. Boon ran inside the gate, leaving me alone. I stood in front of the two guards, feeling all sorts of vulnerable. I almost whistled casually, but figured that would have been a little suspicious. I looked to the ground but still felt their eyes on me. I really hoped they weren't hungry.

"What is that smell?" one klee asked the other in disgust.

"The gar," the other guard snarled. "Filthy animal. Don't they ever clean themselves?"

The first klee walked up to me. I could feel his breath, but didn't dare look up.

"Nice shoes," the klee said. "My hunting gar could use those."

"So get him a pair like that," the second guard said.

"I didn't say he could use a pair *like* that," the first guard corrected. "I said he could use *those*!"

Before I knew what was happening, the klee grabbed me around the neck, choking me.

"Take them!" he ordered the second klee.

The other guard quickly yanked off my shoes. I didn't fight. There were bigger problems to deal with than losing a pair of torn-up cloth shoes. Besides, I didn't want them to bite me. A few long seconds later, I heard the sound of hoofs. The klee guard let go of me and I gasped for breath. I saw Boon trotting up on the back of an incredibly strange-looking horse. I now realized that this tall fence was actually a corral. The animal Boon called a "zenzen" was dark orange, and sort of looked like a regular old Second Earth horse, except that it had impossibly long legs. That's because each leg had an extra joint. I'm serious. Imagine a horse leg, then add a whole 'nother section that was about two feet long, complete with an extra joint, and you'd have what they called a zenzen. It moved strangely, like a spider. But it was definitely a horse.

"C'mon, gar!" Boon shouted to me, as if he were calling a dog. "Good boy, let's go!"

I was totally humiliated, but had to play along. I walked over to the zenzen and looked up at Boon. It's tough enough climbing up onto a regular old horse, but this thing was another few feet higher. Boon reached down and held out his paw.

"C'mon boy, grab on," Boon commanded.

I gave him a dirty look and reached with my hand. Boon grabbed it and pulled me up like a doll. Man, he was strong. He plunked me down in back of him, just behind the saddle.

"Not bad!" one of the klee guards said. "You got that one trained pretty good!"

"But you gotta wash him down," the other said. "He stinks."

"And get him some shoes!" the first guard added with an obnoxious chuckle.

I whispered to Boon, "The stink comments are getting old."

"Sorry," Boon whispered. He then let out a "Yah!" while snapping the reins. I grabbed on to his tunic and we bolted forward and ran faster than I thought any horse could run. That extra length of leg must have acted like a turbocharger, because in no time we were flying. We blasted along the jungle floor, beneath the buildings of Leeandra. Very soon we came upon a wall made of bamboo that looked like the fence around the corral. Only this wall towered fifty feet into the air.

I now realized that Leeandra was built like a fort, with a wall ringing it to keep out the tangs.

"The gate!" Boon yelled ahead.

I looked over his shoulder to see a few klee guards move to open a huge, swinging door. Boon didn't slow down. The guards must have realized he wasn't going to stop, because they scrambled to get the door open. They swung it wide, just in time, as Boon and I galloped out of the safety of Leeandra and into the badlands.

Boon knew how to ride. We charged along the narrow, jungle path as if we were out in the great wide open. Fast was scary, but good. We not only had to beat Saint Dane to the flume, I figured as long as we were flying along, it would be tough for a tang to attack. Still, Boon wasn't taking any chances. Attached to the saddle was one of those long wooden weapons. Once we were out of the city, Boon held the reins with one paw, and grabbed the weapon with the other. He held it forward, ready, in case a hungry tang decided to get in our way.

Now that we were moving, my thoughts turned to what I would do once we caught up with Saint Dane. I was really worried about you guys. Saint Dane's comment about it being your turn, and your having new powers, didn't make sense. The only thing I knew for sure was that it couldn't be good. Saint Dane wouldn't be dropping in on you guys just to say howdy do. And he mentioned Gunny. I felt certain that Gunny was still alive, but where was he? I didn't want to leave Eelong without finding him, but knowing that Saint Dane was coming after you guys was more important. I had to get to you first.

The mad gallop through the forest was uneventful. Not a

single tang showed up. After a few minutes I saw that the stone in my ring was starting to glow. We were getting close to the gate. Boon rode us right back to the giant tree that held the flume and pulled up at the small entrance I had first come through. I had no idea if we had beaten Saint Dane there or not.

"Find Seegen," I said to Boon while climbing down from the zenzen. "He must know where Gunny is."

"No," Boon protested. "I'm coming with you."

"You can't," I shot back. "Only Travelers can use the flume."

"What about acolytes?" Boon asked.

"You're not an acolyte yet," I shot back. "And even if you were, acolytes can't use the flume. It doesn't work that way." I stopped short, my mind racing. My own words rang in my ears: *It doesn't work that way.* Saint Dane had said that the rules were changing, and the walls between the territories were breaking down. Could that be the "new powers" he was talking about? Was it possible that acolytes could now activate the flume?

"Pendragon?" Boon called to me. "What are you thinking?"

"Find Seegen," I said again. "I'll get back as soon as I can."

I had turned for the gate when Boon yelled, "Pendragon!" I looked back and Boon tossed me his wooden weapon.

"Quigs" was all he said.

I caught the heavy stick and felt its weight. It was like a long baseball bat. I had no idea how to use it against one of those human quigs, but it was better having it than not. I nodded to Boon, then dove down to the hole in the tree. I knew the way. I crawled through the narrow tunnel that was choked with vines and found the hole in the floor that led down to the flume cavern. While holding the weapon in front of me, I climbed down the root stairs, stepped over the pile of gar bones, and found myself standing in the grand underground cavern that held the flume. A quick look to the ground showed me the arrow I had scratched into the dirt. So far so good.

I didn't know if I was ahead of Saint Dane, or if he had already gone to Second Earth. Either way I didn't want to waste time, so I didn't change out of my Eelong rags. I put the wooden weapon down on the flat rock next to my jumpsuit from Veelox and dove through the curtain of roots that hid the flume.

When I reached the tunnel, I saw something I hadn't expected. There was a light glowing far in the distance, as if I had already activated the flume. But it didn't grow closer to me, nor did it disappear into the distance. It just sort of hung there as if the flume had been half activated. I didn't know what it meant, but I couldn't spend any time trying to figure it out.

"Second Earth!" I shouted into the tunnel.

The light came for me. A moment later I was pulled in and on my way home. But this was like no other trip I had taken back to Second Earth. Every time I had traveled home, it was always with a feeling like I was going somewhere safe and sane. This time I feared what I would find . . . and I wasn't disappointed. The voyage through the flume was eerily similar to the trip I had taken from Veelox to Eelong. I once again saw transparent images floating in space. This time I saw what looked to be giant chess pieces. There were also beautiful clear blue crystals spinning by that looked like glaze, the precious ore from Denduron. It felt like the star field was teeming with ghosts from all the different territories. I wondered if this had something to do with what Saint Dane had said about the walls between the territories crumbling.

You guys already know what happened when I arrived on Second Earth. When I saw you at the mouth of the flume, I realized I was too late. You looked all sorts of scared, which meant Saint Dane had already been there. I was relieved that you two were okay, but still worried about what it all meant. I'm sorry if I was rough with you guys, but I had so many different thoughts and fears running through my head, not the least of which was that bag that turned out to have Gunny's hand in it. Saint Dane is truly a monster. Once you told me he had returned to Eelong, I knew that I had to return as well. Again, I'm sorry for being such a creep.

My plan was to return to Eelong, then climb back up into the tree and see if I could find my way back to Leeandra. I needed to find Seegen, the Traveler. And ultimately, Gunny. After that we would begin to try and find a way to stop Saint Dane and his quest to obliterate the gars. On the trip back, I carried the bag with Gunny's hand with reverence. I didn't know what I was going to do with it, but whatever it was, it would have to be on Eelong.

But when the flume deposited me back in the cavern on Eelong, my plans immediately changed. I pushed my way through the hanging roots to find myself in the vast underground cavern facing . . .

A jet-black jungle cat. The big cat stood on all fours, facing me. Its amber eyes seemed to look right through me. If this cat had been given the okay to hunt gars, then it had just gotten a surprise snack from out of the blue. Me.

We stood looking at each other for what seemed like an eternity. I saw that my wooden weapon was still on the flat rock where I left it—beyond my reach. Not that I would have known what to do with it anyway. The next move was going to have to be the cat's. I bent my legs, ready to spring out of the way if it charged.

It didn't. Instead the big cat said calmly, "So you're Pendragon."

I immediately realized who it was. I had seen her before and knew I wasn't in danger.

"My name's Kasha," she continued. "My father is Seegen, the Traveler from Eelong." She stood up on her two hind legs, crossed her arms in front of her and added, "He's missing."

I'm going to end my journal here, guys. I'm writing this from the city of Leeandra, where I am staying in the tree house that belongs to Kasha, the daughter of Seegen. But Seegen isn't here. Question is, where is he?

The main reason I'm ending this here is that I need to send you a warning. Whatever happened by losing Veelox has changed the nature of Halla. I'm not entirely sure what that means, but it seems to be okay with Saint Dane, which can only mean it's bad news. You two are acolytes now. I'm proud of you, and I know you're going to support me and the other Travelers when we come to Second Earth. But I'm beginning to think that it means a little more. I can't be sure, but I think you two now have the power to activate the flumes.

Don't do it.

If there was one thing that Uncle Press taught me, it's that the territories cannot be mixed. Remember what happened on Denduron? It was nearly a disaster. I can't even imagine what would happen if acolytes started traveling between territories. I might be wrong about this, but my gut tells me it would cause even more trouble than before. So please, wait for my next journal. Hopefully by the time I write it, I'll have more information to give you. You guys are the best. I don't know what I would do if you weren't there for me, even if it's just on the other end of my journals. Again, I'm sorry for having been so rough when I saw you, but I know you understand.

And I hope that by the next time I write, I'll have some news about Gunny. Until then, think about me, and please be careful.

**END OF JOURNAL #16**

# ☻ SECOND EARTH ☻

*". . . think about me, and please be careful."*

Courtney Chetwynde read the last few words of Bobby's journal out loud and then dropped the crunchy, brown pages onto the table in front of the couch where Mark Dimond sat. They were in the basement of Courtney's house, in her father's dusty workshop. It was the one place they knew they could read Bobby's journals and not be disturbed. Courtney's dad never used the workshop. They called it the "tool museum."

"That sucks," Courtney said with disgust.

"What do you mean?" Mark asked.

"We finally have the chance to help Bobby, for real, and he won't let us."

Mark sat up straight. He hadn't expected this reaction from her.

"Whoa, you were the one who wasn't sure about being an acolyte. Now you're upset because you can't jump into the flume?"

Courtney picked up a hammer from the workbench and pounded it into her open hand, a move that clearly said to Mark that she was upset. She didn't say anything right away and Mark didn't press her. Whatever was on her mind, he knew it had to come out on her terms. Finally, after slamming her hand so many times Mark felt sure she'd break bones, she opened up.

"We're in trouble," she began. "All of us. You, me, our families, Stony Brook, Second Earth, Halla . . . *everybody!* Up until now it's all been like some bizarro dream. But seeing Saint Dane in the flesh, man, that made it real." She threw the hammer down onto the workbench. The loud clatter echoed through the basement. Mark had never seen Courtney like this. She was focused, like when she played sports. But there was something more. Something different. The only thing Mark could figure was that Courtney seemed . . . older. He sensed an odd mix of emotions: intensity, anger, and fear.

"We know what's going on," she continued. "As much as Bobby does. How can we sit around and do nothing but wait for the mail to come in?"

"Because that's what Bobby asked us to do," Mark answered meekly, hoping not to redirect Courtney's anger to him.

"Bull!" Courtney shouted. "Bobby's guessing. He doesn't know for a fact it would be bad if we used the flumes. And I'll tell you something else, has Saint Dane ever told the truth? Things never turn out the way they first appear—that's how he manipulates people. He gives you just enough information to think you know what's going on, then when you jump at his bait, he twists things. You know what I think? It's possible he's messing with Bobby's head again. Maybe Saint Dane is *afraid* for us to travel? Huh? What about that? Maybe he doesn't want more enemies on his butt. Did you think about that?"

Mark let this theory sink in. This was serious stuff. "Okay," he said calmly. "I'm not sure if you're right, but s-suppose you are. What do you th-think we should do?"

Courtney deflated. Mark saw it. The wind went right out of her sails, and she plunked herself down on the couch, sending up a cloud of dust that made Mark cough.

"It's only a theory," she said in defeat. "I didn't say I had answers."

Mark let out a relieved breath. For a second he was afraid that Courtney was going to suggest they go to Eelong. Not only would that be exactly what Bobby asked them *not* to do, the idea of running into one of those tang creatures wasn't exactly a pleasant one. Not to mention the gar quigs . . . or the klees, who were on the verge of legalizing the killing of humans for food. No, Mark figured that going to Eelong would be an aggressively bad idea.

Courtney sat on the couch stiffly, her jaw muscles working. Mark was beginning to think her anger had a lot to do with the trouble she was having at school, and at sports. Courtney wasn't used to failing, and right now she was failing big-time. It occurred to Mark that Courtney's sudden desire to enter the fight against Saint Dane might be her way of proving something to herself. But he wasn't about to share that theory with her. No way. He didn't want to risk her picking up that hammer again and going to work on his head.

"I want to help," Mark said softly. "But we've got to be smart about it."

"I know," Courtney said. "You told me once you hoped the battle with Saint Dane would come to Second Earth so we could be part of it. Remember?"

"Yeah, I remember."

"Well, you got your wish. Saint Dane showed up. He knows who we are. How does that make you feel?"

Mark thought for a second and said, "Scared."

"Yeah, me too," Courtney admitted. "I'm not a total idiot."

"The thing is," Mark continued, "there's nothing we can do. We're not going to go to Eelong because we'd just get in the way, or get eaten. Bobby's barely able to take care of himself. He doesn't need us to worry about."

Courtney nodded.

"And we can't get around the fact that Bobby thinks we shouldn't use the flumes. He might be wrong, but we just don't know."

"So what do *you* think we should do?" Courtney asked.

"I hate to say it but . . . nothing. Until something else happens that makes things a little clearer, we have to wait."

"It's torture," Courtney said between clenched teeth. "Do you know how hard it is to go to school and do homework and take tests and deal with your parents while the universe is crumbling?"

"Well . . . yeah, I do," Mark answered.

Courtney smiled, backing down. "I know you do, Mark," she said sheepishly.

Mark reached for the journal papers and rolled them up. "I gotta get home," he said. "I'll bring this to the bank in the morning. Maybe after school we should get together again and talk about what might be—"

Mark stopped talking. His face went blank.

"What's the matter?" Courtney asked.

Mark dropped the journal and lifted his hand. His ring was activating again.

"Another journal?" Courtney asked. "Already?"

"N-No," Mark answered. They both saw that the dark stone in the center of the ring hadn't changed. Instead one of the symbols that circled the gray stone was glowing. Each of these ten symbols represented one of the ten territories of Halla. The symbol that was now glowing looked like three wavy lines.

"We're getting a message from an acolyte," Mark said, stunned.

When Tom Dorney told them about being acolytes, he explained that the acolytes were able to communicate with one another through the rings. Mark and Courtney had already seen it work when they got a message from the Veelox acolyte, Evangeline. Mark took off the ring and placed it on the table. It quickly grew, opening up a path between the territories. They heard the usual musical notes and saw the sparkling lights. As strange and magical as the event was, it had become familiar. They shielded their eyes from the harsh light, and in a few seconds it was over. The ring had returned to normal. The delivery had been made. Sitting on the table next to the ring was another roll of parchment paper.

"It looks like Bobby's journal," Courtney observed. "But it's short."

Mark picked up the paper and unrolled it to discover a single page.

"Well?" Courtney asked impatiently.

Mark said soberly, "I think we just got our first job as acolytes." He handed the page to Courtney. She read: *"You must come to the flume."*

"That's it?" she asked. "Who's it from?"

Mark took the paper back and rolled it up.

"No clue," he said. "Ready?"

"You want to go now?" Courtney asked, surprised. "It's almost dinnertime."

Mark shot her a "you've got to be kidding" look.

Courtney smiled, realizing her priorities were slightly confused.

"Forget I said that," she said quickly. "I'll tell my parents I'm going to the library. Call your mom and tell her the same thing."

"Okay," Mark agreed.

The two sat for a second, letting the reality of what was happening sink in. Finally Mark said, "I'm, uh, I'm kinda nervous. What if Saint Dane shows up again?"

Courtney jumped to her feet and said, "Then we deal. This is what we wanted, right?"

Fifteen minutes later Mark and Courtney found themselves back in the basement of the abandoned Sherwood house. They had made the appropriate excuses to their parents as to why they had to go to the library and promised to grab something to eat at McDonald's. Neither liked fibbing, but both figured it was justified in that they were helping to save the universe.

"How come the quigs aren't here?" Courtney asked as they made their way through the dark, empty basement. "Not that I'm complaining."

"I don't know," Mark answered. "But from what Bobby said, they only show up when Saint Dane is around."

"Good," Courtney said. "No quigs, no Saint Dane. So far I'm liking this mission."

The two approached the wooden door with the star symbol that marked it as a gate to the flume. It was night. The basement was dark, but their eyes had adjusted enough so they could find their way. Mark had his backpack and dropped it just outside the door. With a quick look at each other, they entered the root cellar that held the tunnel to infinity. They walked up to the huge mouth of the flume, but stopped before setting foot inside. Both gazed into the endless void.

"Tempting, isn't it?" Courtney asked playfully.

Mark nodded. He shot a sideways glance at her, worried that she might leap inside.

"How will they know we're here?" she asked. "Whoever *they* are."

"I don't think they have to know" was Mark's answer. "The flumes put the Travelers where they need to be, when they need to be there. So if somebody needs to see us, it doesn't matter when they enter the flume, they'll be here when we're here."

"That makes no sense," Courtney said, shaking her head.

"I know," Mark agreed. "But so far it's worked out that way, right?"

Before Courtney could answer, a light appeared in the depths of the flume. "I guess you're right," she announced. "Here we go."

The two backed away as far across the root cellar as they could go, which wasn't far. They clung to each other for support. Both were thinking the same thing: The last time this happened, Saint Dane showed up. Gulp. The light inside the flume grew closer, brightening the dank root cellar. The musical notes grew louder and the gray rock walls of the tunnel melted into glorious crystal.

"It's okay," Mark whispered with an oddly confident voice. "I think this is the way it was meant to be."

An instant later the light flashed and disappeared as quickly as it had arrived, taking the music with it. When Mark and Courtney's eyes adjusted back to the dark of the cellar, they looked into the flume to see who had arrived. Both gasped in surprise. It wasn't Saint Dane. It wasn't Bobby. It wasn't any of the Travelers they had met or read about.

It was a huge jungle cat.

Mark and Courtney didn't let go of each other. Though they had read about the klees of Eelong being intelligent, it was totally unnerving to be standing a few feet away from one. This was a beast that could rip them in half and eat them for lunch.

The big cat was on all fours, staring back at them. Its coat was gray-and-white spotted, like a leopard's. The only thing that gave Mark and Courtney a glimmer of hope that they wouldn't be devoured was the fact that the cat wore a tunic, like the ones Bobby described.

"Are you the acolytes from Second Earth?" the big cat said with a firm, male voice.

Neither Mark nor Courtney could speak. They stood dumbly, with their mouths hanging open.

"I said," the cat repeated more forcefully, "are you the acolytes?"

Mark and Courtney nodded.

"Good," the cat said. "My name is Seegen. I am the Traveler from Eelong."

Courtney shot Mark a surprised look.

"W-We got a message to come here," Mark said weakly.

"Yes," Seegen replied. "Sent by my acolyte."

"Your acolyte knows about us?" Courtney asked, surprised.

"The acolytes know of many things," Seegen answered.

Courtney said, "Really? We're acolytes and we're clueless."

"I must see Pendragon, the lead Traveler," Seegen continued. "I have vital information for him. He must come to Eelong."

"Well, I guess your acolyte doesn't know everything," Courtney said. "Because Bobby's already there."

If it were possible for a cat to look surprised, Seegen did. His head wavered, as if he were dizzy. He sat down on his haunches.

"You feeling all right?" Courtney asked.

"You don't look so hot," Mark added.

"Pendragon doesn't know what he's stepped into," Seegen said weakly. "I must find him."

"Tell us," Courtney said.

"I believe I've discovered how Saint Dane plans to decimate

Eelong," Seegen said. "He's going to poison the territory."

"Poison?" Mark said. "The whole territory?"

"I've already seen the signs. Tangs have been dying, by the hundreds. I believe they ate crops that were infected by this poison. Pendragon needs to know!"

"How do you know Saint Dane poisoned the tangs?" Courtney asked.

"Because nothing like this has ever happened on Eelong," Seegen answered. "Mass deaths? It's unnatural. It can only be the work of Saint Dane. No one else but Pendragon will understand that. I must tell him before—"

Seegen didn't finish his sentence. He didn't move. The big cat sat there like a freeze-frame, his cat eyes staring forward.

"Before what?" Courtney asked.

No response.

"Hey, a-are you okay?" Mark asked.

"Seegen?" Courtney called out. "Hel-lo?"

The cat didn't answer. Courtney took a step toward the Traveler. Mark followed close behind.

"Maybe you should go back to Eelong," Courtney told the cat nervously. "Bobby is there looking for you. You can tell him all about the poison."

Still, Seegen didn't move. Courtney reached out to touch him, but Mark grabbed her arm and screamed, "Stop!"

"What's the matter?" Courtney asked.

"Look," Mark said. He was pointing to Seegen's mouth. A thin line of bright green liquid had dribbled out and trickled down his fur. Mark cautiously held his open palm in front of the cat's nose. He held it there for a moment, then declared, "He's not breathing."

Courtney took a surprised step back. "Whoa, no way!"

Mark waved his hand in front of the cat's glassy eyes. They remained fixed. Staring. Unseeing.

"He can't be dead!" Courtney yelled in a panic. "He was fine a second ago. You don't just . . . stop living!"

Indeed, Seegen didn't look any different in death than he had in life. Nothing had changed, except that life had left his body. Mark turned away from the big cat and looked to the ground, his mind lost in thought.

"Mark!" Courtney called. "What are we going to do? This is . . . this is . . . bad!"

"It's worse than bad," Mark answered.

"How's that?"

"I know Bobby's journals inside out," Mark explained. "I've reread each one a dozen times. I remember everything. Every event. Every detail."

"Yeah, so?" Courtney said anxiously.

"We've read about this," Mark continued. "Think. Seegen suddenly died, with no warning, and there's green liquid dribbling from his mouth and—"

"And there's a deadly poison on Eelong!" Courtney interrupted, realizing where Mark was going. "Like nothing they've ever seen. It infects crops and makes them poisonous. You don't think—"

"Yeah, I do," Mark said solemnly. "Saint Dane said the walls between the territories were crumbling."

"Cloral," Courtney said with finality.

"Yeah, Cloral," Mark echoed. "I don't know how, I don't know why, but somehow the poison that Saint Dane tried to destroy Cloral with is still active, and it found its way to Eelong."

"And a Traveler is dead," Courtney added. "What if he's the only one who knew the truth?"

"He isn't," Mark said. "*We* know."

## ● SECOND EARTH ●

### (CONTINUED)

**Courtney grabbed Mark's arm,** pulling him out of the root cellar and back into the big, empty basement of the Sherwood house. Once outside, he yanked his arm back. "What's the matter with you?" he demanded.

"I couldn't stay in there with a dead, a dead—"

"Klee," Mark snapped. "He's called a klee. And he was the Traveler from Eelong."

"Whatever, it was . . . creepy."

"Creepy is the least of our problems," Mark said.

"What are we going to do, Mark?" Courtney asked quickly, her normally calm exterior showing signs of cracking. "Saint Dane has brought that poison from Cloral to Eelong, and we're the only ones who know it."

Mark paced. His mind was full of possibilities. None of them were good.

"It's wrong," he muttered nervously. "He's not supposed to mix things from the territories."

"Saint Dane's not supposed to do a lot of things," Courtney said. "But that hasn't stopped him. Bobby's gotta know!"

"And I know how to tell him," Mark exclaimed. " We can send a note to Boon, the acolyte from Eelong. Dorney showed us how to do that!"

"Good idea, except for one thing," Courtney said.

"What?"

"Boon's not the acolyte. Not yet, anyway. I thought you remembered every detail?"

"Then who sent us the note?" Mark asked.

"Seegen's acolyte. That's not Boon."

"Well, we gotta try!" Mark exclaimed. He grabbed the backpack that he left outside the wooden door and pulled out a spiral notebook and rollerball pen. He nervously flipped through dozens of pages filled with notes from his classes (Mark loved taking notes), until he found a blank page. He spoke aloud as he wrote:

*"This note is for Pendragon, the lead Traveler. Saint Dane brought the mutant poison from Cloral to Eelong. Seegen is dead. He was killed by the poison. His body is on Second Earth. What should we do? Mark and Courtney."*

Mark asked, "Anything else you can think of?"

Courtney shook her head. Mark ripped out the note and folded it in two. He took off his Traveler ring and laid it on the floor.

"Dorney said all we have to do is say the name of the acolyte we want to send it to," Mark said, breathless. He held the note over the ring, cleared his throat and announced, "Boon."

Nothing happened.

"Boon from Eelong," Mark said louder.

The two looked at the ring. It lay there doing absolutely nothing.

"Send this to Boon! The acolyte from Eelong!" Mark yelled.

Still nothing.

"Am I forgetting something?" Mark asked with a hint of desperation.

"Yes," Courtney answered. "Boon isn't the acolyte. Hello! I told you that."

Frustrated, Mark picked up the ring and put it back on his finger. "Then I don't know what to do."

Courtney took the note from Mark, read it, then read it again. An idea was forming. "Mark," she began softly. "Think about what I'm saying before telling me I'm wrong, okay?" Mark nodded.

"Saint Dane said that when the first territory falls, the rest will go over like dominos, right?"

"Yes," Mark agreed. "And I'm getting sick of hearing that."

"From what we've seen and what Bobby wrote, Saint Dane's prediction is coming true. Veelox is doomed, and now weird things are happening. Like those images Bobby saw when he flew through the flume, and the way Saint Dane's hair burned. I think he's getting stronger, and if he gets another territory, there's no telling what might happen."

"I'm with you so far," Mark said.

"Eelong is in big trouble," Courtney continued. "It looks like Saint Dane's got the klees ready to start killing off the gars."

"Hang on," Mark interrupted. "I think Saint Dane is wrong. Sure, if all the gars were killed off, it would throw Eelong totally out of whack, but get real. Even if they made it legal to hunt gars, they couldn't wipe out the entire population."

"Exactly!" Courtney agreed quickly. "That is, unless they had a weapon that was so powerful it could kill off thousands of gars at one time before they even realized what was happening."

The weight of Courtney's words hit Mark hard. The horrible truth was becoming all too clear.

"The Cloral poison!" he shouted. "Saint Dane brought the poison to Eelong to wipe out the gars!"

"It's worse than that," Courtney said with passion. "Think about it. What are the klees going to do after they kill the gars?"

The answer came fast to Mark, hitting him like a punch in the gut. "Oh my god," he said, his panic growing. "They're going to eat them! If some klees don't know about the poison and eat gars who were killed by it—"

"Yes!" Courtney shouted. "They'll be poisoned too. Then the whole food chain thing will be thrown out of whack and . . . Mark, with this poison Saint Dane truly has a chance of bringing down Eelong."

Mark paced nervously. "I can't believe this!"

"I'm not finished," Courtney said, still calm.

"There's more?" Mark asked, incredulous.

"Yes," Courtney said. She took a deep breath and said, "You're not going to like this."

"I don't like any of it. What?"

"Mark, we've got to travel."

Mark froze. He wasn't expecting to hear that.

"Say something," Courtney said.

"No way!" Mark shouted. "That's exactly what Bobby said we shouldn't do!"

"Bobby could be wrong," Courtney countered. "The ball just got slammed into our court. Bobby knows that Saint Dane wants to kill off the gars, but we're the only ones who know how. The Council of Klee may have already revoked the law that forbids the killing of gars—"

"Edict Forty-six."

"Whatever! We know the truth. How are you going to feel when we read in Bobby's next journal that thousands of gars mysteriously died off? I don't want to be the one to tell Bobby we knew it was coming but didn't do anything to stop it."

Mark walked deeper into the vast basement. All he could hear was the sound of his own footsteps, crunching on the gritty floor. The problem was, he agreed with everything Courtney had to say. But the idea of going against Bobby's direct orders was tough to imagine. Even tougher was the idea of shooting through the flume. Sure, he had fantasized about it. But when it came right down to it, he didn't think he had what it took to join this fight. Maybe Courtney did, but not Mark. Mark feared he was way too . . . Mark.

"It's okay if you don't want to go," Courtney said softly. "But I do."

Mark whipped around and saw that Courtney stood with both feet planted firmly. It was at that exact moment that Mark realized Courtney had already made up her mind. The time for discussion was over. She was going to jump into the flume.

"H-Hang on a second," Mark said, trying to restore sanity. "Suppose I agreed with you? I'm not saying I do, but just suppose. I don't know about you, but I've never had to fight a quig or a tang or any other nasty creature that might be lurking around the jungles of Eelong. Heck, my mother's *cat* scares me! I've got the scratch scars to prove it. You're right, Bobby has to know what's going on, but we'd be killed on Eelong before we got the chance to tell him."

Courtney gave Mark a sly smile and said, "Who said anything about going to Eelong?"

Mark gave her a curious look. She had just logically convinced him how important it was to ignore Bobby's wishes and flume to the rescue, only to hear that this isn't what she was suggesting at all.

"Now you lost me," Mark said.

Courtney took Mark's spiral notebook and his pen and began writing another message. She spoke as she wrote:

*"This note is from Courtney Chetwynde and Mark Dimond, acolytes for Bobby Pendragon from Second Earth. We believe that Saint Dane has taken the poison that threatened Cloral and brought it to the territory of Eelong. Acolytes can now travel through the flumes. We are coming to get your help to find a way to stop it."*

Courtney ripped out the page and folded it in two.

"Who are you sending that to?" Mark asked, totally confused.

"An acolyte," Courtney answered. "I think her name is . . . Wu Yenza."

"Wu Yenza?" Mark shouted. "But she's from—"

"Exactly," Courtney announced. "She's from Cloral."

Mark stared at Courtney, stunned.

Courtney held out her hand and said, "Give me your ring."

Mark did as he was told. He was too numb not to. Courtney took the ring and gently placed it on the basement floor. She held the note over the ring and announced in a clear voice, "Wu Yenza!"

Instantly one of the ten symbols that represented the territories sparkled to life. It was a single, squiggly line that looked like a wave. The ring quivered on the ground and grew larger, revealing the tunnel to the territories. Brilliant light shot from the ring, looking like a headlight on the front of an oncoming freight train. The familiar jumble of musical notes grew louder. Courtney looked to Mark, winked, and dropped the note through the ring. The paper disappeared and the ring shrank back down to normal size. Courtney picked it up and held it out for Mark.

"Special delivery," she said with a smile.

Mark took the ring and put it back on his finger.

"You're right about Eelong," Courtney said. "We probably wouldn't get out of the flume tree. But even if we got lucky and found Bobby, there's only one way to stop that poison . . . the antidote that saved Cloral."

"You want to bring the antidote from Cloral to Eelong?" Mark asked.

"Exactly."

Mark's mouth went dry. What Courtney was suggesting went against everything they'd learned about how the territories worked. "But n-nothing is supposed to be moved between the territories," Mark said, his voice barely above a whisper.

"Saint Dane said the rules have changed," Courtney countered. "And he's certainly moving things around. I think the alternative is worse. If we don't do something, he's going to have his second territory."

Mark felt dizzy. He actually had to spread his feet to keep his balance. He looked down at the ground, praying that he'd wake up and this would all be a nightmare.

"I wish you'd come with me," Courtney said. "But I'll understand if you don't."

"I-I'm really confused, Courtney," Mark stammered. "Everything's getting so, so . . . twisted. Did you know that Andy Mitchell does college-level scientific research?"

The surprised look on Courtney's face was almost comical. If Mark weren't so upset, he would have laughed.

"Mitchell? The juvi doofus?"

"Nothing is right with the world anymore" was Mark's answer.

Courtney nodded soberly. "I hear you. Things aren't working out the way I thought they would, either. On any level. I may be totally dumb about this, but as huge as going to Cloral may be, at least it's something we have control over. I'm going, Mark. Will you go with me?"

Mark looked into Courtney's gray eyes and saw the intensity and confidence that had been missing lately. The old Courtney was back and she was ready to roll.

"Can I ask you one thing?" Mark said, though his voice was shaky.

"Sure."

"Wh-What exactly are we going to tell our parents?"

Courtney laughed. "We're going to ride a flume to another time and territory on the other side of Halla to try and save humanity from total destruction. I don't know about your parents, but if I told mine, they'd lock me in the basement until a team of psychiatrists turned my head inside out . . . or I turned forty, whichever came last."

Mark chuckled nervously and said, "Yeah, my mom barely let me out to go to the library tonight."

The two laughed, but it was nervous laughter.

Courtney added, "We'll deal when we get back."

Mark nodded. He wasn't sure which he feared more: jumping into the flume or telling his parents why he'd disappeared. Talk about things changing! Once they took this step, there would be no turning back. When they returned to Second Earth, *if* they returned, they'd have to 'fess up about everything. They'd have to explain about Bobby, and his uncle Press. They'd have to confess to the police that they hid the truth about the Pendragons disappearing for fear of being locked away in a nuthouse. Of course, Mark figured, after revealing all that's been happening, they'd be locked away in a nuthouse anyway. It was a scary step for all sorts of reasons, but the more Mark thought about it, the more he felt Courtney was right. There was no choice. They had to travel.

Courtney walked to the wooden door to the root cellar. She looked at the star that had been burned into the wood, marking it as a gate to the flume. She reached up and touched it, feeling the smooth, burned edges of the symbol.

"Ready?" she asked.

Mark took a deep breath and walked for the door. "Last chance to talk me out of it," he said.

Courtney smiled, opened the door, and said, "Let's go to Cloral."

## ◉ SECOND EARTH ◉

### (CONTINUED)

**Seegen's body sat motionless** in the mouth of the flume, his lifeless eyes staring straight ahead, seeing nothing. Mark and Courtney entered the root cellar and stood in front of this latest casualty in the war against Saint Dane. It was a grim reminder that this was no game. The stakes were high. People died.

Courtney broke the silence by saying, "I've never seen a dead person."

"He's a cat," Mark said softly. "Does that count?"

"Close enough," Courtney answered. "What should we do about him?"

"We should send him back to Eelong," Mark offered. "It's where he belongs."

"Can we do that?" Courtney asked.

Mark shrugged and said, "We can try. But we should say something first. Out of respect."

Courtney nodded and dropped her head. Mark did the same and said reverently, "We only know a few things about Seegen. He came from the territory of Eelong; he has a daughter named Kasha; he was a Traveler; and he died in the battle to protect

Halla from Saint Dane. For that, he was a hero. There's nothing else we can say except that we'll do all we can to make sure he didn't die for nothing."

The two kept their heads down for a moment. "That was perfect," Courtney said.

Mark nodded. "Wait here," he said, and ran out of the root cellar. He quickly returned with a plastic sandwich bag full of carrots from his backpack.

"You want a snack now?" Courtney asked in wonder.

"Hang on," Mark answered, taking out the note he had written to the acolyte from Eelong. He knelt down next to Seegen and cautiously brought the paper close to the dead cat's mouth.

"What are you doing?" Courtney asked nervously.

"We've got to be sure," Mark answered. He used the paper to pull out some of the fur from around Seegen's mouth. "There will be traces of the poison on his fur. On Cloral they can examine it to see if it really is the same plague." Mark stood up and folded the paper several times, making sure the hairs were trapped safely inside. He dumped the carrots out of the plastic bag and put the folded paper inside, being careful to seal the bag up tight.

"That's pretty smart," Courtney said.

"Yeah, I'm a smart guy." He put the bag in his pocket and said, "A really scared, smart guy. Now what?"

Courtney shrugged. "Now we see if this is going to work." She looked into the flume, took a deep breath and shouted, *"Eelong!"*

The flume sprang to life.

"Oh man," Mark said in awe. "What if it takes us, too?"

Courtney pulled Mark to the side of the flume. The two hugged each other as light filled the root cellar along with the sweet musical notes. The flume shivered slightly. Mark and Courtney felt the ground move, as if they were in a small earthquake. They shared a quick look, but didn't think about it again. Both waited to be tugged into the flume. They weren't. The light diminished; the music grew faint; and they were still on Second Earth. Courtney let go of Mark and peered around the mouth of the flume in time to see the light disappearing in the distance. Seegen's body was gone.

"Good-bye, Seegen," Mark said.

The two stood staring into the empty flume. Neither made a move for the longest time. Finally Mark said softly, "Courtney, I am really scared."

Courtney said, "Yeah, me too."

Neither made a move.

"It seems like so long ago," Mark said wistfully. "And sometimes like yesterday."

"What does?"

"The night Osa came to my bedroom and gave me the ring. I put my head back there sometimes. Back before Bobby left. Before we found out about Travelers, and territories, and Saint Dane."

"Me too," Courtney admitted. "I always think about the night Bobby left. It was like a whole different life."

"Yeah, a whole different life," Mark echoed.

The two stood in silence for a few moments, then Mark said, "Are you sure we're doing the right thing?"

"I don't know, Mark. I'd be lying if I said I was absolutely sure. But from all we know, I don't think we have another choice."

Mark nodded thoughtfully. "You know what I think?"

"What?"

Mark stood up straight, looked Courtney square in the eye, and said with as much confidence as he could gather, "I think we're on the wrong territory."

Courtney broke out in a wide grin. "Then say it," she said.

Mark Dimond was ready for an adventure. He was about to get one. After watching Bobby for so long from the safety of the sidelines, he and Courtney were about to step onto the playing field. Mark looked into the flume, took a deep breath, and said in a strong voice, *"Cloral."*

The flume woke up. The walls began to crack and groan. Mark and Courtney could actually feel it moving beneath their feet as it writhed and twisted like a sleepy snake.

"I've never felt it move before," Mark said nervously.

"I don't think it has," Courtney replied.

The light appeared far in the distance. It was on its way in to sweep them up and bring them on a ride that had been long in coming. The jumble of musical notes were heard faintly at first, but grew steadily louder while drawing closer. Mark grabbed Courtney's hand. They both fought the instinct to back away. In the past they would have. Not today. Today their job was to stay put and let the flume take them. They saw the gray rock walls melting into crystal. Soon the entire tunnel would become clear and they'd be off.

*Thunk!*

Mark and Courtney jumped back because a piece of rock the size of a basketball had cracked away from the tunnel over their heads and fallen at their feet. It was heavy, and it nearly hit them.

"That can't be good," Courtney said.

"Something's wrong," Mark said nervously.

*Clunk!*

Another piece of the flume cracked away from the wall and rolled past them.

"Maybe we should bail," Courtney offered.

Too late. They both felt the tug at the same time. The powerful energy of the flume was gently pulling them in. They couldn't back out if they wanted to. The light blasted into their faces, the sweet notes danced around them, the walls turned totally crystal. . . .

"Here we go!" Courtney shouted.

"Whoooooooo!" Mark yelled.

And a moment later, the two were lifted up on a bed of light and rocketed into the tunnel.

## ∞ CLORAL ∞

**The ride was everything they** hoped it would be . . . only better. All that Bobby had described to them in his journals was now theirs to experience. The sensation of floating on warm air, the twists and turns with no fear of bashing into the crystal walls, the vast star field beyond, the musical notes that whipped past—it was all exactly as Bobby had explained it. Mark and Courtney held hands as they flew along. At first they held tight out of fear, but it only took a few moments for them both to relax and enjoy the ride.

"It . . . it's incredible," Mark exclaimed. He looked to Courtney, who floated alongside him, her eyes wide, taking in every detail.

"Look!" she exclaimed while pointing out to the star field.

They saw what looked like a giant fish swimming right up to the crystal shell of the flume and traveling along with them. It was the size of a house, with nearly transparent skin through which they could see the stars beyond.

"It's one of the images Bobby wrote about," Mark exclaimed.

The immense fish shot away and flew toward the stars.

"What is that?" Mark asked, while pointing to the other side of the flume. There was a vast, pyramid-shaped object spinning across space. It too was semitransparent so that stars could be seen through it.

"Maybe it's a Lifelight pyramid," Courtney suggested.

"What does it mean?" Mark asked.

Courtney laughed and said, "Are you kidding? What does *any* of this mean?" She let go of Mark's hand and did a somersault like an astronaut in zero g. "Just go with it."

Mark actually laughed and tried to do a somersault too. But he only got halfway around and the two of them ended up sailing along with Courtney's head up and Mark's head down. They looked at each other and burst out laughing. A moment later they both heard something far ahead. The musical notes grew more furious, along with a new sound that was like . . .

"Water!" Mark exclaimed while scrambling to get his head back upright. "I forgot! The flume on Cloral dumps out into a—"

He couldn't finish the sentence because they were shot out of the flume, twenty feet in the air. Gravity kicked back in and both fell toward a pool of water. Since Courtney's head was up, she was able to get her feet together and hold her nose. But Mark was launched out of the flume head down. He flailed his arms to try and right himself, but it was too late. Courtney knifed into the water, nearly vertical. Mark spun himself heels over head and hit the water with a full-on belly flop that sounded like a cannon going off. Courtney surfaced first, looking for Mark.

"Mark?" she called out. "Mark!"

A moment later Mark surfaced, his long dark hair covering his eyes. He floated there for a second, making Courtney wonder if he was hurt. He then uttered a simple, profound, "Ouch."

Courtney laughed. So did Mark. They had made it. The two swam to the side of the pool and pulled themselves up and out, to sit on the rocky ledge and survey their surroundings. It was exactly as Bobby had described. They were in a rock cavern that had vines laden with colorful flowers growing from its walls.

"We're here!" Mark exclaimed. "I can't believe it." He leaned over and plucked off a dark green, cucumber-looking fruit from a vine. "Bobby made these sound delicious," he explained while snapping it in half. The fruit inside was bright red, like a tubular watermelon. Mark took a greedy bite, the juice dripping down his chin.

"Well?" Courtney asked.

Mark smiled. "Sweet, crunchy, excellent. Bobby's words didn't do them justice."

Mark handed Courtney the other half. The two of them took a moment to enjoy the strange fruit that could only be found on this territory. While they ate, both looked around the cavern, awestruck.

"Cloral. Unbelievable," Courtney said.

Mark added, "It's like we stepped inside a book."

They both dangled their feet in the warm pool of water that was their welcome mat.

"I hope Wu Yenza got the message," Courtney said. "If not, this is as far as we go."

Both knew that in order to get out of this cavern, they would need air globes and swim belts, because they were far below the surface of the waters of Cloral. No way they would be able to hold their breath long enough to swim out. Even if they could, they'd find themselves in the middle of the ocean, with the possibility of quig-sharks lurking around. Courtney was right—if Wu Yenza hadn't gotten their message, the mission to Cloral would go no farther than the gate.

"I think she got the message," Courtney announced.

"How do you know?" Mark asked.

Courtney made her way carefully around the edge of the pool until she came upon a mound of vines. She tugged at them to reveal . . .

"Clothes!" Mark exclaimed. "Cloral clothes!"

Courtney picked up a bright blue shirt that looked to be made of a lightweight, rubbery wet suit material.

"We were expected," Courtney said.

"Awesome!" Mark exclaimed. "I guess all we have to do is wait and—" Mark didn't finish his sentence.

"What's the matter?" Courtney asked.

Mark held up his hand. The gray stone in the center of his ring was starting to sparkle. "We've got mail."

Mark took it off and put it on the rocks while Courtney quickly scampered around the edge of the pool to join him. The light from the stone shot out of the ring and lit up the flower-filled cavern, making it look as if they were standing inside a giant Christmas tree. The ring grew wide as the musical notes bounced off the walls. As always the entire event took only a few seconds. When it was over, Mark and Courtney were left looking at a ring that had returned to normal, with Bobby's next journal lying beside it.

They had been so focused on the event, they hadn't noticed the dark shadow that had been swimming toward them underwater. The shadow moved to the center of the pool and silently surfaced directly behind them.

Mark picked up the rolled-up parchment and said, "At least we'll have something to do while we wait to see if anybody comes for us."

That's when the shadow spoke, saying, "No need to wait."

Mark and Courtney jumped in surprise. They spun quickly to the sound of the voice to see . . .

Treading water in the middle of the pool was a guy wearing

a clear air globe that was form fitted to his head. He pulled off the globe and it instantly returned to its normal, round shape. Now that the globe was gone, Mark and Courtney saw that the guy had long black hair that fell almost to his shoulders. His eyes were almond shaped and he had a dazzling smile that lit up the cavern.

"You must be Mark and Courtney," the guy said. "Sounds as if you've found yourselves in a bit of a tum-tigger."

Mark stammered, "A-Are you—"

"Who else would I be?" the guy laughed.

Courtney uttered, "Spader?"

"Hobey-ho, mates," the Traveler exclaimed. "Welcome to Cloral."

## ∞ CLORAL ∞
### (CONTINUED)

**Mark and Courtney felt** as if they had stepped inside a dream.

They had experienced the wonders of Cloral through Bobby's journals, but now they were seeing it for themselves. Firsthand. For real. It was everything they had imagined.

"I'm proud to meet you, mates," Vo Spader said as he pulled himself out of the pool of water in the cavern. He laid his air globe on the edge of the pool and stood up to his full six-foot height. Mark and Courtney saw that he was wearing his jet-black aquaneer uniform with no sleeves. He held his hand out to Mark and said, "You're both just as Pendragon described."

Mark shook Spader's hand while staring at him with his mouth hanging open, like he was looking at a celebrity. Spader gave him a reassuring wink, then shook Courtney's hand. "That's a right strong grip, Courtney," he said. "Pendragon said you were a handful."

Courtney held eye contact with him and said with a confident smile, "He wasn't lying."

Spader gave her a big smile in return, and said, "I'll remember that."

"D-Did W-Wu Yenza get our note?" Mark asked.

"Yes indeed," Spader answered. "Can't say I was happy about what it said, though."

"There's big trouble, Spader," Mark said quickly. "Saint Dane somehow got hold of the Cloral poison and—"

"First things first, Mark," the Traveler said. "Let's get home and take a look at that new journal."

"Really?" Mark asked in awe. "Home? You mean to Grallion?"

"Is that a problem?" Spader asked back.

"No, I think it's great!" Mark exclaimed. "Can we have some sniggers, too?"

"Mark!" Courtney scolded. "Could you be any more of a geek?"

Spader laughed warmly. "No worries. This must be strange for you, splashing around a territory you've only read about."

"Yeah, it's pretty bizarre," Courtney admitted.

"I'll try to make it as comfortable as I can," Spader said with a wink. "Right?"

"Right!" Mark answered.

The first task was to get Mark and Courtney into Cloral clothes. They each chose a matching set of bright blue two-piece swimskins from the pile. They also picked out pairs of soft swim shoes.

"No peeking!" Courtney teased Spader as she took off her dripping-wet Second Earth clothes.

"Wouldn't dream of it," Spader teased back.

While Mark and Courtney changed, Spader took Bobby's latest journal and sealed it into a watertight pouch that he attached to his belt. Mark saw what he was doing and said, "Put this in there too." He handed Spader the plastic bag that held the fur sample from Seegen. Spader took it without question and sealed it inside the pouch. He then grabbed two air globes that were near the pile of Cloral clothes. The round, clear globes were the size of basketballs, with silver harmonica-looking devices on top that turned water into oxygen.

"Did Pendragon explain how these work?" Spader asked.

"Absolutely," Mark answered. "They form to our heads so we can breathe and talk underwater."

"Right you are," Spader replied.

"We need belts, too, right?" Courtney asked. "To keep us neutrally buoyant?"

"Indeed," Spader answered. "You two really know what you're doing."

"We try," Courtney said.

Mark gave a quick look to Courtney. He realized that she was flirting with Spader, and Spader was flirting back! Mark hoped this wouldn't get icky.

"I've only got one water sled," Spader said, pointing to a device that was floating on the surface of the pool. It was bright purple and roughly the shape of a football with handles. From reading Bobby's journals, Mark and Courtney knew Spader used it to propel himself underwater.

"Only one?" Mark said with disappointment. He really wanted to use one of his own.

"No worries," Spader answered. "It's got enough go to pull us all."

"What about quig-sharks?" Courtney asked.

"Haven't seen one since the natty-do with Saint Dane," the Traveler answered. "Seems as if they're long gone."

Mark and Courtney were ready. Their swimskins fit perfectly, with long sleeves and long pants. Mark checked out Courtney and noticed how good she looked in the skintight Cloral suit. He wondered if Spader noticed too.

"Either of you have trouble swimming underwater?" Spader asked.

"Not me," Courtney said quickly.

"M-Me neither," Mark lied. Truth was, Mark was a terrible swimmer. But he put his faith in the fact that using the air globes was as easy as Bobby described. He wasn't going to let something silly like an irrational fear of a horrific death by drowning stop him from seeing Cloral.

"Right!" Spader announced. "On with the gear."

Mark and Courtney picked up the round air globes and put them on like helmets. Instantly the clear globes rippled and shrank until they fit snugly to their heads. Though Mark knew what was going to happen, the sensation took him by surprise. He took a step back, tripped, and fell on his butt.

"Easy there, mate!" Spader said as he helped Mark to his feet. "You all right?"

"Yeah," Mark said, embarrassed. "Everything's . . . spiff."

Courtney rolled her eyes at Mark's use of the word "spiff." It was a word they knew Spader always used.

"Here's the do," Spader said. "We'll descend a bit to get you used to being underwater. Once everybody's happy, grab on to my belt, hang on tight, and I'll get us to the surface. Right?"

"Hobey-ho!" Mark chirped.

Courtney tried not to roll her eyes again.

Spader laughed and gave them a genuine smile. "Hobey-ho. Let's go."

Spader jumped into the water first, followed by Courtney. Mark eased himself in slowly. Both Mark and Courtney instantly felt their swim belts tighten around their waists, keeping them afloat. They didn't have to kick or move their arms to stay on the surface.

"Let's drop below," Spader instructed. With a quick arm swing, he sank underwater.

"Courtney?" Mark called out.

"Yeah?"

"Can you believe this?"

"Not really," she answered.

"I feel bad about saying it," Mark added. "But this is awesome."

"Don't feel bad; I think so too," Courtney replied. "There's plenty of time for things to get un-awesome."

"Yeah, I guess so."

"Hobey-ho, you geek," Courtney added teasingly.

Mark laughed and the two dropped below the surface. Spader was waiting for them in the sand, about fifteen feet below. Mark and Courtney sank to the bottom and sat on their knees.

"Everything spiff?" Spader asked.

Both Courtney and Mark were surprised that they could hear Spader so clearly underwater. Bobby had explained it all in his journals, but it was still strange to hear it for real. Mark signaled a thumbs-up.

"You can talk, Mark," Spader instructed.

"Oh, right," Mark said. "I'm cool." Truth was, he was so nervous he was having trouble getting a deep breath.

"Courtney?" Spader asked.

"This is freaky," she answered, also breathing hard.

"Relax," Spader said calmly. "Breathe normal. I promise, you'll get used to it."

They stayed kneeling in the sand for a few minutes, adjusting to the sensation of being weightless in the warm water and breathing through the globes. Spader was right. It didn't take long for them to calm down. He instructed Mark and Courtney to grab on to his belt. Once they had a firm grip, he took his water sled with both hands, held it in front of him, and triggered the engine. With a low whine, the sled bit into the water and pulled the trio along. As incredible as it seemed to Mark and Courtney, they were on their way to Grallion. They shot under the long, low ceiling of rock for several minutes, until Spader announced, "Open water ahead!"

They looked forward to see a ribbon of light that was the end of the ceiling they had been swimming under. A moment later they shot out into open water. Mark and Courtney looked around in wonder at the glorious coral reef that lay just beyond the rock shelf. There were schools of colorful fish swimming lazily past, a forest of red sea kelp that swayed with the current, and beautiful coral formations that made the reef look like an undersea sculpture garden.

Mark looked to Courtney. Courtney looked to Mark. They both smiled.

Spader pulled them up to the surface. When their heads popped above the water, Mark saw something that made him laugh out loud.

"It's a skimmer!" he shouted.

Floating on the soft swells was Spader's skimmer craft. It looked to Mark like a large, white snowmobile, with outrigger pontoons for stability. The deck was flat, with low sides so it was easy for them to hoist themselves up and in.

"Off with the globes," Spader ordered. He opened up a hatch to a storage compartment below. There he stowed the gear, along with Bobby's journal in its waterproof pouch.

"Everything spiff?" Spader asked.

"Couldn't be spiffer. Spiffier. More spiff. Whatever," Mark replied happily.

"Can I drive?" Courtney asked.

Mark couldn't believe she was being so bold. But then again, she was just being Courtney.

"Sure!" Spader replied. "Step right up."

The controls to the skimmer were like motorcycle handlebars that you stood behind. Courtney grabbed the handles with the confidence of an experienced aquaneer. Spader stood behind her and showed her the throttle and how to steer.

"Simple?" he asked.

"Simple," she replied. "No more talk. Let's go!"

Mark grabbed the side of the skimmer for safety. He trusted Spader's driving. He wasn't so sure about Courtney's. Spader flipped a switch and the skimmer hummed to life. The pontoons slowly lowered themselves into the water. As soon as they were wet, Spader said, "She's all yours."

Courtney didn't have to be told twice. "Yeahhhh!" she yelled and gunned the throttle. The skimmer shot forward so fast that Mark fell over in spite of the fact he had been holding on. Spader pointed her in the right direction and they were off, flying over the low swells.

"This is off the hook!" Courtney shouted with joy.

Most of the trip Spader spent sitting with Mark, his feet up casually, enjoying the ride. Mark wasn't quite as relaxed. He held on tight to the side of the skimmer, just in case. Both watched Courtney at the controls, her long brown hair flying back in the wind, a huge smile on her face. Mark thought that it was the happiest he had seen her in a long time. He knew their mission wasn't about having fun, but for the time being, he didn't complain.

In no time they arrived at the massive barge that was the farming habitat of Grallion. It's where Spader worked with a team of aquaneers who kept the floating city running smoothly. Spader docked the skimmer and led them through the aquaneer landing, up the stairs, and out onto the surface of the huge barge city. When they arrived on top, Mark and Courtney were blown away by the acres of glorious farmland. They knew that except for the city of Faar, Cloral was covered entirely by water. All their food was grown either on barges like Grallion, or underwater on the farms that were all over the territory. These were the farms that were endangered by the poison that Saint Dane had helped let loose. Seeing this farm and knowing how close Cloral had come to disaster brought Mark and Courtney back to reality. They were there because Saint Dane had taken this horrible poison to Eelong.

They soon arrived at Spader's small apartment that was right on the edge of the city, looking out over the ocean. "Make yourselves comfortable, mates," Spader said cheerily. The furniture was all made from some kind of molded material. There were no cushions, but it was comfortable just the same. "I hope you're hungry. I made some cooger fish for the occasion."

"And sniggers?" Mark asked.

"Sniggers too," Spader answered with a chuckle.

"I'm starved," Courtney said.

Neither had thought much about food since they left Second Earth. But now that they were relaxed, dinner sounded pretty good. Spader brought them plates heaped with the white, flaky fish. It was served cold, which was kind of weird, but delicious just the same. Spader presented a tall glass of dark red sniggers to Mark. Mark took a big, thirsty gulp of the frosty brew and experienced the horrible, sour taste that Bobby had warned of. His eyes went wide and he nearly gagged.

"Ride it out!" Spader said, laughing.

Mark held the foul, bubbly liquid in his mouth and a second later he was rewarded with a wonderful, sweet nutty taste that stayed in his mouth long after he swallowed.

"Awesome!" Mark declared with a big smile.

They all had a laugh over it and finished the meal. The trip had been a fantasy come true for Mark and Courtney, but always tugging at the corner of their minds was the real reason they were there. It wasn't to race skimmers or chug sniggers.

"There's something that needs saying," Spader said, turning to business. "You've read Pendragon's journals, so you know how he feels about me."

"What do you mean?" Courtney asked. "He says you're one of his best friends."

"That's saying a lot," Mark chimed in quickly. "I know. I've been his best friend since we were kids." Mark wanted to establish the best friend hierarchy right away.

"Pendragon's like my brother," Spader said. "But I'm afraid he's lost faith in me, after what happened on First Earth."

Mark and Courtney knew what Spader meant. Saint Dane killed Spader's father and Spader wanted revenge. Badly. His hatred of the demon Traveler was so intense, it often made him lose control of his emotions. On First Earth Spader was so blinded by hate he wouldn't listen to Bobby or Gunny and almost caused a disaster that would have led to the destruction of all three Earth territories. After that Bobby asked Spader to return to his home on Cloral until he could learn how to better control his anger.

"Be honest," Courtney said. "Was Bobby right? I mean, by asking you to go home?"

Mark shot Courtney a quick look. It was a pretty bold question to ask somebody they hardly knew. Spader thought for several seconds before speaking.

"Yes," he finally said. "I nearly made a natty mess of things. But coming home and pretending everything is normal hasn't been easy. I've done it though, just as Pendragon asked. I hope I've grown up some along the way. But I'm a Traveler. I'd be lying if I told you I wasn't living for the day when I can jump back into the flume and rejoin the fight."

"I think that day is today," Courtney said.

Spader couldn't help but break out in a wide grin. "I've been waiting to hear those words! Whatever Pendragon needs, I'm there."

Mark and Courtney exchanged nervous looks.

"Well," Courtney said. "It's not exactly like that. He doesn't know we're here."

Spader blinked once, then twice, as if Courtney's words didn't make sense. "I don't follow," he said. "Pendragon didn't send you?"

"It's worse than that," Mark said. "If he knew we were here, he'd be really angry. He thinks it's wrong for the acolytes to travel. He said it might somehow help Saint Dane."

"But we're not sure he's right," Courtney added quickly. "Saint Dane may have tricked Bobby into thinking that."

"And we took the chance in coming because Eelong is in trouble, and we're the only ones who know the real reason why," Mark explained.

"We talked to the Traveler from Eelong," Courtney said quickly. "His name was Seegen. But now he's dead and he gave us some information that we have to share."

Spader kept looking back and forth between Mark and Courtney, trying to understand it all. He finally couldn't take it anymore and jumped to his feet. "Stop!" he shouted. "This is all coming a bit fast. Let me understand. Pendragon told you not to use the flumes, but you did anyway because of something another Traveler told you?"

"Yes," Courtney said. "But it's more than that. The Traveler died. Right in front of us. It was the poison from Cloral that killed him."

Mark added, "We know you're not supposed to mix things between territories, but it looks like Saint Dane has done exactly that. He's somehow brought the poison that nearly wiped out Cloral, to Eelong."

Spader paced nervously. "This isn't right, mates," he said worriedly. "Keeping the territories separate is almost as important as stopping Saint Dane. The territories are different worlds, in different times. If they start to mingle, well, it would be the biggest tum-tigger there ever was. At least that's what I've been told."

"But Saint Dane isn't playing by the rules," Courtney argued.

"Are you sure?" Spader questioned.

Mark grabbed the watertight pouch that contained Bobby's latest journal and took out the plastic bag with Seegen's fur. "This is a sample of the fur from Seegen's mouth," Mark said. "Take it to your agronomers. I'll bet they can test it and see if it's the same poison."

Spader gave the bag a confused look and asked, "Seegen had fur around his mouth?"

"The beings on Eelong are big animals. Cats," Courtney answered. "Or maybe you don't have cats on Cloral."

Spader stared at Courtney, trying to make sense of what she was saying. "I'm sorry, mates, this is making me uneasy. I'm already on Pendragon's bad side. If I help you, he might never trust me again. Why don't I get you back to the flume, and you can go home before Pendragon finds out you've been—"

"No!" Courtney shouted and jumped to her feet. She got right in Spader's face and said, "Seegen died before he could tell Bobby about the poison. But he told us. We're the *only* ones who know what's going on. If we don't do something, then Eelong is doomed. You're worried about Bobby trusting you? How do you think he'll feel when Saint Dane crushes another territory and he finds out you could have stopped him?"

Spader and Courtney stood nose-to-nose. Neither blinked.

Mark looked back and forth between the two, not sure of what to say.

"Pendragon was right," Spader said. "You *are* a handful."

"I'm just getting started," Courtney shot back. "Are you going to help us or not?"

Spader didn't back off. "Let's give that journal a look, Mark," he said, still staring at Courtney. "I want to learn about this cat world called Eelong."

# EELONG

I've lost all track of time. How long have I been on Eelong? Days? Weeks? It could be months. I don't know for sure. Did I have a birthday? Am I sixteen? Who knows? Time means nothing to me anymore. Sorry if I sound so glum, but things haven't been going well since I wrote my last journal. Some things happened to me that I wouldn't wish on my worst enemy. Okay, maybe I'd wish them on Saint Dane, but that's about it.

Now that I got some food and a little rest, I'm starting to feel human again. Though on Eelong, that's not such a good thing. Tomorrow we're taking a journey that I'm hoping will lead us to some answers, and a way to stop Saint Dane and his insane plan to wipe out the gars. There's a good chance that if this trip is successful, I'll find Gunny. I can only hope that he's still alive. We're not leaving until the morning, so I've got a little time to write my journal. Let me go back and get down everything that happened since I wrote last. It's now, or maybe never.

\* \* \*

I left off when I had just gotten back to Eelong from seeing you guys on Second Earth. I stood at the mouth of the flume, staring at a huge jet-black cat named Kasha.

"So," she said with a superior air. "You're not what I expected." She sized me up and down. I hoped she wasn't wondering what I would taste like.

"Really?" I said, trying to be casual. "What did you expect?"

"I don't know," Kasha replied. "Someone more . . . interesting."

Gee, thanks. I wanted to act all insulted, but I needed to be careful. Kasha may have been the daughter of a Traveler, but I saw how she handled that tang in the jungle. She was tough, and fearless . . . and ate meat. I let the insult go without comment.

"Where is my father?" she demanded.

"You tell me," I shot back. "I haven't met him yet."

"Aren't you the leader of these so-called . . . Travelers?" she snarled, taking an aggressive step toward me. "Shouldn't you know these things?"

I took a step back into the flume. I couldn't help it. I wasn't used to having a man-eating cat make a move on me. Kasha cocked her head curiously.

"Do I scare you?" she asked.

I didn't want to show her that I was weak and frightened, but the truth was, I was weak and frightened. "On Eelong, I'm a gar," I said, trying not to let my voice crack. "But come to my home territory. It's different there." Truth be told, it isn't different at all. I'd be just as scared of her on Second Earth as I was here, but I had to say something to keep a little dignity.

Kasha took another step toward me. This time I didn't back

off, but man, I was scared. She put her nose in my face and stared me down. I tried not to blink.

"If something happened to my father because of this silly game you all play"—she seethed intensely—"I will personally tear you apart."

Gulp.

"This isn't a game," I told her. "And you're insulting your father by calling it that."

Her eyes grew sharp and angry. I feared I had played this totally wrong and was about to get sliced. But what else could I do? She had dissed everything we Travelers were doing to save the butts of people like her. Or cats like her. Assuming cats even have butts.

"You think this is a game?" I said. "Look at this." I held up the dirty bag I had carried back from Second Earth that held the grisly gift from Saint Dane.

"Hey, what's in the bag?" came a welcome, friendly voice. It was Boon. The brown cat padded up behind Kasha and stood at her shoulder. "Did you catch up with Saint Dane?" he asked me.

"Not exactly," I answered. "But he gave this to my acolytes. It's a small sample of what he's capable of."

I held the bag out for Boon. He took it, reached in, and pulled out Gunny's hand. I expected them to be all sorts of repulsed, but they looked at the hand like it was no big deal. I guess they were used to seeing dismembered body parts here on Eelong. But me? I had to turn away. The sight of Gunny's hand made me want to cry.

"It's got a Traveler ring," was all Boon said.

"Take it off for me, please," I asked Boon. Boon took off the ring and handed it to me. I quickly tied it around my neck, along with my own ring.

"Is it the hand of the tall, dark gar? The one you called Gunny?" Boon asked.

"Yes." I looked to Kasha and said, "Still think this is a game?"

She didn't answer. Seeing a dismembered hand didn't faze her. How twisted is that?

"Will you bury it for me?" I asked Boon.

"We have to burn it," Boon answered. "That's what we do here. We can't take the chance that a tang might dig it up and . . ." He didn't finish the sentence, but I knew what he meant. He reverently placed Gunny's hand back in the sack.

"Throw it away!" Kasha demanded. "It's a gar."

"But he's a Traveler," Boon argued. "He deserves better."

"Thanks, Boon," I said. I was really beginning to like this cat.

Kasha shot me an intimidating look. I didn't blink.

"You'll come with me now," she said abruptly. "Tomorrow you'll help find my father."

"Fine," I said. "That's exactly what I want to do."

Kasha turned away, annoyed. She didn't like being stood up to by a gar.

I asked Boon, "Why didn't you tell me Seegen was missing?"

"I didn't know," Boon said defensively. "Last I saw him he was leaving Leeandra with Yorn."

"Yorn? Who's Yorn?"

"Seegen's acolyte. Do you think they're okay?"

"How should I know? I'm new here, remember?"

"Right," Boon corrected himself. "Sorry."

Before leaving the flume I grabbed another pair of raggy shoes off the clothing pile. I took my sweet time tying them on, making Kasha and Boon wait. Kasha didn't look happy about it and that was okay by me. Hey, maybe I was being petty, but it was the only chance I had to have a little bit of control. Pathetic, I know, but I was floundering. When we got outside I saw that the zenzen horse was long gone, so we climbed up through the tree and walked the sky bridges back to Leeandra.

"When was the last time you saw your father?" I asked Kasha as we walked.

"Three days ago," she answered coldly.

"What makes you think he's missing?"

"Because we were supposed to meet this morning, after I got back from the forage," she said. "He never showed up. That's not like him."

Kasha's answers were clipped. I got the feeling she didn't like being questioned but hey, tough. This was important.

"What's a forage?" I asked her.

"It's what I do."

"Me too," Boon added with a little more enthusiasm. "We travel in packs on the jungle floor to hunt or gather fruit or chop trees for building materials or anything else that's needed in Leeandra. It's a dangerous job, and very important."

I asked Kasha, "How much do you know about the Travelers?"

It was one question too many. Kasha stopped short and turned to me, growling. I could see the anger in her eyes. "I'll tell you what I know, gar." She spat out the word "gar" like it was a bad taste in her mouth. "My father was a visionary who helped build cities. Now he's become a silly old klee spinning fantasy stories of time-traveling animals battling an evil gar. He says it's all very dangerous. You want to see danger? Come on a forage. I'd like to see you stand up to a rampaging tang. Then you can tell me you're more afraid of a gar named Saint Dane."

She growled at me, her anger barely contained. I figured it would be a bad idea to argue, seeing as she'd probably bite my head off. Literally. I kept my voice totally calm and said, "If it's all a fantasy, how do you explain me?"

This threw her. She turned away, saying, "You're a freak. When we find my father, I'll prove it to him."

She continued walking. Boon shrugged and followed. We were getting off to a bad start. I didn't know what to make of Kasha. If something tragic happened to Seegen, she'd be the Traveler from Eelong. I didn't look forward to that. On top of that, she'd hold me responsible. I looked even *less* forward to that. All I could hope was that Seegen would turn up okay, and Kasha would only be a minor pain.

I really, really hoped that we'd find Seegen back in Leeandra.

# EELONG

By the time we reached the portal into Leeandra, the sunbelt had dropped below the horizon. Night had settled on Eelong. I looked up through the thick tree canopy and saw stars. Fireflies were everywhere, just like on Second Earth. The small flying bugs would light up for a few seconds, then go dark. But unlike the boring old fireflies on Second Earth, these lit up with every color you could imagine. There were reds and greens and purples and blues, and yes, even some yellows like at home. It was stunning. As I gazed out to admire the light show, Boon stepped in front of me and gave me a sheepish look. I knew where this was going. I put my hands together and held them out.

"Thanks, Pendragon," he said gratefully as he slipped another restraining leash around my wrists. As horrible as this was, I knew I was safer this way. Kasha barely stopped long enough for me to be hooked up. As we followed her into the city, she made a point of staying in front of us. There was no way she was going to be seen walking with a gar. We followed her across several sky bridges and took a few elevators until we reached our destination . . . Kasha's home.

She lived inside a huge hollow tree, but unlike the others I had been in, this home had partitions that separated the space into rooms. We first stepped into the largest room that had a table and chairs for meals, low wooden benches for furniture, and even sculptures hanging on the walls that were made from twisted branches. Unbelievable. This cat had artwork! An archway led out onto a balcony where there was a large stone oven for cooking. Kasha didn't give me a tour of the rest. I think she hated the fact that I was there at all. Maybe she was afraid I'd pee on the furniture or something.

"Gars sleep in the pen out back," she said coldly.

"He's not an ordinary gar," Boon complained. "You can't make him—"

"Yes, I can!" Kasha snapped. "Unless he wants to sleep on the jungle floor with the tangs, he'll sleep in the gar pen."

"No!" Boon insisted. Kasha shot him an angry look, as if she weren't used to being disagreed with. Boon backed down, but not by much. "I'm sorry, Kasha," he continued sheepishly. "You may not agree with your father, but Pendragon is a Traveler. He should be treated with respect. It's what Seegen would want."

Kasha stood staring at me. She really hated to be civilized to an uncivilized gar.

"Fine," she finally said. "Prepare a meal, Boon. I'm going to clean up." She left for another room, leaving Boon and me alone.

"C'mon," Boon said. "I'll make something."

He took off my restraints and led me into the kitchen, where he made dinner. I'd never eaten cat food before, though I didn't think he'd be cracking open a can of Friskies. On the other hand, I was so hungry I was pretty sure I'd eat anything, no matter how gross it was. He reached into a square container on the floor that was some kind of refrigerator. He pulled out three birds that looked pretty much like chickens, all cleaned and dressed as if they came right from the grocery store.

"You eat meat, right?" he asked.

"Depends," I answered.

"On what?"

"On if you're going to cook it or not." I'm happy to report that Boon laughed at that.

"Of course I'm going to cook it!" he said. "We're not animals."

Yeah. Right.

Boon proceeded to cook the chickens, or whatever they were called there, on a rotisserie like at Garden Poultry on the Ave. There was a bed of hot coals beneath that cooked the birds slowly, all the way around. When the smell of the cooking birds hit my nose, my mouth started to water. Man, barbequed chicken. I couldn't wait. Too bad I couldn't have some fries to go with it. While the birds cooked, I took the chance to grill Boon about Kasha . . . no pun intended.

"Why is she so angry?" I asked.

"She loves her father," Boon explained. "He's a hero. He helped build Leeandra from nothing, fighting off the tangs every inch of the way. Everything she learned, she learned from Seegen. So when he started talking about Travelers and intelligent gars and fluming to different territories, her whole image of him fell apart. In her eyes he had lost his mind. Then he told her that when he died, she would take his place. Well, that really set her off. She won't even talk to him about it. The thing is, Kasha is great. She's brave and caring and would do anything to help a friend. But she's also pretty stubborn. If something doesn't fit her idea of the way things should be, it's hard to change her mind."

"But you believe Seegen," I said.

"I've got more of an imagination," Boon answered. "Besides, I'm sitting here talking to you, right? Seegen said you'd come and here you are."

"What about her mother?" I asked.

"She was killed in a tang raid," Boon said softly. "I think that's why Kasha became a forager. She likes fighting tangs. Every time she kills one, I know she's thinking about her mother."

Kasha entered the kitchen and Boon fell silent. "Are we ready to eat?" she asked.

"All set!" answered Boon. The three birds were now crackling brown and smelled delicious. Boon pulled them off the spit and brought them inside the tree, where we all sat around the table. Kasha gave me a quick, dirty look. It must have been hard for her to have a filthy gar sitting at her table, but too bad. I was starving. I sat down politely and waited for Boon to serve. He placed one bird in front of each of us. No knives. No forks. No plates, either. I was kind of hoping for a vegetable and a potato, but I wasn't going to push my luck. The chicken would do me just fine. Kasha and Boon picked up their birds and devoured them. I pulled off a leg and took a big bite. Oh yeah. It was good. It tasted like . . . chicken. No big surprise. It could have tasted like shoes. I didn't care. I tore into the meat and ate, but not quite as ravenously as Boon and Kasha. It took them all of thirty seconds to polish off their birds, bones and all. I had barely finished one leg when they were licking their paws and staring at my bird out of the corner of their eyes. As hungry as I was, there was no way I'd be able to finish the whole thing, so I tore off the other leg, pulled some breast meat off the bone for myself and asked, "You guys want to finish this?"

Boon answered by grabbing the bird quickly, tearing it in two, and giving half to Kasha. These cats may have been civilized, but they sure ate like animals. The strange scene was complete when I heard an odd noise. It sounded like a low engine, but looking around, I didn't see anything that might be making the sound. That's when I realized it was coming from Kasha and Boon. They were purring. How freaking strange is that?

I finished the delicious meat and looked around for a napkin to wipe my hands, but realized that was idiotic. So I followed the lead of my hosts and licked my fingers clean. Hey, why not? At home my mother would kill me for doing that, but I wasn't home. When I finished, I saw that my plate was empty. Both my leg bones had been swooped up by the cats and devoured. Note to self: If you don't want to go hungry around here, eat fast.

"It's late," Kasha announced. "I need rest. Tomorrow we will go to my father's home. Be ready to leave early."

"Where do I sleep?" I asked, really hoping she wouldn't banish me to the dog run.

She glanced at Boon and spat out, "Right here." It killed her to let a beast sleep under her roof. Tough.

Boon said, "I'll get you a blanket."

"I need something to write with," I said. I figured it was time to catch up with my journals.

Kasha looked at me like I had just announced I was going to grow a second head.

"You can write?" she asked, not hiding her surprise.

"Amazing, but true," I answered snottily. "And I can count, too. Want to hear?"

"I'll get what you need," Boon interjected, trying to keep

the peace. Kasha left without saying good night. Boon got me a scratchy blanket, along with some blank parchment pages and a pen. The pen actually had an ink reservoir inside. I didn't have to dip a quill into a well. Eelong was truly a strange place. Much of what I saw was savage, but there were also hints of modern convenience.

"I'll be back in the morning," Boon announced.

"Whoa, you're not staying? What if Kasha decides to slit my throat while I'm asleep?"

Boon chuckled. "She won't. She may not like to be told what to do, but she's honorable."

"I'll have to take your word for that," I said. I planned on being a very light sleeper that night.

"So, tomorrow we go after Saint Dane?" Boon asked hopefully, like he was asking if we were going to Disneyland.

"One thing at a time," I answered. "First we find Seegen and Gunny."

"Right!" Boon exclaimed. "Good night, Pendragon." He got down on all fours, leaped out of the doorway, and ran off into the night.

I sat down on a long couch that had a soft blanket for a seat. It wasn't exactly cushy, but it was comfortable enough. I spent the next few hours writing Journal #16, the one you've already read by now. By the time I finished, I couldn't keep my eyes open. I rolled up the pages, sent it through my ring to you guys, then put my head down to rest. In the few seconds before nodding out, I thought back on the incredible day I had just spent. I had woken up that morning in a mansion on Veelox having slept in a comfortable bed. I ended the day sleeping on a scratchy blanket in a tree house surrounded by predator jungle cats who were getting ready to pass a law that allowed them to kill and eat humans.

Can my life be any stranger?

I wanted to sleep lightly, but my body wouldn't let me. I totally conked out. The next thing I remembered, I had a dream that I was being stalked by a cat. No big surprise, right? The only thing was, the dream felt real . . . so real that it jolted me awake. There was a moment where I wasn't sure where I was, but when I opened my eyes it all came flooding back. That's when I realized my dream wasn't a dream. I slowly opened my eyes to see a big, gray cat creeping across the floor toward me, hunched down, ready to spring. Zing! I went from dead asleep to wide awake in a nanosecond. I was totally defenseless and quickly realized I had only one hope.

"Kasha!" I screamed. I rolled off the couch and scrambled underneath it, pulling the blanket down for whatever pitiful protection it might offer until Kasha came to my rescue . . . assuming she came to my rescue.

She did. The black cat leaped into the room, ready for action. "What?" she snarled.

The big gray cat who was stalking me stood up on its two hind legs and said, "What is this, Kasha? You're now letting gars sleep in your home?" The cat's voice sounded old. His fur was longer than others I'd seen and the gray was from age. This was definitely an elderly cat, but it still looked pretty dangerous.

"Where is my father, Yorn?" Kasha growled at him.

"Yorn?" I exclaimed. "The acolyte?"

The old cat shot me a surprised look. I figured I had to take charge and said, "My name is Pendragon. I'm looking for Seegen."

"Pendragon?" the old cat gasped. "But . . . you're not supposed to be here!"

"Well, surprise," I said, crawling out from under the couch. My heart was still thumping. "Where is Seegen?" I asked him.

Yorn staggered to a bench and sat down. I wasn't sure if it was because he was old and weak, or the surprise of seeing me knocked him for a loop.

"He went to Second Earth, looking for you!" Yorn answered. "He had news of the Traveler you seek. The injured gar."

"Gunny?" I shouted.

"Yes, Gunny."

"Where is he? Is he all right?"

"I don't know," Yorn answered. "He and Seegen left on a journey several days ago. They wouldn't tell me where they went. Then Seegen returned alone. As far as I know, Gunny's harm does not go beyond the loss of his hand. He was attacked by a tang, you know."

I couldn't believe it! Gunny was okay! Now I knew why he lost his hand—he was attacked by a tang. But he survived. That's all that mattered.

"There's more, Pendragon," Yorn continued. "Saint Dane is here on Eelong. He's influencing the Council of Klee to begin a campaign that will wipe out the gars. Seegen went to Second Earth to tell you this and bring you back."

"This is ridiculous," Kasha spat out. "Where is my father?"

Yorn and I shared a look. Kasha didn't have a clue. We ignored her.

"I've got to get to the flume," I said. "If Seegen is on Second Earth, he's in trouble. A big cat roaming around Stony Brook is going to get—"

"Kasha!" came a voice in the doorway. I looked to see a

group of cats entering, led by the big cat named Durgen. It was the same group that was with Kasha when they were attacked by the tang the day before. I quickly backed away from Yorn and bent over like the animal I was . . . or was supposed to be.

"What do you want, Durgen?" Kasha asked, annoyed.

"We've got a forage," Durgen answered.

"No," Kasha protested. "We're off the schedule today."

"Not anymore," the big cat answered.

"Well, I can't," she answered. "There may be a problem with my father and Yorn needs my help to—"

"I'm sure it's nothing the old klee can't handle," Durgen interrupted. "This is a direct order, Kasha."

Yorn glanced to me, but said nothing. Kasha made a quick move for the door.

"Fine," she said. "Let's get out and back fast, all right?"

Durgen asked, "What about the gar? You can't leave him here."

"I'll tend to him," Yorn offered.

"Nonsense," the big cat replied. He grabbed the back of my neck and pulled me to my feet. I felt as helpless as a kitten, which is a strange way to put it under the circumstances. "After the attack yesterday we're short a few gars. We can use this one. We're going to the south country."

Yorn sat up straight, as if hearing this surprised him.

"The south country?" Kasha asked, surprised as well. "There hasn't been a forage there in months."

"Exactly," Durgen answered. "There are acres of ripening fruit about to go bad."

"Yes, but it's dangerous," Kasha shot back. "There are huge packs of tangs in the south."

"That's why we need all the gars we can get," the big cat replied. "We're probably going to lose a few on this one." The cat looked Kasha right in the eye and said, "Since when were you afraid of a few extra tangs?"

Kasha stiffened and said, "Did I say I was afraid? Let's go."

Durgen gave me a shove toward the door. I stumbled but Kasha grabbed me before I could fall. I took a quick glance back at Yorn to see the old klee looking worried. Join the club. I had seen what happens to gars on a forage. Now I was about to experience it for myself.

# EELONG

Up until that moment, my stay on Eelong had been a nightmare. It was about to get worse. Is there a word for something worse than a nightmare? If I could think of one, I'd use it. Saint Dane's plan was clear. He was going to throw Eelong into chaos by thinning the gar population, which would tip the balance of nature and lead to the destruction of the klees. My plan was clear too. I had to find Seegen, the Traveler from Eelong, and get his help to find Gunny. Together, the three of us would try to stop Saint Dane. But as treacherous as that was going to be, I couldn't even get started, because I was being shipped off on a suicide mission to run interference for a bunch of cats so they wouldn't be killed by rampaging tangs while they harvested some fruit. How idiotic was that? The future of their entire world was at stake, and I had to go out and pick fruit in a war zone.

I was really beginning to hate Eelong.

It was morning. The sky was growing lighter. In no time I expected to see the sunbelt appear in the sky. The team of foragers led me and a few other gars down to the jungle floor and toward the corral where they kept the zenzen horses. There were five cats, along with three gars . . . and me. They lashed my hands together and tied me up to the other gars so we had to shuffle along like one of those chain gangs you see in prison movies. I'm not really sure why they did this, since the gars didn't look like they were going anywhere. If there was anybody who wanted to beat feet out of there, it was me. Kasha walked ahead of us with the other klees. A few times she stole a glance back at me. I might be reading too much into this, but I thought I saw a touch of sympathy in her eyes. Maybe even a little worry. She knew I wasn't ready for this. On the other hand, maybe she was thinking this would be a quick and easy way to get me out of her life, and her father's life. Either way, I wasn't real excited about how this day was shaping up.

As we neared the zenzen corral, I looked ahead to see a big wagon with huge wooden wheels being driven toward us, pulled by two zenzens. Sitting in front with the reins was Boon. Loaded in back were a dozen more gars, all looking about as thrilled to be there as I was. Boon brought the wagon to a stop and shouted a friendly greeting. "Morning, everybody!" He spotted me and the smile fell from his face. "Whoa, not that gar. He's useless."

I tried to look useless.

"What's wrong with him?" Durgen asked.

Kasha answered, "He's been sick. He's weak. He won't be able to harvest his weight."

That was good. Kasha was trying to get me out of this too. At least that meant she was on my side. Durgen felt my arms with his paws. I tried to shrink and act all weak, but there was only so much acting I could do. He lifted my chin and looked into my eyes. Finally he grabbed my hands and examined them. "He is soft," the cat exclaimed. "But he doesn't seem frail." He dropped my hands, turned his back to me, and walked away. Suddenly he whipped around and threw his wooden weapon at me. I didn't have time to think, only react. I caught the weapon before it beaned me. It was the wrong thing to do. I should have taken the hit. I gave a quick glance to Kasha, who looked to the ground in disappointment.

"His reflexes are fine," Durgen announced. "Better than most. And he's the biggest one here. Even if he's weak, he'll harvest more than the rest. He comes."

Oh well. Nice try. The other three gars and I were shoved into the back of the wagon, where there was barely enough room to sit down. Most of the gars were men, but I saw a few women, too. They were all sitting on the hard, wooden floor. Not exactly a deluxe way to travel. I found a small opening between two gars. My first instinct was to be polite and ask, "Excuse me, can I sit there?" But I realized it would be a waste of breath, so I nudged my way in and sat down between the two without a word.

"Let's go!" Durgen shouted.

Boon cracked the reins and the wagon lumbered forward. The crude wooden wagon bounced across the jungle floor. My aching butt felt every bump and divot. A few minutes later the giant doors swung open and we rolled out of Leeandra, headed for who knows what danger. Kasha and Durgen walked in front of the wagon, with the other three klees walking to the rear. As soon as we left the safety of Leeandra, the cats tensed up and grabbed their weapons. Their eyes darted back and forth, looking for any hint of danger.

Between the threat of tangs and the bumpy ride, I knew we were in for a long trip. All I could do was try to get comfortable and stare at the pathetic-looking gars who surrounded me. It was totally creepy. I was jammed in with a bunch of raggy-looking people who kept their eyes down. I guess I shouldn't have been surprised, but it was tough getting my mind around the fact that as much as they looked like humans, they weren't. Expecting them to be social would be like expecting a bunch of cows to stand up and sing some reggae. And they smelled too. I don't think any of them had a bath in, well, maybe never.

As we bumped along the dirt road, one of the cats tossed a bag into the center of the wagon. The gars dove for it, tearing it apart and pulling out what looked to be pieces of fruit. They looked like apples, but they were bright blue. The gars fought over them like it was their last meal. The sick thought occurred to me that for some of them, it probably was. I hoped I wasn't one of them. I didn't join the fight. I didn't have much of an appetite.

Have I mentioned that I was really beginning to hate Eelong?

We rode for about an hour. Every so often Boon would glance back from his driver's seat to see if I was okay. All I could do was offer him a weak smile to assure him that I was fine . . . in spite of my aching butt. Boon would nod in sympathy.

We finally broke out of the jungle and rolled into a vast clearing. At first I thought this would be the farm where we'd stop and pick the fruit, but I couldn't have been more wrong. This was a farm, all right. The wagon had stopped on the edge of what looked like a vast cornfield. But rather than green husks shielding yellow ears of corn, these plants grew the same blue apples that were thrown into the wagon earlier.

And there was something else. Lying amid the rows of plants were dead tangs. Lots of them. It didn't look like there had been a fight or anything. All these tangs looked as if they just lay down . . . and died. Not that I felt bad for these monsters, but it was totally creepy.

Durgen took a step away from the wagon and surveyed the carnage. Kasha walked up to him and asked, "What happened here?"

Durgen looked troubled. "There have been reports of some crops turning foul. These tangs stopped at the wrong farm."

"But how could this happen?" Kasha asked. "Did the fruit simply turn rotten from being overripe?"

"That's my guess," Durgen answered. "But whatever the reason, with the food shortage we can't afford to let this happen again. Which is all the more reason to be out here and harvest what we can. Let's keep moving."

The wagon began rolling again. I saw that every few rows held more dead tangs. As horrible as it was, it gave me a slight bit of hope that maybe enough tangs had been killed off so they wouldn't bother us. On the other hand, if the fruit out here had become poisonous, I wasn't too thrilled about having to pick any of it. I was suddenly relieved I hadn't eaten any of the blue apples that were thrown into the wagon.

We soon left the farm and followed the path back into the jungle. I was happy to leave the tang graveyard behind.

"Death place," whispered a weak voice next to me. I was so shocked, I actually jerked back. I looked to where the voice came from but saw only the gars, staring out at the carnage with wide, scared eyes.

Then another voice said, "Time soon."

I whipped around to see another gar.

"You can talk?" I whispered, because I didn't want the klees to hear.

The gar looked at me. For the first time I saw signs of intelligent life. He let out a small smile and said, "Time soon."

I was stunned. The gar could speak! This was incredible. These creatures were being treated like animals, and don't get me wrong, they acted like animals, but they could speak! They had intelligence! Why didn't Boon tell me this? Or Kasha? How could the klees treat gars like cattle when they had an intellect?

I looked at the other gars in the wagon, and froze. They were all looking at me with these strange smiles. I didn't know how to react. They didn't look dangerous or anything. Just the opposite. They all looked at me with what I can best describe as . . . love. I'm serious. You know that look. It's the proud look you get from your parents when you're playing tuba in some lame-o concert at school, and they're thinking you're ready for Carnegie Hall. I had seen that look once before, other than from my parents, that is. It was in the arena on Denduron, when the poor Milago miner was about to be attacked by the quig. Remember that? The old miner saw my face in the crowd, and even though he was about to die, he stood up straight and gave me a smile of strength. It creeped me out then, and it was creeping me out in that wagon on Eelong. What did these people see in me? Did they know I was a Traveler who was trying to save them from Saint Dane? That was impossible . . . wasn't it?

I felt a tap on my shoulder and looked back to the gar who first spoke. He held out his hand. In his open palm was something I recognized. It was a small, amber cube like the one I had seen the two gars petting back in Leeandra. A closer look showed me that it was definitely made of some kind of crystal. But one of the sides was black. I looked at the strange object, not sure of what to do. He didn't want me to take it, it was more like he was showing it off.

"What is it?" I whispered, not sure if he'd understand.

The gar cocked his head, as if he were surprised I didn't know what it was.

"Black Water," the gar said.

I had absolutely no freakin' idea of what he was talking about. Heck, I was still thrown by the fact that he could talk. That's when a gar sitting across from me said, "Black Water."

He too was holding one of the small cubes. I glanced to the front of the wagon and saw that two more gars had cubes. They each held them up with two hands like they were fragile, precious treasures.

"Soon," another gar said, and the others nodded.

"Soon what?" I asked.

"Home," another said.

Before I could ask them any more, the wagon came to an abrupt stop. The gars quickly hid their cubes, which told me they didn't want the klees to know about them. Very interesting. Now I was faced with a difficult choice. I felt as if the only way I'd learn about these cubes would be to ask Boon or Kasha. But if the gars didn't want the klees to know about them, would I be betraying their confidence? Boon and Kasha were on my side. At least Boon was. But they were klees, and klees were about to start hunting the gars, which is exactly what I had to prevent. What was I supposed to do? My head was starting to hurt as much as my butt.

"Everybody out!" shouted Durgen.

He threw open the back of the wagon and we all climbed out. One cat untied our restraints while another handed us each a large, empty sack. Once I got the circulation back in my legs, I looked around to see where we were. Since I had been so focused on the gars in the wagon, I hadn't noticed that we had emerged from the jungle and arrived at another farm. A quick look around showed that there were no tang bodies lying around. Durgen walked up to the first row of plants and plucked off one of the blue apples. He strode back toward the wagon and tossed the fruit to a gar who was standing next to me.

"Eat," he ordered.

The gar looked at the blue apple like it was poison. I didn't blame him. It might have been.

"Now!" Durgen yelled.

The gar closed his eyes and took a bite.

"More!" Durgen commanded.

The frightened gar took a few more bites and reluctantly swallowed. We all watched him, expecting . . . I don't know what. Would he fall down dead like the tangs?

He didn't. The gar looked visibly relieved and hungrily gnawed on the rest of the apple. But he didn't get far because Durgen knocked it out of his hands. I was beginning to have some serious issues with this Durgen character.

"The fruit is fine here," he bellowed to everyone. "This is where we harvest."

Oh joy.

Suddenly I was grabbed roughly by the back of my shirt and yanked away from the group. "Don't try to run away, gar!" a klee hissed at me.

It was Kasha. She pulled me far enough away from the group so they couldn't hear what we were saying. She gave me a rough shove that nearly threw me to the ground.

"Hey, easy!" I complained.

"We need to talk," she said.

"What happened to that farm back there? Why did those tangs die?" I asked.

"I don't know," Kasha answered. "But if you want to stay alive, listen to me. Do what you are told. Be sure to stay near the center of the pack. The tangs attack from the outside in."

"You didn't tell me gars could talk," I said. "They're intelligent. They aren't animals."

"Pendragon, are you listening to me?"

"Yeah, yeah. Outside in. How could the klees want to hunt intelligent life?"

Kasha gave a quick glance behind me. I turned to see Durgen stalking toward us. "Do as I say, Pendragon," Kasha said quickly. She gave me a kick and I fell at Durgen's feet. "I was making sure he will carry his weight," Kasha explained to Durgen.

Kasha was definitely playing this up for Durgen's sake, but I think she was enjoying it a little. Durgen lifted me up by my shirt. I was really getting sick of being handled like a doll.

"Good," he said. "Then he will lead the pack." He shoved me in the direction of the other gars. I didn't know what he meant by leading the pack, but whatever it was, I was pretty sure I wouldn't like it.

The klees herded the gars together, shoulder to shoulder. I was in dead center. That was good. Tangs attacked from the outside in. But I was told to walk forward first, into the tall stalks. The others were to follow me, slightly behind and spread out like an arrowhead. That was bad. I was the tip of the arrow. If there was a hungry tang lying in wait inside those plants, I'd be the first one to reach it. I gave a quick glance back to see Boon sitting in the driver's seat of the wagon, looking helpless. I heard a loud *crack* and felt a sharp, stinging pain on my back. Yeow! I looked the other way to see Durgen standing there with a long strap he used like a whip.

"Now!" he bellowed. "Before the tangs catch a whiff of your stench!"

I got the message. I stepped forward and into the first row of plants. The others followed to either side and slightly behind. I didn't know what else to do, so I started pulling the blue fruit off the stalks and dropping it into my bag. It was mindless work, which was good because the only thing on my mind was the possibility of a tang lying in wait for me. As I picked the fruit I looked back to see what the klees were doing to protect us. The answer was, nothing. Just the opposite, we were there to protect them. While Boon and another klee stayed at the wagon, the others walked behind us, inside the arrowhead, shielded from a surprise attack. Kasha was with them, which gave me a little reassurance. Very little.

When my bag was filled with blue apples, a gar came forward, took it from me, and gave me another empty sack. The gar dragged the loaded bag back to the wagon where he dumped the fruit. They had a couple of gars shuttling loaded sacks. I realized pretty quickly that once the wagon was loaded, there'd be no room for us poor gars to ride on the way back to Leeandra. That is, assuming we survived.

The picking was slow going. I'd say it took about a minute to get all the fruit off a single plant. I quickly learned that after a plant was picked clean, it had to be uprooted and laid down. That meant as our formation moved forward, we cleared a path through the crops that grew wider as we went. I don't know how long we were picking. Two hours? Three? It was grueling and I was getting tired. The klees didn't give us water, either. Or food. It struck me that if the tangs were smart, they'd attack later in the day, once their victims were burned out. I really, really hoped they weren't smart.

I finished another bag and held my hand up to signal a gar to come and take it. But nobody came. They had been pretty quick up till then, so I realized that for some reason the process had slowed . . . or stopped. I looked to Kasha and held up the heavy bag.

Kasha saw it and shouted out, "Here!"

Nobody came to fetch it.

The other gars stopped picking. I instantly felt the tension as they stood up and looked around nervously. The cats reached for their weapons and slowly brought them forward. Uh-oh. Everyone stood absolutely still, not making a sound, only listening. A few seconds went by. The only sound I heard was the wind gently rustling the plants. Where were the shuttling gars? Were they just slow in emptying the sacks at the wagon, or was the answer more ominous?

I looked to my right. Standing a few feet behind me was the gar who earlier showed me his amber cube. His every sense was on alert, listening, looking, smelling. He was scared. I didn't blame him. So was I. The guy looked ahead into the dense crops, but saw nothing but plants. His gaze wandered until he saw me. Our eyes met. Instantly his look went from one of fear, to one of serenity. Seriously. It was like the tension left his body as he broke into a big smile.

It would be the last action of his life.

A second later I smelled the stench. It was the odor of a hungry tang. Another second passed and the tall plants in front of the gar rustled. Something flashed out. It went so fast I can't really describe exactly what happened. One second he was standing there, the next second a green blur wrapped around him and pulled him into the dense plants. I stood frozen, a scream caught in my throat. A moment later I had no trouble screaming, because something came back out. It hit the ground and rolled close to my feet. I looked down to see something I'll never forget for the rest of my life. Lying at my feet was the head of my friend the gar. His lifeless eyes staring up at me.

I screamed . . . and the attack began.

# EELONG

The assault was fast and violent.

The tangs were waiting for us, just as I had feared. As soon as the first gar was killed, it was like the signal had gone out for the others to attack. They sprang from the plants in front of us like guerrilla fighters. These may have been beasts, but they were smart. Their green color blended with the green vegetation so well that we were nearly on top of them before they made their move.

A tang leaped for me. Without thinking, I swung the bag full of apples. It wasn't exactly a deadly weapon, but the heavy bag saved my life. I hit the tang's gut with such force, I heard it grunt. The beast fell back, its scaly tale thrashing. It wasn't hurt, but the move gave me the few seconds I needed to do the only thing possible.

I ran.

It all happened so fast that I can only remember quick, horrible images. I saw another tang leap out and grab the gar who was picking fruit on the other side of me. The gar's scream of pain cut right through me. I never saw him again. All around me, gars had dropped their bags of fruit and were running back toward the wagon. They had no weapons. They were sitting ducks. Or running ducks. The klees didn't do anything to help them. The cats held their wooden staves up as they backed toward the wagon, but it was to protect themselves, not the gars. A few tangs attacked the klees, but the experienced foragers used their weapons expertly, fending them off and knocking a few senseless. There were screams all around me, both from gars who were being attacked, and the tangs who were pouncing on them with a bloodlust. I had no idea how many tangs there were. There could have been ten, or a hundred. It was all a blur.

All I could do was block out the horror around me and get back to the wagon. I pumped my legs, jumping over the crops we had just picked. I didn't dare turn around for fear of what I would see. Besides, it would only slow me down. I've always been fast, but I had no idea if I was faster than a hungry tang.

Up ahead of me, the klees were on the run. They were down on all fours and chewing up the ground to escape. I didn't see Kasha, but I figured she was right there with them, abandoning me. So much for trusting the next Traveler from Eelong. Behind me, I heard tangs crunching across the fallen plants, hungry to catch up. But my confidence was growing. I was faster than they were. I was going to make it to the wagon. My thoughts went to what I would do once I got there. The klees would make a stand, I was sure of that. But could I count on them to protect me and the other gars who were lucky enough to make it back? Could I rely on Kasha? And Boon? I would find out soon enough. Up ahead, I saw the wagon. Boon was standing up in the driver's seat, motioning for us all to hurry. I shouldn't have been looking at him, because it meant I wasn't watching what was in front of me and . . . I tripped.

I stumbled forward and did a complete somersault only to come face-to-face with a dead gar. Blood trickled from his mouth. I jumped up quickly to see what I had tripped over. It was another dead gar. I then knew what had happened to the group that was shuttling the fruit back to the wagon. They had been ambushed by the tangs. A quick look to my right showed me a tang dragging a gar back into the high stalks. He had gotten his prize. I shot a look to where I had come from to see a tang was running for me. Its mouth was open to reveal bloody, sharp teeth. I was like a deer caught in the headlights. The tang was on a dead run. I was just . . . dead. There was no way I could turn and run fast enough to get away. I was tang chow. I backed away, but too late. The tang leaped.

And a blur flashed in front of me, knocking the tang off balance. It was a gar! He fought the tang valiantly, but the poor guy didn't stand a chance. I took a step forward to help him, but it was too late. The tang swept its arm back and stabbed the gar with its long, sharp talons. The three talons went right through his body, coming out his back. It was hideous. The gar writhed in pain, but managed to turn his head and look at me. The guy was in agony, but when he saw me, he relaxed. It was like the pain had magically gone away.

I recognized him. It was one of the gars I had spoken to on the wagon. His eyes looked peaceful. He wasn't in pain anymore. He smiled. I swear, guys, he smiled. This primitive human-animal had sacrificed his life to save mine. But why? Blood started leaking out the sides of his mouth, but he kept his smile. He croaked out two words. He said them with such a soft whisper, I could barely hear.

"Black Water," he groaned.

His eyes closed and he died. The tang pulled its talons out

of the guy, threw him to the ground and looked at me. I wasn't sure if it was going to attack or make off with its conquest. I didn't stick around long enough for it to decide. I turned and ran for the wagon, trying to hold down the sick feeling in my stomach. I expected to feel the tang's talons stab me in the back, but the stab never came. The tang must have stayed with its victim. Gross.

"Hurry! C'mon!" Boon yelled.

The other klees got to the wagon first. Of the twenty or so gars who were brought here, only a handful survived the attack. I was one of them, thanks to the selfless gar who gave his life to save mine

"Durgen! Help!"

I heard the pained cry come from a klee who was still twenty yards from the wagon. He was on the ground, hurt. I saw that both his back legs were bleeding. He could barely crawl forward using his front paws. A tang was slowly creeping up on him, ready for the kill. It approached cautiously, in case the klee still had some fight left. Lying next to the injured klee was his wooden weapon, but he was too weak to use it. The cat was doomed . . . unless somebody helped him. I glanced to the wagon to see the gars were hiding underneath. The klees were standing next to one another, weapons up, ready to defend themselves. None made a move to save their friend. I had a quick thought of the gar who died to save me. It felt wrong not to try and do something to help the injured klee. Before I had the chance to chicken out, I ran for the fallen cat. Stupid move, I know. But I had to do it. There had been enough killing.

"No!" Boon yelled.

As I think back to that moment, I wish I had listened to

him. Things would have turned out much better. But there was no way I could have guessed at the horrible consequences my actions would have. My plan was to grab the cat's weapon and try to fend off the tang. I hoped that if the other klees saw that I was putting up a fight to save their friend, they'd come and help us both out.

It was a totally stupid plan.

I ran to the klee and scooped up the weapon. But as soon as I lifted it up, another tang leaped from the cover of the tall stalks. It had been hiding, waiting for a golden opportunity like this. It lashed out with its scaly tail and whipped against my hands so hard and fast, it felt like I was hit with an electric shock. The wooden weapon was knocked out of my grasp. What an idiot. Now the klee and I were both in trouble. He was injured and I was defenseless—with two tangs standing by, ready to attack.

I heard a sound that can be best described as a whistle. Whatever was making it, it came up from behind me fast and whizzed past my ear. It felt so close I ducked, expecting to get hit in the back of the head. An instant later I saw what it was.

Kasha. She had thrown her lasso with the three stones tied to the end. The stones spun like a buzz saw, flew past me, and wrapped themselves around the neck of the closest tang. Kasha gave a sharp yank on the rope and I heard a sickening *snap*. She had broken the tang's neck. If I wasn't so relieved, I would have been totally grossed out. The beast fell. It was dead before it hit the ground. But there was still one more tang to deal with and Kasha no longer had her lasso.

The tang made the next move. He didn't attack me, or Kasha. He pounced on the injured klee, the easy prey. The lizard jumped on the cat's back and locked its jaws around its neck. The cat reared up and tried to shake the tang off, but the monster would not be denied. The klee was already weak from having lost so much blood. He didn't stand a chance. I watched in horror as the cat fell to the ground hard, with the tang's jaws still clamped on its neck.

I felt a strong hand on my shoulder. I whipped around, expecting another tang attack. But it was Kasha.

"It's over," she said sadly. "We have to go back."

It may have been over for the poor klee, but not for us. Other tangs were still sniffing around, looking to do some damage. We had to get out of there. The two of us ran back to the safety of the wagon. I stole a quick glance back at the battleground to see that the tangs were finished. They got what they came for. I watched as the few remaining tangs dragged their victims back into the tall stalks. Most were gars, but of course, there was the one klee. It now suddenly made all sorts of sense to me why the klees chose to build their world in the trees. The tangs were merciless marauders.

I wasn't sure of what to do when we got back to the wagon. I still had to act like a simple gar, so I decided to hide under the wagon with the survivors. But I didn't get the chance. As soon as we approached the group of klees, Durgen stepped forward and slapped Kasha across the face. Everybody was so stunned, they froze in place. Including Kasha. Durgen stood in front of her, his eyes fixed on her in anger.

"You sacrificed a klee to save a gar?" he seethed. "Are you insane?"

Uh-oh. Kasha had saved me, but it looked as if she was going to pay a price for it.

"He was as good as dead when I got there," Kasha said, not backing down. "If I tried to save him, we would have lost both."

That might have been true, but I wasn't so sure. Durgen didn't think it was true at all. He hauled back and slapped Kasha again. Kasha barely flinched. She was tough. She took the hit but stood tall.

"You don't know that!" he bellowed. "If there was a chance to save him, you should have taken it. But you didn't. And why? To save . . . this?"

Durgen grabbed me by the back of my neck and held me up in the air, my feet dangling a few inches off of the ground.

"It is an animal, Kasha!" he shouted in anger. "An animal!"

He tossed me down hard. I wasn't ready for it and my knees buckled, sending me crashing onto my shoulder. I wasn't so quick to get back up. I didn't want him throwing me around again.

"That klee was your friend," Durgen continued, his voice softening. "You chose this animal over a friend."

Kasha looked down. I think it finally hit her that someone she cared about, a fellow klee, had died.

"I did what I felt was right," she said softly.

"And I will do what I think is right," Durgen said angrily. "Turn the wagon around! Back to Leeandra!"

I looked to Boon. His eyes were wide and scared. He knew exactly why Kasha had chosen me over the klee, but he wasn't about to say anything. How could he? I stood up slowly and looked at Kasha. She walked past without looking back at me. I guarantee she was having second thoughts about what she had done. The trip back to Leeandra was grueling. The wagon was full of blue apples, so we gars couldn't ride. I think the only reason we got to ride out here in the first place was to save our strength to pick the fruit. Now that our job was done, the klee foragers couldn't care less if we even made it back. Boon drove the wagon again, while I walked behind it with the few surviving gar. Kasha walked behind us with another klee. Durgen and the last klee walked in front of the wagon. If we ran into another band of tangs, I don't think anybody would have had the strength to fight.

The walk took a few hours and it gave me time to plan my next move. I still had to find Seegen. I figured the best way to do that was through his acolyte, Yorn. If Seegen was on Second Earth, I thought that maybe Yorn could send a message to you guys, and you could tell Seegen to return to Eelong. It was a weak plan, I know. The chances of you guys finding him were pretty slight. I couldn't imagine a jungle cat wearing a tunic walking through the streets of Stony Brook. He'd either be shot, or captured and put in a zoo. But I couldn't think of anything else. I was too tired.

Thankfully, no tangs attacked on our return trip. When we finally made it safely inside the gates of Leeandra, I figured I would ask Boon if I could stay with him. I was pretty sure Kasha wouldn't want me around anymore. But as soon as the gates closed behind us, my plan went right out the window. Durgen grabbed me by the neck, again. It was getting very, very old. He dragged me away from the group. Boon leaped down from the wagon and jumped in front of him.

"Uhh," he said with a nervous laugh. "What are you doing?"

"Have the rest of the gars unload the wagon at the transfer station," he ordered. "Then return the wagon to the corral." He kept walking, dragging me along with him.

"Yeah, sure," Boon said. "But what are you doing with Kasha's gar?"

Durgen stopped and looked back to Kasha, who stood by

the wagon. Her eyes were wide, but she didn't say a word. When Durgen spoke, it wasn't to Boon, it was to Kasha.

"This gar cost me a dear friend," Durgen said bitterly. "I'm going to make sure I get some value in return."

What was he talking about? Was he going to eat me or something? Kasha took a step forward.

"You can't," she complained. "He's my gar."

"Not anymore," Durgen spat back at her. "I'm selling him to the handlers."

"No!" shouted Boon.

"You can't!" Kasha added.

Durgen gave me a shove. Boon caught me. Durgen went nose-to-nose with Kasha, saying, "And how exactly do you plan on stopping me?"

It was a standoff. Kasha didn't back off. Neither did Durgen.

"What are the handlers, Boon?" I whispered nervously. "Are they going to eat me?"

"Don't worry," Boon whispered back. "We'll get you out of there."

He didn't get the chance to say any more. Durgen stepped back from Kasha and grabbed me again. I had had enough. It was time to stop fooling around and start taking charge of my own destiny. I pulled away from Durgen and stood facing him, trying to look as defiant as possible.

"I am not an animal," I declared. "You don't own me and you sure as heck can't sell me."

I thought this would blow Durgen away. I saw the shock on his face. I doubted if he had ever heard a gar speak a full sentence like that, let alone right in his face. Out of the corner of my eye I saw the other gars looking at me in awe. The only ones who weren't shocked, of course, were Kasha and Boon.

Durgen reacted in a way I didn't expect. He laughed. "Well." He chuckled. "A gar who believes he is more than a gar." He put his hands on his hips and said, "I have bad news for you." He hauled back and hit me with the back of his hand. Hard. It was such a surprise and came so fast, I had no chance to duck or to block it. He hit me square on the side of the head. I saw stars. And colors. I don't think I was knocked out, but I lost touch with reality. Things got fuzzy. I remember being grabbed again, and dragged. It was all a blur. Whoever was dragging me wasn't gentle about it. I remember being knocked around a few times, and hitting my head again, which didn't help matters.

I remember things getting dark. Not lights-out dark, just darker. I remember wondering if night had fallen. I stopped moving, too. Wherever I was being taken, I was there. It felt cold and a little damp. I probably lost consciousness a few times. I couldn't tell for sure. I don't know how long I was out of touch like that, but I do remember my first clear thought. I remember thinking that wherever I was, it smelled insanely bad.

My eyes opened and I focused for the first time since I didn't know when. It was still dark, but it wasn't night and I wasn't outside. I registered stone walls and a high ceiling with an interesting pattern on it. At first I thought it was a checkerboard, because there were boxes floating overhead. That was weird. I laid on my back looking up at this strange checkerboard, trying to make sense of it, when a klee appeared overhead. It wasn't a checkerboard after all; it was a grid. The cat walked on top of it and looked down at me.

"Welcome home," the klee said with a sneer. He poured a bucket of water down through the grid. I didn't have time to react and got hit with a wave of smelly water. At least it woke me up. I sat up, blowing the disgusting water out of my nose, and looked around. I was in a large, dark room with stone walls; the high ceiling was a grid made of crisscrossing bamboo. It was a cage of some sort. And I wasn't alone. Lying against the walls were a dozen other people, gars, looking ghostly white and sickly thin, as if they hadn't had decent food in months.

I looked at one of the gars and asked, "Where is this?"

"This," he said. "End of life."

# EELONG

I was in prison.

I don't think that's what the klees called it. To them, this was a holding pen for animals. Nobody here had committed any crimes, except for being born a gar. To the wretched gars I shared the dungeon with, it was another added bit of cruelty to their already miserable lives. At night the gars huddled against the slimy stone walls, hugging one another, trying to share what little body heat they could generate. During the day, the sunbelt beat down so relentlessly that I now know what a lobster feels like when it's being boiled. And no matter what the time of day was, the smell was vicious.

Along one wall was a water trough dug into the stone floor that we were supposed to use as a bathroom. Nice idea, with constantly running water and all. Trouble was, the water wasn't running fast enough to take everything away, and the klees never set foot inside the dungeon to clean up. So it was like living inside a toilet. Making things worse, the running water gave the cell a damp feeling that cut to the center of my bones. I felt like one big toothache.

There was one wooden door with a barred window, where

I could see klee guards walk past. The only cushioning we had to make the hard floor more comfortable was dirty hay that had probably been dumped there a century before. The stuff smelled so bad I never sat on it. I chose to be uncomfortable rather than nauseous. There was no ceiling, only the bamboo grid that was beyond reach. At least this open ceiling made it possible to see the sky and catch a breath of fresh air. It was good to see the stars at night, clouds drifting by during the day, and the band of sun as the day wore on. Unfortunately it also meant that when it rained, we got wet. At least it helped wash the stench out of the cell.

The food was a joke, though maybe that's a bad way of putting it because there was nothing funny about it. Every so often a klee would appear on the grid above and dump down a load of fruit. The shower of food would hit the stone floor and smash to bits. It was a rotten way to be fed, but the gars didn't care. They scrambled to pick up every putrid crumb they could find. Some even licked the stone floor afterward. I had no idea what most of the stuff was. It all smelled rank. At first I couldn't bring myself to eat, especially after what I saw on that farm with all the dead tangs. But after a while I got so hungry I didn't care anymore and joined the feast. I didn't die. Obviously.

From what I've written so far, you may be wondering how long I spent in this hole. The fact is, I'm not exactly sure. When I first woke up, I didn't think I'd be there for long, so I didn't try to keep track of time. But after a few days I figured I'd better start getting my head together, so each time it got light, I scraped a notch in the floor with a small chunk of rock. But even then, I didn't know how long a day on Eelong was. Was it twenty-four hours like on Second Earth? Or forty-eight? Or twelve or . . . whatever. Time hasn't had a whole lot of meaning since I left home. But as I think back on the gruesome experience of being trapped in that cell, I can guesstimate that by Second Earth standards, I spent at least a month in there. I'm serious. A month. It was a month too long. I'd be kidding you if I said it didn't change me.

With each passing day, I got angrier. I couldn't believe that klees could treat gars so inhumanely, especially since I discovered the gars weren't dumb animals. I'm not saying they were playing chess with the klees or anything. Far from it. But they could think, and they had feelings, and they had a lot more to offer Eelong than what the klees gave them credit for. It wasn't right.

I was also angry at Durgen for sticking me here, and at Kasha and Boon for not getting me out. I was afraid they had abandoned me and left me to die. Most of all, I got angry at Saint Dane. Not that I needed any more of an excuse for that, but he was the real reason I was trapped in this cell. And with me out of the way, there was nobody to stop him from tricking the klees into destroying their own territory.

As long as I'm being totally honest, I have to admit that I was getting mad at Uncle Press, too. He was the one who got me into this Traveler mess in the first place. If it weren't for him, I'd probably be eating a pizza with you guys and catching the Yankees on TV. Or the Jets. What season is it, anyway? Instead, I sat in a putrid prison, grossed out by my own stench, wondering if this was my last stop. Morbid, aye? Sure, but why not? There was nothing else to think about. I had already counted the stones in the walls (8,462), done every math problem I could think of, and even came up with my own lyrics to that old song "Smells Like Teen Spirit," since I never understood the real lyrics anyway. Tell me *that's* not desperate. While Eelong edged closer to disaster, I was stuck in a sewerlike prison, helpless, hungry and making up mind games to keep from going insane.

I shouldn't rant so much about my own feelings, but I'll say one more thing. Once I finish writing this journal I'm going to put the horrible memories of my stay in the gar dungeon away in a safe place. I'll get over it, but I won't forget. And when it all goes down with Saint Dane, I'll bring this nightmare back and use it for strength against him. Bet on it.

Besides describing the horrible conditions, there were a few things that happened during my stay that I need to write down before I forget them. When I was first thrown into the dungeon, I hadn't had any real contact with gars, other than in that wagon on the way to our ill-fated farming expedition. But now, stuck in a confined space, I was officially a gar. I wanted to know more about them. It wasn't easy. They were afraid of me, and maybe a little bit loony from being starved and imprisoned. (They didn't have the outlet of making up lyrics to "Smells Like Teen Spirit." Poor them.) They didn't accept me. Most kept their distance, cowering in the shadows and shivering with fear, as if I would hurt them. It took me a while to realize why. Even though I looked like them, I was way different. I was taller and I walked with the authority of a klee. These little guys were always a little hunched over and afraid of their own shadows. To them I was a freak. When I made a move to pick up some fruit that had been tossed down, the gars would back off and let me take what I wanted before helping themselves.

A few times I heard them whispering to each other. I'd try to join in by saying something simple like "Hello?" or "My name is Pendragon." But they'd immediately shut down and scamper away. It didn't help that I tried to stay in shape. I constantly did sit-ups and push-ups to keep my muscle tone from going south. But every time I'd start exercising, the gars would huddle together and look at me like I was performing some strange ritual. After a while I gave up trying to communicate with them. It was too frustrating.

I soon began to wonder about the point of it all. Why were we being kept here? Durgen said something about getting "value" from me by selling me to handlers. But after being there for several weeks, there was no sign of a handler or of anybody else who might have bought me. I didn't think they were going to eat us. If that were the case they'd be feeding us a lot better. Most of the gars down here were skin and bones, not exactly a tempting taste treat for a hungry klee. It all seemed so pointless.

Then one day, with no warning, the wooden door flew open and two klees leaped in. The gars scampered to the far side of the cell in fear, no big surprise. I didn't. I was too tired to be scared.

The klees scanned the group. One said, "It's a sorry bunch." He pointed at two of the bigger gars and said, "Those two!" Without any deliberation, they pounced on the chosen gars and dragged them out of the cell. The gars were terrified, letting out cries of panic. None of the others did anything to save them. To be honest, neither did I. What could I do? I thought about standing up and blowing these cats away by singing a song, or reciting a poem, or telling them about Madden football. You know, anything that would be un-gar-like. But I decided not to draw attention to myself. My job here was about Saint Dane. I figured I shouldn't do anything that might get me in trouble and stop me from dealing with the bigger picture.

About an hour later the door opened again, and one of the gars was thrown back into the cell. He looked exhausted. He crawled on his hands and knees to a corner and collapsed. He was a mess. Or should I say, a bigger mess than before. I couldn't tell for sure, but I thought I saw a dark stain on his chest. From where I was sitting, it looked like blood. I didn't think it was his, and I never saw the other gar again. Connect the dots. Something nasty had happened.

Days went by. I was losing strength. I had never been hungry before. I mean, *really* hungry. Missing lunch and getting a little rumble in the tummy didn't count. This hurt. I had long since given up being picky about the food and would have eaten bugs if there had been any around. I didn't sleep much, and when I did, my dreams were horrible. I always seemed to be running from some horrible fate. I'd wake up in a cold sweat, relieved that I was safe, and then crushed to realize I was still in this prison.

One night I dreamed that I was lying on my back, looking up at the stars through the ceiling grid. The sky was beginning to lighten, which meant it was morning. The silhouette of a large klee appeared above and stared down at me. I looked up at this big cat, thinking how real this dream felt, when the klee snarled and said, "Good morning, Pendragon. Enjoying the morning air?"

Whoa. I sat up quickly. This wasn't a dream. It was the cat named Timber, from the Council of Klee. Or should I say, it was Saint Dane.

"You really should tidy up a bit," Saint Dane added. "I can smell you from up here."

"You're enjoying this, aren't you?" I asked angrily. "I'm stuck in here where you can keep an eye on me."

"Oh no, my friend," Saint Dane said. "Quite the opposite. I would much rather have you free to match wits. Having you lurking about makes things so much more interesting."

"Then get me out of here," I demanded.

"Ahh, if only I could," Saint Dane replied with mock sincerity. "But it would be wrong to interfere with the ways of the territory. That's against the rules, you know."

"Yeah, right," I said with as much sarcasm as I could generate. "Like that's ever stopped you before."

"I will give you a piece of advice though," Saint Dane added. "There is a way for you to get out. Seize the opportunity when it arrives."

"What is it?" I demanded to know.

"Good-bye, Pendragon," Saint Dane said as he slinked away. "Enjoy your day."

"Saint Dane!" I shouted. I was out of my mind. I jumped up and tried to climb the rock walls, but it was hopeless. They were slick and I only got about a foot off the floor before crashing back down, banging my butt on the stone. I had hit bottom. Literally. I was hungry, I was weak, and Saint Dane had just teased me into losing control. I never liked to show weakness to the demon. I didn't want him to know he was getting to me. But as of that moment, I had officially been gotten to.

"Black Water," came a soft voice next to me.

I looked to my right to see that one of the gars had bravely crept a few feet from me. He held his hand out, palm up. Resting in it was one of the mysterious, amber cubes.

"What is Black Water?" I asked.

"Home," came another weak voice.

The first gar held the cube closer to me, as if he wanted me to take it. I carefully reached out, expecting the gar to pull it away, but he let me take the precious crystal cube right off his hand. I was surprised to feel that the cube was as light as a marshmallow. I handled it gingerly, afraid that if I put any pressure on it, it might crack. I turned it around to examine all sides and discovered that there was a single black side, just like the other cube I had seen.

"Soon," the gar said. "Home."

"What home?" I asked. "What is Black Water? What's going to happen?"

"The Advent," the gar said.

Before I could ask what that meant, the wooden door to the cell screeched open and two klee guards entered. The gar snatched the cube back and tried to hide it in his ragged clothes. Too late. The first klee guard saw it and pounced on the frightened gar.

"What is this?" he shouted. He pulled the cube away from the gar and held it up. "Is it something to do with Black Water? Is that it?"

The gar cowered in the corner, shivering with fear. The klee dropped the amber box onto the stone floor and with one violent move, stomped it. A sickening *crunch* told me the box was indeed as fragile as I had feared. The other gars jumped, as if the klee had stomped on them. The only thing left of the strange little box was a pile of shattered glass. The gars stared at it, as if their last hope had been crushed right along with it.

The klee grabbed the gar he had stolen the cube from. He lifted the poor guy to his feet, holding him by the back of his neck and hissed. "I'm sure the Inquisitors will convince you to tell us. Guard!" A third klee entered the cell. The first klee guard shoved the gar toward them saying, "He had one of those boxes. Take him to the Inquisitors."

The third klee dragged the terrified gar from the cell. The first klee pointed to a gar who was on his knees, shivering and crying.

"Him!" the klee ordered. The second klee guard quickly pulled him to his feet. The first klee looked around again until his eyes fell on . . . me. "And you," he snarled. "You look like you might give us a decent show."

I was tired of playing the role of a primitive, docile gar. I slowly got to my feet and stood up to my full height. I actually thought I caught a look of surprise on the klee's face. He wasn't used to a gar being so big, or acting so brashly.

"If giving you a decent show will get me out of here," I said calmly, "then it's showtime."

The klees stared at me, dumbfounded. I'm guessing a gar had never spoken to either of them like that. I had thrown them off. I liked that. What I didn't like was that the gar who was chosen first now looked more terrified than before. He shook his head violently and cried, "No!"

Uh oh. Had I made a mistake? Saint Dane had said there was a way to get out of here if I seized the opportunity. This sure felt like an opportunity, but was I crazy for believing anything he had to say? A month of confinement and hunger was making my thinking a little fuzzy. Okay, a *lot* fuzzy.

The first klee guard grabbed my arms. I pulled away and said, "You don't have to do that; I'll go wherever you want."

The klee hesitated, then glanced at his friend. The other klee shrugged. Neither knew what to make of me. Then the first klee grabbed me again and pulled me to the door. I didn't fight. I didn't want to waste what little gas was left in my tank. A moment later I was dragged out of the cell for the first time in a month. My legs were wobbly, but it felt good to use them again. Behind us, the other klee pulled the gar along as we traveled through a long stone corridor.

"What's this all about?" I asked. "What are we supposed to do?"

The klee answered by giving me a rough shake. I didn't want my brain rattled anymore, so I stopped asking questions.

We reached the end of the corridor and went through a door that led outside. Feeling the cool morning breeze was awesome. I felt like I was returning to civilization. Sort of. I now got a look at the prison building where we were being kept. It was a square courtyard. The stone building that surrounded it was one story high. I wondered how many other animal pens this building held. Probably lots. The ground inside the courtyard had a few worn grassy patches, but mostly it was brown dirt. In the center was a ring of stones about twenty feet in diameter. This is where we were headed. I saw several klees hanging around the courtyard, doing nothing. When we appeared, they all made their way toward the circle.

When we reached the center, the klees gave us each a shove. I stumbled into the circle but managed to keep my feet. The gar wasn't so lucky. He took a tumble, and stayed on the ground. I was beginning to get an uneasy feeling about this. The gar and I were now alone inside the circle, with more klees arriving to watch. They gathered around, chatting excitedly and laughing. There was a definite air of anticipation. I had the feeling that whatever show they wanted us to put on, it wouldn't involve singing or dancing.

The klee who had chosen me stepped into the circle. He looked me up and down, smiled in satisfaction, and nodded. He walked to the gar who was cowering in the dirt and gave him a sharp kick. The gar whined in pain, but didn't move. The klee faced the assembled audience and said, "Make your wagers."

Instantly the klees started chattering with one another. It was slowly dawning on me that this was going to be some kind of contest between us gars. I had no idea what it would be, but I had to believe that I was the favorite. I was in much better shape than the poor gar who was balled up on the ground. I was pretty sure I was smarter, too. However, I couldn't help but think about the two other gars who had been pulled out of the cell. One came back full of blood, the other never came back. Gulp.

"What's the contest?" I asked the klee.

Everyone grew quiet and stared at me. None could believe that a gar would speak that way to a klee. I was beyond caring.

"You can win your freedom," the klee in the circle answered.

"How?" I asked.

Something was thrown down in the dirt between me and the other gar. I looked at it, and my stomach dropped. It was a knife. But no ordinary knife. It was a three-pronged knife made from the talons of a tang. The blades were long and thin, and looked just as sharp as when they were still attached and used to attack helpless gars.

"One gar leaves the ring . . . free," the klee said with an evil smile. "The other dies."

Before I had the chance to process that sickening piece of information, the gar who a moment before had been curled up like a sick puppy, dove for the tang knife and held it up, ready for action.

"Forgive," the gar said.

The klee jumped out of the circle and the gar jumped at *me*.

The fight was on.

# EELONG

I dodged out of the way and the gar's knife thrust missed me by inches.

If I wanted my freedom, I'd have to kill this gar. Yeah right. Like I could do that. I'd never thrown a punch in anger in my entire life, let alone stabbed somebody to death! But if I didn't do something drastic, and fast, the gar would kill me. From the way he attacked, it was pretty clear that he wasn't faced with the same moral dilemma I was. It was a no-win situation. For me, anyway.

The gar stumbled a few steps but kept his balance. He whipped the knife back toward me, sweeping the air, barely missing. I backed off to the far side of the ring, trying to buy some time so I could figure out what to do. The klees were cheering. This was all sorts of fun for them. "Fight! Fight!" they yelled, and pushed me back toward the gar. I was the favorite, after all. There must have been a lot of bets down on me. The gar now faced me, holding the knife low. His knees were bent, looking for an opening, ready to attack. I circled away, making sure to keep him in front of me. His eyes were wild. For him, this was about survival. I had no doubt he'd kill me.

He lunged again, knife first. I dove the other way, but the gar slashed at me as we crossed. The blades raked three slices into the front of my shirt. My adrenaline was pumping so hard I had no idea if he'd cut my skin. Some klees cheered, others booed. I'm sure I was disappointing those who bet on me. Tough.

The gar was breathing hard. That was good. It meant I was in better shape than he was. I felt sure that if the fight lasted much longer, he'd burn out. That was my best chance. I had to tire the gar out until he couldn't attack anymore and then, and then, and then *what*? There was no way I could kill him. The gar slashed the knife back and forth, cutting nothing but air. He wasn't much of a fighter. The gars who bet on me saw it too. Their boos turned to cheers. The gar charged. I dodged him like a toreador dodges a bull. The gar stumbled and fell to his knees. A few klees picked him up, turned him around, and pushed him back toward me.

The gar was out of gas. Spittle flew from his nose and mouth as he gasped for air. I think he was crying, too. He made another run at me. I dodged out of the way easily, but this time I ducked down, swept my leg in front of him, and tripped the guy up. He stumbled and crashed to the ground. I jumped on him, trying to pin his arm and get the knife. But this was a wild animal. When he realized he was being attacked, he dug down deep into some primal well and found the strength to shrug me off. The move totally surprised me. I was thrown off his back and landed flat on my own. A second later I found myself staring up at a knife that was slicing the air on its way toward my neck.

But I had a little animal instinct as well. I rolled out of the way and the knife stabbed the ground right where my head had been. I scrambled to my knees and quickly moved to tackle the gar before he could pull it out of the ground. But with his free hand the gar backhanded me in the mouth with surprising strength. The punch landed me on my back again, blood dripping from my mouth. The gar was back in charge. He yanked the knife out of the ground and came in for the kill.

I stopped thinking. It wasn't like I meant to or anything; it's just that my reflexes took over. Good thing, because it saved my life. Up until then I had been all tactical in trying to figure out a way to beat the gar and save myself without either of us being killed. But there was something about the combination of fear, pain, and impending death that made me stop reasoning and click into survival mode. I was flat on my back and vulnerable. The gar charged, the knife held high, ready to kill. He leaped for me, and I instinctively threw up my leg. My foot caught him square in the chest, and I flipped him over my head. The surprised gar did a full end-o and landed flat on his back. When he hit the ground I heard him let out a pained *"oof."* The fall knocked the wind out of him. I quickly flipped over and went for his knife hand. The gar was gasping for air and didn't have a chance. I jammed my knee onto his outstretched arm and his hand went slack. He released the knife. I grabbed it.

The klees cheered. At least the klees who bet on me, anyway. I clutched the knife and brought it toward the neck of the gar. Another cheer went up. They sensed the kill. I held the knife there, ready to slash it across his neck and save my life. It was something I never thought I could do, but the heat of battle and the fear of my own death turned me into something else. Something primal. I was an animal whose only concern was survival. I was a gar.

That's when I heard a familiar laugh. It cut through my

insane haze, forcing me to look up. Standing among the cheering klees was Timber, the cat who was Saint Dane. All the cats around him were cheering wildly, coaxing me to cut the throat of the gar. But Saint Dane was calm. It was like everything had gone to slow motion, except for Saint Dane and me.

"This is your way out, Pendragon," he said calmly. "Kill him and you'll be free."

This was the opportunity Saint Dane told me about. I had to kill this gar to save myself.

"Kill him," Saint Dane said. "It's not difficult."

His words triggered something in me. Maybe it was because I had won and was no longer scared. Maybe the adrenaline was wearing off. Or maybe I realized that if I followed through, I would forever be a killer . . . just like Saint Dane. That truth brought me right back into my own head. I grasped the knife tighter, kept eye contact with Saint Dane . . . and backed away from the gar. A second later all hell broke loose as the klees charged into the ring. In the brief moment before that happened, I saw the smug smile fall from Saint Dane's cat face. I wasn't a killer and there was no way he was going to turn me into one.

Score one for me. I had just beaten Saint Dane in this small battle.

Then came the riot. The klees jumped into the ring, angered that I had ruined their show. There was all sorts of pushing and shoving. It was a blur of fur and fury as they argued over how the bets should be paid off. I felt the tang knife pulled out of my hand, then felt a strong, furry arm wrap around my waist and pull me out of the scrum. I was too exhausted to do anything but go along for the ride. The strong cat pulled me out of the mess while fighting off klees who were grabbing at me. Once we were clear, I finally looked to see who my savior was.

It was Kasha.

"Leave him be!" a klee yelled at Kasha. "He's ours!"

Kasha stopped and squared off against the others. "He's not!" she snarled back. "Durgen had no right to sell him."

"Then where's our value?" another klee shouted. "We paid for him."

"You had him long enough and he gave you a good fight," Kasha yelled back. "He owes you nothing more."

"But he didn't kill the gar!" the first klee argued. "The fight isn't over."

Kasha took a threatening step toward the other klees. "The fight *is* over," she snarled viciously. "Unless you want to enter the circle with me."

The klees exchanged nervous looks. Nobody wanted to mess with Kasha.

"Durgen won't like this," the klee said.

"You say that like I should care," Kasha spit back sarcastically.

The klees shrugged and backed off. "Just letting you know, is all," one of them said.

Kasha watched them to make sure they weren't going to come after me, then looked to me. "Are you all right?" she asked.

"I'm alive," I answered. "Where have you been?"

"What? I get no thanks for saving you?"

"Thanks. Where have you been?"

"You need food," she said. "Come with me." She held out a leash for me to slip over my wrists.

"Not a chance," I said, and walked off.

Kasha didn't argue. She dropped the leash and we walked, together, back toward her home. I was weak and hungry and a little wobbly on my feet, but it didn't matter. I had my freedom and I didn't have to kill a gar to get it. For all I knew, being sent to that prison and starved and mistreated was all a Saint Dane—orchestrated setup to get me to kill a gar. If so, it failed. The nightmare was over.

As we walked I saw that the prison was next to the zenzen corral. We walked through the animal enclosure, passing several of the multijointed horses, who were kept in much nicer conditions than the gars, I might add. Being outside for the first time in a month made me appreciate how truly beautiful Leeandra was. Heck, anyplace would have looked beautiful compared to that gar hole.

"We tried to rescue you sooner," Kasha finally said, but it was more of a statement than an apology. "It was impossible. Durgen has many friends among the handlers."

"You should have tried harder," I said bitterly.

"Should I?" Kasha snapped. "You forget why you were there in the first place. It was because I chose to save your life instead of a klee. Now I've saved your life twice. But instead of thanks, you criticize."

I wanted to argue, but didn't think it would help.

Kasha added, "We couldn't even get close to you. We had to wait until they brought you out to . . ." Her voice trailed off. She didn't want to say it.

"To get killed," I said, finishing the sentence. "Why do they keep gars in prison like that? It's beyond cruel."

"It's not a prison," she corrected. "Prisons are for klees. You were in a stable."

"Whatever," I answered angrily. "They treat gars worse

than animals. Why? So they can have their little bloodsport?"

"No," Kasha answered. "Gars have many uses."

"Like?"

"Like working to keep Leeandra operating by clearing the water pipes and replacing power crystals above the trees. The handlers train some for wippen tournaments; or to help blind klees who can't get around on their own. Some go into homes as servants or perform acrobatics in shows for young klees. If a gar doesn't show a particular talent, but is loving, a handler can train them to be excellent pets. Gars are very important to Leeandra."

"And some are used to kill each other to amuse the handlers," I added. "Or to feed tangs to protect the foragers."

Kasha didn't comment.

"Bottom line is, the gars are your slaves," I said. "The klees treat them as totally disposable creatures who do all your dirty work. It's wrong, Kasha, and the thing is, you know it. I saw you save that gar in the jungle when I first got here. You're not the hard case you pretend to be."

"There are many things I don't agree with," she said softly. "I still see all sides."

We walked in silence for a while. I then asked, "Has Seegen turned up?"

Kasha didn't answer, which meant that the Traveler from Eelong was still missing. I was beginning to worry that he might never come back, which would spin my situation into a whole 'nother, scary direction. We didn't say another word for the rest of the walk. I wanted to stay angry at Kasha, but didn't have the energy. If they couldn't rescue me sooner, I had to accept that. Besides, I was too relieved to be out to stay mad at anybody. Except for Saint Dane, that is.

When we got to her home, Kasha gave me some fresh clothes (rags) and allowed me to use the running water in her bathroom to clean up. It was an incredible feeling to shower off the crud that had been building up for the last month. I felt like a snake shedding its skin. Once the filth was gone, I took a look at my body to see I had lost a ton of weight. I actually had a six pack for the first time in my life, but it wasn't because I was in shape, it was because there was no fat to cover the muscle. I looked totally cut . . . but felt horrible. I couldn't look at myself anymore; it was too depressing. I quickly put on my new, clean rags and joined Kasha in the main room of her tree house.

I was overwhelmed to see that while I was washing, she made me a feast. There was a roasted bird, bowls brimming with fresh, nonmoldy fruit, and round loaves of dark brown bread.

"Don't eat too fast," she warned. "Your system isn't used to it."

Tough. I was starved. I sat down and did my best not to be a total pig, but the more I ate, the more I wanted. I chowed, only stopping long enough to let out a belch that felt like it came up from my toes. After that I dug right back in. Kasha stayed in the kitchen, allowing me to enjoy my meal in peace. It didn't take long before I was totally stuffed. I actually didn't eat all that much because I think my stomach had shrunk down to the size of a walnut. There was still a tableful of food left over when I had to call it quits. I thought of forcing myself to puke, just so I could do it all over again, but realized that would have been idiotic. Not to mention rude. So I sat back and enjoyed the sensation of a full belly for the first time in a long time.

"I fear for my father," Kasha said. She was standing in the

doorway to the kitchen. "Boon and Yorn have been taking turns watching that tunnel in the tree."

"The flume," I said.

"They are convinced he will somehow magically appear there," she said. "I don't share their optimism."

Kasha sat across from me at the table. For the first time since I'd met her, she seemed unsure. She wanted answers, and I sensed that she might finally be willing to listen to what I had to say. I may have been a lowly gar, but if it meant finding out what happened to her father, she would listen.

"Believe it or not," I began, "I know how you feel. My life used to be normal. I had a great family; I liked my school; I had excellent friends—it was about as close to perfect as you can get. But I also had an uncle Press. One day he showed up and told me I had to leave home because people needed my help. It didn't take long for me to find out my life wasn't as normal as I thought."

"And where is this Uncle Press now?" Kasha asked.

I quickly realized I had gone down the wrong road. But I had to answer truthfully. "He's, uh, he's dead."

That wasn't what she wanted to hear. Bad move, Bobby. Kasha stood and paced anxiously. It was odd how I couldn't hear her feet making sounds on the floor, but after all, she was a cat.

"I don't know how to say this in a good way," she began.

"Just say it," I coaxed her.

"All right. I don't care. I really don't. All this talk of Travelers and territories and evil demons is nonsense, and it's ruined my father's life. He was respected. He was about to be named to the Council of Klee! But once he found that tunnel in the tree, he changed. He became obsessed with this foolish mission. It consumed his life. And Yorn encouraged him! I tried to get him to see reason, but instead he told me that one day I would have to take his place. I turned to my best friend, Boon, to help me talk sense to him. But instead of helping me, Boon got sucked into the ridiculous fantasy as well. They amuse themselves with tales of battles on other worlds, while ignoring the real problem facing Eelong."

"And what's that?" I asked.

"We're starving," she said bluntly. "The klee population is growing quickly. The number of gars is growing as well. Our ability to grow food crops isn't keeping up with the demand. All the fertile land has been overfarmed for generations. We can't even maintain the level we're used to, let alone increase it. The meal I just prepared for you is a feast that would normally be stretched to feed an entire family of klees for several days. If we don't find a way to turn this around, quickly, our civilization will begin to starve to death. So forgive me if I don't care to chase an evil demon through time and space, when my own home is on the edge of catastrophe."

"Kasha," I said softly. "That's exactly why you have to worry about Saint Dane. He goes to territories, uh, worlds that are reaching a critical time. Like the food shortage here on Eelong. That's perfect for him. He's using it as an excuse to get the klees to start killing gars. Right now, he's on the Council of Klee, trying to get them to repeal Edict Forty-six. Who knows where it will go from there?"

Kasha shot me a look. "There are no gars on the Council of Klee."

"That's because he's taken the form of a klee named Timber," I said. But even as the words came out of my mouth,

I knew Kasha wouldn't believe them. Heck, if I hadn't seen Saint Dane transform myself, I wouldn't believe it either. I decided to change the subject before I lost her.

"Have you ever heard of something called Black Water?" I asked.

"Black Water?" she said incredulously. "Where did you hear that?"

"From the gars in prison. What is it?"

"It's not a thing, it's a place," she answered.

"Tell me about it."

"It's a gar story," she began. "I don't know much about it, but I've heard gars speak of it. It's a place where all gars will someday go for their ultimate reward."

"They called it 'home,'" I said.

"I'm sure they did," Kasha said. "They need something to give them hope for a better life, no?"

"So it's like the promised land? Or heaven?"

"I don't know what those things are," Kasha answered.

"Doesn't matter," I said. "Where is this place?"

"It's not real, Pendragon," she said with a sarcastic chuckle. "It's a fantasy."

"You mean Black Water doesn't really exist?"

"Only in the minds of the gars" was Kasha's answer.

I debated about how much more to tell Kasha. Should I tell her about the amber boxes? Or about the mysterious thing called the "Advent"? Kasha would one day be the Traveler from Eelong, and I would have to trust her, but that time hadn't come. I decided to continue, but cautiously.

"I don't think the klee guards thought Black Water was a fantasy. When I was in that cell, one of the gars started talking about it. A klee burst in and took the gar to the Inquisitors."

Kasha stopped pacing, as if this were surprising news. "A klee took a gar to the Inquisitors to ask about Black Water?" she asked. "That makes no sense."

"Who are the Inquisitors?" I asked.

"It's a division of the security police," she answered. "They interrogate anyone they feel poses a threat to the peace. If you think those handlers who stage gar fights are cruel, you ought to meet the Inquisitors. They're vicious. I never agreed with their methods. But they don't interrogate gars."

"They do now," I said. "And they want to know about Black Water."

Kasha let that settle in. It made no sense to her, and made little more to me. But I was beginning to smell something bad going down, and it had the distinct aroma of Saint Dane.

"Kasha!" came a voice from outside. A moment later Boon walked into the room.

"Boon!" Kasha shouted. "I rescued Pendragon!"

Boon saw me, but didn't react. If he was happy about my escape, he sure didn't show it. That wasn't like Boon. I had only known him a short time, but it was long enough to know something was wrong. He walked slowly into the room without making eye contact with either of us.

"What's the matter?" Kasha asked. "Are you sick?"

Boon sat down and stared at the table. I could see that he had been crying.

"Boon!" Kasha bellowed. "What's wrong?"

Boon looked to me. He seemed scared and a bit lost. I don't know why, but the moment I looked into his eyes I knew exactly what was bothering him. Maybe it was because the news he had was inevitable. That's the way it was meant to be. I hoped I was wrong, but one look at Boon told me I wasn't. I nodded, giving him encouragement and letting him know that I understood. Boon turned from me and looked at Kasha. Kasha's eyes were wide and hungry for an answer.

"Kasha," Boon said as his voice cracked. "I found Seegen."

"Really? Where is he?" she asked excitedly.

"He's dead."

He didn't have to say another word. The rest would be details. All would be important, but not as important as the inevitable truth I now faced.

Seegen was dead.

Kasha was the Traveler from Eelong.

# EELONG

Seegen's body lay in the mouth of the flume.

An hour after Boon delivered the bad news, four of us stood over him, staring down at the former Traveler from Eelong. It was me, Boon, Yorn, and of course, Kasha. His daughter. Seegen was a big cat. He was mostly gray, with many white spots. Even in death I could tell he was a formidable creature. But no longer. We stood there silently. I think we were all waiting for Kasha to speak first. I glanced at her to see that her eyes were tearing up. But she was strong. She didn't break down or anything.

"How did he die, Yorn?" she asked.

The old cat sighed and said, "I don't know. As I told you, he left here for Second Earth, looking for Pendragon. When he came back through the flume, he was dead. What happened there I can't say."

Boon did a quick examination, checking for signs of injury. He found nothing.

Kasha looked to me and said, "You told me klees are treated like gars where you come from. What could have happened?"

"I can only guess," I answered. "If Seegen appeared in my home town, they'd try to capture him. They'd probably shoot him with a tranquilizer to make him sleep. As a last resort they might shoot him with a gun that was more deadly, but there are no wounds. I don't think he died on Second Earth."

"But he left here alive, and now he's dead," Kasha said, trying to contain her emotions.

I felt horrible for her. I knew what it was like to lose a loved one. And I also knew what lay ahead for her.

"I don't know how he died, Kasha," I said sympathetically. "And I know you don't believe in the battle against Saint Dane, but I promise you, it's real. Your father's death is proof of that." I knelt down to Seegen and gently removed his braided necklace. Dangling from the loop was his Traveler ring. I held it up for Kasha to see.

"You're the Traveler from Eelong now," I said. "I'm not asking you to change your beliefs, but I am asking you to help us stop Saint Dane."

"And why should I?" Kasha asked.

"Because it's what your father wanted, and I guarantee Saint Dane had something to do with his death. If you want justice, you'll join us."

Kasha looked at the dangling ring. She glanced to Yorn. Yorn gave her a slight nod of encouragement. She looked to Boon. Boon gave her a weak smile in return. Kasha tentatively reached out and grasped the ring, examining its dark gray stone and the symbols that circled it.

"I believe in things I can see," she said. "Everything I've heard about you, Pendragon, must be taken on faith. But my father is dead and that's about as real as can be." She gave me a piercing look and continued, "What I do is for him. Not you.

Not Yorn or Boon or some misguided mission. As long as you understand that, I'll help you."

"Understood" was my simple answer.

She then dropped the ring in the dirt. "But I am not a Traveler," she said with disdain.

Boon and Yorn looked at me, waiting for my reaction. I didn't get ticked or anything. All I did was bend down and pick up the ring.

"Whatever works for you," I said. I dusted off the ring and added it to the two I already had on the cord around my neck.

It was a tense moment. Yorn broke the silence by saying, "Seegen was my best friend and I was his acolyte. I may be old, but I can still be of use."

"Absolutely," I said.

"Good," Yorn said. "We should first attend to his body. After that we can set our sights on Saint Dane."

We struggled to bring Seegen's body from the underground cavern out to the jungle where a zenzen-powered wagon was waiting for us. We had traveled to the flume tree in this wagon because we knew we would have to bring Seegen's body back. We gently loaded the big cat's body onto the wagon, covered it with a blanket out of respect, and began the long journey back to Leeandra.

"Will there be a ceremony?" I asked. "And a burial?"

"A ceremony, yes," Yorn explained. "But we do not bury our dead on Eelong. Bodies must be burned to keep them from scavenger tangs."

"Like with Gunny's hand," Boon reminded me.

"Yes, Gunny's hand," Yorn added. "I was surprised to have found it after he was attacked. I thought for sure the tangs would have devoured it."

Yorn dropped his head and fell silent, as if the conversation was upsetting him. It wasn't doing much for me, either. The whole subject was depressing and gross. I didn't mind that we didn't talk for the rest of the journey. I was too busy watching out for tangs, anyway. Luckily for us, we didn't run into any. I suppose I should be grateful for that small bit of luck, because it seemed as if the only luck I had been having lately was the bad kind.

Back in Leeandra, I stayed at Kasha's home while the others attended to Seegen's body. I wanted to go, but we all figured it would be tough to explain why a gar was there. It gave me time to collect my thoughts, eat something, and start writing this journal. I didn't get very far. No sooner did I start writing, than I conked out. My body really needed the sleep. The last thing I remember was that it was still daylight when I put my pen down to rest my eyes. The next thing I knew it was dark, and I was looking up at an excited Boon who was shaking me awake.

"Pendragon! You have to come, now!" he said, barely able to contain himself.

"Huh, what?" I asked groggily.

"Kasha told me to get you quickly."

"Why? What's going on?" I asked, trying to kick-start my brain.

He grabbed my hand and pulled me to my feet, saying, "It's about Black Water."

A bolt of adrenaline shot through me. Suddenly I wasn't so sleepy. Boon ran out of the tree house without waiting for me, but that was okay, because I was ready to roll. I caught up and we jogged across several sky bridges. He didn't put restraints on me, and I didn't remind him to. It was nighttime and there weren't many klees around to see us.

"Where are we going?" I asked as we ran.

"Kasha has many friends in government," Boon answered. "She found out where the Inquisitors are questioning the gar about Black Water. We have to hurry."

Excellent. Kasha had only been a Traveler for a short time and she was already helping out. I was very curious about Black Water. Not because it was an interesting fable or anything, but because the klees were so interested in it. A few minutes later we arrived at the tree that held the Circle of Klee. Boon took me to an elevator that brought us much higher into the tree than we had been before.

"Be quiet now," he whispered. "We aren't supposed to be here." He led me along a skywalk that circled the tree, and into a doorway. Inside was a dark corridor that traveled around the inside of the tree. We moved quickly and quietly until we came upon . . . Kasha. She was peering through a small window into the center of the tree.

"We're here!" Boon announced in a loud voice.

"Shhh!" Kasha scolded.

"What's happening?" I whispered to Kasha. I moved to look through the small opening, but Kasha stopped me.

"You must be prepared for this," she cautioned. "You will not like what you see."

"Okay," I said. "Prepare me."

"There's no good way to say this," she said coldly. "They are torturing the gar. Unless he tells them what they want to know, I fear he will die. He may anyway."

"What do they want to know?" I asked.

"They want to know where Black Water is," she answered.

"So it's real?" Boon asked, a little too loud. He quickly

clamped his own furry hand over his mouth. He shrugged an apology.

"The Inquisitors seem to think so," she answered. "Are you prepared?"

"Yes," I answered. I took a deep breath and peeked into the hole. Turned out, I wasn't prepared at all.

We were high overhead, looking down through small slits near the ceiling. We must have been in an observation area for those who didn't have the stomach to be too close to what was happening below. I was one of them. Beneath us was a large room with a table in the middle. Tied to the table was the gar I remembered from the prison. He was naked from the waist up. My stomach twisted when I saw that his torso and arms were covered with hundreds of bleeding cuts. There were two klees in the room. One lashed at the gar with a thin strap that made a sharp, ugly *crack* sound. The poor gar cried out in pain. It left an ugly, bleeding cut on his chest. I had never seen anything this cruel before, and hoped I never would again.

"This can end," the klee said calmly. "If you tell us where to find Black Water."

The gar whimpered, but didn't answer. If he knew where Black Water was, he wasn't saying.

"Don't you have laws against this?" I whispered to Kasha.

"Well . . . no," she said. "They are animals. They aren't protected like klees."

"They aren't animals!" I whispered back angrily, straining not to shout. "And even if they were, that doesn't make it okay to torture them."

"Uh-oh," Boon said. "This just got more interesting."

I looked back down to the torture room. What I saw was

only a small surprise. It made perfect sense and confirmed my interest in Black Water. Stepping up to the gar was the klee called Timber.

"Saint Dane," I said under my breath.

"It isn't," Kasha whispered. "That's Timber, from the Council of Klee."

"That's what he wants you to think," I answered, keeping my eyes on the demon Traveler. "I tried to tell you before. He can transform himself into anything he wants."

I didn't explain further. It wasn't the time to start educating Kasha on the evil ways of Saint Dane. I watched as the klees backed away from their torture victim and let Saint Dane approach. He held something out for the poor gar to see.

"What is this?" Timber asked in a calm, friendly voice.

It was one of the small amber cubes. I knew it had something to do with Black Water, but didn't know what. Neither did Saint Dane. But it was important enough for him to torture a gar to find out.

"Tell me what this is," he said to the gar soothingly. "And your pain will end."

The gar's eyes were wild. Even from where we were, I could tell that he was shaking. It would have been easy for the gar to tell Timber what he wanted to know, but he kept silent. Brave guy.

Timber leaned down to the gar and asked, "Tell me, when will you go home?"

A strange thing happened. As soon as the gar heard the word "home," it was like his pain went away. The word had a calming effect on him. He looked at Timber, and laughed. Right in his face. Whatever "home" meant, it gave him the strength to stick it to Timber. It was a brazen move, but not a smart one. Saint Dane didn't like being dissed. What happened next was something that surprised even the klees in the torture room.

"Tell me!" Timber ordered the gar angrily.

The gar suddenly stopped laughing. His body went stiff. He snapped a surprised look at Timber. Their eyes met and he slowly arched his back as if straining against a heavy weight. The klees looked at each other with curiosity. They didn't know what was going on.

"What's happening?" Kasha asked.

"It's Saint Dane," I said sadly. "He's doing this."

The poor gar strained against the cords tying him to the bench. His whole body went red with the exertion. He lifted up off the table, defying gravity.

"Tell me what this is!" Timber bellowed, losing his cool.

The gar screamed in pain. The two klees backed away. I was pretty sure they had never seen anything like this. I didn't want to watch, but I had to. So did Kasha. This was her first lesson on the evil depths that Saint Dane could sink to. Finally the gar let out a guttural, anguished cry. I heard a sickening *crack*. The gar went limp and fell back to the table. One of the klees felt his neck.

"How did that happen?" the klee asked in wonder. "He's dead."

"No!" Timber screamed in frustration. He grabbed the klee by the throat and shouted, "Find out the purpose of these cubes or you'll be the next one on this table!"

"Y-Yes, I understand," the frightened klee babbled.

Timber tossed him aside and stormed out of the room. I turned away from the small window and looked at Kasha. She was shaken. Boon bent over and puked. It wasn't a kittycat hair ball gaak, either. He totally ralphed.

"Welcome to the wonderful world of Saint Dane," I said to Kasha, trying to control the quiver in my voice. "Was it real enough for you?"

Kasha took a step back and cleared her throat. She tried to speak calmly, but her voice was shaky. "I need to go to my father's home. You are welcome to come. Maybe we will find something of use there."

"Good," I said. I had to get out of there. I was sweating and shaking. Boon's puke didn't smell so hot either. We left the tree quickly and made our way across to the far side of Leeandra, and Seegen's home. None of us spoke. I think we were in shock. I know I was. I wondered if after seeing that horrifying scene, Boon was still enthusiastic about doing battle with Saint Dane. When we arrived at Seegen's tree house, Yorn was waiting for us outside.

"What are you doing out here, Yorn?" Kasha asked.

"I didn't want to go inside until you arrived," the old klee answered.

"That's silly," Kasha said. "You're like family."

Yorn smiled sadly. With the loss of Seegen, their family had just gotten smaller. We all went inside and I saw that the place was set up very much like Kasha's.

"You won't believe what we just saw," Boon exclaimed. "The Inquisitors were torturing a gar to find out where Black Water is."

"Black Water?" Yorn asked with surprise. "Seegen spoke of Black Water. He seemed to think it was real."

"So do the gars," Boon said.

"And so does Saint Dane," I added.

"Saint Dane?" Yorn asked, surprised. "He was there? With the Inquisitors?"

"Yes," I answered. "He's taken the form of a klee named Timber."

"Boon told me," Yorn said, shaking his head sadly. "It's frightening to think he has found his way onto the Council of Klee. Why is he interested in Black Water?"

"That's what I'd like to know," I said.

Kasha didn't say a word. She kept looking back and forth between all of us, trying to understand what it all meant.

Boon asked, "And what are those little brown cubes the gars have? Saint Dane was real interested in those, too."

"Maybe your father has some answers for us," Yorn said.

Huh? Now it was my turn to be confused. "What do you mean?" I asked.

Kasha reached into a fold of her tunic and pulled out a small, wooden key. "My father gave this to me the last time I saw him. He said that if anything should happen to him, I needed to use it right away." She went to Seegen's kitchen table and pulled it away to reveal a bench that was built into the wall. She ran her hand along the bench, just under the seat, until she found a small hole.

"This is where my father kept his most valuable possessions," Kasha explained.

She inserted the key into the hole, turned it, and I heard the *click* of a lock. Kasha lifted the seat to reveal a hollow area beneath. There was only one item inside. It was a wooden box about the size of my mom's jewelry box. I wanted to make a comment about how Seegen didn't have many valuable possessions, but figured that wouldn't be cool. Kasha removed the box, dropped the seat back down, and placed the small chest on the table. I noticed that on top of the box was a folded piece of paper. Kasha opened the note and read it aloud: *"For my daughter, Kasha."*

"It's for you!" Boon exclaimed.

Kasha gave us all a quick, nervous look, then opened the box. She pulled out another note that was on top. She first read it to herself. A tear welled up in her eye. None of us said anything. That wouldn't have been cool. Kasha sniffed, stood up straight, and turned to us, saying, "You should all hear this." She read the letter aloud.

*"My dear Kasha, If you are reading this, it means I am dead. Please do not grieve for me. This was the way it was meant to be. I know you do not believe in the Travelers, and our mission. I don't blame you. But I'm afraid you will soon discover that it is all true. Eelong is in grave danger. If Saint Dane succeeds in his quest to destroy the gars, our home will be crushed. As difficult as this is to believe, Eelong being destroyed would be a small catastrophe compared to what would follow. Saint Dane must not succeed. If you choose not to follow your destiny as a Traveler, I would understand. The fault is mine. I have not done enough to prepare you for this responsibility. But I will ask one thing of you. It is something you must not refuse. A gar will arrive one day who goes by the name of Pendragon . . ."*

Kasha looked at me. I stared back silently, though I was dying to shout: "Keep reading!"

She continued.

*"Share with him the contents of this box. I wish I knew more about Saint Dane's evil plan, but I'm sorry to say I*

*do not. I did discover this much: The gar legend of Black
Water is true. It exists. I know, because I've been there."*

Whoa, that officially made this note a shocker. We all
exchanged looks, then Kasha continued.

*"I believe Black Water is central to Saint Dane's plans.
So does the Traveler named Gunny. He is waiting for
Pendragon at Black Water."*

I stood up straight. My heart raced. Gunny was alive.

*"I need you to help Pendragon get to Black Water. This is
my request to you. Please, please honor it. I'm proud of you,
my daughter, but more than that, I love you.*

Kasha lowered the note. Nobody could speak. Seegen had
reached back from beyond death to finish his duties as a
Traveler. My first thought was that I wished I had known him.
My second thought was voiced by Boon.

"So what's in the box?" he asked.

Kasha reached inside and picked up another piece of
paper. She stared at it for a moment, as if not believing what
she was seeing.

"What is it, Kasha?" I asked softly.

She handed the paper to me, and I examined it to see
hand-drawn symbols and numbers that made no sense.

"I don't understand this," I said.

Yorn took the paper, gave it a quick look, and smiled.
"Could it be?" he asked.

"I think so," Kasha answered.

"What?" I demanded to know.

"It's a map," Yorn answered. "From what Seegen wrote, I'd say it's the route to Black Water."

"Yeah!" shouted Boon.

I was so surprised, I couldn't breathe. We had a piece of information that Saint Dane was desperate to get his hands on. Or should I say, his paws on? He tortured and killed a gar trying to get it, and here it was, right in our laps.

"There's something else in the box," Yorn said.

Kasha pulled out a roll of pages that were tied together with twine. She unfurled the pages and read, *"Journal Number One—Eelong."*

"Seegen's journal!" I exclaimed.

We were now complete. We had the benefit of knowing everything the previous Traveler discovered; we knew where Gunny was; and we were a couple of steps ahead of Saint Dane. For the first time since I landed on Eelong, I felt as if we had a fighting chance. But there was one important question that needed to be answered.

"Kasha," I said. "Where do you stand?"

Kasha thought for a moment, glanced at her father's note, and said, "I'll get you to Black Water, Pendragon."

This is where I'm going to end this journal. I'm feeling better now, though the experience of being a caged animal will stay with me forever. I'm going to use those memories to give me the strength I need to help save the gars from Saint Dane. They've suffered enough. Tomorrow, Kasha, Yorn, and I will leave for Black Water. We've decided that Boon should stay in Leeandra to watch what happens with Saint Dane and the Council of Klee. Hopefully he'll find out more about their plans for the gars.

I'll close this journal by saying I hope Kasha's head is in

the right place. I'm going to have to rely on her if things get tough, and based on history, things *always* get tough. It goes with the territory, so to speak. By the time I write to you again, I'll have news about Gunny. Good news, I hope.

Please be well. Think of me. And though I know I don't have to remind you . . . do not use the flume. There's no telling what will happen if you do.

**END OF JOURNAL #17**

## ∞ CLORAL ∞

*"Please be well. Think of me. And though I know I don't have to remind you . . . do not use the flume. There's no telling what will happen if you do.*

Mark lowered the pages of Bobby's Journal #17 after having read it aloud to Courtney and Spader. Everyone looked pretty grim.

"Did we make a mistake by coming here?" Mark asked solemnly.

"No!" Courtney said with confidence. "Bobby doesn't know the whole story. What about all those dead tangs at the farm? It all fits. It's the poison from Cloral! I'll bet Saint Dane is trying to find Black Water so he can use the poison there, too."

"What do you think, Spader?" Mark asked.

"I think Courtney's right," he answered.

"Thank you!" Courtney shouted in triumph.

"But I'm not sure if bringing the antidote from Cloral is the right thing to do," Spader added.

"How can you say that?" Courtney said quickly. "The rules have changed. Saint Dane told us that himself. If he's mixing the territories, why can't we?"

"Well," Spader said thoughtfully. "Because he's the bad guy."

Courtney couldn't argue with that. Instead, she grabbed the plastic bag with the sample of Seegen's fur in it. "What about this?" she asked Mark. "We brought this from Second Earth. Aren't we mixing things from the territories too?"

"I was going to destroy that," Mark said sheepishly.

"Sure, after you were finished with it," Courtney shot back. "I think things really have changed. Saint Dane ruined his first territory and it's somehow made him stronger. Mixing the territories may be dangerous, but letting him win again might be worse."

"And what about the acolytes traveling?" Mark asked. "Bobby thinks it's wrong."

"He doesn't know for sure," Courtney answered. "But I'll tell you what *is* for sure: Saint Dane is about to wipe out the gars. He's got the klees behind him and he's got the poison. What do you want to do? Go home and wait for Bobby's journal to tell us how he lost again, and Saint Dane's powers have gotten even stronger? Or maybe Saint Dane will stop by to tells us in person, right before he starts messing with Second Earth."

Mark looked to Spader. Spader's eyes were trained on the floor. Mark saw that his jaw muscles were working as he clenched his teeth together. Finally Spader stood and took the plastic bag from Courtney and said, "We're not doing anything until we know for sure. Come with me."

A short while later the three of them stood in the agronomy laboratory on Grallion. They were with Ty Manoo, one of the agronomers who was responsible for accidentally creating the deadly poison that threatened to spread a plague across Cloral. They watched the pudgy little scientist as he busily prepared a microscope slide from the strands of Seegen's fur.

"It was such a noble idea," Manoo explained. "We set out to

make a fertilizer that would double the growth rate of our crops. It would have insured a bounty of food for all of Cloral for generations! But something went terribly wrong."

The others knew exactly what went wrong. Saint Dane.

"The fertilizer ended up mutating the molecular structure of everything it touched. The crops became poisonous. It was horrible!"

Ty Manoo was short and bald, with an elflike face. He was a nervous guy, who constantly licked his lips when he spoke. He was licking overtime now. He didn't like talking about the poison he was partly responsible for creating.

"If it weren't for the good people of Faar who created an antidote to counteract the effects, well, I'd hate to imagine what would have happened."

"Saint Dane would have destroyed Cloral, that's what," Courtney said under her breath.

"Excuse me?" asked Manoo.

"Nothing," Courtney answered.

Manoo finished the slide and slipped it into a microscope. It didn't look anything like a Second Earth microscope. The contraption was round like a volleyball, and shiny silver. It had a flat base and a square window on top to peer down on the magnified image. Manoo looked intently down through this window while slowly spinning the sphere to focus it. "This is a waste of time," he said. "Every trace of the poison was destroyed soon after . . ."

Manoo fell silent. Mark thought he actually saw the color drain out of his face.

"What?" Spader asked.

"Where did you get this?" Manoo asked numbly.

"It doesn't matter," Spader said quickly. "Is it the poison fertilizer?"

"It . . . it can't be," Manoo stammered. "It's impossible."

"But is it?" Courtney demanded.

Manoo looked at them with a mixture of fear and confusion.

"Say something, Manoo," Spader said firmly.

Manoo said sheepishly, "There was a problem—"

"*Problem?*" Spader shouted. "I never heard about any problem!"

"It's not certain," Manoo said quickly. "All the fertilizer was destroyed. All of it. But there was a discrepancy. A mistake—"

"What kind of mistake?" Spader asked, losing patience quickly.

"It was a clerical error. Nothing more."

"Hobey, Manoo! Tell us!" Spader demanded.

"When we did an inventory, the numbers didn't add up," Manoo said nervously. "There were ten tanks of the poison that couldn't be accounted for. We figured somebody wrote the numbers down incorrectly." Manoo fell silent. The horrible reality was sinking in for him that the numbers weren't wrong.

"You're positive it's the same poison?" Spader asked.

"I'd know it anywhere," he answered, licking his lips furiously.

That confirmed it. The Cloral plague was officially on Eelong. Manoo pulled the slide out of the microscope and dropped it on the desk as if it were diseased, which it was.

"Spader, if it wasn't a mistake, and those tanks are floating around somewhere on Cloral, we must—"

"They aren't," Spader said harshly. "You're holding the last of it. Burn it. The fur, the paper, even this bag." Spader shoved the plastic bag into Manoo's sweaty hands. "Burn it all."

"But what about the missing tanks?" Manoo asked.

"They're going to stay missing," Spader said sharply. "What about the chemical antidote? Was that destroyed too?"

"Of course not," Manoo answered. "Every habitat has its own supply, in case, well, in case something like this happened. I can't believe it! What should we do?"

"Nothing," Spader said. "I'll report this to Yenza. Don't tell anybody else; we don't want to cause a panic over nothing."

"All right, Spader, if you say so," Manoo whined. "But please, talk to Wu Yenza."

Spader left the laboratory with Mark and Courtney right on his heels. Once outside he kept walking quickly, passing through a section of the farm that grew luscious-looking yellow-and-purple-striped fruit the size of grapefruits. Mark and Courtney had never seen crops like this, but they didn't stop to marvel. The time for fun was long past.

"Do we have enough proof now?" Courtney asked, as if she were confident of the answer all along.

Spader didn't answer.

"Where are we going?" Mark asked.

"I've got to tell Yenza," Spader said.

"The chief aquaneer," Mark added knowingly. "Your acolyte."

"What's the point?" Courtney asked. "This isn't about Cloral."

Spader stopped short and whipped around to face the other two. He was upset. Mark saw it in his eyes. "It wasn't supposed to be like this," he said. "Pendragon was supposed to come find me when he needed my help. That's what I promised him."

"What's the difference?" Courtney said. "He needs your help now. You're going to give it to him, right?"

"The difference is we're doing the exact things he told us not to do! Okay, maybe the rules have changed and anything goes now, but Pendragon's the lead Traveler. I trust him."

"We all do," Courtney said.

"Then what if he's right?" Spader barked with finality. "What if we're doing the exact wrong thing?"

It was a statement more than a question. They let it hang in the air because the truth was, none of them knew what would happen if the territories started to mingle, or the acolytes traveled.

"I don't know," Courtney said calmly. "But I do know that if those are the rules, Saint Dane isn't playing by them. Yeah, bad guys don't always play fair, but he's about to destroy his second territory. He told Bobby that once the first territory fell, the others would go more easily. So I think we have two choices. First one is: You can stay here, Mark and I can go home to Second Earth, and we can all hope that Bobby will figure out a way to stop the Cloral poison from destroying Eelong."

"It won't happen," Mark said soberly. "From what we've read, they don't have the kind of science on Eelong to create an antidote like they did on Faar."

"Which brings us to our second choice," Courtney continued. "We can take the antidote to Eelong. Hopefully it isn't too late. The rules may be broken and two territories will be mixed, but it's the best shot at beating Saint Dane. The only shot. The real question is, which is worse? Acolytes traveling and mixing the territories? Or Saint Dane winning territory number two?"

The three stood silently for a moment, then Mark said in a soft voice, "You want us to bring the antidote to Eelong?"

Wu Yenza stood on the deck of a large speeder craft that floated gently on the sea. She was giving a final check to the gear that was spread out before her. Yenza was the chief aquaneer of Grallion and carried herself with the kind of confidence needed for the job. She was older, somewhere in her thirties, and in pretty good shape. She had short black hair and wore a black aquaneer uniform like Spader's, only hers had long sleeves with three yellow stripes on the cuffs that showed her rank. Yenza was fully up to speed on all things to do with the Travelers. After she and her aquaneers helped defeat Saint Dane and his raiders in the battle for the city of Faar, Spader told her all he knew about their mission to stop the evil demon. Realizing the importance of the Travelers' mission, she agreed to become Spader's acolyte. And now, standing on an aquaneer craft, she was doing a tech check on three silver cylinders that looked like scuba tanks. But they didn't hold compressed air. They were filled with the liquid antidote for the poison that threatened Eelong.

"Each of these cylinders has a nozzle," Yenza explained to Mark and Courtney, who watched her closely. "The liquid inside is under pressure. Opening the nozzle will let out a fine, wide spray. It doesn't take much to counteract the poison."

"Got it," Courtney said.

Spader climbed up from belowdecks carrying three black backpacks. "We'll each carry one cylinder," he explained. He slipped one of the backpacks on and Yenza dropped a cylinder into it. Spader tugged the straps tight, pulling the silver cylinder snug against his back. "Just like that. Easy-do."

Spader and Yenza helped Mark and Courtney slip into their own harnesses, then dropped the silver tanks into them. The gear was light. They could move around easily without having to lean forward and counterbalance.

"You look like a scuba diver," Mark said to Courtney.

Yenza held up a silver pistol. Mark and Courtney recognized the weapon from Bobby's description in his journals. It fired a short blast of water that was powerful enough to tear through a wall.

"There's one for each of you. With holsters," Yenza said. "I don't care how tough those tangs are on Eelong, one shot from this will knock 'em silly."

"No," Spader said. "No weapons."

"Why not?" Courtney asked. "Eelong is a hairy place."

"So it is," Spader replied. "But we're going there to get rid of a poison that should never have been brought in. That's all. We can't start using whatever we want from other territories."

"I-I hear you, Spader," Mark said nervously. "B-But it's going to be dangerous. We might not make it out of the flume tree alive."

"If we don't," Spader said, "then that was the way it was meant to be. We'll have to take our chances. Still want to go?"

Mark looked at Courtney. He had been having second thoughts about this trip all along. Now he was having third and fourth thoughts.

"Absolutely," Courtney answered with confidence.

"Mark?" Spader asked.

Mark took a breath, then said, "Yeah."

Spader said to Yenza, "Please send a message to Yorn through your ring. He's the acolyte from Eelong. Tell him that Saint Dane brought a poison to Eelong from Cloral and we're coming with the antidote. He's got to get that message to Pendragon so we can join up with him."

"Understood," Yenza said. "Are you sure you don't want me to come?"

"No, I'm not at all sure," Spader answered. "But we've already got two acolytes traveling. If it turns out to be wrong, I don't want to risk sending another."

"It's not wrong," Courtney said defensively.

Spader replied by picking up his water sled. "We'll soon find out. Ready?"

They all grabbed their air globes and placed them over their heads.

"Good luck!" Yenza called to them as Spader and Courtney leaped into the water.

"Thank you," Mark said to Yenza. He sat on the rail of the speeder, twisted his legs over the side, and gently slipped into the warm water of Cloral. The three floated together next to the boat.

"Same as before," Spader instructed. "Grab my belt."

He ducked below the surface, followed by Mark and Courtney. They each grabbed on to his belt, and with the help of his powerful water sled, Spader pulled the trio down underwater toward the gate to the flume. Yenza had positioned the speeder right above the rock ledge, so in no time the three shot underneath. Minutes later they surfaced in the cavern that held the flume. Without a word they pulled themselves up onto the rocky ledge and got rid of their air globes and swim belts.

"We'll wear these clothes in the flume," Spader said. "Then find clothes from Eelong when we arrive."

"It's going to be tough explaining to the klees what these tanks are," Mark said.

"It's going to be impossible," Spader shot back. "Let's hope we won't have to." He slipped back into the water and called out, *"Eelong!"* The flume overhead sprang to life. As the light and the musical notes grew closer, Spader looked to Courtney and said, "I sure hope you're right about this. See you on the other side."

The bright light flashed out of the flume and shot down toward Spader. Mark and Courtney had to squint to see what was happening, and caught a glimpse of Spader being lifted out of the water. A second later the light flashed so brightly that it blinded them. When it disappeared, Spader was gone. All they could hear was the faint sound of the musical notes fading into the depths of the flume. The two stood there, nervously waiting for the other to go first.

"You realize we could die on Eelong," Mark said soberly.

"Nice," Courtney said. "Real positive attitude you got there."

"I'm serious," Mark complained. "Are we ready for this?"

Courtney answered by slipping into the water. "Yes," she said. "You're not going to bail on me just when it's getting interesting, are you?"

"This is a lot of things," Mark said as he dropped into the water. "'Interesting' doesn't begin to cover it."

*"Eelong!"* Courtney shouted.

Instantly the flume groaned. They could hear the rock walls crack and grind as if an earthquake were shaking it. Mark and Courtney looked up in wonder.

"It didn't do that when Spader left," Mark said nervously.

Two rocks fell out of the flume, bounded down the side of the cavern and splashed into the water. Mark and Courtney had to swim out of the way or they would have been creamed.

"This isn't right," Mark gasped.

"Too late now," Courtney shouted back as the musical notes grew loud. More rocks fell, splashing down in the water. The light from the flume circled them both and they could feel themselves being lifted up and out of the pool. A moment later they were whisked into the flume and sent on their way to Eelong.

As they flew, they quickly forgot about the unusual damage that happened to the flume. The anticipation of what was to come was far more exciting, and scary. As with their first flume trip, they saw strange images floating in the star field that surrounded the crystal tunnel. There was a giant castle that looked as if it were built into a mountainside, a silver, cigar-shaped zeppelin that could very well have been the *Hindenburg*, and what looked like legions of tall soldiers, marching together in perfect formation, headed for some unknown war. Mark and Courtney had no idea what any of it meant. They didn't have much time to discuss it anyway, because they soon felt the tug of gravity that meant they were arriving on Eelong. Seconds later they were on their feet . . . and enveloped by the curtain of vines. Each went a different way and quickly got lost in the tangle.

"Ahhh!" shouted Mark in terror as he slashed with his arms to keep them away. "Courtney!"

"Mark!" Courtney called back from somewhere. "It's cool. They're roots, remember? Bobby wrote about them."

Mark stopped struggling. "Right, roots," he said, embarrassed. He felt a strong hand grab his arm and relaxed. He wasn't alone anymore. "Oh man," he panted. "How do we get out of—"

As the hanging vegetation parted, he saw that the hand didn't belong to Courtney. Holding on to his wrist was a yellow-eyed, sharp-toothed, semihuman quig. The two stared at each other, waiting to see what the other was going to do. Mark reacted first.

"Quig!" he shouted and tried to pull away. But the quig held him tight. Mark fell backward into the vines as the quig pounced on his chest. The beast looked down on him, baring his teeth in a hideous smile. It lunged for Mark's throat. Mark threw his hands up to protect himself, and the quig bit into his forearm. "Ahhh!" Mark screamed in pain. Mark wasn't a fighter. Not even close. But the pain kicked him into action. He whacked the quig on the side of the head with his free hand, knocking the little beast away. But not for long. The quig scrambled to his knees, ready to pounce again. Mark was on his butt, backing away on all fours.

"Courtney!" he shouted. "Help!"

The quig sprang, but before it got to Mark, a vine shot out and wrapped around its neck, holding it back. The quig let out a surprised yelp and tore at the noose. At first, Mark thought the vine had come to life and attacked the quig, but a second later he saw the real reason. Spader was clutching the two ends of the vine, holding the monster quig tight.

"Nasty little woggly," Spader said with way more calm than the situation deserved. "I think you should apologize to my friend."

The quig tore at the vine, cutting it in two, allowing it to escape. It took off through the root forest and disappeared. A second later, the vines behind Mark rustled.

"There's more of 'em!" he shouted, and backed toward Spader.

The roots parted to reveal . . . Courtney. "What happened? You all right?" she asked.

"No!" Mark shouted.

Spader looked at Mark's arm to see the damage. "It's not bad," he said. "Just a scratch."

"Easy for you to say," Mark shot back. "That thing better not have rabies!"

"Can we please get out of this jungle?" Courtney asked.

The three stayed close together and pushed their way toward the cavern that Bobby had described in his journal. Courtney emerged from the tangle first, took one look, and said, "Oh man!"

Mark and Spader came out right behind her. Mark had the same reaction, "Oh man!"

"Hobey," Spader said. "I guess it's true."

Standing on all fours next to the flat rock in the center of the cavern was a big, brown jungle cat.

"Are you all right?" the cat asked. "I didn't know the quig was in there. Sorry. That wasn't a very good welcome to Eelong."

They stared back at the animal numbly. Though Mark and Courtney had already met Seegen, seeing a talking predator cat was still pretty strange. And Spader had never seen any kind of cat before, civilized or not.

The cat said, "Are you Mark and Courtney? And Spader?"

Courtney was the first one to get her head back together. "Yes," she said. "Boon?"

"That's me!" Boon answered. He stood up on his hind legs

and held out a pale green leaflike sheet. It looked just like one of the pages Bobby used to write his journals from Cloral.

"This is terrible news," the brown klee said. "Would Saint Dane really bring a poison from another territory?"

"I don't understand," Spader said.

"It's okay," Mark assured him. "Klees are the superior beings here on Eelong."

"No, I'm talking about the note," Spader said. "I asked Yenza to send that note to the acolyte, Yorn."

"She did," Boon answered. "Yorn gave it to me just before they left for Black Water—that's why I'm here to meet you. Is it true? About the poison from Cloral?"

"It's true," Spader answered. "Why didn't they wait for us?"

"There's something else I don't get," Mark said. "How come we can understand you, Boon? I mean, you're not a Traveler. We're not Travelers either, and I'm pretty sure you don't know English. And now that I think of it, neither did Ty Manoo on Cloral."

Courtney said, "Bobby said that things were changing. Maybe something changed in us because we can use the flume now."

"Uh-oh," Mark said.

"Now what?" Spader asked.

Mark raised his hand to show that the stone in the center of his ring was glowing. He took it off and placed it on the dirt floor. The familiar events followed quickly. The music, the lights, the growing ring . . . and the arrival of a roll of parchment pages. Mark reached down and picked up the next journal from Bobby Pendragon.

"Maybe all the answers we need just came in," Spader said.

# EELONG

How does he know?

It's a question that's always bugged me, but now it's pissing me off. Ever since I left home with Uncle Press I've had to accept a lot of things that made no sense. On top of that list of course, is the question of why I was chosen to be a Traveler. But there are a thousand other questions rolling around that have yet to be answered, like: Who made the flumes? How can they shoot us through time as well as space? What is the power behind it all? Where did the rings come from? I could go on forever, but there's one question that's making me totally nuts right now.

How does he know?

I'm talking about Saint Dane. Time and time again he's found the perfect moment in a territory's history to step in and work his evil. Why is that? Can he predict the future? Can he look into a crystal ball and see the entire history of a civilization and pick a moment in time when he can do the most damage? If I ever find the answer to that question, I think I'll unravel the entire mystery as to why all of this is happening. Maybe then I can forget this whole mess and go home for good.

I guess the reason I'm obsessing about it now is because

I'm angry. Mostly at myself because I've been an idiot. We are at a critical turning point in the history of Eelong; an event is about to happen that will alter the course of this territory forever, and Saint Dane is once again ready to step in and push things the wrong way. What makes it all so frustrating is that I had a chance to stop him, and I blew it. The truth was staring me square in the face and I didn't see it. Saint Dane made a critical mistake, and I didn't realize it until it was too late. I should have been smarter. Now Eelong is on the verge of catastrophe, and I don't know what we can do to stop it. I'm feeling totally helpless. All I can do now is go back and write about what's happened since I finished my last journal. At least that way there will be a record of my failure, so that when the history of Halla is written and they get to the chapter on Eelong, they'll know which Traveler was to blame.

Me.

I finished my last journal after we found Seegen's map to Black Water. Our plan was to have Boon stay in Leeandra to spy on Timber and the Council of Klee while Kasha, Yorn, and I followed the map to Black Water. At first I thought only Kasha and I should go because Yorn was kind of, well, old. I don't mean to sound like I'm against old people or anything, but this was probably going to be a dangerous trip, and I wasn't sure if Yorn could handle it. But Yorn told me he wanted to help make sure Seegen's last request was carried out. I figured the real reason he wanted to go was because he didn't trust Kasha. Truth was, neither did I. But Kasha understood Seegen's map. I didn't. To me it looked like a bunch of circles with random numbers and some arrows that represented . . . whatever. But Yorn could read it. I figured if Kasha bailed, Yorn could take over. Besides, I was happy to have somebody along who wanted to be there, as opposed to Kasha, who didn't. So we became a trio.

Kasha guessed it would take a full day, riding on zenzens, to follow Seegen's map to the end. We decided to rest that night and start out at dawn. That was fine by me because my batteries were dead. While Boon and Yorn went out to arrange for the zenzens and stock up on provisions, Kasha and I returned to her home. I was glad to get the chance to talk to her alone. She was the Traveler from Eelong now, whether she accepted it or not. I knew what she was going through, and I felt bad for her, but there were more important things at stake than her feelings. I needed to get her up to speed, fast. So when we got to the privacy of her home, I tried to do just that.

"How do you feel?" I asked, opening the conversation as innocently as possible.

"About what?" was her sharp answer.

I didn't want to push. She got mad easily, and I didn't want her thinking the problem was me and decide to go all klee on me and take my head off. Or some other vital body part. So I tried to make nice. "A lot's happened," I said. "I remember how tough it was when I first found out I was a Traveler and—"

"Stop!" she roared. "I am *not* a Traveler!"

"But, you saw what Saint Dane did to the gar—"

"It was a gar," she shot back. "It wasn't like he was torturing a klee."

"I don't believe you feel that way."

"I don't care what you believe," she spat at me. "My father is dead because of you Travelers. I'm not going to make the same mistake." She tried to walk back to her room, but I cut her off.

"I saw you risk your life to save a gar," I argued. "And you did the same for me, more than once. That's not the way somebody acts when they don't care."

"Look!" she snarled. "I told you I'd help you follow the map. But I'm doing it for my father, not because I'm a Traveler."

"Fine, whatever." I was getting tired of arguing with her. "I'll leave you alone, but I need to see your father's journal."

"You can't. When we burned his body, I threw the pages on the fire."

"You didn't!" I shouted.

"I absolutely did."

"Why?"

"I didn't want anything to remind me of how he wasted his final days. I'll follow his map for you, Pendragon, but then I'm done."

She brushed past me. I didn't give up.

"But Eelong is in danger—"

Kasha whirled on me. "I told you if anything happened to my father because of you Travelers, I'd tear you apart. I meant it. After I get you to Black Water, if I ever see you again, I'll kill you."

She stormed out of the room, leaving me a little dizzy. Not only had I bungled the chance to get her on board, I pushed her into threatening my life. Nice work, Bobby. Real diplomatic. I could only hope that she'd make good on her word. At least the part about getting me to Black Water, that is. The killing me part I'd just as soon she forgot. With that ominous thought in mind, I laid down on the couch and turned my thoughts to the task ahead.

Black Water. What exactly was it? A place? A state of mind? Another dimension? A lost underwater city like Faar? It had to be real, because Seegen had been there and drawn a map. And Gunny was there. It was definitely important enough to the gars that they chose death over revealing its secret. And what did those little amber cubes have to do with anything? I hoped to find some clues in Seegen's journal, but that chance went up in smoke. Literally. But in spite of all the setbacks and uncertainties, I felt sure that Black Water was key to Saint Dane's plan. I had to get there and find answers.

I tried to get some sleep but it was tough. My mind was racing in eighteen different directions. Thankfully my body took over and I nodded out. Sleep is an amazing thing. It heals the body, and the brain, too. Good thing. I desperately needed healing. I even had a dream. Boon was bouncing around wearing a tall, red-and-white-striped hat and saying nonsensical rhymes like: "Where is Gunny? I think he's funny. I don't like eggs all soft and runny." Yeah, I know. Twisted dream. But hey, no more twisted than Eelong. The next thing I knew I was being shaken awake.

"Pendragon," a voice whispered. "It's time."

I was still half asleep, but opened my eyes to see Boon. I said, "Imagine that, you've lost your hat."

"Huh?" was Boon's confused reply.

I didn't bother to explain my bizarre Dr. Seuss dream. "Where's Kasha?" I asked, rubbing my eyes.

"Down with the zenzens," he answered. "She wants to get out of Leeandra early, before anybody asks where you're going."

I dragged myself off the couch and took a couple of deep breaths. Every move I made hurt, because my body was covered with bruises from sleeping in that gar prison. Even my hair hurt.

"I wish I was going with you," Boon said, sounding like a disappointed kid who didn't get the pony he wanted for his birthday.

"I know," I said. "But if anything happens to us, you're the only one who knows what's going on. You'll have to stop Saint Dane yourself."

Boon gave me a long, worried look and said, "Now I *really* wish I was going with you."

I laughed. "Stay close to the Council of Klee, but don't let them know you're watching. Saint Dane doesn't know who you are. Keep it that way. When we get back, tell us where they stand on Edict Forty-six."

"Got it," he said. "Good luck, Pendragon." Boon grabbed me in a big bear hug. Or cat hug. It was kind of scary, but sincere. So I hugged him back. I liked Boon. I liked Yorn, too. It was Kasha I was shaky on. I left Boon and took the elevator down to the jungle floor. Three zenzens were at the base of the tree. Kasha sat tall in the saddle of one; Yorn was in the second; the third was loaded with equipment. Swell.

"I guess the gar walks," I said snottily.

"Only until we leave Leeandra," Yorn said. "It's against the law for gars to ride alone."

"Of course it is," I said sarcastically. "Maybe you should just load the equipment on my back so the zenzen won't have to work so hard. Better yet, maybe I should carry the zenzen."

"Do you want to go or not?" Kasha said flatly.

"Absolutely," I said quickly. "I am *so* over this town."

I was being obnoxious, but I was in a grumpy mood after having just been woken up three years too early, discovered I was one big black-and-blue mark (which Boon's hug didn't help, by the way), and then told I was the only one who had to walk. It wasn't a good way to start the day.

Our little caravan made its way along the jungle floor, headed for the giant gates of Leeandra. I glanced at the zenzens to see a number of vicious-looking weapons lashed to the sides of the strange horses. There were a couple of spears, some short wooden clubs, a few coiled ropes with the three balls on the end, and even a bow and arrow. It all looked good to me. I was pretty sure that at some point we'd need some firepower against a hungry tang. As we trudged along, I saw that the city was quiet. We hadn't passed a single klee, and I was about to ask if I could ride when a dark shadow leaped out of a tree, landing right in front of Kasha. Her zenzen reared back and she had to wrestle it to a stop. At first I thought it was a tang and was ready to go for a weapon, but before I could make a move, it spoke.

"The gar is mine," Durgen said.

Uh-oh. What was *this* guy doing up so early?

"You had no right to take him in the first place," Kasha answered.

"You owed me," he spat at her.

"And you got value for him," she snarled back. "Step aside, Durgen."

Durgen didn't move. This was bad. For me. I slowly moved toward a zenzen and reached for one of the short clubs. I wouldn't stand a chance in a fight against Durgen, but I didn't know what else to do.

"Durgen, please," Yorn said calmly. "You two are friends. Be reasonable."

Durgen spoke angrily through clenched teeth, saying, "The klee who was killed on the forage was my friend too. You, Kasha, have become dangerous. You are no longer a forager. I've had you ejected."

"What!" Kasha shouted, stunned. "You can't do that!"

"I can and I did! And if you continue this subversive behavior, you'll be banished from Leeandra. Now get out of my way and give me the gar!"

Durgen pushed past Kasha's zenzen, headed for me. In that one instant, all the horrible memories of prison came flooding back. It gave me a shot of adrenaline like I had never experienced before. I clicked into survival mode. I yanked the club out from the last zenzen and made a quick decision. Attack. I thought if I surprised Durgen, I might get in a lucky shot. Or not, and he'd kill me. Either way, I was *not* going back to that gar prison. I leaped out from behind the zenzen with the club held low. Durgen didn't expect that. The big cat swiped at me. I ducked. His paw swept over my head so closely, I felt his claws cut the air. Cut was the right word. Durgen wasn't trying to capture me. He wanted to kill me.

I drove the club forward, ramrodding it into Durgen's exposed ribs. He let out a sharp, pained cry that made me think I might have broken something. But it didn't stop him. It made him angry. He came at me with his paws swiping like I was a boxing speed bag. I backed off, using the club to knock away the relentless attack. The big cat hissed angrily. His ears were back. I was way out of my depth. I knew I couldn't defend myself against this onslaught for long. I took another step back and fell on my butt. How pathetic was that? Durgen dropped to all fours and crouched down low. He was a jungle cat who had his prey in sight.

Suddenly he yelped and stood right back up. His eyes were wide and he arched his back as if something had hit him from behind. He snarled and turned his back to me. I saw that sticking out of his shoulder was a round, polished disk the size of a CD. But this was no CD. It had sharp teeth like a miniature buzz saw, and its blades were imbedded in Durgen's back. The cat squealed with pain. He desperately grabbed at the disk to pull it out, but his arms didn't reach.

"Kasha!" he screamed, and yelped in pain as he jolted again. He spun back toward me. I saw another disk imbedded near the top of his other arm. Blood blossomed from his wounds, spreading across his tunic. The dark, wet stain glowed with light from the street lanterns that hung overhead. Durgen fell to the ground, breathing hard, growling in pain.

Kasha walked up to him calmly, holding another killer disk ready to throw.

"You might as well kill me," Durgen said through clenched teeth. "You're as good as dead anyway. You've attacked a forager within the city. A *klee*! You know the penalty for that."

"Death," Kasha said. She put the disk back into a pouch on a belt around her midsection. "You are a good klee, Durgen," Kasha said. "You'll do what you think is right."

Durgen couldn't move. Or maybe he decided not to. He must have known that if he attacked Kasha now, with his wounds, he'd be done. Kasha strode over to the last zenzen and yanked off the saddle bags, revealing the saddle. She tossed them up to Yorn, who sat on his zenzen with wide, stunned eyes.

"Carry that," Kasha commanded.

Yorn caught the saddle bags and fixed them across his own saddle.

Kasha looked to me and said, "Get on the zenzen."

I was too stunned to move. Kasha stared down at me.

"Are you hurt?"

"No."

"Can you ride?"

"Yes."

"Then get on the zenzen, Pendragon," she commanded firmly. "Now!"

I wasn't about to argue. I got to my feet and ran to the strange horse. I wasn't graceful about it, but I was able to climb aboard and get my feet into the stirrups.

"What has happened to you, Kasha?" Durgen screamed. "Don't you see what you've done? And for what? A . . . a . . . *gar*?"

Kasha walked deliberately to Durgen and looked down on him, saying, "What you and the handlers do to these poor animals is criminal. It's bloodthirsty, and it's wrong." She coldly yanked one of the disk weapons out of his arm. Durgen screamed in agony. "I may need this," she said. She stuck the weapon into her pouch, then backed away and leaped onto her zenzen. She gave the animal a kick and shouted, "Don't stop. It's our only chance of getting out."

Her animal reared up and bolted forward. Yorn kicked his zenzen and with a loud "Yaa!" he charged after Kasha. Though I had ridden on the back of Boon's zenzen when I first got to Eelong, I hadn't had to control a horse since my fantasy adventure on Veelox, but I knew how to ride. I could only hope that riding a horse with a few extra joints was the same as riding a regular old Second Earth–style horse.

"Yaaa!" I shouted and gave my zenzen a kick. I sprang forward and galloped after the others, leaving Durgen in a cloud of bloody dust. As it turned out, riding the zenzen was easy. In fact the extra joint somehow made it pretty smooth, don't ask me why. I galloped behind the other two, headed for the gates of Leeandra. We sped past surprised klees who were coming out to start their day. They didn't expect to see three speeding zenzens flying by . . . with a gar picking up the rear. In no time I saw the tall gates to the city. They were open to let out a wagon of foragers. Our luck was holding.

That's when I heard the alarm.

It was a horn that pierced through me like fingernails on a blackboard. A quick look ahead made me realize what Kasha meant when she told us not to stop. Several klees were scampering toward the gate to close it. I didn't know if Durgen had sounded the alarm, or if it was because a gar was riding a zenzen, or both. Either way, the klees now hurried to close the gates.

"Don't stop," Kasha called back.

We were either going to make it, or crash.

# EELONG

The klee sentries scrambled to swing the giant gates closed. I didn't think we were going to make it. We were too far away. But surprise was on our side. The klee sentries took a look over their shoulders to see us charging right for them, and stopped pushing. I didn't know if it was because they were surprised to see us galloping pedal to the metal and about to splat against the closed gate, or because they were shocked to see that one of the suicidal riders was a gar. Didn't matter. All that counted was that a few of them were startled enough to stop pushing the gate. Those few seconds were exactly what we needed. By the time they got their wits back and continued pushing, we blasted through the gate at full throttle, barely squeaking out of Leeandra.

Once outside the city, we didn't slow down. I think Kasha wanted to get as much distance between us and Leeandra as possible in case we were chased. We charged along the wide jungle path as if it were an open field. I had to duck down low like a jockey, for fear of getting lashed by a stray branch. Kasha made a quick turn and galloped onto a connecting trail. It was a good thing I had my eye on her or I would have shot right past the turn. As it was, I barely made it. We galloped on, not slowing down a fraction, flashing past branches that bit at my arms.

Thankfully, we broke out of the trail into a wide, grassy meadow. Going from a closed, dark trail to such a wide-open space took my breath away. The sunbelt was just coming up over the horizon, burning off the morning dew that glistened on miles of dark green grass. Kasha didn't stop pushing. There was no trail, so we fanned out, galloped up a rise and down the other side. Spread out before us was an immense, green pasture. We didn't stop to admire the view. Kasha pushed her zenzen even faster. Its hooves dug up the soft grass, sending clumps of dirt and sod into the air that peppered Yorn and me.

Finally Yorn galloped up beside her and yelled, "We're safe, Kasha! Slow down!"

Kasha looked back, and I immediately realized that her mad gamble wasn't just about escaping from Leeandra. I saw it in her eyes. Kasha was freaking out. She pulled on her reins and slowed her zenzen. Yorn and I did the same until we came to a stop near the far end of the pasture. Kasha immediately jumped off, dropped to all fours, and paced.

I looked to Yorn for a reaction. He was breathing too hard to speak. This was a lot for such an old guy. It was a lot for a young guy too. I was pretty winded. My heart was thumping like crazy. Even the zenzens were spent. Sweat poured off them as they gasped for air. We needed to take a break. But Kasha wasn't even close to calming down. She paced for a few seconds, then stood on her hind legs and shouted angrily at me, "Is this what it means to be a Traveler? Is everything going the way it's supposed to? My father's dead, I'm a fugitive, and now we're at the mercy of the tangs."

Nothing I could have said would make it better. So I chose not to answer.

"Say something, Yorn!" she demanded. "Is this the big battle against evil you've been telling me about? Are you happy now?"

Yorn stammered, "Kasha, I-I—"

"Don't bother," she snarled. "I don't want to hear it." She dropped back down on all fours and continued pacing.

"I'm dead," she said to the wind. "If I go home, Durgen will have me arrested and executed. Everything I've ever known, my whole life, is gone."

We were at a dangerous crossroads. I didn't know how to talk her down. Yorn and I kept looking at each other nervously, hoping the other would come up with something to say, but neither of us rose to the occasion. Kasha paced a bit more, then without warning she sprang for her zenzen, landing in the saddle.

"It's a long way," she announced, sounding slightly more in control. "We don't want to lose daylight."

That was it. The crisis was over, at least for the time being. Kasha coaxed her zenzen into a trot and continued on across the valley.

"I'm too old for this," Yorn admitted.

"Me too, and I'm still a kid," I replied.

"Her whole life has just been twisted," Yorn said. "We can't blame her for being angry."

"I don't," I said. "But if we fail, her life will get a whole lot more twisted than it is now."

I kicked my zenzen into a trot. Yorn followed right behind. We traveled that way for most of the day, with Kasha in front, me in the middle, and Yorn picking up the rear. Kasha kept checking the map and often made course corrections. I was on a constant lookout for tangs. I feared that at any moment we could ride into an ambush. A few times I thought I caught a glimpse of a green tail slithering into the bushes, but when I looked, it was gone. Either they saw our weapons and were afraid to attack, or I was loony and hallucinating. Either way was okay with me, so long as nothing came after us.

When I wasn't totally consumed with scanning for predators, I tried to take in my surroundings. Eelong really was beautiful. We traveled through dense, tropical jungle; crossed lazy streams; climbed steep trails that brought us up and over ridges that gave us incredible views of the jungle below; and even swam across a glassy, warm lake on the backs of our zenzens. Most of the territory seemed to be uninhabited, but every so often we'd pass a village built into the trees, like Leeandra. These small towns were nowhere near as big as Leeandra, though. They were farming villages that existed solely to tend acres of crops that grew beneath their homes. After a few hours of traveling, these villages became fewer and fewer. By the time the sunbelt was directly overhead, all signs of civilization had disappeared. We were headed into scary, desolate territory.

There was wildlife, too. I'm happy to report that we saw many different creatures on Eelong, and for a change, none of them wanted to eat me. There were beautiful, deerlike animals with strong, sharp antlers that must have been used to fend off tangs. I saw more of those funny, green monkeys, along with multicolored birds that chattered in the trees. When we'd pass beneath, the birds would take flight, looking like a chaotic rainbow. There were bugs, too. On the ground, and flying. Some were the size of hummingbirds. A sting from one of those babies would hurt. We passed a large flock of birds pecking at the grass in a meadow. They were hefty things, about the size of turkeys, but with brilliant blue feathers.

"What are those called?" I asked Yorn.

"Rookers" was his answer. "Very tasty."

I realized they were the same birds that had been roasted on the coals of Kasha's kitchen.

Kasha seemed to be pretty clear on where the map directed us. Sometimes we'd traverse a large field with no trails and hit the other side right at another trailhead. Once we had to detour around a truly huge lake. Many times we had the choice of several trails, and after a quick glance at the map, Kasha always seemed to know which one to take. I never questioned her.

From the get-go, my body was sore. After trotting along for several hours, I was totally worked. And hungry, too. I needed a break, but I didn't dare suggest we stop. I was on thin ice with Kasha; it wouldn't have taken much to crack it. Besides, Yorn wasn't complaining. My pride alone made me keep quiet. Finally, after my butt had gone beyond sore into full-on numb, Kasha stopped.

"We've still got a ways to go," she said. "We should rest and eat."

I could have kissed her. If she wasn't a cat and if she didn't want to kill me, I might have. We got off our zenzens, and after walking around to get the circulation back into our legs, we sat down at the base of a gnarled old tree to eat. Yorn had packed food that was nothing more than long, brown strips of dried something.

"I don't care what this is," I said. "So long as it isn't gar."

"It's not." Yorn chuckled. "It's a mixture of fruit and rooker meat."

"The blue birds?" I asked.

"Exactly. It's mixed together, dried, seasoned, pounded

into strips and then dried again. It may not taste like much, but it's good for you, and it's light for traveling."

I bit off a piece and chewed. It was tough, but after a few chews it softened up. It actually tasted pretty good, too. On the other hand, I was so hungry, the rags on my back would have seemed tasty.

"We have something like this on Second Earth," I said. "We call it jerky. I'm not sure why. Maybe the guy who invented it was a jerk." I chuckled. Nobody else did. So much for clever conversation.

Kasha didn't say a word as we ate. She sat with her back to us, staring at a mountain range far in the distance. Yorn and I made small talk about the birds, but my mind was on Kasha, wondering what she was thinking. She was the Traveler from Eelong. We needed her. Eelong needed her. Heck, Halla needed her. I wished I knew how to convince her of that. When she finally did speak, I was surprised at her question.

"How many territories are there?" she asked.

"Ten in all," I said. "At least that's what I've been told. They're all part of Halla."

"Explain to me what Halla is," she said. It was an order more than a question. I didn't know why she suddenly had this interest, but if she was willing to listen, I was ready to talk.

"The way it was told to me, Halla is everything. Every time, every place, every person and creature that ever existed. It all still exists."

"And you understand that?" she asked.

"Well, not entirely," I answered honestly.

"But you're willing to risk your life and the lives of those around you to protect Halla from Saint Dane?"

Good question. I'd asked myself the same question more than once.

"I wasn't at first," I began. "Far from it. I didn't want any part of Travelers or flumes and especially of Saint Dane. But since then I've been to a bunch of territories and seen the evil he's capable of."

Kasha scoffed and said, "Evil? You're a fool, Pendragon. A tang is evil. What possible evil could a gar cause that's worse than that?"

"I'll tell you," I said. "He's killed more people than I want to count, all in the name of creating chaos. He fueled a war on Denduron and tried to poison all of Cloral. Then he nearly crushed three territories at once, my home territories of Earth. But each time the Travelers stopped him. Until Veelox. We failed on Veelox. An entire civilization is going to collapse, millions will die, all because we failed. And Saint Dane will be there to pick up the pieces. Or step on them."

"It's all mildly interesting," she said calmly. "But like I said before, it has nothing to do with me. I don't care."

That's when I snapped. Okay, I admit, maybe I should have been cool, but Kasha's total lack of concern had finally gotten to me. I jumped to my feet and said, "Well you'd better start!"

"It's all right, Pendragon," Yorn said calmly. "Relax."

"Relax?" I shouted, getting more amped up by the second. "Why? So I won't upset Kasha? She *should* be upset. People have died fighting Saint Dane. People I've loved, people *she's* loved." I looked right at Kasha and said, "You don't care? I'll tell you what I don't care about. I don't care that your life is a mess. Sorry, it's true. You've got way bigger problems coming, kitty cat. You want to pretend like none of this affects you? Fine. You're wrong. If we fail, Eelong will crumble and everything you care about will crash along with it. And whether you like it or not, you're a Traveler. So why don't you just grow up and accept it!"

I glanced at Yorn to see his eyes were wide. He couldn't believe I had just gone off on Kasha like that. But I couldn't help myself. The time for pussyfooting around was over, no pun intended. I looked back to Kasha and saw that she was reaching into the pouch around her waist. Uh-oh, she was digging out one of those round, projectile weapons. I froze. She was going to kill me! Yorn saw it too, and lunged for her.

"Kasha, no!" he shouted.

He was too late. Kasha flicked the killer disk. I instinctively threw up my arms to protect my head and closed my eyes, ready to get hit. But the hit never came. Instead I heard a screeching sound of agony come from behind me. I whipped around quickly to see a tang lying on the ground, writhing in its last moments of life. The disk was lodged in its head. Kasha had just saved my life . . . again. I slowly turned back to see Yorn had his arms wrapped around her. He looked just as stunned as I felt.

"Oh," was all he said.

"Nice shot," I croaked.

Yorn dropped his arms and Kasha stood up. "Those mountains," she said, pointing. "That's where we're headed. We need to get there before dark."

We mounted up and continued the journey as if nothing had happened. Still, there was a strange tension in the air. I was embarrassed that I'd lost control, but since Kasha was still leading us along the map route, I guessed it didn't matter. The real question was, had anything I said sunk in?

The closer we got to the mountains, the less vegetation there was. The ground went from soft brown earth to rocky scrabble. The trees were no longer lush and leafy, but now scraggly and dry. A few times my ears popped, which meant we were gaining altitude.

Yorn rode up beside me and said, "I don't know anyone who's ever come this far. It's definitely not on any map, other than Seegen's."

That made sense; we hadn't been on a cut trail for hours. Kasha seemed confident in the route, though. She'd check Seegen's map against the terrain and the sunbelt, making slight adjustments. The steep, gray mountains loomed high before us and stretched out far to either side. If Black Water was on the far side of these huge peaks, it would take days for us to go around. But I didn't dare say that. I had to trust the map, and Kasha's ability to read it.

"There!" Kasha finally announced, pointing.

I looked ahead to the steep, craggy rise of the mountains and saw . . . nothing.

"I see it!" Yorn exclaimed.

I was feeling a little handicapped. I didn't have sharp cat eyes to see whatever they were pointing to.

"I don't see anything," I admitted, more curious than embarrassed.

"A trail," Yorn answered. "Cut into the mountain."

Kasha made a slight change in direction and headed for the invisible trail that apparently only cats could see. As far as I was concerned, we were marching straight for a steep, rocky dead end. But as we got closer, I began to make out a thin, zigzag line in the craggy face of the mountain. Sure enough, before I knew it, we were walking on a narrow path. It was the first sign of civilization we had seen in hours. My heart started to race. Could this be the trail to Black Water? The rocky trail took a sharp turn and got very steep. We climbed, single file, in one direction for a while, then hit a switchback that sent us around the other way. The whole time we kept climbing higher and higher, zigzagging our way up.

The scary thing was that the trail was nothing more than a narrow ledge cut into the steep mountainside. In no time we were up so high that my palms started to sweat when I looked down. I found myself leaning into the mountain, just in case the zenzen stumbled.

We reached another switchback, and I expected to make the turn and continue climbing in the opposite direction, but the trail didn't go that way. Instead it led to a narrow gap that looked like the mountain had been wrenched apart. The opening was so narrow that it blended in with the terrain and couldn't be seen from below, even by sharp klee eyes. We were about to walk *in* to the mountain! Kasha didn't hesitate and walked her zenzen right into the fissure. Yorn and I followed close behind. The gap was barely wide enough for the zenzen. I had to concentrate to keep my animal walking straight because my knees kept scraping against the rock walls to either side. I was glad to be off the ledge, but didn't especially enjoy having my legs shredded.

A couple of times I heard the sound of falling stones coming from above. I quickly looked up and saw pebbles bouncing down toward me. I ducked, and the pebbles missed, but it gave me a bad feeling. What caused them to fall? Was it coincidence? Or did something up there kick them loose? If we were attacked by a pack of tangs, we'd be trapped and slaughtered. I tried not to think about it and went back to concentrating on protecting my poor knees.

Thankfully, it didn't take long for us to arrive on the far side of this gap. I was actually surprised that it was so quick, because there was no way we could have traveled all the way through to the far side of the mountain range. When I directed my zenzen out into the light, I saw the reason why.

We were still in the mountains. The three of us stood on a wide ledge, looking down into a beautiful, enclosed valley. It was like being on the inside of a volcano. Unlike the gray, rocky terrain we had been traveling through for the past few hours, the inside of this bowl was covered with lush plant life. I counted seven waterfalls that began near the rim of the bowl and cascaded down to a large, mountain lake that took up much of the bottom.

"Is this Black Water?" I asked.

"No," she answered.

Kasha looked at her map, then looked to the sky.

"What are you doing?" Yorn asked.

"According to the map," she answered, "this is the exact time we need to be here."

"I don't understand," Yorn said.

"The sunbelt needs to be at a certain angle," Kasha explained.

I looked around. I'm not sure why. I had no idea of what to look for. A few minutes passed. Still nothing. Kasha kept checking the sky. I kept looking around like an idiot. A few more minutes crept by. The sunbelt dropped lower. Soon it would be resting on the rim of this crater, and then it would be dark.

"You're sure this is the right spot?" I finally asked.

Kasha scanned the inside of the bowl, then announced, "There!"

She pointed to the far side of the bowl. I had been staring out there since we had stopped and didn't expect to see anything different, but I was wrong. Something was different with the waterfalls. They were all about the same height. The water appeared white as it crested the top and fell all the way down to the lake. But now, with the sunbelt at just the right angle, the light must have been blocked by a rock formation or something. For now, the second waterfall from the right no longer appeared white. The water had gone dark. It totally stood out from the other six. There was only one way to describe it.

"Black Water," Yorn whispered in awe.

# EELONG

"That's our destination," Kasha confirmed.

The three of us sat on our zenzens, staring at the dark waterfall on the far side of the valley. It was our guidepost to the mysterious place called Black Water. Yorn reached over to Kasha and took Seegen's map from her. He looked at it with a smile, shaking his head in wonder.

"There are times when I feel older than the ground I walk on," Yorn said. "You'll find that as you grow older, there is one gift you will cherish most dearly, because it doesn't come often."

"What's that?" I asked.

"Surprise," Yorn said with a big smile—the first smile I'd seen from him since we'd met. "Surprises keep you young, and right now, I feel like a child. Yahhh!" Yorn shouted with excitement and kicked his zenzen forward. He galloped down the grassy hill that led from the crevice we had entered through, charging toward the waterfall.

"He reminds me of my father," Kasha said. "Even at his age he's always looking for the next adventure."

"And you're not like your father?" I asked.

Kasha took a sad breath and answered, "Things were

simple for him. He felt strongly about what was right, and wrong. What was fair and what wasn't. He was a builder. But where others used gars for the more difficult or dangerous work, he always did the work himself."

"Did he tell you why?" I asked.

"He always said that he didn't think it was fair to force a gar to do something they wouldn't benefit from. It was a simple sentiment, but said so much."

"Maybe you're more like him than you think," I said.

Kasha didn't reply to that.

"Is this where you leave us?" I asked.

"We haven't gotten to the end of the map," she said, and kicked her zenzen forward. Together we galloped down the steep, grassy slope to the bottom of the valley. I felt like a cowboy charging across some awesome, uncharted territory. The sunbelt cast a warm, late-afternoon glow over the valley that made the place look like a painting. For those few minutes, I can actually say I was having fun. We soon hit a dense stand of trees and had to slow down. Yorn had disappeared into these trees long before we reached them and was nowhere to be seen.

"I hope he went the right way," I said.

"If he keeps his eye on the black waterfall, he'll be fine," Kasha answered.

It was getting dark. The sunbelt had dipped below the rim of the crater. We only had a few minutes of light left. I was really worried that if it got too dark, we'd be lost until daybreak. I hoped klees could see in the dark like the cats at home.

"Yorn?" Kasha called.

All we heard back was the roaring sound of the waterfalls. Not good. At best we were separated and would have to deal with finding each other. At worst, well, I didn't want to think the worst.

"Look," Kasha said.

A soft mist was rising off the ground, making it even more difficult to see anything. I was about to ask Kasha what she saw, when something appeared through the trees ahead of us. It was a large, dark shape moving slowly toward us. But it was too dark and the shadow was too far away to make out what it was.

"Oh no," Kasha gasped.

At least one question was answered. The cat in Kasha had way better vision than the gar in me.

"Is it a tang?" I asked.

Kasha didn't have to answer, because a second later I recognized it. Trotting toward us through the trees was Yorn's zenzen . . . without Yorn. Kasha walked her zenzen up to the beast and retrieved the spears that were strapped to the saddle. She tossed one to me.

"Whatever happened, happened fast," she said, all business. "Yorn never got to his weapons."

Kasha held her spear to the side, low, and walked her zenzen forward slowly. "Stay beside me," she ordered.

I did what I was told and brought my zenzen alongside her, also holding my spear ready. We walked together through the trees, headed in the direction that Yorn's zenzen had come from. I was a raw nerve. Every little thing I heard sounded like a tang charging through the trees to attack us. A cracking twig, rustling branches, even the distant roar from the waterfalls. Everything made me jump. But nothing attacked us. Yet.

We reached the end of the stand of trees and walked into the open to discover we were on the shore of the lake. That meant we were at the very bottom of the crater. The waterfalls loomed over us. We were so close I could feel their cool mist. Stars were starting to appear in the sky. Their light reflected in the smooth, clear lake. I would have thought it was beautiful, if I weren't so freakin' nervous.

"That way," Kasha pointed.

I looked to see a break in the trees farther along the lake that must have led to the dark waterfall. Black Water. If Yorn made it this far, that's the way he would have gone. We walked our zenzens along the shore, toward the opening. We took a few steps, then I heard something that nearly made my heart stop. I shot a quick look to Kasha. She had heard it too. After all, she was a cat. The two of us whipped around to look out on the lake and saw . . .

The once still water was churning. Something down below was rising up. It looked like several things, actually. There must have been twenty dark shadows that broke the surface of the water and moved quickly toward shore, headed for us. Attacking.

"Go!" Kasha commanded.

We kicked our zenzens and bolted forward toward the opening in the trees. I charged into the woods first, not sure of where I was headed. All I knew was I wanted to get away from whatever monsters had been lurking underwater, waiting for us. The woods were totally dark. All I could do was follow the sound of the waterfall. I thought for sure I'd hit something. A few seconds later, I did. One second I was galloping on my zenzen, the next second I was falling through the air. My first thought was that I had hit a branch sticking out onto the trail. I slammed into the ground hard, still clutching the spear in a death grip. The shaft dug into my side. Ouch. I thought for sure I'd broken a rib, but that was the least of my problems. I stayed focused and looked up at what I had run into. It wasn't a branch.

Dangling over me, hanging from a tree, was a net. Or should I say, it was a trap, and it had been sprung. Caught in the swaying net was Yorn.

"Stop Kasha!" he yelled. "It's a trap!"

Kasha came charging up from the lake. I couldn't think fast enough to stop her as she pushed her zenzen on. A second later another trap was sprung. A net came flying down from the trees, catching Kasha. Her zenzen kept running, but Kasha was now caught and dangling, only a few feet from Yorn.

"Pendragon," Yorn cried. "Run!"

I looked back to the lake to see dozens of the dark shadows running toward us. The lake monsters were on the attack.

"Go!" Kasha screamed.

I went. There was nothing else to do, not that I was thinking clearly anyway. I staggered to my feet and ran toward the waterfall. I had some strange idea that if I made it to the waterfall, I'd be safe. The gars called Black Water "home." Maybe this was like playing tag. When you were home, you were safe. I know, dumb thought, but I wasn't exactly in my right mind. It was so dark I could only go by the sound of the waterfall. I took a few steps, expecting to run into a tree, when my feet suddenly got pulled out from under me. Something had grabbed me and swept me up into the air, feet first. I quickly realized that my last-ditch escape attempt landed me right in another trap. I hung there, upside down, swinging in the air, helpless. Now the three of us were caught, powerless against the marauding beasts.

I watched, upside down, as the dark forms ran toward me. They didn't look like tangs. They were more like formless shadows. Dark ghosts. They ran right past Yorn and Kasha, headed for me. Lucky me. They stopped about five feet away, making a circle around me. They didn't attack, they just stood there. It gave me hope that maybe they weren't mindless beasts looking for their evening meal. I didn't move. I didn't breathe. I figured maybe if I played dead, they'd go away. Yeah, right.

The circle opened up and a much larger shadow stepped in. It was bigger than the others at least a foot. It was hard to make out exactly what it looked like because it was so dark and, well, I was upside down. The shadow walked up and stood there, looking at me. At least I thought it was looking at me. I couldn't see its eyes. The others crowded behind it. As they got closer, I saw that the reason they looked shapeless was because they were all wearing long, dark cloaks from head to toe. These weren't wild animals. They weren't ghostly shadows, either. They were wearing clothes. But what were they? Or who were they?

The leader reached for my face. I winced, expecting something painful to happen. But instead, it reached out with a strange-looking arm that was rounded on the end and wrapped with a rag. This guy was too big to be a klee. And definitely not a tang. But I couldn't imagine what kind of animal had long arms that were rounded on the end. My heart pounded. I wanted to say something, but the words choked in my throat. I stared at this strange, rounded arm as it poked me to see if I was conscious. That's when I realized it wasn't a rounded, alien arm at all. It was a regular old human arm. We had been attacked by a cloaked gang of gars, and this was a normal human poking me. And his hand was missing. He spoke with a deep, soft voice that was something out of a dream—maybe the most incredible dream I'd ever had.

"What're you doin', shorty?" the voice said with the hint of a chuckle. "Just hangin' around?"

He pulled the cape from over his head to reveal the most welcome sight I could have imagined. He smiled warmly and added, "I thought you'd never get here, Bobby."

I reached around my neck and pulled out the necklace with the Traveler rings. I held the largest ring out to him and said, "Just dropped by to return your ring, Gunny."

# EELONG

"You look like you've been through the war, shorty," Gunny said as he held me by the shoulders so the other gars could cut me down.

"Me?" I said. "What about your hand?"

"Ahh, just a minor inconvenience," he said casually, though I didn't believe him for a second. "Where did you find my ring?"

"You don't want to know."

I was lowered to my feet and stood facing my friend, the tall African-American guy who was the Traveler from First Earth, Vincent "Gunny" Van Dyke. He looked good for a guy in his sixties. But he also looked tired, with a bit more gray in his hair. No big surprise. Eelong did that to people. He put his ring on the finger of his right hand, then looked to me and shook his head. "You look older than when I saw you last."

"I am," I said. "Man, it's good to see you." I threw my arms around him and hugged him tight. A huge wave of relief washed over me. Gunny was alive and I was no longer alone. I didn't want to let him go, but an angry snarl brought me back to reality. I looked to see a few gars poking at Kasha and Yorn as they dangled in their net traps.

A gar ran up to Gunny and said, "We will kill them now, while they're trapped."

I don't know what was more of a shock, knowing that Yorn and Kasha were about to be killed, or hearing a gar speak fluently.

"No!" I shouted quickly. "They're friends."

"Klees are not friends," the gar said. "They will die now." The gar pulled a weapon from beneath his cloak. It looked like a long arrow, almost a spear, that was loaded in a simple contraption with a band pulled taut, like a spear gun. He raised the tip, and I saw it was very large and very pointy. He headed for the dangling klees, ready for an execution.

"Gunny," I shouted in desperation. "Seegen is dead. The black klee is his daughter, Kasha."

"Aron, wait!" Gunny shouted to the gar. The gar, Aron, stopped. Gunny looked to me and said, "Seegen's dead? How?"

"I don't know," I answered. "But Kasha is the Traveler now."

"Gunny!" Yorn called. "It's me, Yorn. Seegen's acolyte."

Gunny walked quickly over to the traps where Kasha and Yorn were dangling.

"What happened to Seegen?" Gunny asked Yorn.

"He went to Second Earth and came back dead," the old klee snapped, sounding irritated. "Now would you mind instructing these gars to cut us down before I injure something."

"In a second," Gunny answered, then looked at Kasha. "I don't know you. But I can't let you loose until I know you won't harm these gars."

"Gunny!" Yorn exclaimed in surprise. "It's Seegen's daughter!"

"My father asked that I bring Pendragon to you," she growled. "That's what I did. I have no interest in these gars."

I jumped in, saying, "She's already saved my life a dozen times over." I took a chance and added, "There's only one problem."

"What's that?" Gunny asked quickly.

"Kasha doesn't want to be a Traveler." I figured I'd lay it all out for Gunny, in front of Kasha. What did I have to lose? "She says she doesn't care about the gars, but then she helps them every chance she gets. She's worried about the future of Eelong, but doesn't believe in the threat of Saint Dane. She's the Traveler, but I don't know how to convince her that by helping us, she's helping Eelong."

Gunny said to Kasha, "You're in a tough spot, missy. These gars would kill you both without a second thought. I'll let them do it, too . . . unless you do what I say."

"I'm listening," Kasha growled.

"Come to Black Water with us."

"No!" shouted the gar named Aron. "No klee has ever been to Black Water!"

Like the other gars, Aron wasn't much taller than five feet. He had long dark hair that fell to his shoulders and even though he looked like an older guy, his face didn't have the hint of a beard. It was weird, because I doubted if these guys shaved. They were like adult children. But more interesting, unlike the gars from Leeandra, there was intelligence behind their eyes. They stood straight and moved with purpose. It was just one more proof that gars weren't animals to be hunted and slaughtered.

Gunny spoke to Aron like a wise parent. "I need you to trust me, Aron. My friend and I are here to help you, but we can't do that without these klees." Gunny spoke softly, and convincingly. It was like listening to Mister Rogers . . . or a Traveler using his powers of persuasion. Could Mister Rogers have been a Traveler? Interesting.

"I will take responsibility," Gunny continued, addressing all of them. "They won't harm you, I promise."

The gars looked nervously between Gunny and the trapped klees. It seemed like they wanted to believe him, but their natural fear of klees made it tough.

"But they might tell others of the secret of Black Water," Aron said worriedly. "We cannot let that happen."

"It won't," Gunny assured him. "If they try to reveal the location of Black Water, I'll kill them myself."

Whoa, strong words from Gunny. He definitely had more of an edge than the last time we were together. Then again, I think I did too. Constant fear does that to people. I glanced to Kasha. Her ears went back.

"Do you trust me?" Gunny asked Aron.

The small gar looked to the others. They all nodded.

"Good," Gunny said. He looked to Kasha and asked, "What's it going to be, missy?"

Kasha's ears were still back. She didn't like being cornered. "I don't see that I have a choice. I'll go with you."

"Wonderful! Would you please cut us down now," Yorn begged.

"Cut them down!" Gunny said to the gars. "Be gentle; they're our guests."

The gars used small knives to cut the klees down, but they weren't gentle. Kasha and Yorn hit the ground hard. Their legs were all tangled in the net so they couldn't even do the cat thing and land on their feet. The gars quickly surrounded them, ready to attack if they so much as growled. They all had those spear weapons that were loaded and ready.

"Let's all take it easy," Gunny said. He walked deliberately into the circle of gars and stood next to Kasha and Yorn. "It's late. We should get back." He motioned for everyone to join him and we all started toward the waterfall. I couldn't call it "black" anymore, because the sunbelt was long gone and pretty much everything was black. But the stars were out and we were able to find our way without walking into any trees. Gunny, Kasha, Yorn, and I walked together, with the gars behind us, keeping a watchful eye.

"How did you get to be chief gar, Gunny?" I said, half joking.

Gunny chuckled and said, "I'm not. But they listen to me. They're scared, and from what I've heard, they should be."

"So they know the klees want to start hunting them?" I asked.

"Yes, they do," Gunny said. "They send scouts to Leeandra all the time. It's a frightening thing, being declared food. I figure Saint Dane must have his hand in this somewhere."

"He does," Yorn answered. "Seegen discovered that."

"I don't understand," Kasha said. "These gars are, are—"

"Intelligent?" Gunny said. "Is that the word you're looking for?"

"Yes," Kasha admitted.

"I think there's a whole lot about the gars you don't know about, that's why I want you to come to Black Water."

We approached the pool at the base of the waterfall. Gunny led us around to the rock wall next to it and continued walking . . . on top of the water! At first I thought he was actually walking on water, but when I looked closer, I saw there were flat stones lying right below water level. I watched as Gunny walked directly toward the waterfall, then made a sharp turn and walked *behind* the water! Awesome! I went next, carefully making my way across the rocks, trying not to slip off and get wet. I stayed focused and when I looked up, I found myself behind the waterfall.

"This way, shorty," Gunny called. He was standing on dry land at the mouth of a cave that disappeared deeper into the mountain. I joined him, then turned around to watch Kasha, Yorn, and then Aron and the gars enter from outside. Gunny picked up something that looked like a black tube about a foot long. He broke it in two. Instantly the two halves glowed bright yellow.

"It's like phosphorous," Gunny explained.

Light filled the cavern, making the waterfall sparkle. I saw that the ceiling stretched high above us and that the cave went farther into the mountain. The light also revealed that we weren't alone. I jumped back in surprise when I saw that several more gars were standing deeper in the cave, gathered together silently like a bunch of dark bats. Their spear weapons were ready for business.

"Guards," Gunny explained. "I wouldn't want to try and get past them if I wasn't welcome." Gunny walked toward them, announcing, "It's all right. The klees are with us."

The guards didn't move.

Aron announced, "We're going to allow these klees to enter Black Water. Do not let them leave unless I tell you otherwise."

This was their insurance. If the klees started making trouble and tried to escape, they'd run into this bunch of lethal bat munchkins. Gunny tossed the second phosphorous stick to Aron and continued the procession into the cave. The guards stepped aside and let us pass. Creepy. The passageway was winding and narrow. Gunny and I had to duck slightly for fear of hitting our heads. The gars didn't have to worry about that, and the klees walked on all fours. Lucky them.

"The gars from Leeandra called Black Water 'home,'" I said. "What does that mean?"

"You'll see," Gunny answered.

After winding our way through the cave tunnel for another few minutes, I started to feel fresh air. Up ahead I caught sight of a starry sky. We were nearing the end. Gunny led us out of the mouth of the cave, and I stood looking down on an incredible sight. Spread out before us, lit by the bright moon, was Black Water.

"Everything you think you know about the gars, forget," Gunny said.

Yorn and Kasha stared in wide-eyed shock.

"What you see here is the truth," Gunny added. "And if Saint Dane finds it, Eelong will be lost."

# EELONG

We stood on the side of a steep hill, looking down on a big, busy village. There was a grand building in the center, with hundreds of smaller huts built out in straight lines like the spokes of a wheel. The cross streets were circles that got bigger and bigger the farther they were from the center. The huts all looked like round log cabins with thatch roofs. Though it was nighttime, I could see it all plainly, because the moon was full and there were lamps burning on posts at most every intersection. Lights glowed inside the huts too, making them look warm and inviting.

It's hard to guesstimate exactly how big the town was, but I'd say it was spread out over a couple of square miles. It was tucked into a hidden valley, surrounded by steep, rocky cliffs. A huge waterfall cascaded down on one end of the valley, feeding a river that wound its way through the center of town and continued out the far side. I couldn't tell for sure, but it looked like farmland stretched out beyond the huts.

The town was a strange oasis tucked into the mountains of nowhere. The only thing that would have made it more surprising was if there had been snow and a guy with a red suit who made toys and drove a sleigh. The streets were busy with gars hurrying about like, well, like humans. Some rode bicycle vehicles, others drove wagons pulled by zenzens. Their clothes were sturdy and clean, nothing like the rags worn by the gars outside of here. I saw women and children and even some elderly gars, which was surprising, because none of the gars in Leeandra lived long enough to become elderly.

"I'm totally confused," I stammered out, "I thought gars were . . . were—"

"Animals?" Gunny said. "They are, everyplace but here."

I noticed that Kasha and Yorn were standing close together, on all fours, looking stunned. They seemed a whole lot more like animals than earlier that day. Just like that, our roles had reversed.

Aron, the gar, approached Gunny, saying, "We should get to town."

Gunny said, "I'd like to take my friend and the klees to the hut where I've been staying. They've come a long way; they'll need rest and food."

Aron looked to the klees nervously. "And what if they escape?" he asked.

"I believe your guards at the waterfall will make sure they don't."

It was clear that Aron wasn't cool with having klees here at Black Water.

"If that's what you want," he said. "But please keep a few guards with you. We don't want anything going wrong when the Advent is so near."

"Thank you," Gunny said.

Aron went back to the group of gars to give them orders.

"What is the Advent, Gunny? " I asked. "The gars on the outside talk about it."

"Not now," Gunny said softly. "Wait till we're alone."

The group of gars dispersed, headed for the village. Two gars remained with us to keep their eyes on the klees. Their spear guns were out and ready for trouble. At least they didn't insist that the cats wear leashes. Score one for the gars on the hospitality scale.

"Who's hungry?" Gunny asked cheerily.

"I'm starved, " Yorn answered.

"I could eat too," I added.

Kasha didn't answer.

"Good," Gunny said. "Let's go to my hut and see what I can find."

The four of us descended the rocky slope along a twisting path that led to Black Water. The two guards followed close behind.

"I have heard the stories of this place," Yorn said. "But I dismissed them as fantasy."

"Evolution took a different path in Black Water," Gunny explained. "The way it was told to me is that many generations ago, a gar stole food from a klee. As punishment, the klee beat him. But the gar fought back and killed the klee. The gar was going to be put to death, but managed to escape with several others. They eventually found this hidden valley, settled, had children, and learned how to take care of themselves."

"They created a whole separate civilization?" I asked.

"Exactly," Gunny answered. "Once they were out from under the klees' control, they evolved into intelligent beings."

"So this is a society spawned from murderers and criminals," Kasha said with disdain.

"You could look at it that way," Gunny said. "Or you could say it's an example of what can happen when individuals are given the freedom to grow."

My thoughts went right back to that horrible gar prison. It pissed me off to know the gars were capable of building their own society, yet the klees treated them like dirt. I didn't want to hate the klees, but it was hard not to, after seeing Black Water.

We reached the first street of the village and continued along a grass strip that was the road. In fact all the roads were covered with short, firm grass that was like artificial turf. To either side of the road were huts. Delicious food smells drifted from some, along with music that sounded as if it were being made by a flute. Each hut was pretty much the same as the next, except for the well-kept flower gardens in front. Some were elaborate and colorful, others had nicely trimmed hedges. All the plants and the grassy roads made the town feel as if it were a living thing.

I was beginning to get used to this peaceful little village, when the calm was interrupted by a strange hissing noise that quickly grew louder. We all stopped, ready for anything.

"What's that?" Kasha asked nervously.

"Don't worry," Gunny assured us. "It's watering time."

Sure enough, there was now a wet mist in the air. I saw that the lampposts doubled as sprinklers. A fine spray of water shot out just beneath the burning lamps in a three-sixty arc, sending moisture into the air. A look down the street proved all the lampposts were active.

"Every inch of Black Water is covered," Gunny explained. "It's very impressive."

It wasn't rain, but more like a fine mist. Probably just enough to keep all the flowers and shrubs happy.

"Unbelievable," Kasha uttered in awe.

We passed several gars along the way. Their reaction to the

klees was always the same. Fear. They ran to the other side of the street. Some picked up their children to protect them, or slammed the doors of their huts. I felt nervous eyes peering at us from windows everywhere. Nobody seemed happy about having two klees strolling through Black Water.

"Ow!" Yorn yelled.

Somebody had thrown a rock at him and run away. Kasha stood up and snarled angrily, but Gunny quickly blocked her way.

"Easy now, missy," he said. "Remember, you don't have friends here. If you pick a fight, you'll lose."

"I'm fine, Kasha," Yorn assured her.

Kasha's ears were back in anger, but she didn't do anything about it.

"This is my hut," Gunny said. "Let's all relax and go inside."

The two guards stayed outside, one at the door, the other near the single window. When we entered, I saw that the hut was pretty simple. There was only one room with wooden furniture. Gunny went to the area that was the kitchen and opened up a locker that was stocked with fresh fruit and vegetables.

"Make yourselves at home," he said. "I hope you're as hungry as I am."

We all sat down and Gunny put a load of fruit and a loaf of bread on a low table in front of us. He and I dug in. We broke off big chunks of bread and I ate pieces of this awesome fruit that was as sweet and juicy as anything I'd tasted at home. Yorn and Kasha didn't move.

"Please eat," Gunny said warmly. "We're all friends."

"I thought you said we had no friends here," Kasha said snottily.

"Outside this hut, you don't," Gunny said. "But in here, we're on the same side."

"Then as long as we are among friends," Yorn said, "I'm going to eat." He reached forward and grabbed himself some fruit.

Kasha grudgingly picked up one of the blue apples and nibbled on it quietly. As we ate, I brought Gunny up to speed with what happened on Veelox. He needed to know that Saint Dane had crushed his first territory, which made our task on Eelong that much more important. He couldn't be allowed to win again. I went into a ton of detail about Lifelight and the Reality Bug and how Saint Dane nearly caused the deaths of millions of people. I did it for Gunny's sake, but I also wanted Kasha to hear how dangerous Saint Dane could be.

Gunny, in turn, told us about his time on Eelong.

"When I stepped out of that tree with the flume," he began, "my, my, I was taken with Eelong. I'd never seen a place so beautiful. I was swept away, which was a mistake because I let my guard down. I went looking for the locals and came upon a band of gars. 'Course, I didn't know they were called gars at the time. Two of 'em picked wild berries while three others stood guard. They were all looking around, like they were doing something wrong, or scared something was about to happen. That should have been my first hint that Eelong wasn't exactly paradise. Just as I was about to talk to them, I was attacked. It was so fast I didn't have a chance to defend myself."

"Was it a tang, or a quig?" I asked.

"It was one of them sneaky lizards. It did a real number on me. It's how I lost this," he said while holding up his injured arm. "It could have been worse. If it weren't for the gars, I'd be a memory. They came to my rescue, and the next thing I knew,

I woke up here in Black Water." Gunny chuckled and added, "They thought I was some kind of king from a distant land, being so tall and dark. I let 'em go on believing it too. They fixed me up and took care of my arm." He looked at his arm with sadness. "It's strange. I feel like my hand is still there until I reach for something and then . . ."

His voice trailed off. I couldn't imagine what it would be like to lose my hand. I felt horrible for him.

"The gars explained to me about how the klees were running the show. It took me a while to get my mind around the idea that cats could be so smart. I'm still having trouble with it, no offense."

"None taken," Yorn said.

"How did you meet my father?" Kasha asked.

"That's where I came in," Yorn answered. "Gunny returned to the flume. I met him there, and took him to meet Seegen."

"So you already knew Black Water was real?" Kasha asked Yorn.

"No, I didn't," Yorn answered.

Gunny said, "I only told Seegen, the Traveler. But this is where things start getting interesting."

"It's already pretty interesting," I threw in.

Gunny said, "I need to show you all something. If you've had enough to eat, let's go for another walk."

We left the hut and Gunny led us toward the center of town. The gar guards followed, keeping a close eye on Kasha and Yorn. Gunny brought us to a large, four-story building that was designed like all the other log huts, only it was huge. It's hard to say for sure how big it was, but I'm guessing it covered a couple of acres.

"They call this the Center," Gunny explained. "It's where the village rulers meet. In one section they manufacture clothes and tools. Another area is for recreation, where they have concerts and such. They're pretty good, too." Gunny said to the guards, "Wait for us here, please."

The guards didn't like that. "But—"

"I said, wait for us here." Gunny was a persuasive guy, though I suppose it helped that Travelers knew how to use the power of suggestion. I wasn't so good at it, but Gunny looked as if he was a master. The gars backed off and we went inside. We walked down a long corridor with many doors on either side and ended up at a large, black door that looked kind of ominous. Gunny stopped there and turned to us, saying, "Behind this door is not only the future for the gars, but it could very well be the future for all of Eelong."

"I'm intrigued," Yorn said.

Gunny opened the door and we stepped into a massive room that I can best describe as a giant greenhouse. Looking up, I saw that the high ceiling was made of glass. Stars could be seen twinkling in the night sky. On the floor were long rows of different sized plants, all holding the most incredible, healthy-looking fruits and vegetables I'd ever seen. There were vines with long, yellow, tubular fruits; bushes laden with orange-size berries; stalks that held the familiar blue apples, but ones twice the size of those I had picked; and trees that were hanging heavy with long, red ropelike fruits that pulled the branches toward the ground. Gunny picked off one of these long fruits and broke it into several pieces, offering them to us. I took a bite to find it had the snap of an apple's texture, but tasted more like citrus. It was the closest thing to chewing lemonade that I could imagine.

"I guess you could call this a laboratory," Gunny explained. "The gars have figured out a way to grow plants in air."

"In air?" I exclaimed. "No dirt?"

"And no water," Gunny added.

Gunny pushed aside a plant to reveal a heavy, black frame. It reminded me of the thing my grandfather used to grow roses on. It was like a grid, with six-inch squares. I looked around the room to see that all the plants were growing on these black grids. Some were flat on the floor and the plants grew up from it. Others were on end, like a wall, and the healthy plants grew all over it.

"It's all about this material they invented," Gunny explained. "They call it 'Virloam.' Whatever it's made of, it somehow takes moisture and nourishment out of the air. Don't ask me how, but it does. The plants love it. They grow like crazy. Look at how big the fruit gets!"

"So they don't need water?" Kasha said, as if she couldn't believe it was true.

"Except for what the virloam gets out of the air," Gunny said. "They don't need fertilizer, either. It's amazing stuff. The gars have more food than they know what to do with."

"This is incredible!" Kasha exclaimed. "Virloam could help feed all of Eelong!"

"It could," Gunny said. "But it won't."

"Why not?" Kasha demanded.

"There's more to see, c'mon," Gunny said.

We walked through the greenhouse, passing by hundreds of plants with the most incredibly healthy-looking fruits and vegetables I could imagine. Kasha was right. This technology could save Eelong.

"I don't get it, Gunny," I said. "If the food problem goes

away, then the klees won't have to overturn Edict Forty-six and start hunting gars."

"That's true," Gunny said. "But the gars have other plans."

We arrived at the far side of the greenhouse and another large, black door. Gunny said, "You asked me why the gars call Black Water 'home'? The answer is in here."

# EELONG

Gunny opened the door and we stepped into a gigantic room that was completely filled with row after row of neat, orderly, bunk beds. There had to be thousands of them. All new. All empty.

"There are four more rooms just like this," Gunny said.

"What is the point?" Yorn asked.

"The gars have been preparing for a long time," Gunny explained. "They haven't abandoned their brothers outside of Black Water. They plan to rescue them."

"Are you serious?" I asked, stunned.

"Absolutely. They call it The Advent. They plan on bringing every single gar on Eelong here. There's more than enough food for them, and plenty of room. They've got schools set up to help educate and civilize children as well as adults. It's quite remarkable. The Advent is all about rescuing and nurturing an entire race. Eelong will never be the same."

"But the klees would never allow that!" Yorn exclaimed. "They need the gars to survive."

"They don't have a choice," Gunny said. "Black Water is

protected by these mountains. The klees won't be able to get close . . . present company excepted."

"So you left here to tell Seegen about the Advent?" I asked.

"I had to," Gunny answered. "Seegen may have been a klee, but he's the Traveler. This is a major turning point in Eelong's history and Saint Dane is here. That's why I left for the flume. I met Yorn, Yorn brought me to Seegen, and I brought Seegen here. He only got as far as the black waterfall, though. He never came inside. You two, Yorn and Kasha, are the first two klees to ever set foot in Black Water, and I'm going to guess that you'll be the last."

"But, how can it be done?" Kasha asked, stunned. "How could they possibly make this Advent happen and get all the gars to come here?"

"That's the last surprise," Gunny said with a sly smile. He took something from his pocket and held it in the palm of his hand. It was one of the mysterious, amber cubes.

"What *are* those things?" Kasha exclaimed.

"Saint Dane wants to know too," I added.

Gunny led us back out and through the greenhouse. We went all the way back to the long corridor we had first walked through and went into one of the side doors. Stepping through, we entered a much smaller room that was completely dark, except for a truly strange-looking device. There were six huge amber crystals that went from floor to ceiling. They were tube shaped and about three feet in diameter. Each tube gave off a soft glow of light and a slight electric hum. In front of the crystals was a table made of polished wood. On top were three rows of crystals that were fixed into the wood, like buttons. They were all different colors and shapes, and like the amber tubes, they glowed with light from within.

"It's cool-looking," I said. "But what is it?"

"They call it 'Link,'" Gunny answered. "We have another name for it at home. We call it a 'radio.'"

"A radio?" I exclaimed.

"That's right," Gunny said. "The gars took klee technology and did it one better. This is the first broadcast station on Eelong. Basically, it's a powerful transmitter."

"And the amber cubes are receivers!" I exclaimed.

"Radios? Receivers?" Kasha repeated, confused. "I don't understand."

Gunny took Kasha's paw and held it out flat. He put the cube on it, making sure the black side faced her. He stepped to the crystal control board, pressed a triangle-shaped crystal and said, "Hello, Kasha!"

The cube in Kasha's hand lit up. Gunny's voice came through it like a miniradio.

"Yaaah!" Kasha screamed and dropped the cube. "It's magic!"

"It's not magic," Gunny said. "It's a radio. This is the turning point on Eelong. The first radio broadcast. Using this device, the gars can communicate with one another. They can coordinate their movements and escape from the klees by the thousands, all at the same time. This radio is going to make the Advent possible. There's no way the klees can stop the gars if they all leave at once. All they have to do is give the word, and the gars will come home."

"My oh my." Yorn laughed. "I am stunned, and it takes a lot to do that. This has turned out to be so much better than I expected."

"You think it's funny?" Kasha said, still upset. "The gars have the technology to save Eelong, but they're only going to use it to help the other gars!"

"Can you blame them?" Yorn replied. "They've been

treated horribly for generations. You can't expect them to turn around and help their tormentors."

"Maybe not," Kasha replied. "But it's not something to laugh about."

"Oh, that's not what I'm laughing about," Yorn said. "I'm laughing in relief."

"Relief about what?" Gunny asked.

"About you, Pendragon," Yorn answered, still chuckling.

"Huh?" was all I managed to get out.

"I made such a silly mistake," Yorn said. "I was worried you'd catch it, but as it turns out, you weren't as observant as I gave you credit for. No harm done."

Uh-oh. I didn't like that tone. A prickly, familiar feeling of dread started to creep up my spine.

"What are you talking about?" I asked.

"Gunny's hand!" Yorn exclaimed. "Think! When we were bringing Seegen's body back to Leeandra, I stupidly told you it was sheer luck that the hand was found and not devoured by the tangs. How could—"

"How could you have known that?" I said. The realization hit me like a punch in the head. "Unless you're the one who found it and gave it to Saint Dane."

"Well, something like that," Yorn exclaimed with a small chuckle. "I thought the game would be over when I made that silly slip, but here I am!"

"What about my hand?" Gunny asked, confused.

"That's how I got your ring, Gunny," I said soberly. "It was on your hand. Saint Dane brought it to Second Earth and gave it to Mark and Courtney. I got it from them. But the thing I never asked myself was—"

"You never asked how Saint Dane got it in the first place," Yorn exclaimed. "I must admit, it was a fluke. The hand was right in the spot where Gunny was attacked. I think the tangs left it alone because they were afraid of the ring."

"I'm lost," Kasha said.

"More than you know," Gunny said to her. The horrible truth was starting to sink in for him, too.

"Yorn?" Kasha shouted. "What are you talking about?"

"Yorn is dead, you stupid girl," the old klee exclaimed. He yanked off the necklace that held Yorn's ring. "It really was a bold move, if I do say so myself. I've never taken the place of an acolyte. I thought I played the role quite nicely."

He tossed the ring at Kasha, who caught it awkwardly. She still didn't know what was happening. But I did.

"Show her," I shouted at the old klee. "Don't just tell her, show her."

"As you wish," the cat responded. He took a step back from us as his body transformed. I had seen this before, but that didn't make it any easier to take. Yorn stood up on his back legs as his body went liquid. First his legs, then his chest, and then his arms became human. He grew to his full seven-foot height. I saw that he still wore the familiar, black suit. Then his head transformed. You guys told me his face had changed, but nothing prepared me for this. He no longer had shoulder length gray hair and cold blue eyes. He was now completely bald, with angry red scars running across his dome, from front to back, that looked like lightning bolts. But what I couldn't stop looking at was his eyes. They were nearly white. I felt as if they were burning holes in me.

Saint Dane was back.

Kasha stood frozen with wide, stunned eyes.

"Thank you, both, so much," Saint Dane said. "I've been trying to discover the location of Black Water for so long; it was so kind of you to show me the way."

"It's too late, Saint Dane," Gunny seethed. "They're ready to call the gars home. Getting rid of Edict Forty-six won't do a thing."

Saint Dane laughed. I know I've said this before, but I *hate* it when Saint Dane laughs. It means he still knows more than he's telling.

"Oh, you simple Travelers," Saint Dane chuckled. "You haven't even begun to understand my plan. Ask your friends Mark and Courtney. Perhaps they should be the Travelers from the Earth territories, they are so much more clever than you."

"Leave them alone!" I shouted.

"What they do is their decision," Saint Dane said innocently. "The same as all of you. Don't blame me for the choices they make."

Gunny took a step backward and touched one of the crystals on the control panel. Instantly a sharp horn sounded.

"What's that?" Kasha asked in surprise.

"That alarm will lock down the Center," Gunny answered. "In two minutes there'll be an army of gars in here."

"Give them my best, won't you?" Saint Dane said, and ran out the door.

Kasha looked at Gunny and me with wide, wild eyes, saying, "He's trapped in here, right?"

"You can't trap Saint Dane," I said.

"We can try!" Kasha said, and leaped for the door.

Gunny and I followed her into the corridor. A quick look showed the door to the greenhouse slamming shut. We all ran for the door, threw it open, and jumped in. A dark shadow swooped past our heads. We ducked as the shadow barely missed us and flew up toward the glass ceiling. It was a bird. A huge, black bird. I had seen that bird before, so had Gunny. It was outside the Manhattan Tower Hotel on First Earth, right after Saint Dane had leaped off the penthouse balcony.

"What is that?" gasped Kasha.

"That," I said, "is why we're here."

"There's no way out," Gunny said.

As if in response, the giant bird shot straight for the ceiling. It hit the glass right above our heads and smashed through, sending a storm of shards raining down on us. Gunny pushed us out of the way as the glass crashed to the floor. The three of us looked back at the ceiling to see the hole that Saint Dane had made, and escaped through.

"What do you think he'll do?" Gunny asked.

"I don't know" was my answer. "But whatever it is, it's got to do with Black Water. He's been desperate to find it . . . and we led him here."

"What do Mark and Courtney have to do with this?" Gunny asked.

"I don't know that, either. I've got to go back to Second Earth. Saint Dane keeps pointing me toward them. We've gotta find out why."

Kasha held Yorn's ring in her furry hand. She stared at it, as if the stolen ring could give her some answers. "Let me have it, Pendragon," she said, all business.

"Let you have what?" I asked.

Kasha looked me right in the eye. I saw an intensity there that made me shiver.

"My ring," she said. "I'd like it now, please."

I reached to my neck and pulled the cord over my head. Dangling on it were two Traveler rings—mine and Seegen's. I took mine off and put it on my finger where it belonged.

"No more pretending," I said, and held the necklace out to Kasha.

She looked closely at the ring she had so callously tossed

aside. Her father's ring. Her ring. Kasha took the necklace reverently, threaded Yorn's ring onto it and put it over her head. She would wear them both.

Once again, there was a Traveler from Eelong.

That's where I'm going to stop writing, guys. I finished this journal back at Gunny's hut. Tomorrow we're going to go to the flume, and I'm going to meet you guys on Second Earth. I don't know why Saint Dane keeps pointing me toward you, but it's time to find out. I hate that he's dragging you into this. It's my fault. If I never sent you journals, you wouldn't be in danger right now. Seems as if a lot of things are my fault lately. I have no idea what day it is at home, or if you're in school, or if you're even in Stony Brook. But I'll find you. You may not believe this after seeing what a dope I can be, but I swear I'm going to figure out a way to keep you guys safe.

Be looking for me. I'm coming home.

**END OF JOURNAL #18**

# ∞ EELONG ∞

**Bobby Pendragon never made it home.**

He and Gunny and Kasha left Black Water, made the long journey back toward Leeandra and got as far as the tree that held the flume. They entered the small tunnel at its base, crawled through the vines, descended the root stairs toward the underground cavern, stepped over the pile of gar bones, and came face-to-face . . . with Mark, Courtney, Spader, and Boon.

Bobby stood there in stunned silence, not fully understanding what he was seeing. There was a long, tense moment where everyone stared at one another. It was Mark who broke the ice first.

"S-Surprise," he said meekly.

"What are you guys doing here?" Bobby said with dismay. "I told you not to use the flume!"

"We didn't have a choice," Courtney said.

"Why not?" Bobby shouted. "Did Saint Dane pick you up and throw you in?"

"Don't be angry, mate," Spader said. "Listen to what they have to say."

Bobby focused on Spader. Seeing him was almost as surprising as seeing Mark and Courtney. "Spader! Did you bring them here?"

"Yes," Spader said. "But—"

"There's no buts!" Bobby shouted. "This is wrong! The territories aren't supposed to be mixed. Get them out of here before—"

"Seegen died on Second Earth," Courtney said calmly. "We were there."

That got Bobby's attention.

"You saw my father die?" Kasha asked. "What happened?"

Courtney and Mark explained everything they had been through, from getting the note to go to the flume, to Seegen's death, to their fearing it was the poison from Cloral that killed him. Spader explained how Mark and Courtney came to Cloral with a sample of Seegen's fur. They tested it and confirmed it was the Cloral poison. No mistake. Finally Spader said that ten tanks of the deadly poison were missing.

"Seegen was fine when he left for the flume," Boon announced. "But he went with Yorn, and since Yorn was really Saint Dane, that means—"

"Saint Dane poisoned my father," Kasha said as if spitting it out.

"And the poison is here on Eelong," Courtney added.

"How bad is this poison, Spader?" Gunny asked.

"It's a nasty-do," Spader answered. "It works on living things, turning them deadly. Eat something infected and you'll be dead before you know you're in trouble." He looked to Kasha and said, "It's how my father died, too."

"All those dead tangs on the farm!" Boon exclaimed. "That fruit didn't just go bad. Saint Dane must have been testing the poison!"

"That's what Seegen thought," Courtney said.

"What if this poison touches a klee, or a gar?" Kasha asked.

"Instant death," Spader answered. "At least, that's what my brainy mates on Cloral tell me."

"Bobby," Mark said, "Saint Dane said he was going to w-wipe out the gars, but there was no way he could do that just by getting klees to hunt them. But with this poison, he can kill thousands."

"That doesn't make sense!" Boon interrupted. "If it's so deadly, he can't use it on the gars without poisoning the klees, too!"

"So maybe he'll just poison everybody and get it over with," Courtney suggested. "He is a bad guy, after all."

"No," Gunny said. "That's not how he works. He wants the people of the territories to bring about their own destruction. All he does is push them into making foolish choices. He'll get the klees to use the poison on the gars, all right. I don't doubt that."

"But how can he get the klees to poison so many gars without getting poisoned themselves?" Boon asked.

Nobody jumped in with an answer. There was a long silence, then Mark said softly. "It'll be easy."

Everyone looked at Mark. Mark cleared his throat and continued, "We read it in Bobby's last journal. I think it's why Saint Dane is here right now. This is the turning point of Eelong. When the radio message is sent from Black Water to start the Advent, every gar on Eelong will go there."

The horrible truth suddenly became obvious to everyone in the cavern. It was Gunny who said it out loud. "If the gars are all in one place, then it would be nothing short of—"

"Genocide," Bobby whispered. "That's what Saint Dane promised. That's his plan. Genocide."

"That's it," Gunny said, stunned. "If the klees poison Black Water after the Advent, they'll not only wipe out the gars, they'll destroy everything the gars learned about growing enough food to feed the territory. The klees will be killing off their only hope of survival."

Bobby's head was spinning. This was all too much to believe, even for him. He sat down on the flat rock, stunned. Courtney sat next to him.

"You okay?" she asked.

"He told me everything," Bobby said, reeling. "He told me what he planned to do, like he was daring me to stop him. He even said that you and Mark figured it out."

"And we can stop him," Courtney said. "We brought the antidote from Cloral. All we have to do is figure out how to use it."

"You brought the antidote?" Bobby asked, surprised. "But Uncle Press said never to mix anything between territories."

"Press is gone, Bobby," Courtney said firmly. "Things have changed. You don't want Saint Dane to get another territory, do you?"

Bobby closed his eyes, as if the thought actually hurt to be inside his head. He jumped to his feet, walked to the far side of the cavern, and huddled down, hugging his knees. The others watched him nervously, not sure of what to say. Spader made a move to go after him, but Gunny held him back.

"Leave him be," Gunny said. "He needs to work this through."

The tension in the cavern was intense. Nobody was sure what the next move should be, or if Bobby could get his act together and help figure it out.

Courtney approached Kasha and said, "I'm sorry about your father."

Kasha nodded in appreciation.

Mark joined them and said, "He didn't s-suffer or anything. One second he was fine, then he was gone."

"That's how fast the poison works," Courtney said. "Saint Dane really could wipe out the gars."

"I'm finally beginning to understand that," Kasha said somberly.

Every so often they'd glance toward Bobby to see that he hadn't moved.

Spader whispered to Gunny, "Time's wasting."

Gunny nodded and walked to Bobby. When Bobby looked up at him, Gunny saw in his face how troubled and confused he was. Gunny sat next to him, and the two had an intense conversation that nobody else could hear. Bobby nodded often, as if he were getting sage advice from a wise old friend, which is exactly what was happening. Finally, Bobby stood up, wiped his eyes, took a deep breath, and walked back to the group.

"I want to say something," he announced.

The others gathered around, not sure of what to expect.

"None of us want to be here," he began with a low voice. "If it were my call, we'd all go home and pretend none of this ever happened. But we can't. Some of us don't even have homes to go back to. I don't know about you guys, but the more I learn about this idiotic war, the more confused I get. Uncle Press told me the number one rule was never to mix the territories. He said each territory has its own history and destiny. 'That's the way it was meant to be,' he'd always say, and I believed him. But if that's true, how come Saint Dane doesn't know it? Why do we have to play by the rules, if he doesn't?"

As he spoke, Bobby's voice grew more assured. The others felt it. Without meaning to, they all stood up a little straighter.

"But you know what?" he continued. "We've beaten him. More than once. He took away most everything I ever cared about, but we beat him. He killed my uncle, but we beat him. He uses every trick possible to confuse us, but we still beat him. And

I'll tell you what, here on Eelong, we're going to beat him again."

Spader smiled at Courtney and winked. Things were getting interesting.

Bobby continued, "If he says the rules have changed, fine. That means they've changed for everybody. This may not be the way it was meant to be, but it's the way it's *going* to be. We're not waiting for his next move. We're taking the fight to him."

"Yes!" Boon shouted.

"Mark, Courtney," Bobby continued. "I'm sorry I doubted you. You were right to bring the antidote here. When we save Eelong, it'll be because of you guys."

Mark beamed. This was exactly the kind of moment he had been dreaming about since he read Bobby's very first journal.

"But I want you to go home now," Bobby added. "This is way too dangerous for you guys."

"No!" Courtney said adamantly. It was so quick that everybody turned to look at her. "We've come too far to wuss out now. We want to see this to the end. Right, Mark?"

Mark gulped. "Right," he said with a shaky voice.

Bobby nodded and gave them a small smile. "That's what I figured you'd say. All right, then. I'm glad you're here. You earned it."

Courtney beamed. Mark smiled weakly.

Bobby turned to Spader and said sharply, "Spader?"

Spader stood up straight. He nervously said, "Look, Pendragon, I know you told me to go home and wait for you but—"

"Welcome back to the show, mate," Bobby said with a smile.

Spader let out a relieved breath and said, "It is so very good to be back."

"Tell us about the antidote," Bobby said.

"With pleasure," Spader replied. He knelt down next to the

three tanks in their black harnesses. "The agronomers tell me the poison may be nasty, but it's fragile. A single whiff of the liquid in these tanks will make it harmless."

Gunny asked, "How do you think Saint Dane will use the poison against Black Water?"

"From what I've read in Pendragon's journal," Spader answered, "Black Water is inside a giant, natural bowl, right?"

"That's right," Gunny answered.

"That's good and bad," Spader continued. "The poison is a liquid gas that clings to anything it touches. If Saint Dane and his klee wogglies release enough of it into the air of Black Water, the surrounding mountains will trap it. The result? Every living thing inside would die."

Everyone exchanged nervous glances.

"So what's the good part?" Boon asked nervously.

"The mountains can help us, too," Mark answered. "If these canisters of antidote are released inside the bowl, the mountains will help keep it from blowing away and let it do its work against the poison."

"Right," Spader concurred. "The tricky part is the timing."

"Gunny and I have a plan," Bobby announced. "If Saint Dane is going to attack Black Water, we've got to get the antidote there as fast as possible. Boon, can you get five zenzens and more weapons?"

"Say the word," Boon answered proudly.

"Good," Bobby acknowledged. "You're going to Black Water, tonight, with the antidote tanks. Gunny will lead you there, along with Spader, Courtney, and Mark. First thing Gunny will do is try to convince the gars not to make that radio broadcast. If the rest of the gar population stays away, that's half the battle."

"Why so many of us?" Courtney asked.

"It's a long way back," Gunny answered. "A lot can happen between here and there."

They all knew what Gunny meant. Eelong was a dangerous place. There was no guarantee they would all get there safely. The more people who went, the better chance they had of somebody arriving with the antidote.

"W-What about the tangs?" Mark asked. "Isn't it kind of dangerous to travel at night?"

"No," Kasha answered. "Tangs don't usually attack at night."

"Then we'll get there before daybreak!" Spader offered optimistically.

"What about you, Bobby?" Courtney asked.

Bobby took a deep breath, as if he didn't like what he was about to say. "Please don't be ticked," he said. "But I can't tell you what I'm going to do. After what happened with Yorn, I can't be sure that one of you isn't really Saint Dane."

The others broke out with surprised responses. "What? Impossible! That can't be. You're not serious!"

"Saint Dane can do a lot of things," Bobby said, trying to restore order. "But I'm pretty sure he can't split himself in two. That means Gunny and Kasha are clear. But as for everybody else, I just can't take the chance. I'm sorry."

Courtney bit her lip. Spader smiled and shook his head. Boon laughed as if it were the most outrageous thing he'd ever heard.

"It's okay, Bobby," Mark said. "You're right."

"I'll tell you one thing," Spader said. "I'm not looking forward to wearing these rags." He held up one of the smelly, rotten pieces of fabric that the gars called clothes.

"Don't," Bobby said defiantly. "If we're throwing away the rules, we're throwing them *all* away. Keep your clothes from Cloral."

"Now we're talking!" Courtney said with relief.

"Are you sure, Bobby?" Mark asked meekly.

"Absolutely," Bobby answered.

"We should get going," Gunny said. "Time may be precious."

The group split up, each preparing for the mission in their own way. Spader strapped on his tank with the help of Gunny while Bobby helped Mark and Courtney gear up.

"Are you sure about this, Mark?" Bobby asked quietly. "If you want to go home, no harm, no foul. You're already a hero."

This was the moment of truth for Mark. He had wrestled with conflicting emotions since Bobby began his adventure so long ago. Part of him wanted to be right there with his best friend, battling Saint Dane and protecting Halla. It all sounded so exciting. But the practical side of his brain kept reminding him that he wasn't a fighter; he wasn't athletic; and he wasn't particularly brave.

"I'm pretty scared," Mark said. "But I'm more scared about what'll happen if Saint Dane comes to Second Earth. One way or another, I'm going to have to face him. It might as well be here. Maybe we can stop him for good, before he gets a shot at my family."

"Trust us, Bobby," Courtney said. "We're going to do this."

Bobby smiled and said, "I believe you."

Courtney added, "And neither of us is Saint Dane, you dork."

Across the cavern, Boon approached Kasha. "Is it true?" he asked. "Is Yorn dead?"

Kasha nodded sadly and said, "Saint Dane changed himself to look just like him. If I hadn't seen it for myself . . ." She didn't finish the thought. "It's not that I didn't believe my father, it's just that, I didn't want to."

Boon said, "You know what he told me? He said that when Saint Dane made his move, you'd be the one to bring him down.

He told me you'd complain, and argue, and come up with a hundred reasons not to be involved, but he knew in the end it wouldn't be him, but you who would save Eelong."

Kasha began to tear up at the thought of her father. She wiped her eyes quickly and took off her necklace. Dangling from the string were two rings. She took one off.

"Yorn's ring," she said. "If I'm the Traveler from Eelong, then you're the acolyte." She held it out to Boon. Boon took it reverently and slipped it into his tunic.

"I won't let you down," he said.

Gunny finished strapping Spader's tank on his back, making sure it was snug. "How's that feel, Flash Gordon?" Gunny asked.

"Snappy-do," Spader replied. "Just like old times, aye, Gunny? It's good to be back with you."

Bobby stepped up to the two and said, "I guess I don't have to say anything. You guys know how important this is."

"No worries, mate," Spader said cheerfully. "You've got the A team in now."

Gunny and Bobby exchanged looks, and smiles. They were used to Spader's cockiness. "Then there's only one thing left to say," Gunny announced. "Hobey-ho, let's go."

"Hobey-ho!" Spader echoed. He gave Bobby a clap on the back and started for the stairs.

"You be careful now, shorty," Gunny said to Bobby.

"Yeah, right," Bobby replied.

Spader called, "Last one back buys the sniggers!"

"You're on," Bobby replied.

Gunny followed Spader to the stairs. Mark and Courtney walked up to Bobby. Mark said, "You know I've been dreaming about this for a long time."

"I know," Bobby said. "But this is no dream, Mark. It's on. For real."

Mark gave him a small, unsure smile.

"Don't worry about us," Courtney said. "Only one thing's got me nervous."

"What's that?" Bobby asked.

"What the heck are we gonna tell our parents when we get home?"

Bobby laughed. Courtney did too. Mark's stomach flipped.

"Like we don't have enough to worry about?" Mark said.

Courtney leaned over and gave Bobby a kiss. "See ya," she said with a wink. She was ready. The two joined Gunny and Spader, and the group pushed through the hanging vines, disappearing up the root stairway, leaving Bobby alone in the cavern with Kasha.

"Well?" she asked. "Are you going to share your big secret plan?"

"Are you in?" Bobby asked with dead seriousness. "I mean *really* in? Because if you have doubts, tell me now."

Kasha said, "I don't understand who you are, Pendragon. Or how you got here, or what it means to be a Traveler. But some things are very clear to me. The klees are going to starve. That's a fact. I also believe the gars deserve better treatment. If the klees can be made to understand that, then I believe the gars of Black Water will share their knowledge and help feed all of Eelong. At least that's what I hope. It may be our only chance to survive."

"I think you're right," Bobby said.

"I still don't know what Saint Dane is," Kasha continued. "But I now believe he's real too. He killed my father and he killed Yorn. From what I've seen, I don't doubt for a second he'd use that poison to destroy Black Water. So given all that, Pendragon, I can say with total confidence . . . I'm in."

"Good," Bobby said.

"So what's the plan?"

Bobby smiled and said, "If we're lucky, it won't matter if the others get the antidote to Black Water in time."

"Because? . . ."

"Because we're going after Saint Dane."

**"I'm not a killer,"** Kasha said as they hurried along the sky bridge back to Leeandra. "If that's your plan to stop Saint Dane, get another plan."

"Give me a break. I'm not a killer either," Bobby assured her. "Even if I was, killing Saint Dane wouldn't stop him."

"Explain that, please," Kasha said.

"Uncle Press told me that killing Saint Dane's body wouldn't kill his spirit. He'd just show up in another form. I don't know how that's possible, but I believe it. You've seen the way he can transform himself. He isn't human, I mean, gar."

"That I believe," Kasha said.

"The thing is," Bobby continued, "when Saint Dane targets a territory, he doesn't do the dirty work himself. He tricks the people of a territory to do things that'll bring about their own ruin."

"And you think he's going to convince the Council of Klee to use the poison on Black Water?"

"Exactly," was Bobby's answer. "So if we want to beat Saint Dane, we've got to beat him at his own game."

"Okay, how?"

"What's the name of that viceroy guy?"

"Ranjin?"

"Right, Ranjin," Bobby repeated. "He's the boss. We've got to convince Ranjin it would be disaster for Eelong if they attacked Black Water."

"So let me understand," Kasha said. "You want us to sneak into Leeandra—where we're both fugitives—get an audience with the viceroy, tell him that one of his trusted inner circle is a shapeshifting gar demon who travels through time and space, and convince him that repealing Edict Forty-six and attacking Black Water would be the downfall of Eelong? That's your big plan?"

"Everything but the demon part," Bobby said. "I don't think he'd understand that."

"I don't think he'd understand any of it!" Kasha snarled. "We need a better plan."

"But that's the way Saint Dane operates," Bobby argued. "We've got to start thinking like him."

"I am thinking like him," Kasha shot back. "He thinks he's beaten us, and if that's the only plan you've got, I'm thinking he's right."

"You have a better idea?" Bobby asked.

Kasha thought, then said, "My plan is to hope the others get the antidote to Black Water because we sure aren't going to be any help stopping the attack."

While Bobby and Kasha hurried toward Leeandra, the others took a different route back to the city in the trees.

"We'll enter Leeandra through the wippen stadium," Boon explained. "There are no games tonight, it will be quiet."

The whole way back, Mark and Courtney barely said a word. Once again they were seeing the pages of Bobby's journals come to life around them. Their journey across the sky bridges was lit by thousands of multicolored fireflies that drifted on the breeze, making the jungle sparkle with life.

"Am I dreaming?" Mark asked Courtney.

"If you are, then we're having the same dream," Courtney answered.

The trip went quickly, and they arrived at a tree that looked down on a large, grassy field that was mostly surrounded by a tall fence. One side of the fence was much taller than the rest. It was part of the wall that surrounded Leeandra.

"What's wippen?" Spader asked.

"It's a game played on zenzens," Boon explained. "Two teams. Each player has a stick with a net on the end. You have to scoop up a ball and get it in your opponent's net."

"Sounds like lacrosse on horseback," Courtney said.

"It's tricky because there are also gars on the field," Boon explained. "They can steal the ball and toss it to their team. Or block the other team."

"Or get trampled by zenzens," Gunny pointed out.

"It's dangerous for gars, yes," Boon said somberly. "Sometimes deadly."

"Let's not play wippen, okay?" Mark said.

Boon cracked open a large, corral-style door, took a peek inside to see if there were any klees around, then led the group inside and across the playing field. They kept close to the fence, trying not to be seen by any klees that might be out for some evening air, or tangs who might be out for an evening snack. They arrived at the corral gate that led into Leeandra.

"Wait for me here," Boon instructed. "I'll bring out five zenzens."

"What about weapons?" Gunny asked.

"If we're lucky, nobody will hear us and we can go to the forager area and pick those up next," Boon answered.

"We're in your hands," Spader said. "Or whatever it is you call those furry things on the ends of your arms."

Boon opened the corral gate and crept inside. The others waited outside, trying to be invisible.

"I've got a problem," Mark whispered to Courtney.

Courtney rolled her eyes and said, "If you gotta go, go."

"No, I don't have to go to the bathroom," Mark whispered. "I've never ridden a horse."

Courtney gave him a surprised look. "You're kidding, right? Never?"

"Not unless you count getting my picture taken on a pony at my fifth birthday party . . . and I fell off. And now that you mention it, I *do* have to go to the bathroom."

"Guys," Courtney whispered to the others. "Mark can't ride."

Gunny and Spader shot Mark a look. Mark shrugged. If there were more light, they would have seen his face was red with embarrassment.

Spader asked, "You can't, or you think you don't know how?"

"What's the difference?" Courtney asked.

"Well, I've never ridden a zenzen, but I'm sure I can do it," Spader said with confidence.

"And why's that?" Courtney challenged.

"It can't be any harder than playing spinney-do on Cloral," Spader answered. "If I can ride a wild fish, I can ride a trained zenzen."

"Let's hope so," Courtney said. "But what about Mark? I don't think he's been doing any wild-fish-riding lately."

They were interrupted by what sounded like a loud, snarling, catfight inside the gate. But it was louder and angrier than any catfight heard on Second Earth. Something was happening inside, and it wasn't good. Someone shouted, "Stop! Right there!" An alarm horn tore through the quiet night. The sound of pounding hooves could be heard coming toward the fence. The time for secrecy was over.

"Open the gates!" Gunny ordered.

Spader and Courtney threw the gates wide open as four zenzens with saddles on their backs came charging out to the wippen field. Behind them was Boon riding a zenzen, herding the animals like a cowboy.

"Mount up!" he shouted.

Spader instantly caught a zenzen and mounted it as easily as a spinney fish.

"Open the far gate!" Boon ordered Spader.

Spader kicked his zenzen and took off to the far side of the arena. The other zenzens tried to follow, but Boon expertly headed them off and brought them back around so the others could reach them. Courtney was about to grab the reins of one when she felt a sharp slap on her back, along with a metallic *clang.* Falling at her feet was an arrow. The tank of antidote on her back had saved her life.

"They're shooting at us!" Courtney yelled.

Standing on top of the fence were several klees with bows and arrows. More arrows hit the ground, sticking into the grass. One klee yelled, "Don't shoot. You'll hit the zenzens!"

Courtney took advantage of the cease-fire and jumped for a zenzen. She grabbed the reins and climbed aboard. She wasn't an expert rider, but she had been on horses enough to know what to do. Boon stopped another zenzen and Gunny quickly took the reins. Being an older guy, he wasn't as agile as the others, but he was still able to swing his long legs up and over to take control. He took a quick look back at the gate to the corral to see that a group of klees were running toward them, swinging ropes over their heads to lasso the zenzens.

"Here they come!" Gunny shouted.

Mark was still on foot. He was too far away from Gunny to jump up with him, so he made the snap decision to try and ride. Boon corralled the last zenzen and held it for Mark.

"Let's go, hurry!" he shouted.

Mark grabbed the saddle and hoisted himself up. He got his chest on top and was about to swing his leg over when a klee threw his lasso. The rope hit the zenzen in the head. The loop missed, but the surprised animal panicked and bolted . . . with Mark half over the saddle. The zenzen charged across the wippen field, with Mark clinging on for his life.

"Heeeelp!" he shouted as he bounced along, barely hanging on.

Spader had opened the gate to the jungle. Mark's zenzen ran for it. The only thing that kept Mark holding on was the fear of broken bones. Gunny, Boon, and Courtney trailed behind, helpless. Mark's zenzen charged out of the gate without slowing down. Spader kicked his zenzen forward and galloped up next to Mark.

"I've got you, mate," Spader said as he maneuvered his zenzen alongside. He reached out with one hand and grabbed Mark by the back of his pants. "Hang on tight," Spader ordered.

"Like . . . I . . . haven't . . . been . . . already?" Mark yelled back.

Spader reined his own zenzen in, slowing them both down. The two zenzens came to a stop, but Mark didn't let go. "I think my hands are fused to the saddle," he said.

"Unfuse them," Spader ordered. "We've got to go."

Mark let go and slid off as the other three charged up and stopped.

"What about the weapons?" Courtney asked.

"You want to go back there?" Boon asked.

They all looked back at the wippen arena to see the klees running for them, pulling out arrows, ready to shoot again.

"We'll take our chances without them," Gunny said.

"Up we go, Mark," Spader said. He held out his hand, Mark took it, and Spader hoisted him up behind him.

An arrow shot by, slicing the air between Gunny and Courtney.

"Can we go now?" Courtney asked.

In answer, Boon kicked his zenzen and charged off. The others followed, barely staying ahead of the wave of arrows.

It wasn't the smooth start they had hoped for, but they were on their way to Black Water.

Bobby and Kasha climbed down the last tree before the city and approached the tall gates on the jungle floor.

"How do we get in?" Bobby asked.

"I don't know," Kasha answered. "This is your plan, remember?"

"Don't you have some secret way we can slip in without anybody seeing us?"

"No."

"You're not helping."

"What can I say? I've never had to do this before."

Their argument was interrupted by the sound of an approaching wagon. Bobby and Kasha saw that a group of foragers was returning with their day's bounty. A single zenzen pulled a rickety wagon that was half full of fruit—a pitiful haul. The famine on Eelong was getting worse. Two klees led the wagon on foot. Two more followed. Bringing up the rear was a straggly pack of exhausted gars.

"Walk with the gars. Keep your head down," she ordered, and sprang into the bushes.

"Hey!" Bobby yelled.

Too late. She was gone. Bobby didn't have time to think. If he didn't move right away, the opportunity would be gone. He quickly and quietly ran up behind the group of gars and nudged his way into the center. None of the gars looked at him. They were too tired. Bobby put his head down and shuffled along, pretending to be as exhausted as the others. He peeked forward to see the giant gates to Leeandra opening up. As long as none of the klee guards recognized him as Kasha's gar, he'd be in. Bobby held his breath as they trudged through the gates. He expected an alarm to sound, or a rough paw on his shoulder pulling him back. But neither happened. The klee guards were too busy scanning the jungle in case a tang tried to rush the open gate.

Bobby kept walking with the gars until he heard the giant doors slam shut behind him. After a quick glance to the klee foragers to make sure they weren't watching him, he leaped away from the group and hid behind a thick, flowering bush. He was in.

"Okay, now what?" he whispered to himself.

His answer came instantly. A dark shadow leaped in front of him, hitting the ground and nearly making him scream in surprise.

"That was easy," Kasha declared.

"I thought you didn't have a secret way in?"

"I didn't," replied the cat. "I crawled up the outside of the fence and climbed over."

"And I couldn't have done that?" Bobby asked.

Kasha held out her hand, showing her very sharp claws. "Not unless you've got a set of these."

"Good point. Where can we find Ranjin?"

"It's late. He should be in his home. He lives in the viceroy's residence, above the Circle of Klee."

The two of them made their way cautiously through Leeandra, keeping to the shadows.

"This is odd," Kasha said. "The city is empty, even for this late hour."

As they drew closer to the tree that held the Circle of Klee, the answer to why the city was so quiet, became clear. They heard the sounds of a noisy crowd coming from inside the tree.

"They're having another meeting," Bobby said. "Is there a way to listen in without being seen?

"Maybe," Kasha answered.

They avoided the elevator. Instead they climbed a stairway inside the tree that led to a room behind the stage.

"This is where they dress in their robes before meetings," Kasha explained.

"Are you serious?" Bobby exclaimed. "We're in the lion's den . . . for real."

"Anywhere else we'd be seen," Kasha said. She crept across the room and cautiously peered out a small window that looked onto the circle. Bobby joined her and saw they were quite close to the stage. The big room was once again full of klees. Onstage was the red-robed Council of Klee sitting in their chairs. On one side sat Ranjin in his deep blue tunic, clutching the wooden staff with the carved cat's head on top. Standing at the edge of the stage, addressing the crowd, was Saint Dane in the form of Timber, the cat with dark brown fur, black spots and a long, perfectly combed mane.

"I've seen the truth," Timber announced to the crowd with passion. "Black Water is not a fable concocted by desperate gars. It is real. And as sure as I stand before you today, the beasts who inhabit this secret lair have plans to change the future of Eelong."

The crowd erupted angrily.

"He's not lying," Bobby whispered to Kasha. "The gars could change the future of Eelong. They could save it."

"That's not the way Timber made it sound."

"Exactly," Bobby said. "That's how Saint Dane works."

"Ending this problem would be simple," Timber continued.

"I'm not suggesting a war, or to put klees in harm's way. It would take only two klees to deliver the toxic gas to Black Water while the rest of us remain here in the safety of Leeandra. The brave klees would be out and back in a single afternoon, and our way of life would be preserved."

The crowd murmured in agreement.

"This isn't going so hot," Bobby said nervously.

Ranjin, the viceroy, stood and quieted the crowd. "Explain to me how you came upon this poison gas, Timber," he said.

"It was developed as a fertilizer," was Timber's answer. "The fact that it mutated into a poison was purely by accident . . . a fortunate accident that can mean the difference between life and death."

"Again, the truth," Bobby said. "Except that it mutated on Cloral. He left out that little nugget of information."

"And using it would be the death of Eelong," Kasha added. "He is very clever."

"Forgive me for sounding like a weak old klee, but I have trouble ordering the extermination of so many gars," Ranjin continued somberly.

"Do you have equal trouble allowing the destruction of the klee race as we know it?" Timber countered. "The gars are planning a revolution. If we don't act quickly, we may soon see an animal on the Council of Klee wearing the blue robe of viceroy."

The klees in the crowd erupted with howls and shouts of anger.

"He really is a demon, isn't he?" Kasha gasped.

"The time is coming!" Timber shouted to the crowd. "We can rid ourselves of the gar menace with a single strike. If we take this positive action, our children will never again be hungry, or live in fear."

The crowd screamed its approval. Timber turned his back to

them and looked to Ranjin, expecting a response. Ranjin took a few steps toward the edge of the stage and looked out on the frenzied crowd as they chanted, "Lee-an-dra! Lee-an-dra!" Ranjin lifted his wooden staff and the crowd quieted.

"I have ruled the Council of Klee proudly for longer than any other viceroy in the history of Leeandra," Ranjin began. "I am proud of the work I've done, and I am grateful for the confidence you've had in me. However, I cannot give my blessing to this course of action."

The crowd murmured its disapproval.

Ranjin continued, "I feel that the mass slaying of living creatures, no matter how low a life-form, goes against the very nature of a civilized society. But it is clear to me from your reaction here today, my opinion is not a popular one. It makes me feel that perhaps I've grown too old to make the difficult decisions necessary to lead the klees. Times are changing, and I'm afraid I cannot change with them. That is why I am stepping down from the position of viceroy."

Bobby and Kasha exchanged nervous looks.

Ranjin held out his long wooden staff, the staff that represented the power of the Council of Klee . . . and handed it to Timber, saying, "I am passing it to the next generation of leaders, and to Timber. I can only wish that the course you choose is the wise one."

The crowd went berserk, cheering and screaming its approval. Timber took the staff, barely able to contain a smile. He grasped the staff with both hands and held it over his head in victory. The crowd was in a frenzy.

"No!" Bobby hissed and moved to jump out onto the stage.

Kasha held him back. "Don't be foolish," she whispered. "They'll tear you apart."

Bobby pulled away from her and said, "Don't you realize what happened? Ranjin just handed Saint Dane his next territory!"

Kasha pulled Bobby away from the window. "We've got to go," she ordered. "Before the Council of Klee comes back here and—" She turned for the door and walked straight into . . . Durgen.

"I'm speechless, Kasha," Durgen said. "I was told you were seen coming in here, but I didn't believe you would be so foolish. Imagine my surprise to find it was true. And with your pet gar as well."

"Durgen, please listen to me," Kasha pleaded. "Timber must be stopped. The gars of Black Water are civilized. They have the ability to end our famine."

Durgen stared at Kasha, dumbfounded. He laughed, "You can't expect me to believe that."

"You've known me forever," Kasha continued with passion. "We've fought side by side more times than I can count. I'm begging you, forget what happened the last few days and listen to me. Timber is evil. If he goes through with his plan to destroy Black Water, it'll be disaster for the klees and all of Eelong. He must not be allowed to rule the Council."

Durgen shook his head sadly and said, "I used to know you, Kasha. It pains me to see how you've been duped by these revolutionary gars."

"Revolutionary gars!" Bobby shouted. "Wake up! If Timber wipes out the gar population, the klees will be next!"

"Security!" Durgen yelled.

Instantly four klees pounced into the room. Kasha tried to bolt for the door, but three of them caught her and held her down. It only took one to hold Bobby.

"I know how impatient you are, Kasha," Durgen said. "Your trial will be quick."

"Don't do this!" Kasha shouted.

"You have such sympathy for these animals," Durgen said

with a touch of venom. "I think it's only fitting that you spend your last days among them."

He nodded to the security force. They dragged Bobby and Kasha out of the room.

"Please, Durgen," Kasha begged. "Timber isn't who he claims to be. It's going to be a disaster."

"If it is," Durgen replied, "you won't be around to see it."

Bobby didn't argue. He knew it was useless. The security force dragged them out of the tree, across the jungle floor of Leeandra, and brought them to the absolute last place on Eelong where Bobby wanted to be.

The gar stable where he had been held prisoner.

He and Kasha were thrown in among several dirty gars who huddled in the corners. For Bobby, being back in this putrid prison slashed open all the emotional wounds from his previous stay. He fell to his knees in defeat.

"Welcome back, Pendragon!" came a voice from above.

Kasha and Bobby looked up to see a dark brown cat with black spots looking down on them through the grid. It was Timber. It was Saint Dane. It was a nightmare.

"It seems as though revealing my plans to you made no difference," Saint Dane chuckled. "The only question now is what will happen first? The destruction of Black Water, or your execution?"

## ∞ EELONG ∞
### (CONTINUED)

**"You're making this far too easy,** Pendragon," snarled the cat who was Saint Dane. "It's almost no fun anymore. Almost."

Kasha leaped at the stone wall, desperately trying to climb and get at the villain. The gars cowered in fear. They weren't used to being trapped with an angry klee. Kasha got halfway up the wall, but gravity took over and she fell to the stone floor, landing on her feet.

"What are you?" she shouted at Timber. "Why are you doing this?"

Timber shook his head like a disappointed parent. "I sympathize with you, Pendragon. This new generation of Travelers certainly isn't helping you much. Then again, Seegen wasn't much help either, except to me. His map to Black Water was exactly what I needed. I wish I could thank him. It was such a pity I had to feed him that poisoned apple before he left for Second Earth."

Kasha let out an anguished howl and jumped at the wall. Her claws scraped the stone, but once again, she fell. This time landing on her back with a sickening thud.

Bobby knelt by her and put his hand on her back. "He's trying to get to you," he said softly.

"He's right, my dear," Timber said. "I always know what you Travelers are thinking. It must be quite unnerving." The klee rolled over on his back and licked his paw in a very catlike manner. He was totally relaxed and enjoying himself. Bobby thought he could hear the demon purring, which totally creeped him out.

"Don't listen to him," Bobby said to Kasha calmly. "He doesn't know as much as he pretends to."

"Oh?" Timber said. "Was I right about your friends from Second Earth? I'm sure they're on Cloral right now, searching for the antidote."

Bobby and Kasha exchanged quick glances. Saint Dane may have known about Mark and Courtney, but didn't know how far they had gotten.

"They'll be too late," the demon klee added. "By the time they bring the antidote here, Black Water will be a graveyard and the second territory of Halla will be mine. After that, there's only one thing left for me to worry about."

"What's that?" Bobby asked.

"I've got to decide which territory to visit next! Perhaps I should go to Quillan. It's such an amusing place. Or maybe it's time to drop in on Zadaa so we can be done with that Traveler you have such affection for . . . Loor." Timber rolled over and looked down on Bobby, saying, "I don't suppose you're having second thoughts about joining me?"

"What do you think?" Bobby snapped back, making himself clearly understood.

"Just as well," Timber replied with a dismissive shrug. "I wasn't making the offer. I must leave you now. After all, I'm the Viceroy of Leeandra. I have duties. I must prepare to deliver our welcome home gift to Black Water."

"This isn't over, Saint Dane," Bobby said through gritted

teeth. "No matter what happens here, I'm not giving up."

Timber leaned down through the grid and broke into a wide, evil grin. "Of course you aren't, Pendragon," he hissed. "I wouldn't have it any other way." He straightened up and pounced off, disappearing into the night.

Bobby looked at Kasha. The confident attitude he put on for Saint Dane was gone. "We've gotta get out of here!" he said nervously.

Kasha jumped for the door and shouted, "Guard! Guard! I demand to see Durgen!"

A klee appeared in the window and said, "You have no right to make demands, traitor."

Kasha stepped back from the door, stunned. "Traitor?" She turned to Bobby and said, "They think I'm a traitor."

"I'm sorry, Kasha," Bobby said. "That stinks, but we've got bigger things to worry about." He paced the cell like a caged cat, which was ironic. Kasha once again tried to climb the stone walls, this time with more control. Like a rock climber on a steep pitch, she found crevices to dig her claws into and slowly moved higher. She made it halfway up the wall and Bobby thought she might actually make it. But her back foot slipped, her balance was gone, and she crashed to the ground again.

"I wish you were the one with claws," Kasha said, rubbing her sore shoulder.

"Saint Dane said something at the meeting I didn't understand," Bobby said. "He said two klees could deliver the poison and be back within the afternoon. It takes a full day to get to Black Water. What was he talking about?"

"He was probably talking about using a gig," Kasha answered. "That's what I'd do."

"What's a gig?" Bobby asked.

Before Kasha could answer, they were interrupted by a low, humming sound.

"What's that?" Bobby asked, looking around.

The sound was soft at first, but grew in volume. Seconds later the hum changed to the sound of four musical notes played over and over. It was a sweet little tune that sounded to Bobby like the sound from a flute.

"Have you heard that before?" Bobby asked.

"No!"

"Then what is it?"

The answer came from an unexpected source. The gars who had been cowering in the corners of the cell, stood up. Moments before, they had been groveling like animals. But once the sound began, they seemed to transform. They stood erect, straighter than any gar Bobby had seen outside of Black Water. Bobby and Kasha moved out of the way as the gars walked to the middle of the cell to form a circle. As one, they reached into their rotten clothing and pulled out their amber cubes.

The cubes were glowing.

"Uh-oh," Kasha uttered.

"Yeah, uh-oh," Bobby agreed. "It's starting."

The gars held their cubes out in front of them. The warm, amber light lit up their faces as if they were standing around a campfire. They no longer looked like frightened animals. These gars had a calm come over them that made them seem almost . . . human. The four notes played through a few more times, then stopped. The cell fell silent as the light from the cubes grew brighter. A few moments passed, and a voice came from the cubes. It was the first radio broadcast on Eelong. It was the turning point.

"The time has come," the friendly, female voice said. "Salvation is at hand."

There was a long pause. The gars stared at the glowing cubes. Bobby and Kasha stood in the shadows, watching with wide eyes.

The voice said, "Use the link. Listen to my words and follow my voice home."

Mark bounced on the back of Spader's zenzen as they traveled along a rocky path in the woods. They were right behind Gunny, who was in the lead since he knew the way to Black Water. It was a totally uncomfortable ride for Mark because Spader had the tank on his back and it pushed him even farther back on the haunches of the zenzen. Mark held on to Spader's tank with both hands, with his legs stretched out over the widest part of the creature. He wasn't even sitting in a saddle. Mark didn't want to complain. After all, he was the one who didn't know how to ride. But after balancing like this for several hours, he was ready to scream.

"Can we stop for a second?" Mark finally called out.

Gunny pulled his zenzen to a stop at the end of the trail before it opened into a clearing. The others stopped behind them.

"What's up?" Courtney asked.

Mark jumped off and walked around to get his blood flowing again. "I don't mean to complain," he said. "But I feel like a wishbone trying to balance on a bouncing basketball."

Boon said, "I don't have a tank, you should ride with me."

"Gladly," Mark said. He rubbed his legs one last time, then climbed up on the back of Boon's zenzen. "Thanks," Mark said. "This'll work."

They were about to continue riding when Spader said, "Wait, what's that sound?"

They all listened.

"Sounds like a flute," Mark said.

"There's a farming village ahead," Gunny announced.

They trotted their zenzens out of the woods and across the clearing until Gunny held his hand up, stopping them. Ahead they saw what looked like a swarm of giant fireflies hovering a few feet off the ground. More lights dropped down from the trees and joined them. As a group, the lights moved toward the trail.

"What is it?" Boon asked.

"It's the beginning of the end," Gunny said soberly.

A closer look showed that the lights weren't fireflies at all, but dozens of glowing, amber cubes being carried by gars who were climbing down from the trees to join the others already on the path.

"Link has been activated," Gunny said. "The Advent has begun."

"The . . . that means they're headed for Black Water," Mark exclaimed.

"The gars back in Leeandra must be doing the same thing," Courtney added.

"How do they know the way?" Spader asked.

"The link cubes," Gunny answered. "They glow brighter when faced toward Black Water."

"Like a compass," Mark added. "It's so simple."

"The fuse is lit," Gunny said softly. "Now that the gars are on their way, there's no telling when Saint Dane will unleash the poison."

"But they're not there yet," Spader exclaimed. "Let's pick up the pace, mates!" Spader kicked his zenzen forward and galloped along the trail. Gunny and Courtney followed right behind him.

"You comfortable?" Boon asked Mark.

"No," Mark answered truthfully. "So let's get there fast, okay?" Mark hugged the furry klee, and Boon kicked his zenzen into motion. The goal was clear. They had to beat the gars to Black Water.

In the prison cell, the gars erupted into cheers and hugged one another as if they had just won the World Series. Some were weeping with joy. Bobby and Kasha stayed in the shadows.

"I don't know what they're so happy about," Bobby said. "They're just as stuck in here as we are."

The gar celebration ended, but their adventure was just beginning. As if they had been rehearsing this for a long time, they put away their amber cubes and went to work. Several quickly formed a human pyramid against one wall that reached up toward the ceiling. With practiced precision, they climbed on top of one another, higher and higher, until two gars reached the bamboo grid. Bobby and Kasha watched in fascination as a gar on the ground pulled out a loose stone in the floor to reveal a cache of sharp tools. The gar handed them up the pyramid to the gars on top. Quickly the top gars began sawing through the bamboo grid.

"They were planning this," Kasha declared.

"You think?" Bobby shot back with a touch of sarcasm.

The bamboo bars were cut through in seconds. With a couple of quick *cracks,* two bars fell to create an opening big enough for a single gar to crawl through. One gar poked his head up through the opening to the outside and . . .

"Hey!" came a shout from above. "Get back in there!"

It was a klee guard. But the gar was ready for him. With incredible speed and the advantage of surprise, the gar grabbed the klee and pulled him down through the opening in the grid. The surprised guard plummeted down into the cell head first. He hit the stone floor hard.

Bobby winced.

The klee guard rolled over, moaning. The gars on the floor

quickly jumped him and took his wooden club and lasso. Bobby looked back to the ceiling to see that the gars who had been on the top of the pyramid were gone. They had escaped. The rest climbed down quickly.

"Now what?" Kasha asked.

An alarm sounded. Outside the cell could be heard the sounds of confusion. Whistles were blown. Klees snarled angrily.

"Sounds like those two gars are getting busy," Bobby said.

The gars in the cell gathered around the door as if they knew exactly what was going to happen next. A second later the door to the cell slammed open and a klee guard was thrown into the room, unconscious. The gars didn't waste any time. They fled from their putrid prison, taking their first steps toward freedom.

"We're outta here!" Bobby announced and ran for the door. Kasha was right behind him. They jumped out of the cell . . .

And into a riot. The same escape that the gars pulled off in Bobby's cell was being duplicated throughout the animal pens. Bobby and Kasha saw cell doors being thrown open all around the courtyard. Gars streamed out, screaming like banshees to intimidate their klee captors. It wasn't hard. The gars outnumbered the klees ten to one. Some brave klees tried to fight, but they were overwhelmed by the charging gars as they ran for the corral doors that would lead them to the zenzen pens and out of this prison.

"We should find Ranjin," Bobby said. "Maybe this will convince him to become the viceroy again and—"

"No," Kasha interrupted. "We're past that. We've got to get to the forager operation center."

"Why?" Bobby asked.

Before Kasha could answer, a squad of klees came charging into the courtyard with a huge net, trying to recapture some gars. Several gars were caught in the net, but they weren't giving up without a fight. These were no longer docile animals. They had been waiting a long time for their chance at freedom and weren't about to give it back easily. They tore at the netting, trying to get at the klees, who did their best to contain them. The klees desperately pulled on the net, but the gars refused to be controlled. They tore the netting away from the klees and turned it back on the cats, tying up the frightened cats and trapping them in their own net. With a cheer of victory, the gars ran for the corral doors.

"Follow me," Kasha ordered and ran for the same doors. She kept to the walls to avoid the mayhem. Bobby was right behind her. When they ran through the doors into the zenzen corral, they were confronted with another form of chaos. Gars were stealing zenzens. They had thrown open the paddock and released all of the horselike animals into the corral. Frightened and confused animals barreled around wildly. Gars leaped for them. The lucky ones landed on a zenzen's back and took control. The unlucky ones missed and got trampled by the terrified animals.

Again the klees were outnumbered. They came at the gars with their wooden clubs and with whips, but ended up getting jumped by several gars and beaten with their own weapons. The gars were on a rampage. Bobby wasn't sure if they were motivated by the chance to escape, or by the desperate need for revenge. Probably both. It was a frightening madhouse. He and Kasha tried as best as they could to steer clear of the mayhem and get across the pen and out to Leeandra. But they were like salmon swimming upstream. Hundreds of gars were flooding in the opposite direction.

Bobby and Kasha faced different dangers. Bobby needed to avoid the klees who were trying to recapture gars, and Kasha had to keep away from the gars who wanted to hurt any klee they ran into. Kasha crept past an open zenzen stall. Bobby was following close, and just as he was about to pass the same pen, a frightened zenzen charged out, nearly hitting him. He had to dive back or get trampled. He wasn't hurt, but when he looked up, Kasha was gone. She had kept going, not realizing Bobby wasn't following.

"Swell," Bobby grumbled under his breath. He ran for the gate to Leeandra, but got only a few feet when he was tackled from behind. He was slammed down to the ground, sending up a cloud of dust. He scrambled around to look up at his attacker and saw that staring down on him, pinning his shoulders with his massive paws, was Durgen.

"Here's one gar I'll make sure won't get away," he snarled while lifting his paw into the air. His claws were out and ready for business. Durgen wound up, ready to slash, when a streaking blur appeared and knocked the klee off Bobby. Bobby scrambled away and jumped to his feet. He was sure he had been saved again by Kasha. But when he looked back, he saw that his savior wasn't the klee Traveler. It was a gar. Two more gars jumped Durgen and tied him up with his own lasso. The first gar backed away from the trussed cat and looked at Bobby.

"Thank you," the gar said.

Bobby didn't know how to react. Why was this gar thanking him? He had saved Bobby's life, not the other way around. The gar stood opposite Bobby, breathing hard. This seemed strangely familiar to Bobby. A second later he remembered why. This was the gar Bobby had been forced to fight for the amusement of the handlers. Bobby let him live. Now the gar had returned the favor.

"Go home," Bobby said.

The gar clapped him on the shoulder and said, "Black Water." He ran deeper into the zenzen corral. Bobby never saw him again.

Bobby left Durgen and ran toward the gate into Leeandra. The wooden doors had been torn down by the rampaging gars. Bobby ran into the city to see that the orderly world of the klees had been turned on its ear. Several huts in the trees were on fire. Gars were flooding down by the hundreds, screaming with joy. A few klees tried to contain them, but most had given up and kept to the trees and out of the way. There was no stopping this flight to freedom. Some gars pushed toward the zenzen corral, but most joined the flood toward the giant gates of Leeandra. There were so many gars, it looked to Bobby like the start of the New York City Marathon.

"What happened?" Bobby heard, and spun to see Kasha standing there. "I thought you were behind me."

"I thought you ditched me," Bobby shot back.

"C'mon," Kasha ordered, and took off running, deeper into the city. Bobby followed, running hard to keep up. At first it was tough because of all the fleeing gars. But soon the crowd thinned and they were able to move quickly. Kasha led him to a tree where they jumped into an elevator and shot up.

"Where are we going?" Bobby asked.

"The forager operation center," Kasha answered.

"Okay, why?"

"You want to stop Saint Dane?" Kasha asked.

"Well, yeah."

"This is where we'll do it."

Bobby didn't question her again. He figured the answers would come soon enough. The elevator brought them up to a high point in the tree and dropped them off at another circular balcony.

"You're the one who figured it out, Pendragon," Kasha said.

"I did?"

"You remembered that Saint Dane promised the council that two klees could deliver the poison to Black Water and be back within the afternoon. As far as I know, there's only one way that's possible."

Kasha led him along the balcony until they came upon a tall, arched door.

"Right! You said it was a gig," Bobby said. "What does that mean?"

Kasha said, "A gig is a tool the foragers use when we go to a remote part of the jungle. With a gig we have access to places it would be too dangerous to go on foot, or even to bring gars. It's the only way I know of to get out and back quickly to a place as far away as Black Water."

"Okay," Bobby said. "What's a gig?"

Kasha pushed open the large door and stepped back for Bobby to enter. Bobby peered into the huge, hollow tree to see a room that was five times as large as the Circle of Klee.

"Oh man," Bobby breathed in awe. "You're right. This is exactly how he's going to do it."

Facing Bobby in neatly spaced rows was a squadron of small, two-seater vehicles.

Helicopters.

"**No way!**" Bobby exclaimed as he stepped into the cavernous room that was the helicopter hangar. "You guys can fly?"

"Gigs have been around forever," Kasha explained. "They're simple, really."

Bobby examined the first gig he came to. The body looked like a bumper car from an amusement park, only narrower. There were two seats in an open cockpit, side by side. The body itself looked to have been molded out of a natural resin material that was hard, like plastic. The craft was a deep yellow color. Half of the gigs were the same yellow and the rest were a deep, forest green. Rising up from behind the cockpit like a triple umbrella were three rotors. The blades of each were only a few feet across, rather than a single, large rotor like Second Earth helicopters. There were two more small rotors on either side of the body, below the cockpit. Each of these rotors was encircled by a ring of the same hard, resin material that the body was made out of.

"No wheels?" Bobby asked.

"Rollers," Kasha said, and gave the gig a push. The light little craft moved forward a few feet. "It's powered by the same type of crystals that light the city." She pointed out two clear, crystal panels that were built into the body in front of the cock-pit, and behind. She reached into the cockpit and squeezed a handle in front of the right seat. "Look to the front," she said.

Bobby looked to see a set of pincer claws attached below the rounded nose—they looked big enough to grab a good-size pumpkin. As Kasha squeezed the handle, the pincers opened and closed like a lobster claw.

"We can pluck fruit from the highest treetops and drop it in a container hanging underneath."

"Isn't it kind of . . . dangerous?" Bobby asked.

"It's safer harvesting with a gig than fighting off tangs. Except we can't carry as much as a wagon, so it's not always practical."

"Can you fly this thing?" Bobby asked.

"All the foragers can. There's only one problem with the gigs. The crystals can't store enough solar energy to spin the blades. So we can only fly during the day."

Bobby looked to the far side of the hangar where there was a huge opening that looked out onto the forest. A large platform was built out from the tree, where Bobby figured the gigs were launched. But what he focused on was the sky. It was turning from black to deep blue. Daytime was coming.

"I think this is how they'll do it," Kasha said somberly. "Two klees can fly over Black Water with the Cloral poison attached to the front. It would be simple to fly down low over the village and dump it. We do it all the time with fertilizer over farms. Black Water would be destroyed before they made the turn to come back."

"And Saint Dane and the klees could stay here all safe and comfortable while an entire race was wiped out."

"With the rest of Eelong soon to follow."

Bobby took a few steps toward the giant hangar door and looked out at the early-morning sky. "They can't fly until it gets light?"

"Exactly, which means we don't have much time," Kasha said.

"To do what?"

She gestured to the neat rows of helicopters and said, "Sabotage."

Gunny looked ahead to see the faint outline of the mountains that held Black Water. That was the good news. They were getting close. The bad news was that he could see them at all. It meant daytime was coming and with it, the chance of a tang attack. They had been riding through the night, constantly coaxing the zenzens to gallop, trying to beat the gars who were making their way to Black Water. The animals were at the point of exhaustion and so were the riders. It was a grueling journey.

"Ho!" Gunny shouted, and pulled his zenzen to a stop. Soon the others galloped up and stopped. They were at the point where the jungle began to grow sparse and give way to dry, rocky terrain.

"It's going to be light soon," Gunny announced. "This is our last chance to take a break."

"Gladly!" Courtney shouted and hopped off her panting zenzen. "I've been bouncing so much I think I'm two inches shorter."

Everybody dismounted and stretched. "How much farther, Gunny?" Mark asked as he did a deep knee bend to get the circulation back.

"At this pace I'd say we'll hit the trail into the mountains in about an hour. Then maybe another hour from there until we're inside Black Water."

"We're going to make it!" Spader exclaimed. "Saint Dane won't attack until the gars get there and we're way ahead of them."

"Maybe," Gunny said. "We don't know what he's planning."

Boon added, "And we're not there yet."

"Hobey!" Spader exclaimed. "Let's be positive."

"Okay," Boon said. "I'm positive we're not there yet."

Spader laughed and said to Boon, "I like you, mate. When this is over I want to show you Cloral."

"You sure about that?" Courtney asked. "Can klees swim?"

"No, we can't," Boon answered. "Would I have to swim if I went to Cloral?"

Courtney, Mark, and Spader exchanged glances, and burst out laughing.

"What's so funny?" Boon asked, confused.

Spader answered, "Maybe a trip to Cloral's not such a good idea after all—"

The attack came without warning. A tang leaped from some low bushes just off the trail. It had crept as close as possible before making its move. Its target . . . was Mark.

"Ahhh!" Mark screamed as the beast jumped on his back, throwing him to the ground. The lizard opened its mouth and lunged. But instead of soft flesh, the tang got a mouthful of broken teeth when it clamped on the steel tank.

Boon leaped and tackled the lizard like a linebacker. With one quick move, he lashed at the surprised tang's throat with his sharp claws. The tang didn't stand a chance.

Spader swooped in and pulled Mark to his feet. "You all right, mate?"

Mark's eyes were wide with fear. He was breathing fast, but able to nod and say, "Y-Yeah."

"Back on the zenzens!" Gunny ordered.

Gunny and Courtney mounted up while Spader helped Mark climb onto Boon's animal. They all looked back toward Boon. What they saw made them turn away just as quickly. Boon was backing away from the dying tang, his paw glistening with blood. Tang blood.

"Boon!" Courtney yelled. "C'mon."

Boon kept his eyes on the tang to make sure it didn't jump up and fight to its last breath. A sharp hiss of exhalation told Boon he needn't bother. The tang was finished. The entire event took no more than twenty seconds.

"I . . . I've never killed a tang before," Boon said with a quivering voice. He was truly shaken.

"You picked the right time to start," Spader said. "You saved us all."

"Pull yourself together, Boon," Gunny said with authority. "It's getting light and there are more tangs where that came from. No more stops until Black Water. Yah!" He kicked his zenzen and galloped off. Courtney was right behind and Spader behind her.

Boon climbed onto the zenzen in front of Mark and grabbed the reins.

"Th-Thank you," Mark said. "You saved my life."

"Thank me later," Boon replied, still a little shocked. "We're not done yet."

Boon kicked the zenzen, and they galloped after the others.

*Smash!*

Kasha used a heavy metal tool to crack the crystal power source on the front of a gig. She dug out the broken pieces with the clawlike device, then moved to the back and smashed the rear crystal. Bobby had his own tool and was doing the same to another gig. It was a slow process because the crystal was diamond hard. They had been working for nearly half an hour and had sabotaged only ten gigs.

"It's getting lighter," Bobby announced as he looked out the hangar door. The sky was getting bright. Daylight painted the treetops. It was going to be a nice, clear day, unfortunately.

"Keep working," Kasha ordered. "We don't know when they plan to—"

They both heard the door opening at the same time. Kasha and Bobby ducked down behind a gig and looked to the hangar door. Two klees entered, looking relaxed and casual.

"You piloted the last two missions," one klee complained. "It's my turn in the command chair."

"Who's the senior forager here?" the second klee asked patiently.

"Well, you, but—"

"And who's responsible for the success of this mission?"

"Okay, you are, except—"

"This is history!" the second klee said. "When they write about this day, nobody's going to remember who was in the command chair. They're only going to remember that two hero klees saved Eelong."

"Really?" the first klee asked with a big smile.

"Yes, really," the second answered.

"Yeah, well, I still think it's my turn," the first klee complained.

"Live with it," the senior forager snapped back.

The two klees went to the front row and pushed a yellow gig out of line toward the edge of the launch platform. It was one of the helicopters that Bobby and Kasha hadn't yet sabotaged.

"I know them," Kasha whispered. "They're the two best flyers we have."

"Figures," Bobby said, deflated.

Three more klees entered the hangar. The first was the new viceroy of Leeandra, Timber . . . Saint Dane. He was followed by two klees who struggled to carry a shiny, golden tank. It was the size of the propane tank Bobby's dad had used to fuel their barbeque at home. The tank must have been heavy, because it took two klees to carry it. They got to the end of a row of gigs, turned the corner, and one klee caught the back of his leg on a side rotor. It threw him off balance, and he fell.

"Look out!" the klee called as he let go of the tank.

"Help!" the second klee said in a panic.

Timber reacted with incredibly quick reflexes. He spun around and caught the tank just before it hit the floor. The other klees stood frozen, holding their breaths.

"Sorry," the fallen klee said sheepishly.

"Sorry?" Timber repeated. "You nearly killed every klee in Leeandra and all you can say is . . . 'sorry'?"

The klee looked down, ashamed.

"Leave," Timber commanded. The clumsy klee skulked away. Timber carried the tank the rest of the way himself.

"I think we almost died," Kasha whispered.

"If that's the Cloral poison, we almost did," Bobby agreed.

The two crawled cautiously forward to get a better look at what the klees were doing. They watched as the two pilots took charge of the golden tank and attached it to the pincer claws on the front of their yellow gig. They ran black tubing from the tank and attached it to the body beneath.

"They're setting it up like they're going to spray fertilizer over crops," Kasha whispered.

"Or death over Black Water," Bobby whispered somberly.

When the job was finished, the two pilots stood at attention in front of their new viceroy.

"You must fly into the wind," Timber instructed. "Come in close to the rim of the canyon, drop down low, and release the chemical. One pass will be enough. Do not circle back or you will meet the same fate as the savages below. Understood?"

"Yes. Understood," the pilots answered.

Timber continued, "Once you have passed over Black Water, set your sights on the gars that are traveling toward the mountains." Timber chuckled and added, "They think they have saved themselves by fleeing from Leeandra, but all they've done is separate themselves from the klees so we can cut them down more efficiently."

The klees chuckled at the irony. Timber held out a map. Seegen's map. "The mountain range is vast," he instructed. "Follow this map precisely or you'll miss your target."

The copilot took Seegen's map and said, "Don't worry, Viceroy. I'll get us there." He folded the map and put it inside his tunic.

"After your mission, you will forever be heroes in the minds of klees everywhere," Timber said. "I thank you, and your fellow klees thank you."

"The light is high enough," the commander said. "We can fly right away."

"Not yet," Saint Dane said. "We want to make sure that most of the gars have reached the killing ground."

Bobby felt his stomach tighten. They were talking about mass murder as casually as if they were discussing sports.

"Be ready," Saint Dane said as he turned to leave. "I will return to send you off momentarily." The other klee followed him out, leaving the pilots alone. The two pilots relaxed and smiled.

"We're going to be heroes!" the copilot shouted with giddy enthusiasm. "Will we get medals?"

"Don't start writing any speeches yet," the commander said as he climbed aboard the gig. He sat in the left-hand, pilot's seat. "Let's fly the mission first." He toggled three switches and shouted, "Clear!"

The copilot took a step back from the gig. With a low whine, the three overhead rotors began to turn. In no time they were up to speed and whirring softly. Bobby was surprised at how quiet they were. They sounded more like powerful fans than the helicopters back home.

"Now's our chance," Kasha said as she crept forward.

"Whoa, to do what?" Bobby asked.

"To steal the gig, of course," she said, and tossed her lasso at Bobby. "Take out the copilot," she ordered, and sprang from their hiding place. Bobby caught the lasso awkwardly and followed her.

"Take out the copilot?" he said to himself quickly. "Yeah, right."

As Kasha ran, she reached into her belt pouch to retrieve her lethal disks. The klees had no idea what was coming. Kasha silently flung the first disk, hitting the commander square in the shoulder. He screamed and looked around with surprise.

Bobby ran for the copilot, having no idea what he was going to do. He had never thrown a lasso in his life. He clutched the rope near the three balls. The confused copilot was turning to look back at what all the screaming was about. Bobby figured this was his one shot at catching him by surprise. He flung the lasso. The three balls flew toward the copilot, catching him on the legs and tripping him up. It was the best Bobby could have hoped for.

Kasha quickly threw another disk at the commander and caught him in the other shoulder. The stunned klee struggled to power up the gig, but he was too late. Kasha pounced. She yanked him out of the craft and threw him to the ground.

Bobby didn't know what to do next. He grabbed one end of the lasso and tried to run around the copilot in a desperate attempt to tie up his legs. It was a lame effort. The copilot quickly got his wits back and lashed at Bobby with his claws. Bobby dove away, barely missing being sliced. He was helpless against this deadly cat.

Kasha scrambled into the gig. She was halfway in and already throttling up. The rotors hummed faster, blasting wind across the platform.

"Stop her!" the injured commander shouted.

The copilot forgot about Bobby and leaped for Kasha.

"Kasha, look out!" Bobby yelled.

Too late. Kasha's attention was on the gig controls. She wasn't prepared for the attack. The copilot yanked her out of the seat and with a mighty heave, sent her spiraling backward toward the edge of the platform.

Bobby grabbed the lasso and bolted for her. On the run, he tossed the balls.

"Kasha!" he yelled.

Kasha grabbed wildly at the lasso as the balls flew past her and caught the rope. Bobby planted and held on to the other end, ready to be yanked, praying he could hold on. The rope went tight and Bobby dug his heels in. Kasha pulled back and was saved only two steps before tumbling over the edge. Bobby pulled her back onto the platform, safe. They were instantly hit with a blast of wind. They both looked up in time to see the gig lifting off, with the copilot at the controls. The side rotors that had been parallel to the ground, rotated until they became perpendicular. They whined to life, and the gig shot forward, right for Bobby and Kasha. The two dove for the deck as the gig shot over their heads, barely clearing them. The small helicopter sailed out over the city of Leeandra, throttled up, and was gone.

Kasha and Bobby lay together on the platform, out of breath, staring at the little helicopter as it grew smaller in the distance.

Kasha said, "Do you think the others will make it in time?"

"I don't know," was Bobby's honest answer.

Kasha looked back at the rows of gigs. Bobby saw her eyes sparkle, as if she were hit with an idea.

"Pull a gig out here *now*!" she ordered while getting to her feet.

"What? Why?" Bobby asked.

"We're going after him."

Bobby didn't allow himself to think of all the reasons why this was a bad idea. He ran to the first gig he saw, a green one. He made sure its crystals were intact, then rolled it out onto the platform. When he got near the edge, he saw that Kasha had tied the klee commander up with her lasso.

"Why, Kasha?" the pilot asked. "This is treason!"

"Killing the gars will mean killing off Eelong," Kasha answered. "Timber knows it—that's why he wants to wipe them out." She looked to Bobby and ordered, "Get in."

Bobby obediently sat in the right, copilot seat. Kasha settled into the pilot's seat and toggled the power switches. The overhead rotors began to turn.

"That's insane. Why would he do that?" the klee commander asked.

"Because he's a monster," Kasha answered. "I swear to you, it's true."

The rotors whined faster and the little craft shook.

"How do you know?" the klee asked.

"I've been to Black Water," she answered. "The gars can save Eelong, but only if I can stop the poison from being dropped."

"Can you?" Bobby asked.

"We'll find out, won't we?" Kasha said, and grabbed the joystick between the two seats. She twisted the handle, the rotors whined, and with a slight bump, the gig lifted off. Bobby instinctively held on to the side for support. The craft hovered a few feet above the platform. Kasha toggled a switch and Bobby looked down to see the side rotors rotate into position. Bobby realized that the overhead rotors gave the gig lift, but the side rotors moved them forward.

"Ready?" Kasha asked.

"Always," Bobby answered.

Kasha pushed the joystick forward and the gig shot off the platform, high over Leeandra, in pursuit of the killer gig.

## ∞ EELONG ∞

(CONTINUED)

**The sunbelt had cleared** the horizon. It was full daylight on Eelong.

The riders bringing the antidote tanks to Black Water were close to the end of their journey. They had made it to the rocky, switchback trail that snaked up the side of the steep mountain. Gunny was still in the lead, followed by Boon and Mark, then Courtney and Spader. They were nearly at the crevice that would lead them to the crater of waterfalls. Every rider was exhausted, sore, and still terrified that another tang would attack, but the higher they climbed the more they felt as if Spader was right—they had made it. Looking back down into the barren valley they had just galloped through, they could see the beginnings of the first wave of gars that were still far behind, hours from Black Water.

"We're nearly there," Gunny called back to the others. "It's time to think about what we're going to do once we arrive."

"How about a Jacuzzi?" Courtney shouted. "My butt's killing me."

Nobody laughed.

"Just kidding," she added.

"Boon, stay close to me," Gunny said. "They don't trust klees."

"Understood," Boon said.

Gunny was first to arrive at the split in the rock that led to the narrow fissure in the mountain.

"This is it!" Gunny exclaimed. "Stay in single file. We'll talk on the other end."

Gunny entered the crevice. Boon and Mark were right behind. But as they entered the fissure, something spooked Boon's zenzen. The animal reared up on its hind legs, whinnying out a complaint. Mark grabbed tight around Boon's middle, or he would have fallen off.

"Whoa! Easy there!" Boon coaxed.

"What's the matter with him?" Mark asked.

"I don't know. Maybe he doesn't like tight spaces."

Boon regained control and steered his zenzen into the crevice. Courtney followed, then Spader. They traveled along the tight corridor, trying their best not to scrape their knees against the rocky walls. Boon was having a tough time keeping his zenzen under control. The animal kept shying, not wanting to go farther.

"This is making me nervous," Mark said.

Courtney started to have problems with her zenzen as well. The animal stopped dead in its tracks, refusing to take another step. "C'mon!" she commanded. "Giddyap. Let's go." The animal didn't budge.

Boon and Mark kept moving. Spader stopped behind Courtney and said, "They might be tired. We've been riding them pretty hard."

"I'm tired too," Courtney said. "You don't see me resting. C'mon, zenzen, we're almost there!" She gave the animal a kick, but the zenzen stood firm.

Mark turned around to see they were leaving Spader and

Courtney behind. He called back, "Maybe if you got off and walked him, he would follow—"

Something hit Mark on the top of his head. It didn't hurt, it was only a small pebble that had fallen from above. But it was enough to make him look up to see where it came from. What he saw nearly made him fall off the zenzen.

Looking down on them from high above was a band of tangs. At first Mark was so stunned, he couldn't speak. But when he saw the tangs pushing large boulders close to the edge, his brain kicked back into gear.

"TANGS!" he shouted.

The tangs pushed the boulders over.

Everybody looked up to see an avalanche bouncing down the steep walls toward them. One boulder careened right for Mark. He leaned forward into Boon and the boulder barely missed hitting him in the head, but it bashed into the tank strapped to his back, knocking him off balance. He started to fall off the zenzen, but Boon grabbed him.

Gunny shouted, "Move!" He kicked his zenzen and galloped through the narrow crevice to escape the rockslide. Boon and Mark shot after him. Their zenzen took off so fast that Mark nearly fell off again. More boulders crashed down. Courtney didn't know what to do. If her zenzen decided to go forward, they'd be crushed by the avalanche. But there was no reverse on a zenzen. She was trapped.

"Jump off!" Spader ordered.

Too late. The boulders hit the ground in front of them, causing Courtney's zenzen to rear up. Courtney wasn't ready for that, and she tumbled off the animal, hitting the ground, tank first. The hard tank dug into her back, making her squeal with pain. Spader jumped off to help her scramble away from the tumbling boulders.

The tangs continued pushing heavy stones down on them, but that wasn't the worst problem. Courtney's zenzen was out of control. It kept rearing up in the narrow space, whinnying and stomping in fear as the boulders crashed down in front of it. Courtney and Spader were in way more danger of being stomped by the frantic zenzen than hit by a boulder. The animal reared up, twisted its body, and came down facing Spader and Courtney.

"Get up!" Spader yelled, and pulled Courtney to her feet. The zenzen charged, desperate to escape from the avalanche. Spader pushed Courtney roughly to the side. They flattened themselves against the rock wall, bracing to be slammed by the rampaging zenzen. The animal brushed by them and ran straight into Spader's zenzen! Both animals wrestled and whinnied. Spader's zenzen went up on its back legs, using its front legs to defend itself. Spader and Courtney were trapped between two huge boxing animals on one side, and an avalanche of boulders on the other.

Courtney's zenzen would not be denied. It fought through Spader's zenzen, knocking the poor animal onto its back, and galloped back toward the entrance of the crevice. Spader's zenzen kicked frantically at the air. It finally rolled over onto its feet, with its head pointed toward the entrance. Once the animal realized it was back in control, it took off, leaving Spader and Courtney alone in the crevice . . . with more boulders thundering down on them. Dust was everywhere, making it hard to see.

"We have to move!" Spader shouted over the roar of falling rocks. Courtney nodded. She had her wits back. She and Spader backed off, away from the danger zone, out of harm's way. Moments later it was over. The thunderous, grinding sound stopped. Spader and Courtney, bruised and cut, stood still, waiting for the thick cloud of dust to settle.

"It was a trap," Courtney said, coughing. "They were waiting to drop those rocks on us!"

"No worries," Spader announced. "They missed."

The dust settled, revealing a sight that was hard for even Spader to put a positive spin on.

"Yeah, they missed all right," Courtney said in a shaky voice. "But I don't think they were trying to hit us."

So many boulders had fallen, the crevice was completely sealed off. There was no way Courtney and Spader could follow the others. Black Water had been cut off from the rest of Eelong.

"Now what do we do?" Courtney asked.

That's when they heard one more sound. It was as if one more boulder had fallen. But this one was behind them.

"Uh-oh," Courtney said. "Are they gonna try to trap us in—"

Courtney and Spader slowly turned around to see that it wasn't a boulder that had fallen. It was a tang. It stood with its teeth bared, blocking the way out.

Gunny pulled his zenzen to a stop, still inside the crevice. Boon and Mark stopped right behind him.

"It was the t-tangs!" Mark gasped. "If I hadn't looked up . . ." He let the thought trail. They all knew what would have happened. It would have been ugly. They all looked back into the crevice, expecting Spader and Courtney to ride up.

Gunny jumped down from his zenzen and said, "Wait here." He squeezed past Boon's zenzen and jogged back the way they had come. It didn't take long for him to arrive at the dead end that had been created by the avalanche. He knew there was no getting past, so he hurried back to the others.

"Wh-Where are they?" Mark asked.

"The crevice is sealed off," Gunny answered.

Mark's panic was rising. "A-Are they okay?" he squealed. "Courtney's zenzen wouldn't move! She could have been—"

"I don't know what happened, Mark," Gunny said firmly. "I think there's a good chance they're okay, but stuck on the other side."

"You know what that means?" Boon said nervously.

"Yes," Gunny said as he remounted his zenzen. "It means we're down to only one tank of the antidote and it's not doing any good out here. Let's go!"

Gunny gave his zenzen a kick and trotted toward the crater of waterfalls.

Boon looked back to Mark and said, "Guard that tank with your life."

Mark was faced with a frightening truth. The future of Eelong and quite possibly of Halla, was strapped to his back. His stomach did a flip.

Bobby and Kasha quickly gained altitude as they flew out of Leeandra. Bobby had a flashback to the last time he was in the air. It was with the pilot Jinx Olsen on First Earth, in her rickety Coast Guard seaplane. He was happy that the gig was actually a lot more comfortable than his last flying experience. The rotors overhead whirred, but it was a pleasant sound, like a fan. It was nothing like bouncing under the seaplane engine of 1937 Earth. He and Jinx had to scream at each other to be heard over that monster. By comparison, the gig was like hovering along in a skilift gondola. He saw that as Kasha moved the joystick, all five rotors moved slightly. The positioning of the rotors is what steered the gig. In all, it was a very pleasant experience . . . except for the fact they were in pursuit of another gig that held enough poison to destroy a territory.

Bobby hadn't said much since they took off. He wanted Kasha to concentrate on flying. But now that they were under way, things needed to be said.

"You remember the route to Black Water?" Bobby asked.

"No problem," Kasha answered.

Bobby nodded. He really didn't want to ask the next question.

"What are we going to do when we catch up?"

Kasha made a few adjustments and checked over the side to see if they were on course. Bobby wasn't sure if she was busy, or didn't have an answer. Or didn't want to give the answer she had.

"You did your job, Pendragon," Kasha finally said.

"What do you mean?" Bobby asked.

"I mean you convinced me. It took a while, but I get it. I know we have to stop Saint Dane."

"That's good. So . . . how do we do it?"

Kasha cleared her throat. While still looking ahead she said, "I'm going to catch that gig and crash it. The poison will do whatever damage it does to the jungle, but at least it won't be used on Black Water."

Bobby nodded. "Okay, good plan. But . . . how? This gig doesn't have any weapons, does it?"

"Let me ask you something, Pendragon," Kasha said, avoiding the question. "How important is this? I mean, if the worst happens and Saint Dane destroys Eelong, what does that mean for the rest of Halla?"

Bobby shrugged. "I don't exactly know. I think Saint Dane got more powerful after wrecking Veelox. I can only imagine that he'd get stronger still if he won on Eelong, and it would be that much harder to stop him."

"And if he isn't stopped? I mean, if he gets what he wants and takes control of Halla. What does that mean?"

"I've asked myself that question a million times," Bobby said. "I've only heard bits and pieces, so I don't even come close to understanding it all, but I believe there's a more powerful force at work in Halla. It's a positive force. I think it's what makes things right. Don't ask me what I mean by that, because I'm not sure myself. But I think that's what the war with Saint Dane is all about. I believe he's trying to destroy whatever it is that makes things right. It's way bigger than the problems of any one territory. I think if Saint Dane takes control, there will be no more order. I'm not even sure what that means, but it won't be good."

Kasha thought about his answer for a moment, then said, "So if you're right, stopping Saint Dane is the single most important task in the history of everything."

Bobby nodded. "I guess you could say that."

"Then it's worth dying for," Kasha said.

Bobby snapped her a look. In that one moment he came to a realization. Kasha may have been the most difficult Traveler to convince of the importance of their mission, but now that she understood, she saw it more clearly than any of them. Nobody had put it out there as plainly as that. Kasha wasn't in it for the adventure, or for revenge, or because she wasn't given a choice. Of all the Travelers, Kasha now believed in their mission so wholeheartedly, she was willing to die for it. The question immediately sprang to Bobby's mind: Was he willing to do the same?

"Does this mean you don't know how to bring down that gig without getting us killed?" Bobby asked nervously.

Kasha looked ahead. Her eyes narrowed. "There it is," she announced.

Bobby scanned the sky. He soon made out a small speck of yellow in the distance. They were catching up.

* * *

The tang had Spader and Courtney backed into a dead end. They both smelled the putrid odor it gave off when it was ready to feed.

"Two on one," Courtney said.

"Could be worse," Spader said bravely.

Three more tangs dropped down from above, making Courtney jump back in surprise.

"Just got worse," Courtney said weakly.

The tangs stood in twos. They slowly stalked forward, their vile smell making Courtney gag. "Is it gonna end here?" she asked, her voice cracking.

"If it does," Spader said, "it won't be because we didn't give 'em a go."

With one quick move, Spader reached both hands back over his head, grabbed the shoulders of his harness, and pulled it up and over, tank and all. He bashed one end of the tank on the ground, hard enough to smash off the nozzle. A jet of high-pressure liquid shot from the broken valve like a portable water cannon. The chemical spewed at the tangs, making them scream and back away. The surprised beasts waved at the rush of chemicals with their lizard arms . . . and fled.

"We got 'em!" Spader shouted, and took off in pursuit. Courtney followed right behind. Spader kept the spewing tank aimed at the squealing lizards. When the tangs reached the mouth of the crevice, they kept going and jumped right off the ledge, tumbling down the side of the steep mountain to escape from the attack. Spader kept the high-pressure tank aimed down at them until the chemical finally ran out.

"That was awesome!" Courtney yelled. "How did you know it would work?"

"I didn't," Spader answered with a chuckle. "Lucky us."

Spader tossed the empty tank aside and said, "Except now we're down to two tanks."

"Wrong," Courtney corrected. "We're down to one tank, and Mark's got it. The tank on my back's no good if we can't get it to Black Water."

Spader put his hands on his hips and looked back into the crevice. He stared into the opening, then his eyes traveled up the craggy face of the mountain.

"What are you thinking?" Courtney asked.

"Those wogglies got up there somehow."

"You're kidding?" Courtney said. "You want us to climb over this mountain?"

"Well, like you said, this tank's not doing any good out here."

Courtney glanced up at the mountain, imagining what it would be like to climb up the rocky face. She had been to the climbing gym back in Stony Brook many times, and was pretty good at it. But that was always with a rope for safety. And a big thick pad on the floor.

"If you can't make it, I can go myself," Spader said.

Courtney Chetwynde never, ever backed down from a challenge. She wasn't going to start now.

"I'll lead," she said, and began climbing up the craggy face.

## ∞ EELONG ∞
### (CONTINUED)

**The small, yellow gig** grew larger in front of Bobby and Kasha as they sped to catch up. Bobby looked to the ground below where thousands of gars were making their way along the route to Black Water. They looked to Bobby like an army of ants, all moving toward the same goal. Bobby nudged Kasha and pointed down. She looked and nodded. "It really is incredible" was all she could say.

Far ahead, the gray mountains that held Black Water were in sight.

"Don't worry," Kasha said. "We'll catch him."

"Then what?" Bobby asked.

Kasha didn't answer. Bobby truly felt as if her plan was to pull a kamikaze stunt and crash into the gig to knock it out of the sky. The idea terrified him, of course, but he was torn. If this was the only way to stop Saint Dane, then maybe this is what had to be done. He could only hope that Kasha was a good enough pilot to land their gig once it was crippled by a collision. One thing he knew for sure: There were no parachutes on board. He wouldn't be able to bail out the way he did with Jinx Olsen's plane. If the gig went down, they were going down with it.

They were near enough to the yellow gig so that Bobby could see the klee pilot was looking down, probably to check Seegen's map against the terrain. Bobby figured that the pilot was so intent on carrying out the mission, he never thought there might be somebody chasing him. Kasha kept their gig directly behind him so there was less chance of him catching sight of them if he looked off to either side.

"I don't want to have to crash into him," Kasha said, as if reading Bobby's mind. "But I will if I have to. There's a chance we'd survive, but I wouldn't bet on it."

"Me neither. Is there a Plan A?"

"The gigs have a tool package underneath," Kasha explained. "That's where we keep the net for harvesting and a few other cutting tools."

"Can we get to them?" Bobby asked.

"No," Kasha answered, smiling slyly. "But we can dump them. I wonder what would happen if they landed on his main rotors?"

Bobby smiled with relief. Kasha had a nonsuicide plan after all. If they could fly over the gig and dump the tool package, the netting and the other tools might foul the klee's rotors.

"I like this," Bobby said. "Can you get on top of him? He's going pretty fast."

"I can catch him anytime I want," Kasha said. "I was waiting until we hit . . . that." She pointed out in front of them to the huge lake they had detoured around on their previous trip to Black Water. "It's better if he crashes in the water than on a bunch of innocent gars."

Bobby chuckled. Kasha knew exactly what she was doing.

"Strap in," she ordered. "This might get bumpy."

Bobby quickly slipped the safety straps that were built into the seats around his shoulders. Kasha did the same. A quick look down told them that the klee pilot was nearing the shore of the lake. They would have a short window of opportunity when he was flying directly over the water. After that he'd be back over the streaming mass of gars on the far side. They had to make their move now. Kasha reached for the throttle. Bobby felt the gig shudder. He had thought they were flying under full power. He was wrong. The little gig shot forward with such force that Bobby was pressed back into his seat. Kasha nosed the craft up and they rose higher. Timing was going to be critical. They needed to fly directly over the other gig, which was pretty dangerous in itself, and drop the tool package before the klee pilot realized what was happening. Then they had to hope it would do enough damage that the gig would crash into the lake.

Bobby held his breath. Kasha maneuvered their gig closer to the klee. They were only a few yards behind the yellow gig when Kasha toggled a switch on her control panel. Bobby heard a mechanical sound, along with a bump. It reminded him of the sound he heard on passenger planes when they dropped the landing gear. He figured that Kasha had opened up the tool hatch below.

Kasha eased their gig forward. She flew with one hand on the joystick and the other on the control panel, fine-tuning the rotors. Bobby's heart leaped. They were actually going to do it!

But there was one thing Kasha hadn't counted on—the sun-belt. The band of light in the sky was behind them. As soon as they got above and behind the yellow gig, their shadow crept over their quarry. The klee pilot saw the looming shadow and spun around in surprise. Busted.

"Drop the tools!' Bobby shouted.

"We're not over him!" Kasha shouted back.

The klee pilot instantly dove down and away to his left. Kasha didn't panic. She dove right after him. The quick drop made Bobby's stomach lurch. Now it was a true chase, because their prey was on the run. The klee pilot was good. He made quick, evasive maneuvers to try and ditch them. Kasha matched him, turn for turn. They were like two jet pilots in a dogfight.

"Don't lose sight of him," Kasha ordered.

The klee pulled out of his dive into a steep and sudden climb. Kasha wasn't fooled. She stayed with him, pointing the nose of their gig to the sky. The sudden change pushed both of them back into their seats with such g force that it slammed Bobby's head into the back of the seat. It felt like a ten-ton giant just sat in his lap. The only thing he could move were his eyes.

"Look!" he shouted.

The klee's gig suddenly began to fall straight down, as if he had lost power. It plummeted toward the ground, twisting in the air like a feather.

"What happened?" Bobby shouted. "Is he crashing?"

"No, he cut the rotors," Kasha said. "He's good. I'm better."

Kasha didn't use the same maneuver. Instead she went into a power dive that was so sudden, it made them both go weightless. Seconds later, after Bobby fought back the urge to puke, he looked around for the yellow gig. It was nowhere to be seen.

"Where is he?" Bobby shouted.

Kasha had lost sight of him too. She looked around quickly, then shouted, "There!"

Sure enough, the yellow gig was back under power. It had righted itself far below them and was headed in the opposite direction, back toward Leeandra.

"He's going back," Bobby shouted. "He's giving up!"

Kasha watched the yellow gig, trying to guess her quarry's thoughts. "He knows he can't outmaneuver us with that heavy tank in front."

"Exactly! That's why he's going back."

They both watched as the yellow gig dropped low to the

ground, barely at treetop level. The side rotors twisted to the horizontal position, parallel with the body, which slowed the gig down considerably.

"Why's he slowing down?" Bobby asked.

"Because he's not going back," Kasha exclaimed. "He's setting up for a run."

"What does that mean?"

"He's getting in position, as if he were going to spray fertilizer," Kasha said.

"But why would he—" Bobby didn't finish the question because the answer hit him a second later. The klee pilot knew he didn't stand a chance against Kasha, so he was going to make sure he was successful in at least one part of his mission. He was going to go back and dump the poison on the thousands of gars on the ground.

Gunny trotted out from the crevice on his zenzen and looked out over the beautiful crater of waterfalls. He was followed right behind by Boon and Mark.

"Wow" was all Mark could say as he got his first glimpse of the wooded valley and the seven waterfalls that fed the lake at the bottom. The sunbelt had made its way up over the rim of the crater, bathing the lake in light, making the waterfalls sparkle.

"It's more beautiful than Pendragon described it," Boon said. "Which one is the entrance to Black Water?"

"Second waterfall from the right," Gunny answered.

"Should we wait for Courtney and Spader?" Mark asked.

Gunny frowned. "We can't risk it," he answered. "We don't know how much time is left. I'm sorry, Mark."

Mark was pained, but chose not to argue. The thought of leaving Courtney behind was horrible. A wave of guilt washed over him for having gotten her involved in the first place, but he pushed it out of his head. He knew he couldn't look back, at least not yet. They had to get the antidote to Black Water.

"Stay close together," Gunny said. "We're almost there."

He coaxed his tired zenzen off the rocky ledge and down the steep slope. Boon and Mark followed close behind. The two animals were near exhaustion, so they let gravity do most of the work. They descended along the grassy slope and into the trees that became more and more dense as they drew closer to the lake.

"Once we get into Black Water," Gunny said, "we should find Aron. We've got to explain to him the danger that's headed this way and get him to—" Gunny never finished the sentence.

The tang didn't let him.

With no warning the beast leaped from the thick underbrush and knocked Gunny off his zenzen.

"Gunny!" Mark shouted as the tall Traveler hit the ground.

Boon instantly leaped off his zenzen to help Gunny. On his way down he slapped the animal on the backside and shouted "Yeahhh!" The animal bolted forward, with Mark still on board.

"Get out of here!" Boon shouted.

Mark lunged forward to grab the saddle so he wouldn't fall off and break his head. He took one quick glance back to see Boon leap at the tang. But turning around threw him off balance and he nearly fell again. He turned back forward as the zenzen charged through the thick forest, out of control. He dug his fingers under the front of the saddle in a death grip. Branches whipped by, tearing at his arms and legs. The zenzen may have been exhausted, but surprise and fear gave it a second wind. Mark knew he had to get control before he was knocked off, or thrown off, or crashed into a tree. He gripped the saddle even tighter with his right hand and tentatively let go with his left. He reached forward to grab the reins, but they bounced freely on the zenzen's neck, out of reach. If he was going to get them, he was going to have to move forward and let go of the saddle.

The zenzen flew past a tree branch so closely, it hit Mark's shoulder, nearly knocking him off. It was the last bit of convincing he needed. He had to act. He gripped the saddle with his hands and let go with his sore legs, pulling himself forward and into the seat. He locked his legs around the animal and let his hands leave the saddle, lunging for the reins. His chest hit the zenzen's neck, snapping his head back and making him nearly bite through his lip, but he grabbed hold of the reins with both hands.

"Whoa!" he screamed, and pulled. The zenzen didn't stop. Mark pulled harder, but the zenzen kept galloping through the forest. Finally Mark wrapped the reins around each of his hands, got a tight grip, and yanked both straps as hard as he possibly could. "I . . . said . . . WHOA!"

The zenzen bucked, whinnied, and finally jogged to a stop. Mark sat in the saddle, exhausted but still in one piece. He felt the tank to find it hadn't moved. He was still in business. He glanced around to find he was in the middle of an unfamiliar forest. He had no idea how long his wild jaunt had gone on, but he knew he was nowhere near the spot where Gunny was attacked. Looking up, he saw that he wasn't far from his destination—the base of the waterfall to Black Water. Mark knew his mission. He had to get the tank to Aron.

But he also knew that Gunny may be hurt. Along with Boon. And if he was being totally honest with himself, he'd admit that he was terrified to go ahead without them. So rather than press on toward the waterfall, Mark grabbed the reins the way he had been watching Boon do for hours. The zenzen responded. It was too tired not to. The animal turned around. Mark gave it a kick, and they trotted back toward the spot where they had been attacked.

Courtney scrambled up the rock face as quickly and expertly as if she were climbing a jungle gym at home. There were plenty of places for her to find handholds and spots to wedge her toes. Her soft, rubberlike Cloral swim shoes were almost as good as climbing boots. They weren't much protection, but they allowed her to feel the rock and find safe purchase.

Spader climbed beneath her, doing his best to keep up without taking dangerous chances. He didn't have the experience that Courtney did, but what he lacked in technique, he made up for in strength.

"There's only one rule," Courtney shouted down to him. "Keep moving and don't look down."

"That's two rules," Spader said.

Both tried not to think how a single misstep would be disaster.

"How did the tangs get up here? I thought they couldn't climb?" Courtney asked.

"Maybe there's an easier way up," Spader offered.

"And we're not on it because?"

"Because we don't have time to look for it," Spader answered quickly. "Less talking and more climbing, please."

"Don't climb directly under me," Courtney warned. "Just in case."

Spader knew what she meant. If she fell, there was a good chance she'd knock him off the face too.

"That's three rules," Spader said. "Now you're getting bossy." He stayed right under her. If she fell, he was going to do his best to save her . . . and the tank of antidote on her back.

"We've still got a shot," Kasha said.

She dropped the gig so quickly, Bobby felt as if they were in a free fall. She clutched the joystick. Her eyes locked on her prey.

The yellow gig was flying low over the lake, lining up for its killer run at the gars. Without the use of its side rotors, the yellow gig flew slowly. Kasha nosed their gig down and picked up even more speed. The force made the fragile craft shudder. Bobby nervously gripped the side of the cockpit, though he knew it was a worthless precaution.

"You can pull out of this dive, right?" he asked nervously.

"I think," Kasha said. "I've never tried it before."

Bobby swallowed hard.

Kasha continued, "The trickier part will be timing the drop. If we miss, we won't get a second chance."

"Then don't miss," Bobby said flatly.

Kasha gave him a quick sideways glance, then focused back on her quarry. The yellow gig with the poison was still over the lake, flying very low. The klee pilot kept looking back over his shoulder to see how close his pursuers were.

"If he dumps the poison at that level, he'll kill thousands," Bobby said.

"Hang on," Kasha shouted.

She leveled out the gig, once again pushing them both back into their seats with the added g force. She jammed the throttle to its limit. They screamed over the lake, gaining quickly on the yellow gig. Bobby glanced down at Kasha's furry hand on the joystick. It looked as if she were battling to keep it under control.

"Little more . . . little more . . . ," she coaxed.

The yellow gig was nearing the shore. In seconds it would be over land, and soon after, it would be in range of the gars.

"See that lever below the console?" Kasha asked between gritted teeth.

Bobby looked to see a dark, curved lever sticking up from the floor.

"Yeah," Bobby answered.

"When I say pull . . . pull."

Bobby reached down and grabbed hold. "Got it," he said.

The klee in the yellow gig was focused on his deadly mission. Bobby glanced ahead to see they were getting so close to the gars, he could see their faces. He knew that in a few seconds, they could all be dead. Kasha pushed the joystick forward. The last bit of speed put them directly over the klee's gig.

"Pull!" Kasha yelled.

Bobby yanked the handle and heard what sounded like a clatter of metal, followed by a horrifying, wrenching sound. Kasha pulled back on the stick and they climbed quickly. Bobby struggled against the force of the climb to turn around to see if they were on target.

They were. The rotors of the yellow gig were torn apart by the pile of tools that landed directly on them.

"Bull's-eye!" Bobby shouted.

The net got wound up and caused two of the rotors to seize. It wasn't total destruction, but enough to make the gig about as flight worthy as a watermelon. The klee struggled out of the cockpit and leapt for his life. Bobby figured he didn't want to be anywhere near the spot where the poison landed. The klee plummeted straight down as the gig sailed forward. The klee hit the water first. Bobby saw him go under, then surface and swim frantically for shore. A few seconds later the gig splashed down. The damaged rotors continued to turn, frothing up the water like an outboard motor. The craft quickly flipped on its side and sank.

Kasha and Bobby sailed over the startled gars, who pointed up at them like they were some kind of prehistoric flying beast. The happy gars had no idea their journey had nearly ended in death. Kasha banked around and flew back over the spot where the gig sank. The only sign of it were the gentle ripples that spread out across the lake.

"Do you think the tank ruptured?" Bobby asked.

"Maybe not," Kasha answered. "They're pretty strong."

Bobby finally took a deep, relieved breath and said, "You're good."

Kasha gave him a smug smile. "Do you think it's over?" she asked. "Was that Saint Dane's play?"

Bobby thought long and hard about the answer. "It could be," he said. "But whenever I think Saint Dane is done, he isn't."

"So what should we do?" Kasha asked. "Back to Leeandra?"

"He's still got nine tanks of that poison," Bobby said somberly. "Back to Leeandra."

Kasha banked the gig and set a course back to the jungle city.

"Let's hope we don't have to go through that nine more times," she said as she gunned the throttle.

Mark was taking a crash course in learning how to ride a zenzen . . . self-taught. After struggling to figure out how to steer the animal and nearly hitting into more than one tree, he finally got the knack. It helped that the zenzen was too exhausted to put up much of a fight. Between riding in circles for a while, and not being sure of where he was in the first place, it took Mark a good half hour to find his way back to where they had been ambushed by the tang.

The only sign of the attack was a shredded piece of cloth lying on the jungle floor. There was no Gunny and no Boon. Mark sat on the zenzen, feeling more alone than he had felt in his entire life.

"This wasn't the way it was supposed to be," he said to himself.

Mark had dozens of different fantasies about what it would be like joining Bobby in the fight against Saint Dane. None of them involved being left alone, lost, fearing that Courtney was dead, with the last hope for saving a territory strapped to his back. As he sat on the zenzen, he truly didn't know what he was going to do. He came dangerously close to crying.

That's when he heard a sound. It had been there before; he just hadn't registered it. It was a steady, white noise kind of sound. Mark looked to where it was coming from to see the top of a waterfall rising above the trees. *The* waterfall. Second from the right. Mark took a deep breath and blew it out to calm himself. He took hold of the reins and gave the zenzen a kick. Using his newly found expertise, he directed the animal to carry him on the final leg of his journey.

To Black Water.

# ∞ EELONG ∞

## (CONTINUED)

**Kasha and Bobby were** cruising high over the jungle, headed back toward Leeandra when Kasha spotted something far in the distance, just above the horizon.

"Do you see that?" she asked.

Bobby strained to look and saw what appeared to be a dark line in the sky running parallel to the ground, headed toward them.

"Yeah, what is it?"

"Birds, maybe," Kasha answered. "We'll fly above it." She pulled back on the control stick and the gig ascended quickly.

The dark line moved steadily forward. Kasha flew high above to make sure there was no danger of a collision. They both strained to look down at the mysterious line as it drew closer, trying to recognize what it might be.

"Could be a flock of rookers," Kasha said. "But they look bigger than . . . uh-oh . . ."

"What uh-oh?" Bobby asked quickly.

"Those aren't birds."

They were close enough to the mysterious line to see that it wasn't a straight line at all. It was a formation of gigs, with one in the lead and the others fanning out like an arrow behind it. They flew with military precision, equally spaced. As Bobby and Kasha flew high over them, they counted nine gigs. Light from the sun-belt reflected off the golden tanks that were attached to the front of each.

"Oh man," Bobby said, stunned.

"Nine," Kasha said. "That's not a good number."

"It's a bombing run," Bobby uttered. "They're going to unload on Black Water."

"Pendragon, I can't knock nine gigs out of the sky!"

Bobby thought fast. "Can we beat them to Black Water?" he asked.

"I think," Kasha replied. "They're loaded, so they're flying pretty slow."

"Then we gotta get there," Bobby exclaimed.

"And do what?" Kasha asked.

"We've got to make sure the others get there with the anti-dote," Bobby answered.

"I'm not sure how, but . . . okay," Kasha said. She banked the gig into a one-eighty and set them on a course to Black Water.

Mark walked his zenzen toward the base of the towering waterfall, stopping close enough to feel the spray on his face. He was exhausted and sore and more than a little bit scared as he swung his leg over the zenzen and dropped to the ground for the last time.

"Thanks, guy," he said to the animal, and rubbed its head. "I'm not gonna miss you."

He tried to remember Bobby's description of how to enter the hidden portal to Black Water. Walking around the pool of water at the base of the falls, he scanned the surface, looking for the stepping stones below. He didn't see anything, until he thought to shade his eyes from the bright sunbelt. Instantly he saw a faint outline under the water about the size of a pizza. He tentatively stepped on it, put his weight down, and didn't get wet. He found the path. A few cautious steps later he found himself walking across the water, behind the waterfall, and into a cave.

"Welcome!" a voice shouted from the dark.

Mark nearly peed in his pants. He stood rock still, fighting the urge to turn and run as a shadowy figure walked toward him. It was a gar who was so genuinely thrilled to see Mark, he held his arms out wide and hugged him.

"You are the first!" the gar exclaimed. "Where did you come from?" The gar spoke slowly and clearly, as if talking to a child. Mark realized the guy was expecting a slew of gars who weren't used to normal conversation. He decided not to freak the gar out, so he spoke slowly and simply, pretending to have trouble finding the words.

"Uh, thank you," Mark said slowly. "Need help. Must see Aron."

The gar gave him a surprised look. "Aron? How could you know Aron?"

Mark had the answer, but didn't want to give it. "Must see Aron," he repeated.

The gar looked at Mark's clothing and frowned. He was expecting the incoming gars to be wearing rags, not slick-looking swimskins.

"Please!" Mark begged. "Important!"

The gar nodded. "All right, come with me," he said.

Score. Mark was on his way.

Courtney crested the summit of the rocky cliff and collapsed in exhaustion. Her arms were screaming from the exertion. Her hands had long ago gone numb from the constant climbing, and her legs were cramped, but she had made it.

Spader followed soon after and fell down beside her.

"I suppose I should have offered to take the tank," he said.

"Why?" Courtney asked. "Don't you think I'm capable?"

"No, no," Spader assured her. "Just thought it might be polite."

The two sat together, catching their breaths.

"So you've got a thing for Pendragon, aye?" Spader asked.

Courtney shot Spader a look and said, "That's a strange thing to ask now."

Spader shrugged and said, "Just staying loose."

Courtney said, "Define a 'thing.'"

"Weren't you two all lovey-do before Pendragon became a Traveler?"

"If you mean do we like each other, yes," Courtney said. She thought for a moment and asked, "Does he talk about me?"

"All the time. He thinks you're natty. I can see why."

Courtney looked closely at Spader. She thought he looked pretty handsome sitting there in his black swimskin with no sleeves, his long dark hair blowing around in the wind. She shook the thought away. "Seems to me he's got a thing for that other Traveler girl," Courtney said coyly. "What's her name? Oh, yeah. Loor."

"Define a 'thing,'" Spader said.

Courtney answered with a coy smile.

"Couldn't say one way or the other," Spader answered. "But if you ask me, he'd be crazy to bother with anybody else if he's got a girl as spiff as you. I mean, you risked your life to help him. That's special, it is."

Courtney shrugged. "You've helped him more than once yourself."

"And the other way 'round. But that's my job, being a Traveler and all."

"Yeah, well, I'm not here just for Bobby. I kind of wouldn't mind if Saint Dane were stopped before messing around with Second Earth."

"I hear you, mate," Spader said, and stood up. "Let's get back on that."

He looked in the direction they needed to go. Ahead was a long, flat mountaintop that could pass for the surface of the moon. It was barren and scattered with huge boulders.

Courtney said, "There could be tangs hiding behind any one of those rocks."

"I suppose," Spader answered. "But they'd have to be pretty desperate to be looking for food up here. I've got no worries."

"Good," Courtney said with a smile. "Then you go first."

Spader gave her a wink, and started on his way.

Kasha and Bobby flew low over the barren valley on the last leg of their flight to Black Water. The idea was to keep a watchful eye out for Gunny and the others, in case they had run into trouble and needed help transporting the antidote. Every second was precious. They were able to fly much faster than the squadron of killer gigs and would arrive long before they made their lethal bombing run. The question was, would it be enough time to save the gar village? They were rapidly approaching the mountain range. Kasha took a quick look up to the sky to get her bearings.

"We've got a problem," she announced.

Bobby didn't see anything out of the ordinary. "What do you mean?"

"I told you how the gigs are powered by the crystals, right?"

"Right."

"I also told you the crystals couldn't store power. They need constant light."

Bobby took another look at the sky. The problem suddenly

came clear. Thick, gray storm clouds formed a line across the sky. It was moving toward the sunbelt.

"Are you serious?" Bobby exclaimed. "What happens when the clouds cover the sunbelt?"

"First we lose light," Kasha said. "Then we lose power."

Bobby glanced ahead to the mountain range. It suddenly looked a lot farther away than it had a few seconds before.

"Can we make it?" he asked.

Kasha gunned the throttle. "We're going to try."

Mark was led by the gar through the tunnel into Black Water. After having read Bobby's description of the village, he felt as if he knew the place. Still, seeing it firsthand was an incredible experience. He was brought to the vast building that was called the Center. The whole way he kept his eyes down, hoping that his gar guide wouldn't ask him any questions. All he wanted to do was get to Aron and tell him what danger the village was in, so they could figure out how to use the antidote he had strapped to his back. The gar guide brought Mark into a giant room that was full of empty cots. Bobby had described this room. It was where many of the gars would spend their first night of freedom.

"Wait here," the gar instructed. "I'll get Aron."

"Thank you," Mark said, and sat on a cot. It was like heaven to finally get the chance to rest. He started to take off his harness with the tank, but decided against it. He wasn't there to chill and get comfy. This was business. A few minutes later a door opened on the far side of the room. The gar had returned, along with another gar. This new gar was short, with long black hair that fell to his shoulders and no trace of a beard—Bobby's description of Aron.

"Hello," the gar said. "I am Aron. How is it that you know me?"

Mark debated with himself about how honest to be. He

quickly decided the time for being cagey was over.

"My n-name is Mark Dimond," Mark began. "I'm a friend of Gunny's."

Aron and the other gar straightened up. Mark wasn't sure if it was because he had mentioned Gunny's name, or because they were surprised to hear a gar from the outside speak so fluently.

"You know him, right?" Mark asked.

Aron nodded tentatively.

"G-Gunny and me and some others were attacked by tangs, and I don't know where anybody is now. There was a rockslide in the crevice leading into the mountains, and it's totally blocked off. You've got to send some gars out there to clear it, or nobody's gonna get through."

Aron gave the other gar a quick look, and a nod. The gar hurried off. Hopefully, Mark thought, to get somebody on the job of clearing out the crevice.

"This is why you had to see me?" Aron asked.

"There's more," Mark answered. "Black Water is in danger. Big-time. The klees are going to attack as soon as the gars from the outside arrive."

"We are prepared for that," Aron said. "Black Water is well protected."

"N-Not from this kind of attack, it isn't! They're going to unload a bunch of poison that will kill every living thing in Black Water." Mark pulled off his tank and held it out to Aron. "But the chemical in this tank can stop it. We've come all this way to bring it to you and help you save Black Water."

Aron looked at the tank curiously. Mark wished he could think of a better way to describe the danger to him. If he couldn't convince Aron, Black Water was doomed.

"Gunny knows about this?" Aron asked.

"Yes, and two other friends of mine, and a klee."

On hearing the word "klee," Aron perked up.

"You brought a klee to Black Water?" he asked.

"Yes. His name's Boon. He's a friend. Gunny would tell you the same thing, but I don't know where he is. I don't know where anybody is! Please, I'm telling you the truth. We've g-got to figure out a way to use this antidote."

Aron nodded. "Come with me."

"Excellent!" Mark said with relief. He gladly followed Aron out of the room.

Mark was beginning to think their plan was going to work. They had made a treacherous journey that might have cost the lives of Courtney, Gunny, Spader, and Boon, but against all odds, he, Mark Dimond, had made it through and delivered the antidote. But Black Water wasn't safe yet. They still had to figure out a way to use it. Mark tried not to worry about the others. There would be plenty of time for that. He set his mind to the challenge of using the antidote.

Aron led him out of the room full of cots and down a long corridor to a closed door where a gar stood in front.

"Please," Aron said. "This way." He motioned for Mark to enter the door. The gar standing there opened the door, and Mark went inside. What he saw made him catch his breath.

It was Boon, wrapped in a net.

"Boon?" Mark shouted.

*Slam!* The door closed behind them. Mark spun around to see Aron looking at them through a small window in the door.

"Please forgive me," Aron said. "I do not understand what you are doing here, and right now it does not matter if you are friends or foes. I cannot let anything interfere with the Advent. Once we are settled, I will return for you, and we will discuss your intentions. Perhaps in a few days."

Mark put his face up to the window and screamed, "No! We d-don't have a few days!"

Aron shrugged an apology and left. The gar outside the door didn't turn around. It now came clear to Mark why he was standing there. He was a guard.

"Uh, little help, please?" Boon said. The brown klee was on the floor, tangled up in the net, unable to move.

"A-Are you okay?" Mark asked.

"I've been better," Boon answered.

"What happened to Gunny?"

The thick band of gray clouds was getting dangerously close to the sunbelt. Bobby and Kasha were flying low to the ground in case their power suddenly cut out. But they were nearly at the mountain range.

"Decision time," Kasha said. "Land now, or risk flying up and over."

Bobby glanced at the clouds and said, "We're not going to do any good out here."

"Then we go!" Kasha said. Without wasting another second, she pulled back on the joystick and they shot straight up. They were so close to the craggy wall of rock that Bobby could almost touch it. Higher and higher they climbed, racing time. Finally they cleared the peak and Kasha jammed the throttle. They jumped forward and flashed over the top of the mountain. Bobby kept his eye on the clouds. The leading edge was about to reach the sunbelt.

"Hurry, please," Bobby said.

The gig flashed over the bleak, flat mountaintop, racing the line of clouds. They were nearly at the far side when Bobby felt the gig hesitate.

"What's that?" he shouted.

"We're losing power," Kasha said in a calm voice.

Bobby looked up to see the cloud was moving faster. Sunlight was still coming through, but it was filtered through the leading edge of the storm.

"We won't lose it all at once," Kasha said. "But when it goes, it'll go fast."

Bobby held his breath as the gig shot off the mountaintop. They were flying high above the ground once again. The gig lurched. The whine of the rotors was noticeably slower.

"I've got to put down," Kasha announced.

She dropped the nose and descended so quickly, Bobby's ears popped. He feared they were descending faster than gravity would have pulled them. But he wasn't the pilot so he kept his mouth shut.

A second later the line of clouds covered the sunbelt, and the gig lost power.

# ∞ EELONG ∞
### (CONTINUED)

**The green gig** whistled through the sky, plummeting toward the ground, past Courtney and Spader, who were carefully making their way down the steepest part of the inside of the crater.

"Whoa, what was that?" Courtney yelled, almost losing her grip.

"A flying machine!" Spader announced.

"More like a falling machine," Courtney corrected. "Could it be Saint Dane's attack?"

"We'll know soon enough," Spader answered.

"Really, how?"

"We'll be dead."

Kasha struggled with the control stick to keep the gig upright and prevent a tumbling free fall. The craft bounced back and forth as she expertly coaxed every last ounce of lift from the failing rotors.

"If I can keep us upright, we've got a chance," Kasha said, sounding strained.

"The lake!" Bobby shouted. "Can you put us down there?"

"Maybe," Kasha said. "But I can't swim."

Bobby shot her a quick look and said, "Let's hope we have that problem." The gig abruptly fell a few more feet, sending Bobby's stomach into his throat. "Seriously, we've got a better chance landing on the lake than crashing into a tree or a rock . . . or the freaking ground."

"All right," she said nervously. "But if we land safely and I drown—"

"I won't let you drown," Bobby said with such conviction that Kasha actually smiled.

"I believe you," she said, and guided the falling gig toward the lake. They were buffeted back and forth inside the small cockpit so violently, Bobby feared his arms would be too bruised to swim. Kasha forced the gig into a tight spiral, desperately trying to slow their descent so the craft wouldn't break up on impact. Bobby glanced to see they were over the lake. The water was coming up fast. Very fast. It was going to be a rough landing.

"Brace yourself," Kasha yelled.

The gig slammed into the lake with such force, Bobby felt like his brain had broken loose inside his head. Kasha had maneuvered the craft so that they landed square on its bottom, like a space capsule splashing down. The impact caused a huge wave of water to shoot out all around them. Bobby thought sure the force of the landing would drive them so deep, they'd be swamped. But the gig bounced back. Like a cork, it lifted back to the surface, still in one piece. Bobby and Kasha were still in one piece too.

"You okay?" Bobby asked, shaken.

"I think. You?"

"Yeah," Bobby shouted. "You did it!"

The gig tipped over and water poured into the cockpit.

"Sort of . . ."

"Get me out of here, Pendragon!" Kasha screamed. It was

the first time Bobby saw her scared. He quickly unlatched his seat belt and reached to release hers. Water filled the gig quickly. Kasha panicked. She scrambled over Bobby to get out, forcing his head underwater. He felt her fur brush over his head and prayed that one of her claws wouldn't lacerate him. Bobby was good in the water. His junior lifeguard training was permanently ingrained. Once Kasha cleared the gig, he resurfaced and looked around the sinking craft for something to help her float.

"Pendragon!" she screamed, gulping water. She was floundering, which meant more trouble for Bobby. If he wasn't careful, they'd both drown. The seats of the gig were padded. Bobby took a chance and yanked one loose. A quick test showed that it floated.

"Kasha here!" Bobby shouted, and held the pad out to the drowning klee. "Grab on to this. Relax. It'll help you float."

She grabbed the pad like it was her last chance at life, which it probably was. It wasn't a perfect flotation device, but it definitely gave her enough confidence that her panic came down a notch.

"It's okay," Bobby said soothingly. "Hold it against your chest. Lean back. It'll keep you up."

Kasha did what she was told and was soon floating on her back, staring up at the sky, trying to calm herself.

"I'm going to tow you in, okay?"

"O . . . kay," Kasha said weakly.

Bobby didn't want to get too close to her. If she panicked again, he'd be in trouble. So he spun her around and towed her in by pulling on her back paws. They weren't far from land. It only took a few minutes to get to where it was shallow enough for them to stand. Kasha awkwardly got her balance and dragged herself out of the water, her fur dripping, and collapsed on the sandy shore. Bobby fell down next to her, exhausted.

"You're a great flyer," Bobby said, gasping for breath. "But you gotta work on the swimming."

They both burst out laughing. It was a complete release from the terror that had gripped them for the last leg of their flight.

"Thanks," Kasha said. "I'll remember that." She looked to the sky and said, "This is good. The gigs can't fly until the cloud passes. I'm sure they put down back in the valley. That gives us a little more time."

Bobby stood up, did a quick look around and said, "There's our waterfall."

Courtney and Spader slid down the last steep portion of the rocky wall and took their first steps inside the crater of waterfalls. They found themselves a few feet from the opening of the crevice they would have come through if they hadn't been ambushed by the tangs.

"We're not dead," Courtney said. "I guess that wasn't the attack."

"Then we've still got time," Spader said as he scanned the inside of the vast crater. "There it is!" he said, pointing.

"Second waterfall from the right," Courtney declared.

*Boom!*

A huge explosion erupted from inside the crevice, knocking Courtney and Spader to their knees. Seconds later, a cloud of dirt blew out of the narrow fissure.

"What the heck?" Courtney coughed.

"Somebody's trying to clear the rockslide," Spader said. "I think the first gars have arrived."

"Or Saint Dane and his klees," Courtney said.

"Either way, we gotta go."

The two got back on their feet and ran down the steep incline of the crater, headed for the waterfall.

It took Mark a long time to untangle Boon from the net. He wasn't good at tying knots. He was worse at untying knots. As he worked, Boon told him what had happened in the crater of waterfalls.

"I jumped on the back of the tang and pulled him off Gunny," he said. "But that monster was ferocious. I mean, he was crazed."

"Is Gunny okay?" Mark asked.

"I don't know," Boon answered. "I slashed at the lizard and caught him across the arm. It jumped back, and I yelled at Gunny to run. The tang started after him, but I jumped on its back and bit it in the neck. Man, do you know how bad tang tastes?"

"Uh . . . no."

"I hope you never find out."

"I'm not worried," Mark said.

Boon continued, "I clamped onto its neck and it kept thrashing around, trying to throw me. But I wouldn't let go. He threw me around real good, too. I finally got so tired that he spun me off."

"Did he attack you?"

"No, I must have hurt it pretty bad, because it ran off into the jungle. I figured Gunny would try to circle around to the waterfall, so that's where I went. Big mistake. I found the cavern behind the falls, but the gars jumped me. I told them I was with Gunny and we were there to help protect Black Water, but they didn't want to hear it. They tied me up in this net and threw me in here. Can you believe it? I'm here to save them, and they threw me in here like I'm a criminal."

"I know the feeling," Mark said.

"What are we going to do, Mark?" Boon asked.

Mark untied the final knot and pulled the net off Boon.

"We're gonna get outta here" was his answer.

* * *

Bobby and Kasha worked their way through the forest at the bottom of the crater, headed for the waterfall that would lead them into Black Water. Bobby kept glancing up to check the movement of the clouds. The storm that had first been their enemy and forced them to crash was now buying them time. As long as the sunbelt stayed covered, the poison-carrying gigs would be grounded.

"The clouds are moving," Bobby announced. "But I can't tell how fast . . . oops!" Bobby's attention was so focused on the sky, he wasn't looking where he was going and tripped over something. He stumbled and hit the ground.

"Look out!" Kasha screamed, and leaped in between Bobby and the thing he had tripped over. "Tang!" she growled, ready to attack.

Bobby jumped up quickly, ready to run. But one look back told him he had nothing to fear. It was a tang, all right. A dead tang.

"I thought it was a rock," Bobby said with relief.

The two crept closer to the dead tang. It was covered with multiple slashes, with one seriously nasty gash on the back of its neck.

"Those are the marks of a klee," Kasha announced. "I'm thinking Boon's been through here." She reached down and touched the lizard's body and said, "It didn't die long ago."

Bobby felt something wet drip on his cheek. He brushed it away and said, "It's starting to rain."

"Good," Kasha said. "Maybe the storm will be around for a while."

Another drip fell on Bobby's cheek. He wiped it off and looked at his hand to see . . . blood. "Hey, I'm bleeding!" he exclaimed.

Kasha gave him a quick look and said, "No, you're not."

"Then what's this?" Bobby said, holding out his hand with the bloody smear. "I must have cut something when we crashed."

Another drip of blood fell on his hand. Kasha and Bobby both realized it didn't come from Bobby, it came from up above. They both slowly looked up to see . . .

Dangling high in the trees was a net trap, with its victim still inside. Bobby dodged back to get away from the dripping blood. The trees above them were so thick it was hard to see the trap, let alone what was caught in it. Bobby strained to see. Once his eyes adjusted, his heart sank. There was a gar arm poking out from the net. A dark gar arm.

"Gunny!" Bobby shouted.

Kasha sprang for the tree that held the trap, climbed up by digging her claws into the bark, and reached the rope that held the suspended net. She slashed at it with one claw, while holding the rope with the other.

"I'll lower him down," she announced as she slowly let the rope slip through her hands. Bobby stood beneath to guide the net down gently and lay Gunny on the ground.

"Help me get this off!" he shouted to Kasha.

She jumped down from the tree and slashed at the net, freeing the unconscious Traveler.

"Gunny!" Bobby called. "C'mon, man. It's me!"

Bobby felt Gunny's neck, checking for a pulse. Kasha held up Gunny's arm that was missing the hand. "He was cut," she said. Bobby saw that the arm had a few deep tang cuts on it, which accounted for the dripping blood.

"He's alive," Bobby announced. He gently tapped Gunny's cheek. "Wake up, Mr. Van Dyke, we need you."

Gunny stirred. His eyelids fluttered and opened. He looked around with confusion until he focused on Bobby.

"No offense, shorty," Gunny croaked. "But I was kind of hoping

I'd wake up in my bed at the Manhattan Tower Hotel."

"Sorry, we're not done here yet," Bobby replied with a relieved smile. He helped Gunny sit up while Kasha used some rags to dress his wounds.

"Are you hurt anywhere else?" Bobby asked.

"Nah. I got a pretty good headache, though."

"What happened?" Kasha asked as she worked.

"We got jumped by a tang," Gunny explained. "Mark and Boon and I. Boon saved my life. He pulled that monster off me and cut it up pretty good."

"Yeah, no kidding," Bobby said, pointing to the dead tang.

Gunny looked at the body of the lizard and shook his head. "Violent place, this Eelong."

"Where are the others?" Kasha asked.

"Boon sent Mark off on the zenzen toward Black Water. He told me to run. I couldn't do much to help him, so I did. I tried to circle around toward the waterfall, but the tang was tracking me. Those beasties must like the way I taste. The tang jumped at me; I backed off and stepped right into the trap." Gunny chuckled. "Never thought I'd be so happy to do something so stupid. I must have banged my head when I hit the ground, I don't remember. But it pulled me up and away from that beast. Last thing I remember is looking down to watch it leaping up at me. But I was out of reach. Then I guess I passed out."

"He must have bled to death trying to get you," Kasha said.

"Serves him right," Gunny said.

"What about Courtney and Spader?" Bobby asked.

Gunny frowned. "The tangs caused a rockslide in the tunnel leading here, Bobby. I can't say if they were hurt, or trapped outside."

"Neither!" came a familiar voice.

Bobby, Kasha, and Gunny looked over to see a welcome sight: Spader and Courtney jogged toward them through the trees.

"You can't stop a couple of intrepid types like us with a couple of rocks and a mountain, no sir!" Spader said with a wide smile.

Courtney ran right to Bobby and gave him a hug. Bobby was more than happy to hug her back.

"Are you okay?" Bobby asked.

"I am now," Courtney answered. "Was that you in the helicopter?"

"Yeah, nice entrance, aye?"

"Where's Mark and Boon?" Spader asked.

"I don't know," Gunny answered. "In Black Water, I hope."

Kasha said, "We're running out of time."

Bobby pulled away from Courtney and got back to business. "Here's the deal. Nine helicopters are grounded back in the valley, loaded with the Cloral poison. As soon as the clouds clear, they'll have the power to take off and make their run on Black Water."

"We lost one tank of the antidote, mate," Spader announced. "Couldn't be helped."

Kasha said, "Without Mark, we've only got one tank left."

"Can you walk, Gunny?" Bobby asked.

Gunny struggled to his feet. He was weak, but determined. "You don't think a little conk on the head and a couple of cuts is going to slow me down, do you? Follow me!"

The team was reunited, sort of. Gunny led them on the final leg of their journey through the crater of waterfalls to the entrance to Black Water. They arrived at the second waterfall from the right, following Gunny across the underwater path of stones. Bobby was the last of the group to step behind the waterfall. He took one last look at the sky to see the thick clouds were still covering the sunbelt. No gigs could fly. But he also saw something new . . . the trailing edge of the large, dark cloud. Behind it was clear blue sky.

The clock was ticking.

## ∞ EELONG ∞
(CONTINUED)

**Boon stood on a chair** to examine the window of the small room where he and Mark were being held captive. "This room wasn't built to be a prison," he declared. "I think I can pry this hinge off with my claw."

"Do it," Mark whispered. He was standing guard at the door to make sure the gar outside wouldn't see them trying to escape.

"What do we do once we get out?" Boon asked as he worked.

"One problem at a time," Mark answered.

"Welcome!" exclaimed the gar behind the waterfall when he saw Gunny and the others approach. "You're home now, you've got nothing more to worry about!" The gar froze when he saw that one of the new arrivals was a klee.

"Klee!" he shouted. Instantly ten more gars appeared, all carrying spear guns.

"It's all right," Gunny assured him. "You know me, my name is Gunny. We've been here before. So has the klee."

The gar was suspicious, until Gunny held up his handless arm. "Remember now?" Gunny asked.

The gar relaxed a little and waved off the other gars. "I

remember," the gar said. "You were with Aron."

"That's right," Gunny said. "We're friends. All of us."

"You realize that the Advent is under way," the gar guard said. "Soon there will be thousands of gars arriving. If they see a klee, they might not enter."

Gunny kept eye contact with the gar. He spoke softly, but forcefully. "Everything will be fine, but you must let us enter. We are on an important mission to make sure the Advent succeeds."

Bobby knew that Gunny was using his Traveler powers of persuasion.

"There's a problem with the Advent?" the gar asked worriedly.

"Not if you help us," Gunny continued. "We need to get to the Center. Can you bring us there?"

The gar's head shook slightly, as if he needed to jiggle the idea around inside until it landed right side up. "Yes," he finally said. "I can help." He turned to the other guards and commanded, "Take my post. I will lead our friends to the Center."

Gunny looked to Bobby and winked.

Bobby said, "You're really getting the hang of that."

Gunny said, "It helps that the gars are simple people."

"Come!" the gar commanded. "Follow me." He walked quickly into the tunnel that led to Black Water, followed by Gunny, Bobby, Spader, Courtney, and Kasha.

"You have a plan?" Bobby asked Gunny quietly.

Gunny put a finger to his lips to shush Bobby. "I'll explain once we get there. No sense in causing a ruckus."

Bobby nodded in understanding. He realized that telling the gar that Black Water was in danger of being wiped out by a poison from the sky might cause enough of a panic to slow them down, and anything that slowed them down wasn't good. The group walked through the narrow, dark tunnel until they arrived at the entrance to Black Water.

"Hobey!" exclaimed Spader when he got his first view of the hidden village. "All this for us?"

He was looking at hundreds of gars gathering on either side of the path that led down to the village. It was like they were getting ready for a parade.

"I think they're here to greet the gars," Bobby said.

A little blond girl who looked no more than five, with beautiful blue eyes, ran up to Bobby and handed him a single, white flower. "Welcome to Black Water," she said sweetly. "We've been waiting for you."

"Thank you," Bobby said, taking the flower.

Spader chuckled and said, "There you go! Maybe it's a little bit for us too."

"We should hurry," Gunny said to the gar who was leading them.

They traveled quickly down the path, past the assembled gars. It was a festive atmosphere with music playing and gars cooking food on either side of the road. Most of the gars backed away from the path when they saw Kasha, but Spader tried to relax them by smiling and waving, as if he were the grand marshal of the Macy's Thanksgiving Day Parade. Many gars waved back, others even cheered as if welcoming returning heroes.

"You should be a politician," Courtney said.

"You're right!" Spader answered. "What's a politician?"

Bobby and Kasha were more concerned with the weather. They kept glancing up at the sky as the trailing edge of the dark storm cloud grew closer to the sunbelt.

"Whatever we're going to do," Kasha said, "we'd better do it fast."

The gar escorted the group through the town to the Center. "Here you are," the gar announced. "Do you need more help from me?"

"No," Gunny said. "Thank you. You should get back to your post."

The gar smiled broadly and said, "It's a very exciting day, isn't it?"

"You have no idea," Courtney said sarcastically.

The gar didn't know what she meant, so without a word he jogged off.

Bobby looked up to see the storm was moving quickly. "We don't have much time," he said. "When that cloud clears the sunbelt, we're done. We'd better figure out a way to use this antidote right now."

"I already know how to use it," Gunny said.

"Really?" Courtney exclaimed.

"I'm surprised you didn't figure it out yourself, shorty," Gunny said. "You and Kasha were here. You saw their irrigation system."

Bobby and Kasha exchanged confused looks. They had no idea what Gunny was talking about.

"Remember when you first got here?" Gunny asked. "When we were walking into the village—"

"The sprinklers!" Bobby exclaimed. "On the light posts."

"They have sprinklers on light posts?" Courtney asked.

"What's a sprinkler?" Spader asked.

Gunny walked to a tall light post and tapped it, saying, "Black Water thrives on the river water that runs through the village. They built a vast, underground watering system that channels the river water to the entire valley."

"I remember," Kasha exclaimed. "The water came from the poles."

"Exactly," Gunny said. "There are thousands of outlets like this one. Every square inch of Black Water can be reached and watered by the mist that comes from the irrigation system. It's like they create their own rain."

"It's brilliant!" Spader declared. "Can we send the antidote through this system?"

"I'm counting on it," Gunny answered. "The trick will be to time it so that Black Water is being sprayed just as the poison is dropped. If this antidote is as powerful as you say, it should act like an umbrella and make the poison harmless."

"You're a genius!" Courtney shouted, and threw her arms around Gunny. "We did it!"

Gunny shook his head and said, "We haven't done anything but get here. Now we've got to feed the antidote into the system."

"You know how to do that?" Bobby asked.

"No," Gunny answered. "But I know who does."

Gunny led the group into the Center and back to the large greenhouse room. As they entered, Bobby and Kasha took a quick look up to the glass ceiling to see the hole Saint Dane smashed open when he escaped in the form of a bird.

"I was hoping I had imagined that," Kasha said soberly.

Gunny led them through the rows of plants growing on vir-loam, to a distant corner of the room, where one whole wall was taken up by a series of pipes and valves.

"Irrigation control?" Bobby asked.

"Yup," Gunny answered. "They got somebody manning this all the time. Let's hope he didn't take the day off for the Advent."

Gunny left the group to go in search of the gar who ran the irrigation system. Courtney took the tank off her shoulders and gently placed it on the floor.

"I gotta be honest," she said. "I didn't think we'd make it."

"Mark *didn't* make it," Bobby said.

Courtney frowned. She had been worried about Mark ever since they split up.

"Neither did Boon," Kasha added.

"If anything happened to them . . . ," Bobby said, but didn't finish the thought. The idea of his best friend getting hurt made Bobby's heart ache.

"First things first, mate," Spader said to Bobby. "Once we're done here, we'll find them. I promise you."

Bobby nodded, but wasn't any less worried.

"Everybody, I'd like you to meet Fayne," Gunny said as he approached them. He was leading a woman who looked no more than twenty years old. But being that the gars of Black Water all looked young, she could have been any age. She was small, with short black hair. She looked to Bobby like someone who was used to hard work. Her rough hands and strong arms were a dead giveaway. "Fayne is on duty today," Gunny explained. "She's going to help us."

"Yeah," Fayne said, none too happily. "Biggest day in the history of Black Water and I'm stuck in here." She stood with her hands on her hips and her feet planted. Fayne was full of no-nonsense. But as tough as she was, when she spotted Kasha, she quickly backed off.

"Whoa, klee!"

"It's okay," Gunny assured her. " Kasha is a friend of Aron's. She's here to help the gars."

Fayne kept a suspicious eye on Kasha. "Never saw a klee who gave one tick about gars."

"I'm special," Kasha said impatiently. "Can we move along here?"

Courtney handed the antidote tank to Gunny. Gunny addressed the group, saying, "I was explaining to Fayne how there's concern that the new gars might be carrying dangerous bacteria or viruses that would infect Black Water." Gunny winked at them, asking them to play along.

Fayne said, "I thought about that too! I mean, they live like animals. They could have all sorts of diseases."

"That's why we need this tank hooked up to the irrigation system. When the gars arrive, we can send this . . . this . . ."

"Disinfectant?" Bobby offered.

"Right, *disinfectant* through the entire system. It's very mild, but it will kill any germ that might cause trouble."

Gunny handed the tank to Fayne. Fayne examined it suspiciously and said, "You say Aron wants me to do this?"

"He's very concerned that the Advent goes smoothly," Bobby offered. "And he wants everybody to be safe."

Gunny looked Fayne right in the eye and used his most convincing Traveler voice to say, "It's very important that you feed it into the system right now. If you don't hurry, it will be too late. Can you do that?"

They all watched Fayne to see if she would accept the ruse.

"Sure," she said with a shrug. "Don't want none of them germs getting us sick or nothing."

Everyone breathed a sigh of relief as Fayne took the tank to the irrigation controls. Spader went with her, just to be sure everything went well.

"We're almost there," Courtney said, barely containing her glee.

Bobby stepped away from the group and looked over the vast room full of plants that were growing in air. For the first time since he set foot on Eelong, he felt as if he had a little bit of control back. It was a relief, yet strangely disturbing to him.

"What's the trouble, shorty?" Gunny asked, walking up to him. "We're about to save Eelong and knock Saint Dane back down a peg or two. You should be happy."

"I am, but I'm worried about Mark," Bobby answered.

"Try not to," Gunny said. "I'll bet Boon is watching out for him right this very minute."

Bobby nodded. "And I'm worried about the future."

"Why's that?"

Bobby looked up to the hole in the glass ceiling. "Have the rules really changed, Gunny? I can't stop thinking about what Uncle Press said. We weren't supposed to mix the territories."

"I thought we went through this," Gunny said. "If Saint Dane can do it, why not us?"

"I know, but what if that's the whole point? We're the good guys. We're supposed to do things the right way. I mean, when is it okay to break the rules? When it's important enough? But who's to say what's important?"

"I think saving a territory is pretty important," Gunny said. "I hate to bring up a sore subject, but you remember the *Hindenburg*. If we had saved that ship, it would have been doomsday for Earth."

"This is different," Bobby said quickly. "The *Hindenburg* was *supposed* to crash. Who knows? Maybe Black Water is supposed to be poisoned?"

Gunny didn't have a reply to that.

Bobby continued, "What I'm saying is that if we start playing on Saint Dane's level, I mean *really* playing on his level, where will it end? What else will we have to do in the name of stopping him? If we have to keep doing things that aren't right, does that make us as bad as he is? Is that the way things were meant to be?"

A dark, worried look crossed Gunny's face. Bobby's words had struck a frightening note of truth.

"She's ready!" Spader announced. "Let's put Saint Dane out of business." He led them all over to the irrigation controls.

"We're gonna beat him with seconds left on the clock!" Courtney said to Bobby.

Bobby didn't react.

All eyes went to Fayne, who was adjusting the antidote tank. The tank itself was lying on its side, underneath a panel that had a series of valves and gauges. Fayne had attached a heavy, metallic tube to the nozzle.

"Is this going to work?" Bobby asked abruptly.

"Sure," Fayne answered confidently. "I've never seen a valve like this, but I made a few adjustments. The seal is solid. Are you sure there's enough juice in there to do the job? I mean, the tank is pretty small."

"No worries, the antidote is very powerful," Spader said.

"Antidote?" Fayne asked.

"Disinfectant," Gunny said quickly. "Fayne, can you release a small amount to make sure it's all hooked up properly?"

"It is," Fayne said.

"Humor me," Gunny said more forcefully.

Fayne shrugged and said, "Whatever you want. I just do what I'm told." She stood up to the control panel and twisted a few heavy levers.

"What're you doing?" Courtney asked.

"Opening up the valves so the entire system is activated. That's what you want, right?"

"It has to reach all of Black Water," Gunny said.

"And that's what it'll do," Fayne assured him. "Here we go." Fayne took hold of a large, black lever and turned it from left to right.

Nothing happened.

Fayne stared at her gauges with a frown. She reached forward and flicked her finger on one gauge to unstick it. The needle didn't budge.

"This doesn't make sense," Fayne said. She flipped a few more levers and tapped a few more gauges. Her frown deepened.

"What's the trouble?" Gunny asked.

"Hang on," Fayne snapped. She left the control panel and pulled the tank out from underneath. She lifted it up on end and unscrewed the metallic hose. The others exchanged nervous looks. Fayne removed the connector and examined the tank's nozzle.

"Ah! Here's your problem," she announced. "There's a crack at the base of the nozzle."

"A crack?" Courtney shouted in dismay.

"It was fine when we left Cloral," Spader said. "Nothing happened to it since."

"But it did!" Courtney said nervously. "It got hit with an arrow on the wippen field. And, and, I landed on the tank when I fell off the zenzen during the rockslide. I got hammered! It could have damaged the nozzle!"

"Can you fix it?" Gunny asked.

"Sure," Fayne answered.

"See?" Spader said. "No worries."

"But it won't do no good," Fayne added.

"Why not?" Courtney asked.

Fayne answered by unscrewing the nozzle and throwing it to Courtney. "Because your tank's empty. The juice inside leaked out through that crack. I hope you got another one because there ain't nothing in here."

They all exchanged stunned, helpless looks.

Something caught Bobby's eye. It was on Kasha's face. Something was happening that didn't make sense. Kasha's black fur had suddenly changed color. He stared at her for a moment, not comprehending what he was seeing, until Kasha lifted her head and looked to the ceiling.

"Oh, no," Kasha whispered.

The truth hit Bobby hard. Kasha's face hadn't changed color. The change happened because she was suddenly bathed in light. Light from the sunbelt. The greenhouse was soon aglow with bright light that shone down through the crystal ceiling. Everybody raised their eyes to the sky, all thinking the same thought:

The gigs had power.

## ∞ EELONG ∞
### (CONTINUED)

**Mark and Boon slipped out** the window of the room where they had been held captive. It was remarkably easy for Boon to unscrew the window hinges with his claw and remove the frame. It wasn't a room designed to keep klees locked inside. The two quietly eased themselves out, so as not to alert the guard, and cowered against the outside wall.

"Now what do we do?" Boon whispered.

"We've got to get this tank to somebody who knows how to use it," Mark answered.

"Okay, who?" Boon replied. "Aron was the only gar Gunny told us about, and he threw us in jail."

"I don't know," Mark said nervously. "M-Maybe we should try to find Aron and convince him again. Or maybe Gunny made it to Black Water by now. Or maybe we can figure out a way to use it ourselves. Or maybe—"

"Or maybe we have no idea of what to do," Boon interrupted.

"Or that," Mark said, defeated.

Two gars rounded the corner of a building across the road and froze in surprise when they spotted Mark and Boon. All four stared at one another, not sure of what to do. Finally . . .

"Klee!" shouted one of the gars. He took out a whistle and blew it frantically. The other gar reached behind his back and whipped out a speargun.

"Uh-oh," Boon shouted. "Time to be someplace else."

The gar fired the weapon and the spear shot across the road. Boon shoved Mark out of the way, and the spear stuck into the wooden wall.

"Wait! We're friends!" Mark shouted at the gars while waving his arms.

The gars didn't believe him. Another spear was launched. Boon hit the ground as the missile sailed right over his head.

"Run!" he shouted to Mark.

"But we're here to help them!" Mark shouted back.

"We can't do it dead," Boon yelled. He stood and pushed Mark to get him running. A quick look back showed him that the two gars were reloading their spears. A moment later a loud horn sounded an alarm.

Inside the greenhouse the group heard the alarm horn.

"What's that?" Courtney asked.

"Could the gigs have gotten here so fast?" Bobby asked.

"No," Kasha answered. "They have to regenerate their power first."

"What is that horn, Fayne?" Gunny asked.

Fayne backed away from the group, saying, "I'm getting nervous about all this. I'd better find Aron."

"Why?" Gunny pressed. "Is it an alarm?"

"Look," Fayne said. "I know you said that klee is friendly, but having two around is two too many."

Spader leaped at her, making her jump in surprise. "What do

you mean 'two'?" he asked. "There's only one klee here."

"Yeah? That alarm says there's another one. I'm getting Aron." With that, Fayne ran out of the greenhouse.

Spader turned back to the group. They all stared at one another, thinking the exact same thing. Spader said it first, "Boon!"

"Yeah, and Mark," Bobby exclaimed, and took off running.

"Stay close to me," Gunny ordered Kasha as they all ran from the greenhouse. When they got to the street outside, they saw a group of gars running with their spearguns drawn.

"What's going on?" Bobby called to them.

"There's a klee on the loose," one answered.

Bobby didn't hesitate. He took off, running after the gars.


Mark and Boon desperately fled through town, trying to outrun the pursuing gars. The village was empty since everyone was lined up on the other side of town, ready to welcome the exodus of gars arriving at Black Water. Mark tried to open the door of a hut. It was locked. Boon tried another; it, too, was locked. He moved away from the door as another spear stuck into it with a solid *Chunk!*

"Keep moving!" Boon shouted.

The two dodged in and around the huts, trying to lose their pursuers.

"Take the tank," Mark said, breathless. "You can get away. You're faster than me."

"But I'm the one they're shooting at," Boon returned. "We've got to get rid of them."

"I can't run much more," Mark panted. "My side is killing me."

"Turn here!" Boon commanded and pushed him into a quick left turn. He grabbed Mark and pulled him down behind a low, stone wall. The two held their breaths, trying not to make a sound that would give them away. A few seconds later they heard the footsteps of the two gars running past. The gars had made the turn, but didn't know Mark and Boon had stopped. Mark needed air, but he did his best to control his breathing until he was sure they were out of earshot. Boon took a peek over the stone wall and saw the two gars still running down the street.

"Unbelievable," Boon said, panting. "It worked."

They both stood up and jumped over the wall to head back the way they had come.

"I think we better split up, " Boon said. "As long as you're with me, you'll be in danger."

The two walked back to the intersection where they had made the turn.

Boon continued, "I'll keep looking for Gunny and—look out!"

Three more spears flew at them, whizzing past their ears. The second wave of gars was on their trail. Without a word Mark and Boon started running again. They jumped off the street and ran along a row of huts, hoping that the trees in the front yards would shield them from incoming spears. The odds weren't with them. This second group had four gars. It would only be a matter of time before one of them took a good shot.

"There!" Mark shouted, and made a quick left turn between two huts. Behind the huts was a stand of trees.

"Maybe we can lose them in the trees," Mark reasoned.

They entered a miniforest that was so dense, it forced them to keep running along the path. With each step, the path grew narrower and narrower until they soon had to run shoulder to shoulder. Fifty yards ahead of them, they saw that the forest ended.

"When we get to the end, we'll split up," Boon declared. "They won't know which way to go."

"If we're lucky," Mark added.

The two sprinted to the end of the path, broke out into the open . . . and stopped short.

"We're not lucky," Mark declared.

They found themselves on the bank of the river that ran through the center of Black Water. There was no turning left or right. It was a wet dead end. Behind them the group of gars was closing fast. Mark took a look at the water to see it was running fast, maybe too fast to swim.

"I'm not a good swimmer," he declared.

"Really?" Boon said. "I can't swim at all. I'm a klee, remember?"

"But we gotta," Mark said nervously. "There's no other way."

Behind them a gar stopped and pulled out his speargun.

"What'll the water do to the stuff in the tank?" Boon asked.

"I-I don't know! Boon, we gotta go!"

The gar knelt down on one knee and raised his speargun.

"I can't, Mark. I'll drown."

The gar took aim, setting his sights directly on Boon.

"They'll kill you!" Mark cried.

"I got a better chance here than in the river," Boon cried. He put his hands on Mark's shoulders, ready to push him in. "You go!" Boon ordered.

Boon was strong. Mark knew he couldn't fight back if the big cat pushed.

"I won't let you drown!" Mark promised. "We can go together and—" Mark looked past Boon into the woods and spotted the gar who was about to shoot. "Look out!"

Boon turned. The gar tightened his finger on the trigger and . . .

Bobby Pendragon came running up behind the gar and launched himself, feet first. "Yahhhhh!" he shouted, and nailed the gar square in the back.

The gar pitched forward, shooting his spear into the ground. He scrambled back to his feet to see Bobby. "What are you doing?" he shouted. "The klee is getting away!" He pulled another spear from his carrier. But before he could load it, he was wrapped in a bear hug by Spader.

"That's all the shooting for today, mate," Spader said.

The other gars ran up, drawing their spearguns. Bobby jumped in front of them and held out his arms.

"Stop!" he commanded. "They're friends."

One gar yelled, "Klees are not friends."

Kasha walked up behind him and put a furry hand on his shoulder. "Some are," she said calmly. The gar looked at her and dove away in fright.

Gunny jogged up, out of breath. He stood next to Kasha and held his hand up to the gars. "It's all right," he said calmly. "It's true. These two klees are friends."

Gunny was a forceful presence. The gars didn't know how to react, or what to believe.

"Bobby!" Mark yelled, and ran to meet his friend wearing a huge, relieved smile.

Bobby grabbed him by the shoulders and said, "Are you okay?"

"We are now! Man, I can't believe you're here! Spader too! Is Courtney okay?"

"She's fine," Bobby answered. "She's back at the Center."

Boon walked up, saying, "I owe you one, Pendragon."

"Bobby, it was unbelievable," Mark said quickly. "I tried to bring the tank to Aron, but he locked us both up! We didn't know what to do so we—"

"Wait!" Kasha said. "Listen."

Her ears perked up. The others listened too.

"All I hear is that alarm back at the Center," Bobby said.

"I hear it," Spader said. "It sounds like . . . like . . . that's impossible. It sounds like a speeder boat."

"It's not a boat," Kasha said as she looked up to the sky.

Everybody else looked up. Through the trees they could see clear blue sky. The storm cloud was long gone.

"I hear it now," Bobby said.

Soon after, they saw them. They flew in a perfect "V" formation, like a flock of geese. They passed directly over Black Water, their rotors making the familiar whirring sound . . . times nine.

"What are they?" Mark asked in wonder.

"Flying death" was Kasha's answer.

# ∾ EELONG ∾

(CONTINUED)

**The formation of gigs** passed high, flying directly over Black Water.

"We're done," Bobby said, defeated.

"Not yet," Kasha said. "They won't spray the poison from that far up, the wind would take it away."

"They must be flying over to scout the place," Gunny suggested.

"Or waiting until the first bunch of gars arrive," Boon said ominously.

"Whatever," Spader said quickly. "It means we've still got time."

Bobby looked to Mark and asked, "Can you keep going?"

Mark stood up straight and said, "Absolutely."

They started back to the Center, but the gars stood in their way, holding up their spearguns.

"Stop!" the gar commanded. "Until we hear from Aron, you are all being held in confinement."

"You are going to hear from Aron right now!" Aron and a few more gars walked quickly along the path. "Gunny! What is happening here?" he demanded.

"Aron, those flying machines are going to drop a poison on Black Water. We can stop them, but we've got to get back to the Center."

"I told you!" Mark added, pointing to the tank on his back.

Aron frowned. "But the Advent—"

"The Advent is what they've been waiting for," Bobby interrupted. "They want you all in one place."

"Please, Aron," Gunny begged. "You've got to let us go back."

The gars looked nervous. They shuffled back and forth, not sure of what to do. Hearing that Black Water was about to be poisoned wasn't exactly a comforting piece of news. They looked to Aron, waiting for his response. Aron looked to the sky, watching the gigs disappear in the distance.

"They'll be back," Gunny said. "And they'll rain death on Black Water. The Advent will forever be known as the day that gars became extinct."

Aron shot a look at Gunny. "I have trusted you from the moment I met you, Gunny," he said. "Do not make me regret it."

"You won't," Gunny said with absolute confidence.

"Then go," Aron said. "Escort them back, hurry!" he ordered the gars.

The gars went from pursuers to protectors. They sprinted back along the path, running interference for the band of Travelers and acolytes who now had their last chance to save Eelong.

They ran quickly through the village, back toward the Center. Each stole nervous glances to the sky, expecting to see the gigs flying on their final, deadly pass. When they were nearly at the Center, they heard a huge cheer go up in the distance.

"It has begun," Aron announced with pride. "The first gars have arrived."

It was a moment of triumph. The gars had come home.

Generations of horror and oppression were at an end. No one yet knew how final that end was going to be.

Outside the Center, Courtney paced anxiously while Fayne relaxed against the building.

"You're making me nervous," Fayne said.

"That's the least of your problems," Courtney said.

Before Fayne could ask what she meant, the others ran up. Gunny quickly took the tank from Mark and handed it to Fayne. "Hook it up *now*!" he ordered.

Fayne looked to Aron. Aron nodded his approval. Fayne shrugged and headed inside. Courtney followed her, just to be sure nothing went wrong.

"Look!" Mark said, pointing toward the side of town that held the entrance to Black Water. In the distance they saw a steady stream of gars emerging from the tunnel. They were getting their first look at Black Water. Home. Greeting them were the gars of Black Water, cheering them like conquering heroes. It was a triumphant sight. Bobby stole a quick look at Aron to see his eyes were tearing up.

"Hobey!" Spader shouted. Everyone looked to him. Spader pointed to the sky. "Here they come!"

They all turned their attention to the mountains above the tunnel entryway to Black Water. Like an ominous dark cloud, the formation of gigs appeared. They were much lower this time, barely clearing the craggy peaks.

"We're too late," Boon cried.

"No we're not," Kasha declared. "They're still too high. And they're flying with the wind. They'll pass over once more then turn and head back. That'll be the killer run."

"Then let's be ready for 'em," Gunny declared, and led them all inside.

Inside the greenhouse Fayne was quickly and expertly hooking up the third and final tank of antidote. The others stood watching. The tension was enormous, but nobody said anything for fear of distracting Fayne. The woman finally looked up at them and frowned. "You're all making me nervous, you know," she said shakily. "I don't usually work with an audience."

"You're doing fine," Gunny said. "Do we know if this tank is full?"

Fayne threw a lever on the control panel and one of the gauges shot all the way from left to right.

"To the top," Fayne answered. "I can't believe it's so light, but it's full."

Everyone let out a relieved breath.

Courtney put her arm around Mark and gave him a quick hug. "You did it, man," she said.

Fayne reached for the lever that would release the antidote into the system and said, "Should I? . . ."

"No!" everyone shouted at once.

Fayne jumped back in surprise. "All right, all right!"

"We have to wait until the right moment," Gunny explained.

"And when is that?" Fayne asked.

"Very soon," Kasha said, pointing up. "They're coming back."

Through the crystal ceiling they could see all the way to the mountains on the far side of Black Water. The formation of gigs had returned once again. They were so far away that they looked like flying ants. But there was no mistake. This time, when they cleared the mountain top, the angels of death dipped down into the valley. At the same time, they spread out quickly, opening up huge gaps between each gig to cover as much ground as possible.

"This is it," Kasha announced. "This is the run."

"Do it!" Courtney shouted.

Fayne reached for the lever and was ready to throw it when . . .

"Stop!" Bobby shouted.

Everyone whipped a disbelieving look at him.

"Shorty, it's now or never," Gunny warned.

Bobby walked to the irrigation control and stood by the lever.

"What are you doing, Bobby?" Courtney asked nervously.

Bobby looked at the group and said, "I don't believe this was the way it was meant to be. But it's the way it is. This may be the totally wrong thing to do, but since it's going to happen, I'll be the one to do it." He reached up for the lever and wrapped his fingers around it. He looked back to the group and said, "I don't think the rules have changed. But we have."

Bobby pulled the lever.

## ∞ EELONG ∞
### (CONTINUED)

**The gigs flew** their attack run with perfect precision. The moment they crested the mountain into Black Water, they spread their formation out wide to cover as much ground as possible. At the same time they swooped down quickly and turned their side rotors parallel to reduce their speed. The klee pilots knew exactly what they were doing. They had made this kind of run many times to drop fertilizer over the vast farms of Eelong.

This time they weren't dropping fertilizer.

At the entrance to Black Water jubilant gars flooded into the secret valley. The line of gars stretched back through the tunnel, out from under the waterfall and all the way through the crater to the fissure through the mountain. The line continued past the spot where the tang's avalanche ambush had been cleared, out the other side and halfway down the steep switchback trail. Thousands more made their way through the rocky valley beyond to join the long line that would bring them home.

Inside Black Water the atmosphere was carnival-like. There was music playing and long tables loaded with fruit and bread to feed the hungry arrivals. As the gars entered with their link cubes glowing, they were greeted with warm hugs and tears. It was like a long-awaited reunion of a huge family. They were weary from the long journey, but reenergized by the thought of beginning a new and better life. Some of the incoming gars were tentative—after all they had lived their entire lives being treated like animals. But their fears were soon erased when they experienced the wonderful reception and learned that the promise of Black Water was a reality.

The klee pilots looked left and right to be sure they were spaced correctly. The pilot flying at the point of the arrow was in charge of coordinating the assault. He raised his furry hand over his head. The pilots on either side of him saw this and did the same. The pilots just outside of them followed, as did the next pilots out, and finally the pilots flying on the far edge of the formation. They were ready.

The lead pilot dropped his hand to give the signal, and the attack began.

Each of the pilots flipped the valve in his gig to release the Cloral poison. The deadly liquid shot from the tanks in the form of a heavy, green gas. It came first from the lead gig, followed quickly by the others. The gas from each gig trailed behind to join with the gas from the other gigs, until it formed a dense, green cloud that grew larger as they flew on. The deadly cloud hovered, barely moving, for it wasn't much heavier than air. The poison gas from all nine gigs drifted together, growing thicker by the second. When the cloud grew so thick that it blocked nearly all the light from the sunbelt, it began to slowly settle toward the ground.

The Black Water gars began to lead the first arrivals down into the village. They needed to keep the crowd moving to make room for the multitude of gars who were still to come. As they walked along the path, they spotted a curious sight on the far horizon. It looked to them like a small flock of birds. The surprising thing was that these birds seemed to be dragging a green cloud behind them. The Black Water gars watched in wonder, glancing to one another to see if anyone else might know what this strange event was all about.

The newly arrived gars laughed and pointed. Since everything for them was a new and exciting experience, this was simply another marvel of Black Water.

The klee pilot on point looked back to see the vast, green cloud that he and his team were laying down. He didn't see a single break in the dense gas. He quickly estimated that it was spread wide enough to cover all of Black Water. They couldn't have done a better job. He smiled in victory.

The Black Water gars experienced yet another surprise. A loud *hissing* sound could be heard that seemed to come from everywhere and nowhere. It was a familiar sound, but not one they expected. Normally it was only heard at night. Never in the middle of the day, especially on such an important day as this. But as strange as it may have been, the sound was real.

The central irrigation system was coming to life.

The sprinklers were everywhere. On light poles along the streets, on the farms that surrounded the village, even on the trees in the forests. The water was released in the form of a mist that spewed so much moisture into the air, the gars were soon soaked to the skin.

The new gars treated this as yet another marvelous treat. They cried for joy as the water washed away so many horrible memories. They danced, they splashed in the puddles, some even fell to their knees and scooped up handfuls of water to quench their thirst.

At the Center, Bobby and the others ran outside to learn that the sprinklers were working. They were instantly soaked by the heavy mist. It was like a rainstorm that began twenty feet above their heads.

"If this doesn't work, isn't it safer to stay inside?" Mark asked.

"If this doesn't work, being inside will only delay things," Gunny answered. "I'd rather get it over quick."

"This is a lot of water," Bobby said to Spader. "That antidote is going to be spread pretty thin."

"No worries, Pendragon," Spader answered with confidence. "Manoo told me it wouldn't take much to stop the poison."

"And you trust him?" Bobby asked.

"Well," Spader said with a sly smile. "Not much I can do about it now."

"We'll find out soon," Boon announced. "Look!"

He pointed to the sky as the nine gigs sailed directly over-head, spewing their poison, turning the sky as green as if they were dragging a carpet of artificial turf over their heads. Everyone stared up at the dark ceiling of poison that was slowly falling toward them.

"Is this g-gonna hurt?" Mark said, barely above a whisper.

"If it gets us," Bobby answered, "it'll be fast."

"Gunny," Aron said, visibly frightened. "I don't understand what is happening."

"I'll explain it all in a couple of minutes," Gunny answered. "If we're still around."

As the formation of gigs passed over the giant crowd, the happy gars cheered and waved at them, as if to thank them for the spectacular air show welcome.

"Look," Kasha announced. "Their tanks are nearly empty."

A quick look up at the formation of gigs showed that the stream of gas coming from the lead gig was thinning out. So too was the gas coming from the others. The noxious cloud was as big as it was going to get, which was plenty big enough. The gigs had reached the far side of Black Water. As soon as the gas from the outermost gigs was spent, they rose together, flying up and over the mountain, leaving Black Water behind. Their evil mission was complete.

"That's good news," Kasha said. "They won't be able to target the gars outside."

"It would be better news if the antidote worked in here," Courtney said.

All eyes went back up to the green cloud that was dropping ever closer. Boon stood near Kasha. The two exchanged nervous looks. Courtney walked to Bobby and took his hand. Bobby gave her a weak smile and squeezed. Mark stood on Bobby's other side.

"We tried," he said.

"I know," Bobby agreed.

The group continued to stare up at the sky. It was an eerie feeling, since the joyous sounds of the celebrating gars acted as a backdrop. The happy music didn't fit with the reality that every living being in Black Water was seconds away from death.

The green cloud fell gently toward the ground. The Travelers and the acolytes waited. And waited.

"Breathe deep," Gunny said somberly. "The faster the better."

Gunny's suggestion had the opposite effect. Everybody held their breaths. The water from the misters dripped into their upturned eyes, but nobody looked away. If these were their final moments of life, they wanted to make them last.

Mark said softly, "Is . . . is it getting brighter?"

Nobody reacted.

Above them the green blanket seemed to be a bit less dense.

"It is!" Courtney shouted.

"It's breaking up!" Boon shouted.

Seconds later the unmistakable shape of the sunbelt could once again be seen. And felt. Light was coming through.

"Hobey!" Spader declared. "The poison's getting eaten up when it hits the mist!"

In a matter of seconds, the sky went from dark green, to lighter green, to vapor white, and finally . . . to blue.

"Hoooweeee!" Gunny shouted, and spun around in a little dance. It was the first time Bobby had seen him happy since they left the Earth territories. "We're alive! Black Water is alive!"

Everyone had different reactions. Gunny danced in the rain like a happy scarecrow. Aron watched him with a frown of confusion. Fayne thought they were all crazy and left to go back to her post.

Spader ran to Courtney and gave her a big hug, spinning her off her feet. "We did it," he shouted with joy. "We beat him!"

Mark finally let his guard down. Now that the pressure was off, he couldn't help himself. He cried.

Boon and Kasha's reactions weren't as huge. The acolyte touched his Traveler on the shoulder and said, "Seegen was right. You were the one."

Kasha gave him a sad smile.

Rather than joining in, Bobby chose to walk away from the group and watch the happy gars who continued streaming into Black Water. Their celebration continued at full throttle, getting bigger as more gars arrived.

Gunny approached Bobby and watched the festivities for a

few moments, then said, "How does it feel to witness the birth of a new civilization?"

"It's awesome," Bobby answered. "I'm happy for them. I'm pretty happy for us, too. It's good not being dead."

The two chuckled.

"We did the right thing, Bobby. Especially after what happened on Veelox. Eelong is safe. Saint Dane won't have his next territory."

Bobby let that sink in a moment, then said, "You're right. We didn't have a choice. But this war isn't over. I'm just worried about what we might have to do to beat him next time."

Gunny nodded thoughtfully. "I better go inside and figure out how to explain this all to Aron."

Gunny left Bobby alone with his thoughts. They had beaten Saint Dane. Again. Eelong had reached its turning point and all signs now indicated a bright future for the territory. There was still work to be done. The rift between the gars and the klees wouldn't be mended easily, but Bobby felt sure that without Saint Dane around to mess things up, it would be possible. Yet Bobby was still troubled. Saint Dane had dared Bobby to stop him. He went so far as to tell Bobby exactly what his plan was for Eelong. That's how confident he was that his evil plan would succeed.

But it didn't. Bobby beat him. It took the help of Mark and Courtney, acolytes from a different territory, but they saved Eelong from destruction. Bobby asked himself if that was all there was to it. He wanted to believe it was true. Certainly there was plenty of proof in front of him. The oppressed race of gars was not only safe, they had the chance to save all of Eelong from starving. It seemed so right.

Yet Bobby didn't feel right.

He watched the joyous gars, trying to draw proof from the scene that all was well. They were dancing in the jammed streets in the most amazing street party Bobby had ever seen. Everyone had a smile on his face and a happy tear in his eye.

All but one person.

It was a little, blond girl who looked to be no more than five years old. She stood alone, on top of one of the huts. She stood out from the others in that she wasn't dancing or singing, or hugging any of the gars. She looked strangely familiar, but Bobby didn't know why. He took a few steps closer to get a better look, when the little girl turned and stared at him.

Bobby stood stone still. He remembered her. She was the little girl who welcomed him when he returned to Black Water. She had stepped out from the crowd of gars and handed him a white flower. Bobby remembered the flower, and he remembered her eyes. They were blue. Piercing blue. And as she looked at him now, her blue eyes seemed sharper than he remembered. More intense. It was like she was looking right through him.

A cold chill crept up Bobby's spine. His mind went to a place he didn't want it to go. But he had no choice, because a moment later the little girl started to laugh. It wasn't a happy laugh. It had a touch of lunacy that cut through Bobby's soul.

The little girl called out to him. She said three words. Three words that meant nothing to any of the gars who danced beneath her. They meant nothing to most every living being on Eelong. But it didn't matter. The words were meant for Bobby, and Bobby alone. When he heard them, his knees went soft.

The little girl cried out, "On to Zadaa!"

"Saint Dane!" Bobby shouted and ran for her. But when he reached the hut and climbed on top, the little girl was gone.

## ∞ EELONG ∞
### (CONTINUED)

**Gunny was right.** They had witnessed the birth of a new civilization.

Once the multitude of gars completed their journey to Black Water, their hosts took on the huge task of settling them down, giving them a place to sleep, and providing meals. The logistics were staggering, but the Black Water gars had been preparing for years. They were ready. The bigger challenge would come next, as they worked to educate their primitive cousins and set them on a course toward a civilized life.

But this alone wouldn't be enough to cure Eelong. The gars still had to confront their enemies, the klees. Though some gars wanted revenge for the history of horrible treatment, those with a larger vision understood that for Eelong to prosper, the two races had to coexist.

Gunny and Bobby went a long way toward mending fences by explaining to Aron how one single klee was responsible for the attack on Black Water. Timber. They convinced him that once Timber was thrown out and the klees were shown how the gars could help end the food problem on Eelong, the klees would no longer feel threatened and begin to look at the gars as equals. It was a good theory, one that Aron hoped would prove true.

Aron never told any of the gars how close they had come to destruction. He wasn't entirely sure he believed it himself. He wanted to look forward, rather than worry about the past. Aron would prove to be a wise leader. But the task still remained to confront the other side—the klees.

That job fell to Kasha and Boon. The Travelers and the acolytes made the long journey back to Leeandra, along with Aron and a few of the Black Water leaders. Kasha and Bobby were still fugitives. Boon was too, for having stolen the zenzens. They didn't want to arrive back in the city only to be arrested, so they returned with an impressive show of force that the klees could not ignore. No less than fifty gars marched on Leeandra. Each rode on zenzens (even Mark), wearing dark cloaks and body armor. They also carried spearguns. They had no intention of using them; they wanted to put on a show that would prove to the klees that they were a force to be reckoned with.

Leading the group were the klees, Kasha and Boon. They boldly led the others into the wippen stadium to demand a meeting with the Council of Klee. What they found was something they never could have predicted.

Leeandra was a city in shambles.

Once the gars fled, the klees discovered how integral they were to running the city. The gars had done all of the menial jobs the klees weren't interested in. Now that they were gone, the elevators and trams broke down; the flow of water was stopped because the elaborate system of pipes wasn't kept clean; and worst of all, food was becoming even more scarce because the foragers weren't willing to risk their lives to go outside Leeandra without the gars to protect them. Leeandra was paralyzed.

It was the perfect situation for Kasha and Boon. Together with Aron, they went immediately to the Circle of Klee to find Ranjin, the former viceroy. Ranjin was quick to grant them an audience. The group learned from Ranjin that after the failure of the attack on Black Water, Timber disappeared. (No big surprise.)

Kasha told Ranjin the truth about the gars. He listened closely as she explained how the gars were actually intelligent beings. She described how the gars had developed advanced farming techniques that could mean the end of the food shortage. Aron made sure that Ranjin understood the gars would help feed the klees, but only if they were treated as equals. The klees would have to put aside all their old prejudices and accept that the gars were not animals.

Ranjin listened to all that Kasha and Aron had to say with keen interest. Kasha said that for the gars to begin helping the klees, they needed a show of good faith. A symbol. Without it, they would leave the klees to starve.

"What is it I can do?" Ranjin asked.

"You must once again become viceroy of Leeandra," Kasha said. "You have proven to be the lone voice of reason. That voice must be heard again."

Ranjin agreed to once again wield the staff of viceroy, and do all he could to forge an alliance with the gars.

After that, events happened quickly. Aron and Ranjin spent days talking about the future of their two races, and of Eelong. They found common ground in the technology that each race had created. The link radio would prove to be an invaluable tool to coordinate forages and track the movement of tangs, so the danger of surprise attacks would be diminished. The link could also be used aboard gigs, allowing the helicopters to travel greater distances without fear of losing power, for they could receive information about clouds and storm patterns. Of course, at the center of their plans was the gar invention of virloam. Using this remarkable substance for farming would guarantee enough food to meet the needs of a growing territory. Neither Aron nor Ranjin expected the road ahead to be without bumps, but each felt certain that traveling down that road was in the best interest of all.

Four weeks after the failed attack on Black Water, Eelong was on its way to becoming a safe, peaceful territory with a bright future.

Bobby and the Travelers stayed on Eelong long enough to make sure the healing process began. At first Bobby wanted Mark and Courtney to return home, but they asked to stay. They had risked their lives to help save Eelong and wanted to see the payoff. Bobby didn't argue. They had earned that right. After the Advent, they first spent two weeks in Black Water, marveling at how the gars quickly adapted to their new lives. Mark was fascinated with the technology the gars had developed, and spent days at the Center, learning about virloam and the link radio. Courtney had a great time teaching the gars how to play soccer. She got Spader involved and the two formed a small soccer league, with Spader and Courtney the captains of opposing teams.

Two weeks later they made the trip to Leeandra for the historic meeting with Ranjin. While the important meeting and negotiations were taking place, Mark and Courtney stayed at Seegen's house. They explored the town, marveling at the incredible city built in the trees. They did this with no small feeling of pride. Since Bobby first left on his adventure, they had longed to play a more important role in protecting the territories. On Eelong their wishes came true. If not for them, Saint Dane would have destroyed Eelong. Courtney's self-confidence had returned, and Mark finally got the adventure he had longed for.

But it was time for the adventure to end.

One evening the three visitors from Second Earth were in Seegen's home, sharing a meal. Mark had appeared nervous all night. When they finished eating, he said what was on his mind.

"Guys," Mark said, "I think it's time to go home."

Courtney hadn't expected that. "Why? It's awesome here!" She asked, "What's at home? School? Homework? Parents ragging about school and homework?"

"Well . . . yeah," Mark answered. "I miss that."

"And what are we going to tell our parents? 'Sorry we've been missing for a month, folks, but we had to flume to another territory with Bobby Pendragon and stop a race of cat people from destroying a secret village in the mountains. Pass the salt.' I don't think so!"

"We knew that was going to be a problem when we left," Mark countered.

"Yeah, but that was before we kicked Saint Dane's butt!" Courtney shot back. "If it weren't for us, Eelong would be a giant litter box. The war is just starting. Bobby needs us. Right, Bobby?"

Bobby didn't answer. Courtney didn't like that. "You do want us to help, don't you?"

"You've been helping since day one, " Bobby said calmly.

"We've been librarians!" Courtney shouted, jumping to her feet. "We can't go back to that now that we've had a taste of the action!"

"But you have to," Bobby said with no emotion.

This stunned Courtney. "What? Why?"

"Because I need you to," Bobby said. "You're right; you saved Eelong. If it weren't for you guys, I don't know what would have happened. You were amazing. But I don't know what I'm going to find next and—"

"And what? You don't think we can hack it?" Courtney said, insulted.

"I don't even know if *I* can hack it!" Bobby barked so quickly that it made both Mark and Courtney jump.

"Something's been bugging you, Bobby," Mark said. "What is it?"

Bobby tried to put his thoughts together before answering. "Something's not right," he finally said. "Eelong is safe. I believe that. But still, I've got this horrible feeling that I've missed something. I know that everything you guys have done was to help, and I'll never be able to thank you enough. But I'm still trying to figure out the rules here, and if they're really changing, and what the hell I'm even doing here in the first place!"

By the time he finished the sentence, he was shouting. Courtney sat back down, surprised by Bobby's outburst. They hadn't realized he was such a raw nerve. He hadn't shared his worries with anyone since Black Water was saved. He never even told anyone about seeing Saint Dane in the form of the little blond girl. But it had been weighing on him, and now he was letting the emotion spill out.

"Please don't give me a hard time about this," he continued. "I'm barely keeping my head above water here. I can't watch my butt and yours too. So please, go home. I'll take you to the flume tomorrow."

Bobby stormed out of the hut, leaving Courtney and Mark stunned. Neither said anything right away; they had to let Bobby's tirade settle in.

"Well," Courtney finally said. "That's pretty ungrateful. We nearly get killed about twenty times over and all he says is 'thanks' and then sends us on our jolly way? That's bull—"

"It's not," Mark said forcefully. "He's right. We're not Travelers, Courtney. We don't belong here."

"Who says?" Courtney argued.

"Well, Bobby's uncle Press," Mark answered.

"Press is gone!" Courtney shot back.

"Yeah, but I think Bobby is still hanging on to him. Press was the guy Bobby trusted above everybody. He was the one who brought him up to be a Traveler, and the only one who knew what it all meant."

"Yeah, I guess," Courtney said grudgingly.

"Think about all Bobby's been through. I couldn't have done it. And I'm sorry if this is an insult, but I don't think you could have either. Bobby is a special guy, but he's just a guy. I think when things get scary for him, he thinks back to what Press taught him about being a Traveler. And us coming to Eelong and bringing the antidote doesn't fit."

"But if we hadn't come, Saint Dane would have won," Courtney countered.

"It seems like that, but who knows for sure?"

"I do," Courtney said quickly. "There was no other way. And you know what else? Spader wants us to stay."

"Does he?" Mark asked. "Or does he just want *you* to stay?"

Courtney snapped Mark a surprised look.

Mark added, "I'm not an idiot. He likes you."

Courtney didn't argue.

Mark stood up and said, "But it doesn't matter. Spader isn't in charge. Neither is Gunny or Kasha or you or me. Bobby's the guy. And you know what? As much as I want to go home, if Bobby asked me to stay, I would. But he wants us to go, so I'm going. And you should too."

When Bobby left Mark and Courtney, he walked onto the balcony of Seegen's house to calm down and breathe some air. He jumped back when he saw a dark shape climbing up to the platform, but relaxed when he realized it was Kasha.

"I'm glad you're here," Kasha said. "Please, come with me."

Kasha led Bobby to the far side of the balcony, where a ladder stretched farther up into the tree. Bobby followed the klee higher and higher until they emerged onto a small platform that was so high it swayed with the breeze. Though it was a frightening perch, it offered a spectacular view of Leeandra.

"It's beautiful," Bobby said as he looked down on the night lights of the city.

"This was my father's favorite place," Kasha said. "He often slept here. He used to say that from up here he felt like he could reach out and hold Leeandra in his hands."

The two looked out over the beautiful city.

"I'm not good with change," Kasha finally said. "I like things orderly and logical. I thought my father did too. He was a brilliant klee. A visionary. But more than that, he could get things done. I wanted nothing more than to be like him. But when he started telling me about Travelers and Saint Dane, I couldn't accept it. Nothing he said fit with anything I knew about Eelong, or about him. I thought he had gone crazy. But now I realize he hadn't changed at all. He was the same dedicated, concerned klee he always was. He had simply adapted to what life threw at him, where I couldn't."

"But you did," Bobby said. "It just took a little longer."

"Yes, too late," Kasha said with sorrow. "I turned my back on him. He died thinking I had lost respect for him, and it couldn't have been further from the truth."

The two stood in silence for a moment, then Bobby said, "When my uncle Press died, he promised me that we would see each other again. I really can't say what he meant by that, or how it would happen, but if there's one thing I've learned about being a Traveler, it's that just when you think you've got it all figured out . . . you don't. When things get tough, I think about those last words of his. If what he said is true, and I believe it is, then you'll see your father again."

Kasha said, "I want to believe that too."

"Then do," Bobby said. "It sure makes things easier."

Kasha said, "I don't know what other territories are out there, or what more a klee Traveler can do, but I'm with you, Pendragon. Not just for my father. For you."

Bobby smiled and nodded in thanks. He noticed that Kasha held a small, wooden box. "What's that?"

Kasha said, "I've been waiting for the right moment to do this. My father's life was about Leeandra. He'd be proud of the changes that are happening. I want him to be a part of it, forever."

She opened the box and tossed its contents into the air. Carried away on the breeze were Seegen's ashes. They quickly spread and were taken away to settle over the jungle village.

"He would have liked you, Pendragon," Kasha said. "I'm glad you were here to share this moment."

Early the next morning the team of Travelers and acolytes made one final journey together. They walked across the sky bridges of Eelong, back to the huge tree that held the flume. There was a feeling of finality to this trip. They had saved Eelong. They had defeated Saint Dane. And now, they were splitting up.

"This is tough," Bobby said to the group as he stood in the center of the underground cavern, outside the flume. "We've beaten Saint Dane. All of us played a huge part. I wish this were the end, but it isn't. I know I've said this before, but no single one of us has a chance against him. It's only the strength we have together that gives us hope. If you need proof of that, remember what happened here on Eelong."

"So that means we're staying together?" Spader asked.

"Yes," Bobby answered.

"Hobey! That's what I like to hear!"

Bobby added, "But not you, Kasha, I'm sorry to say. You wouldn't exactly go unnoticed on other territories."

"I understand," the klee Traveler said. "We've plenty to do here on Eelong. But you know if you ever need me . . ."

She didn't finish the sentence. Bobby knew.

"Where to, shorty?" Gunny asked.

"I think it's time to pay Loor a visit," Bobby said.

"Zadaa!" Spader announced happily. "That Loor's a handful, she is."

Bobby turned to Mark and Courtney. Neither looked happy, especially Courtney. Bobby pulled them aside so they could have a private moment between friends.

"I'm sorry about last night, guys," Bobby said. "I was way out of line."

"It's cool, Bobby," Mark said. "We get it."

"But?" Courtney asked.

"But I still want you to go home."

Mark nodded. Courtney looked away, peeved.

"Can I still count on you guys to take care of my journals?" Bobby asked.

"Are you kidding?" Mark said quickly. "Bring 'em on."

"I need to know something else," Bobby said. "This isn't over. If I ever get to understand things a little more, will you guys come back?"

Courtney's face lit up. "So you're not closing the door entirely?" she asked.

"How can I do that?" Bobby said. "I'm winging this. I've got to keep every option open."

Courtney threw her arms around Bobby and hugged him tight. "We'll be waiting," Courtney whispered into his ear.

Bobby looked to Mark over Courtney's shoulder. Mark said, "Just say the word."

Courtney pulled away from Bobby. Bobby gave Mark a hug. "Thank you, guys. I don't know what else to say."

"That's enough," Mark said, nearly in tears.

Mark and Courtney made their good-byes all around. When Courtney hugged Spader good-bye, she said, "So you think Loor is a handful, aye? Isn't that what you said about me?"

Spader backpedaled, saying, "Oh, well, in a different way. I mean, she's a warrior, trained and all, and you're, uh, you're really smart and—"

Bobby burst out laughing. "Spader, this is the first time I've seen you nervous."

"It's the first time I've ever *been* nervous," Spader said with an uncomfortable chuckle.

"We'll see each other again," Courtney said. "And then we'll see who's a handful."

Gunny gave them both a big hug, then they made their good-byes to the klees.

"Thank you for everything," Kasha said.

"Absolutely," Boon added.

"Hey, it goes with the job," Mark said cockily.

Courtney gave him a playful shove. "Yeah, right. Let's go."

Bobby walked the two of them through the curtain of vines and stood with them in the mouth of the flume. "What are you going to tell your parents?" he asked.

"Good question," Mark said.

"Any suggestions?" Courtney asked.

"Yeah," Bobby answered. "Lie."

The three joined in one last hug, then Mark and Courtney backed into the flume. "Write soon," Mark said.

"You know it," Bobby answered.

"See ya, Bobby," Courtney said, then she and Mark turned to face the tunnel to infinity.

"Ready?" Mark asked.

"There's no place like home," Courtney replied.

"Second Earth!" Mark called out.

And things were never the same.

The flume began to collapse.

The light appeared in the distance, along with the usual musical notes, but the stone structure of the flume was crumbling.

"Wh-What happened?" Mark shouted.

The stone flume writhed and shuddered. The sound was deafening. Giant chunks of rock fell from overhead. The whole tunnel shifted. Mark was knocked off his feet. The light grew brighter. Bobby ran in and helped Mark to his feet. All around them, the rock lining of the flume came tumbling down.

"Run in!" Bobby shouted over the roar. "Meet the light!"

He gave them both a shove, sending them running into the flume. A crack appeared between Bobby's feet, opening up a deep chasm beneath. The flume was breaking apart. Bobby dove to his right, hitting the floor of the tunnel with his shoulder. Above him, another rock broke loose and fell. Bobby rolled out of the way, and right to the edge of the crack that was now a chasm. He glanced back into the flume to see that Mark and Courtney were nothing more than silhouettes running into the light. Above him, rocks continued to break loose and rain down, crashing all around him. He crawled away from the edge of the chasm in a desperate attempt to get out of the flume, when the floor beneath him crumbled.

An instant later Mark and Courtney were gone.

# ◉ SECOND EARTH ◉

**The light from the flume** blasted into the root cellar of the abandoned Sherwood house, along with the jumble of musical notes. A second later Mark and Courtney came running out of the tunnel, safe. They turned around quickly to examine the flume.

"It's still in one piece!" Mark announced.

The light and music quickly receded, leaving the tunnel dark and quiet. Courtney felt the stone at the mouth of the tunnel.

"Solid," she proclaimed. "Mark, what happened?"

"I-I don't know! It was like an earthquake."

"What should we do?" Courtney said, frantic. "Should we go back?"

"No!" Mark yelled. "We b-barely got out of there. Why would we go back?"

"But what about Bobby and the others?"

Mark didn't have an answer. "Let's just . . . relax. And think. We can't go back. All we can do is wait. That's what Bobby said, right?"

"But Bobby didn't know the flume was going to collapse!"

"I know, I know! But, what can we do?"

Courtney deflated. "Nothing. This is going to be torture."

The two changed out of the Cloral swimskins they had been wearing, back into the Second Earth clothes they brought to the flume so long ago. Courtney didn't even make fun of Mark for wearing the bright yellow sweatshirt with the "Cool Dude" logo. They left the basement not even worrying if they'd run into a quig-dog. When they stepped outside the abandoned mansion, they discovered that it was nighttime in Stony Brook. They were able to scale the wall surrounding the mansion and get back to the quiet, suburban street without being seen. As soon as they hit the ground, their thoughts turned from what had happened on Eelong, to what was about to happen on Second Earth. By their estimation they had left for Cloral over a month before. Neither could begin to imagine how frantic their families were.

"Now what?" Courtney asked, as they walked. "You realize we're about to catch hell."

"I know," Mark said. "I've got a plan. We've got to be together on this or it'll never work."

"I'm listening."

"Let's tell everybody we ran away together, you know, to go on an adventure."

"Well, we did."

"I'm not saying we tell the truth! Give me a break. I'm saying we tell everybody we got sick of having to be the good kids all the time and school was too intense and we were being pressured by peers into doing stuff we didn't want to do and, I don't know, all those things they say on TV talk shows make kids go crazy. We'll say we needed a break before we did something really stupid, so we ran away to go to, I don't know, to California. To surf!"

"That's ridiculous," Courtney said.

"Why? Kids run away all the time."

"I know, but nobody will believe you and I did it together."

Mark stopped walking and gave Courtney a sour look.

"I'm kidding," she said. "It's a good idea, but it'll get us in huge trouble."

"Maybe. Or maybe our parents will feel sorry for us because we're troubled youths."

"Yeah, right."

"Whatever. We're in huge trouble no matter what we do. At least this way we might have a chance of sliding by without having to talk about flumes and territories and Travelers—"

"And get locked up," Courtney said, finishing the thought.

"Exactly."

"It's a plan."

They decided to go to Courtney's house first, since it was closer and Courtney was already having big arguments with her parents. They figured her parents would buy it quicker than Mark's, since Mark had never done anything remotely spontaneous in his life. At least as far as his parents knew. On the way to her house, they fabricated an incredible story of how they put enough money together to take the bus to California, then spent a few weeks on a beach just north of Mexico trying to learn how to surf and pretend like they weren't who they were. They worked in every detail they could think of—the towns they went through, the food they ate, the people they met. Everything. It didn't take long for them to feel confident enough with the bare bones of a story to run it by Courtney's parents. Finally they made the long walk up the path to Courtney's house.

"Let's ring the bell," Courtney said. "I don't want to barge in and give them a heart attack."

"Good luck," Mark whispered.

She rang the bell. A few seconds later Courtney's door opened. Mr. Chetwynde stood there, staring at them, as if he couldn't believe he was actually seeing them. Mark and Courtney weren't sure how to begin, so they didn't say anything. They had already figured that it was better to react than to offer any info. They stood that way for a good thirty seconds, when Courtney's father finally spoke.

"What happened?" was all he asked.

"It's a long story, Dad," Courtney said, trying to sound tired and remorseful.

"Very long," Mark added.

"Was the library closed?" Mr. Chetwynde asked.

Mark and Courtney didn't know how to answer that one. They had figured out answers for most every question that could have been thrown at them, but not that one.

"Excuse me?" Courtney asked tentatively.

"The library," Mr. Chetwynde said. "Weren't you guys going to the library?"

"You mean, like a month ago?" Courtney asked.

"I mean a half hour ago when you left the house," Mr. Chetwynde said, confused.

Mark asked, "Courtney left here half an hour ago? Was I with her?"

Mr. Chetwynde frowned at Mark. "Unless you've got an identical twin. Am I missing something?"

Courtney said, "Well, yeah! We've been—"

"No!" Mark jumped in. "You're not missing anything. The library was open, but we were starved so we went to McDonald's first and ended up getting our work done there. It didn't take as long as we thought."

"Oh," Mr. Chetwynde said, satisfied. "Not exactly a long story. I'm sorry to hear it though."

"Why?" Courtney asked, still trying to understand what was happening.

"It's not good to eat junk food for dinner. It's not good for your health."

Mark and Courtney gave each other a sideways look. "I can think of a lot of things bad for your health," Courtney said. "Burgers aren't high on the list."

"Don't be a wise guy. You know what I mean," Mr. Chetwynde said with a half smile.

Mark tugged on the back of Courtney's shirt and said, "Uh, I left something on my bike I meant to give you."

He tried to pull her away from the door, but Courtney stood firm. "Bike? You don't have a—"

"Yeah!" Mark interrupted. "The bike I left out front so we could walk together."

Courtney was reeling. Nothing was making sense to her.

"C'mon, Courtney," Mark said vehemently through clenched teeth. He turned quickly and hurried away from the house.

"Be right back, Dad," Courtney said, and jogged after Mark. When she caught up, Mark kept walking. "What's going on?" Courtney said under her breath.

Mark's answer was to show Courtney his hand. The center stone of his ring was glowing.

"Oh man," Courtney gasped.

Mark clapped his hand over the ring to hide the pyrotechnics. When they got to the street and out of Mr. Chetwynde's sight, Mark ran next door and ducked behind a huge bush in front of the neighbor's yard. By the time he got the ring off, it was already growing. Mark placed it on the ground and stood next to Courtney. The two watched it grow to Frisbee-size, opening up the conduit between territories.

"This is too much. I'm going mental," Courtney gasped.

The bright light shot out of the hole inside the ring, along with the sweet musical notes. With a final brilliant flash, the event ended and the ring returned to normal. Lying on the ground next to it was a rolled-up piece of parchment paper. Mark moved to pick it up, but Courtney stopped him.

"Wait," she said. "One thing at a time. Did my father snap or what? That was not what I expected from a guy whose daughter was missing for a month."

"Because I don't think we were gone for a month," Mark answered.

Courtney gave Mark a blank look. "No way. That wasn't some *Wizard of Oz* dream we had. I've got the black-and-blue marks to prove it."

Mark laughed. "No, we spent a month on Eelong, but I think we were brought back here only a few minutes after we left."

Courtney shook her head, confused. "You mean, like time stood still while we were gone?"

"No. I think we went to a territory that existed in another time. When the flume brought us back here, it was to the same time we left."

"So . . . we're not in trouble?"

"Not with our parents, anyway."

The implication was there. Parents were the last thing Mark and Courtney had to worry about. They both looked down at the rolled-up parchment paper.

"That was fast," Courtney said.

"For us. Who knows if Bobby wrote it in the past, or the future."

"Don't go there," Courtney scolded. "My brain already hurts."

Mark picked up the parchment. It was crunchy brown paper,

wrapped and tied with leather twine. Mark's hands were shaking as he untied the knot.

"What happened to the flume, Mark?"

"Maybe this will tell us," he said, unrolling the pages. He took a deep breath and glanced at the first page.

"From Bobby?" Courtney asked.

"Uh-huh," Mark answered.

"Where is he?"

# ZADAA

It was a trap.

Everything that happened from the first moment I set foot on Eelong was about leading me into it . . . and I went. The poison from Cloral, Seegen's death on Second Earth, Saint Dane's boasting to me that he would wipe out the gars, the attack on Black Water; everything! It was all about setting the trap. The thing is, I felt certain that Saint Dane was up to something more, but I wasn't smart enough to figure it out.

Now it's too late.

I'm real good at looking back and putting the puzzle pieces together. It's looking ahead that I'm not so hot at, and we paid the price. Mark, Courtney, I want to go back and tell you exactly what happened from the moment you left Eelong for Second Earth. You need to hear it all. Be warned, this is going to be tough to read. I wish I didn't have to tell you. But you're in this now, more so than ever. We've had a lot of victories over Saint Dane. For that, we deserve to be proud. But we've also made mistakes, and we have to accept those, too.

This is what happened.

"Run in!" I shouted to you guys as the flume crumbled around us. "Meet the light!"

I saw that the flume light was coming and wanted to make sure you'd make it, so I gave you both a shove to go deeper into the flume. That's when the tunnel started to break up. On the ground between my legs a huge crack appeared. If I hadn't thrown myself to the side, I might have fallen in. I hit the bottom of the flume with my shoulder. The pain shot all the way down into my leg, but I couldn't worry about it just then, because above me the rocks of the flume were breaking up and falling down . . . on me. I rolled out of the way just as a boulder hit the ground where my head had been. But I nearly rolled right into the crack in the floor that was already a couple of feet wide, and growing. I grabbed on to the edge and stared down into nothing. Absolutely nothing. That crack may have opened up a hole to the center of Eelong for all I knew. I tried to crawl away, but the floor crumbled beneath me. One second it was solid, the next I felt it break loose, and I fell with it.

"I've got you!" shouted Kasha. She had fought her way through the curtain of vines and into the crumbling flume. It was a good thing, because she snagged the back of my clothes with her claw, just in time. She saved my life. Again. I was able to twist around and grab on to the craggy ledge of rock. Beneath me the crumbled ledge fell to oblivion.

"I got it," I told her as I pulled myself up.

The horrible, wrenching sound got louder. It was like being inside a thundercloud. Rocks were being torn apart by some incredible above-ground earthquake.

"Get out of there, Pendragon!" Spader shouted.

I looked to see that he and Gunny were outside the mouth of the flume.

"Stay back!" I shouted. But I didn't need to. Another crack appeared in the floor in front of Spader and Gunny, cutting them off from the flume. But worse than that, it kept Kasha and me from getting out. All around us, the flume was falling down and the ground was crumbling away. We were moments away from being crushed, or plunged into the dark pit. There was only one way we could escape.

"Zadaa!" I shouted into the flume.

The light sparkled from deep within, coming to our rescue. It would be a race. Would the light get us out of there before the flume collapsed on our heads?

"Run!" I shouted to Kasha.

She tried to help me to my feet, but it was like trying to stand up inside a washing machine. We both fell again. I heard the musical notes coming closer.

"Hurry, Bobby!" Gunny shouted from outside the flume. "Run toward the light!"

Everything changed in a single second. One second. A second is nothing. A tick on the clock. Seconds pass all the time and we never think about any one of them. But a second can be an eternity. I got back on my feet and reached down to help Kasha up. I had her hand. I was a second away from pulling her to her feet. One stupid second. If I had been a second earlier, the falling rock would have missed her.

I wasn't.

Before I could pull her to her feet, a chunk of rock fell down from the ceiling and hit Kasha square on the head. It was so loud in the flume that I didn't hear the sound it made, and I'm glad for that. But I will always remember the sight. Kasha's head jerked to the side, and her body went limp.

I didn't allow myself to think about what had happened. I pulled on Kasha's furry hand, knelt down on one knee, and draped the big klee over my shoulders. I was operating on pure adrenaline.

"Go, shorty, go!" Gunny shouted.

I took a quick look back to see Gunny pulling Spader away from the mouth of the flume. They disappeared back through the curtain of hanging vines. Safe.

The floor of the flume was rumbling so hard, I nearly lost my balance again. But through sheer force of will I was able to stay upright and put one foot in front of the other. I was desperate to get us deeper into the flume and away from the destruction. The light blinded me . . .

"Hobey-ho, Pendragon!" I heard Spader yell.

And we were on our way. The last sound I heard from Eelong was a shriek and a huge *boom* as the flume disintegrated behind us. I braced myself, expecting the entire flume to collapse. But it didn't. All the damage was done at the gate. The rest of the flume was intact.

I don't remember much about the trip to Zadaa. Kasha and I sailed along side by side. I held her in my arms, cradling her head. Blood was starting to blossom through the black fur above her left eye, turning it slick. I put my hand over the wound, thinking direct pressure might stop the bleeding, but then I was afraid of putting too much pressure on her damaged skull.

"Kasha?" I said.

She opened her eyes, but couldn't focus.

"We'll be there soon," I assured her. "Loor can get us help." I was scared to death. I knew that Loor would do what she could, but I had no idea what the doctor situation was on Zadaa, let alone if they would treat a giant predator cat. I wondered if they had such things as veterinarians. All I could do was hold Kasha tight and wait for the trip to end.

It only took us a few minutes to get there, but it felt like days. Finally the musical notes grew faster and I felt the tug of gravity. I held Kasha tight to help ease her down once we arrived. Moments later I carried her out of the flume and into the large, underground cavern made of light brown stone—the sandstone of Zadaa. I laid Kasha down on the floor as gently as I could, then turned my thoughts to helping her. I quickly realized how tough that was going to be. To get out of this cavern, we needed to climb up through a cleft in the rock using footholds that were dug out of the stone. There was no way I would be able to climb out of there with an unconscious, two-hundred-pound cat. I decided to leave her and go for help.

"Pendragon?" Kasha whispered.

Her eyes were open and barely focused.

"Don't talk," I said. "I'm going to find somebody to help you."

"No," she said. "I don't want to be alone."

"But if I don't get help—"

Kasha cut me off by squeezing my arm. One look into her eyes and my heart sank. Her once-sharp eyes were becoming glassy. Blood flowed from her wound. The grim truth was that Kasha didn't need help. She needed comfort. I sat down next to her, lifted her head and put my hand under it, to act as a cushion against the hard, dirt floor.

"Tell me again," Kasha whispered.

"About what?"

"Tell me what your uncle Press said," she answered weakly. "I need to hear it."

It took every bit of courage I had to keep it together, and answer. "Uncle Press was a lot like your father," I said, my voice cracking. "People loved to be around him because he was the kind of guy who never had problems, only challenges.

He never gave reasons, or excuses why things couldn't be done. He just went out and did them."

"Just like Seegen," Kasha whispered.

"And Uncle Press was a Traveler. He taught me a lot about what being a Traveler meant, but he didn't even scratch the surface. He knew a lot more, but never got the chance to tell me. The last thing he said, as he was dying, was not to be sad because one day I'd see him again. He promised. He never broke a promise to me and I don't believe he's going to now."

"I wish I knew him," she said.

"I wish you did too."

Kasha swallowed and said, "Am I going to see my father now?"

I almost lost it. "Yeah," I said. "You are."

"I'm proud to have known you, Bobby Pendragon. And to have been a Traveler."

"You'll always be a Traveler," I said.

Kasha smiled, closed her eyes, and died. I felt the life go out of her as her head slumped into my hand. I kept staring at her, refusing to believe it, hoping that her eyes would open. But they didn't. The harsh reality landed like a heavy weight on my shoulders. Another Traveler was gone. I knew of others who died before her: Osa, Seegen, Spader's father, and of course, Uncle Press. But this was different. Kasha was the first Traveler from my generation who died. The last generation.

Saint Dane's true purpose on Eelong was suddenly coming into focus.

"Hello, Pendragon," came a voice from deeper in the cavern.

I knew who it was without looking.

"Hello, Loor," I said.

The tall, dark-skinned warrior girl stepped out of the shadows and stood over Kasha and me. "I knew you would be coming," she said softly. "But I did not expect this."

"Nothing is the same, Loor," I said, trying not to let my emotions take over. "We saved Eelong. The territory is safe. But I don't think Saint Dane cares one way or the other."

"Then what was the point?" Loor asked.

"He wants to change the way things were meant to be," I answered. "Saint Dane is doing all that he can to tear Halla apart. On Eelong, we helped him."

"Please explain," Loor said.

I gently laid Kasha's head down, stood up, and walked to the mouth of the flume. I took a step inside and called out, "Eelong!"

Nothing happened.

Loor stepped in and tried herself. "Eelong!"

The flume remained quiet.

"The gate on Eelong is destroyed," I concluded.

"How did Saint Dane do that?" Loor asked.

"He didn't. *We* did. Uncle Press always said that mixing the territories was wrong. What happened on Eelong is proof. Saint Dane may have lost a territory, but we lost three Travelers."

I saw the surprised look on Loor's face. She was too stunned to ask what I meant by that. I walked back to Kasha's body and knelt down. Gently I took the Traveler ring from around her neck. "Kasha was the Traveler from Eelong," I said. "Since we're the last generation, Eelong no longer has one." I put the cord that held Kasha's ring around my neck and stood to face Loor. "And since the gate on Eelong is destroyed, Spader and Gunny are trapped."

For the first time ever, I saw surprise in Loor's eyes. "But they are safe?" she asked.

"I think so. But they aren't going anywhere. Saint Dane

said the rules have changed, but they haven't. He's just decided not to follow them."

Loor and I brought Kasha's body out of the cavern and smuggled it through the twisting caves and tunnels beneath the city of Xhaxhu. I had been here twice before and remembered the route. But there was one very big difference. Xhaxhu was an oasis city surrounded by a vast desert. Its water supply came from a complex series of underground rivers. These rivers were the lifeblood of Xhaxhu. Without this water, the city would dry up and blow away. We had to pass one of these rivers on our way out of the tunnels, but when we came to it, I was stunned to see that the river was absolutely, totally dry. Instead of the fast-flowing waterway that I remembered, I saw a deep, empty trough with a few inches of dry dirt in the bottom. I rested Kasha's body down and stood on the edge of what had once been a deep canal. I was speechless.

"This is why I knew you were coming," Loor said. "But now is not the time. We must complete our task."

I shook off the image of the dry riverbed. We picked Kasha up to continue our journey. When we climbed up into the city, I saw that it was the dead of night. The streets were empty. That was good. It would have been tough to explain what we were doing. We brought Kasha to the ceremonial center where the fallen warriors of Zadaa were cremated. Since the klee tradition was to cremate their dead, I thought it was the right thing to do. We wrapped Kasha's body in a white cloth and gently placed her inside the stone structure where the fire would be set. Loor took on the tough task and lit the ceremonial fires. I had to step outside until it was done. I didn't have the strength to gut this one out. It didn't take long. Soon after, Loor came out of the crematorium carrying a silver urn that held Kasha's ashes. I took it, felt its weight, and made a promise to Kasha that I would do all I could to one day scatter her ashes from Seegen's perch, high above Leeandra.

"You must grieve for your friend," Loor said. "I will grieve as well, for we have lost a Traveler. But we must quickly put it behind us, for there is much to do."

"Saint Dane is coming here," I said.

"Tell me something I do not already know," Loor answered. "The war that I have feared for so long has begun. You saw the dry river below. The Rokador and Batu tribes have already spilled blood to control the rivers of Zadaa."

There would be no time to rest. No time to grieve. No time to think back on the meaning of all that had happened and recharge our batteries for the next encounter with Saint Dane. I wasn't surprised.

"And so we go," I said softly.

"So we go," Loor agreed.

This is where I'm going to end my journal, guys. I'm writing it in Loor's small home in the warrior complex of Xhaxhu. Mark, Courtney, there are three things I want you to take away from this journal, and from what happened on Eelong.

The first, and maybe the most important, is that what happened was not your fault. Saint Dane gave us no choice but to do what we did. I believe he poisoned Seegen as the klee was leaving for Second Earth, so that you would discover the Cloral poison. You did exactly what you needed to do. If you hadn't gone to Cloral to get the antidote, Eelong would have been doomed. Beyond that, Gunny and Kasha and I would probably have died too. Either way, we would have lost three Travelers.

Saint Dane manipulated us all. He told me his plans to wipe out the gars so that once we discovered the Cloral poison, we'd do all we could to stop him. Allowing an entire race to be killed is something he knew we'd never let happen. But this brings me to the second thing you must know.

I believe there is a balance to Halla, and to the territories. That's why I'm now convinced that what Uncle Press told me so long ago is still the truth. Mingling the territories is wrong. Saint Dane did it because he's trying to create chaos. But we can't follow. He lured you guys into using the flumes, which was wrong. Each time you used a flume, it grew weaker. When you left Eelong, it was the last straw. That's why the gate collapsed. Whatever force holds Halla in balance was disrupted. I believe this was Saint Dane's plan all along. It's why he met you on Second Earth and gave you Gunny's hand. He tempted you into using the flumes, then gave you a reason to do it.

Saint Dane's goal wasn't to destroy Eelong, it was about forcing us to change the way things were meant to be. He wants to disrupt all of Halla. So I will repeat what I've said before. Do not use the flumes. I'm saying this now with more certainty than ever. If you do, what happened to the flume on Eelong might happen on Second Earth.

The final thing I want you guys to know, is that I am incredibly proud of you. I mean it when I say this wasn't your fault. You two were brave and resourceful. Words can't begin to describe it. I know you did this to help me, and for that I will always love you both. But I also know that you understand how important it is to stop Saint Dane. To risk your lives the way you did, man, I am in awe of you two. If there was one thing I wish, it would be that you were both Travelers. I'd give anything to have you here with me. But you can't. I can only hope that you will continue to be my acolytes and protect my journals.

As I'm writing this, I have to admit that I'm really disturbed about the future. Our adventure on Eelong kicked this war with Saint Dane into another gear. Telling right from wrong, good from bad, isn't so easy anymore. We broke the rules on Eelong. But we did it because we thought it was for a greater good. And it was. But we paid a steep price for it. My problem is, I'm afraid I won't know what I should do when faced with this kind of decision again. Do I allow an entire race to be wiped out in order to play by the rules? Worse, do we let Saint Dane destroy a territory to save all of Halla? I still have nightmares about the *Hindenburg*. We're the good guys, but how moral is it to allow people to die, no matter what the reason? When I think like this, I wonder if I'm truly the right person to be the lead Traveler. I've done my best, I can say that for sure. But when the next difficult decision has to be made, will my best be good enough? I guess we're all going to find out.

Be well, my friends. Try to go back to living your normal lives, though I'm not sure what normal is anymore. After what you went through on Eelong, I'm sure you're going to have the same problem. For that, I'm sorry. When I write next time, I'll bring you up to speed on the nightmare that I have found here on Zadaa.

Because it is a nightmare.

And so we go. Again.

**END OF JOURNAL #19**

*To Be Continued*

**D. J. MacHale** is a writer, director, executive producer, and creator of several popular television series and movies which include: *Are You Afraid of the Dark?; Chris Cross; Encyclopedia Brown, Boy Detective; Tower of Terror; Ghostwriter;* and multiple Afterschool Specials. In print D. J. has cowritten the book *The Tale of the Nightly Neighbors,* based on his own teleplay, and written a poetic adaptation of the classic folktale *East of the Sun and West of the Moon.* Visit him on the Web at www.thependragonadventure.com.

# PENDRAGON

## JOURNAL OF AN ADVENTURE THROUGH TIME AND SPACE

*Coming in Summer 2005*

Bobby Pendragon continues his pursuit of Saint Dane in

## The Rivers of Zadaa

Bobby Pendragon has followed Saint Dane to the territory of Zadaa, where Saint Dane's influence has fueled the fire of discontent between two warring tribes: the Rokador and the Batu. This is also the territory where the Traveler Loor lives, and together she and Bobby work to thwart Saint Dane's efforts to destroy Zadaa.

**Look for *The Rivers of Zadaa* wherever books are sold.**

**A** remarkable fantasy sequence by Susan Cooper, described by *The Horn Book* as being "as rich and eloquent as a Beethoven symphony."

*The Dark Is Rising*
**A Newbery Honor Book**
0-689-71087-9 (rack)
0-689-82983-3 (digest)

*The Grey King*
**Winner of the Newbery Medal**
0-689-71089-5 (rack)
0-689-82984-1 (digest)

*Greenwitch*
0-689-71088-7 (rack)
0-689-84034-9 (digest)

*Silver on the Tree*
0-689-71152-2 (rack)
0-689-84033-0 (digest)

*Over Sea, Under Stone*
0-02-042785-9 (rack)
0-689-84035-7 (digest)

*The Dark Is Rising* **boxed set** (includes all titles listed above)
0-02-042565-1

ALADDIN PAPERBACKS/SIMON & SCHUSTER CHILDREN'S PUBLISHING
www.SimonSaysKids.com

# Aladdin Paperbacks is the place to come for top-notch fantasy/science-fiction! How many of these have *you* read?

**The Tripods, by John Christopher**

- ❏ Boxed Set • 0-689-00852-X • $17.95 US / $27.96 Canadian

- ❏ The Tripods #1 *When the Tripods Came* • 0-02-042575-9 • $4.99 US / $6.99 Canadian

- ❏ The Tripods #2 *The White Mountains* • 0-02-042711-5 • $4.99 US / $6.99 Canadian

- ❏ The Tripods #3 *The City of Gold and Lead* • 0-02-042701-8 • $4.99 US / $6.99 Canadian

- ❏ The Tripods #4 *The Pool of Fire* • 0-02-042721-2 • $4.99 US / $6.99 Canadian

**The Dark is Rising Sequence, by Susan Cooper**

- ❏ Boxed Set • 0-02-042565-1 • $19.75 US / $29.50 Canadian

- ❏ *Over Sea, Under Stone* • 0-02-042785-9 • $4.99 US / $6.99 Canadian

- ❏ *The Dark Is Rising* • 0-689-71087-9 • $4.99 US / $6.99 Canadian

- ❏ *Greenwitch* • 0-689-71088-7 • $4.99 US / $6.99 Canadian

- ❏ *The Grey King* • 0-689-71089-5 • $4.99 US / $6.99 Canadian

- ❏ *Silver on the Tree* • 0-689-70467-4 • $4.99 US / $6.99 Canadian

**The Dragon Chronicles, by Susan Fletcher**

- ❏ *Dragon's Milk* • 0-689-71623-0 • $4.99 US / $6.99 Canadian

- ❏ *The Flight of the Dragon Kyn* • 0-689-81515-8 • $4.99 US / $6.99 Canadian

- ❏ *Sign of the Dove* • 0-689-82449-1 • $4.50 US / $6.50 Canadian

- ❏ *Virtual War*, by Gloria Skurzynski • 0-689-82425-4 • $4.50 US / $6.50 Canadian

- ❏ *Invitation to the Game*, by Monica Hughes • 0-671-86692-3 • $4.50 US / $6.50 Canadian

## Aladdin Paperbacks
## Simon & Schuster Children's Publishing
## www.SimonSaysKids.com